THE ARIUMS OF EARTH

THE HELIOSPHERE TRILOGY
BOOK 2

E.M. RENSING

Copyright © 2023 by E.M. Rensing

ISBN: 979-8-9869182-1-1

Cover Design: Ryan Meeks

Cover Font: "Ailerons," Adilson Garcia

All rights reserved.

No part of this book may be reproduced in any form or by any electronic or mechanical means, including information storage and retrieval systems, without written permission from the author, except for the use of brief quotations in a book review.

Generative AI was not utilized for any component of this book; narrative outlining, drafting, editing, formatting and cover art creation were all tasks completed by humans. Some writers like to claim spell check features in word processors are AI. I'd turn that crap off too if I could—huge pain when you're writing SF anyway.

For my Dad

PROLOGUE

THE AIR WAS the first thing she noticed.

Heavy air, laden with moisture, warmer than anything she'd felt in a long time.

It also stank, a combination of wet plant matter, decaying protein, burnt hydrocarbons. Salt. The passage of thousands of human bodies.

Very, very few places on Mars had that kind of smell. One of the port towns down in the Marineris Delta, perhaps.

But it was wrong.

Wrong.

Rain was falling.

Not through a window or translated through LEDs. Present. Around her. Catching in her hair. Wet, warm on her cold skin.

Rain.

Real planetary rain.

Falling.

And she was falling along with it.

Through empty corridors. Through open void, brilliant in its darkness. The light of the sun flowed around her, through metal and glass, through flesh and time.

She grabbed for a handhold there, anywhere, but only sand flowed through her fingers. Red, then white, slipping away, subsiding beneath her. Warm waves lapped at her feet and pulled at her body, sand slipping through her desperate fingers.

Caught in the wind.

Piling up.

Drifting.

The rot smell was gone.

Sand was covering everything, taking everything away, into the darkness of the void.

A man was staring at her, head cocked, like he was trying to size her up. As she stood on the deck of a small ship, the sun setting behind the ocean. As she collapsed into emptiness, the blackness of that sand.

For a moment, the scene shifted. No longer a rain-swept deck, but a tight dome of fractured sandstone and red sand, a body half-subsumed, sinking deeper and—

Stars shone overhead, the burning path of the Milky Way, seen from the surface of some world that wasn't Mars.

He was watching her.

The Flet, she realized.

Beyond him was a glow. Above the nighttime waters. Like a bonfire from a far distance. A sunset, still fading after all else had gone dark. A glow, and a noise. Roaring, roaring like the ocean itself, even though the surface was quiet.

She had a glimpse of herself, then.

Walking.

Across the frozen atmosphere of Eris.

Through white sand, streaked red.

Towards that sound.

"I can't hold this position much longer, Tharsis. This orbit's decaying." Words desperate, his eyes far too old for the young face he was wearing. "We need to deal with this." The man ran a hand across his head, sweeping rain off his cadet's haircut. "Tharsis, right now, I need you to listen very carefully to—"

But the Flet was gone.

The cabin was gone.

The smell was back. Stronger now.

Tharsis realized she was still walking.

Naked, feet unsteady on the rough concrete beneath them.

Tharsis blinked up into a man-made canyon of glass, shining towers that reached up forever. Beyond, the street opened out onto a wide bridge, shimmering waters, rimmed with parkland, impossibly green. People were everywhere. The noise of human civilization, the sound of life, was overwhelming.

It wasn't Mars.

But if it wasn't Mars…

Legs gave out.

Vision tunneled.

The blackness took her again.

BOOK ONE

NERITIC

CHAPTER
ONE

"YOU TOLD ME HE WAS AWAKE."

"He is."

"He's catatonic."

"He isn't dead anymore. That's something, isn't it, sir?"

Maybe it was. Maybe it wasn't. Stag wasn't convinced any of this was worth his time. He had a deepvoider with a barely functioning quant and a scat-ton of burnt-out circuitry to deal with. Not to mention the intermittent riots still raging across New Stockholm.

Last thing he needed was that damn historian from INSHOALCOM playing semantics with him.

"I have more important scat to deal with today," he said. "Like that problem out in the Shoal Bar. You are aware of the current body count, aren't you?"

"I know, Colonel Orlani, but—"

"It's Lieutenant Colonel," he said absently, staring through the glass of the small isolation room. At the motionless body of the Landlord. "And the name's Stag."

What a fucking mess.

Lieutenant Chen's broadcast, and the consequential cessation of the growing Propagation, had left most of the Heliosphere reeling. On places like 4Vesta, that had translated into bloody rioting. It had taken a Herculean effort on the part of Yip and his Marines to retrieve the bodies of the Landlord and his dog. The base commander was dead as well, but unlike the other two, he wouldn't be waking up.

Why the Rallarhu hadn't stopped the rioting was a matter of intense concern for the ASDF. As was why she had made no attempt to save the Rossen. Even if the bulk of the Arran population hated her, the two Landlords were reliable allies.

It didn't matter. Instead of a seasoned sergeant with decades of experience with the current state of the Heliosphere, Mars was now stuck with a corporal. One who woke up angry and barely spoke their language.

There were protocols for this, for the Landlord coming back after dying. It had happened so many times, the ASDF's Historians' Office had it down to a science. Procedures, checklists. A whole trained team. A team they couldn't get.

Every divedrive in the fleet was tied down at the moment. Including the *Barachiel*. Combat duty. The few civilian craft with dive cores were involved with evacuations. Mars was on the other side of the sun, too far for a conventional fusion drive to make the trip in time.

They'd gotten the backup plan. Daevid Adair, the INSHOALCOM headquarters historian. Arrived on the general's personal cessna with the rest of the small relief force. A working knowledge of Silicone English, he'd promised, but not much else to offer. Now he was Stag's problem to deal with.

Just like the Landlord.

"Doc," Stag said. "What's your take on this?"

"We're still in a variable period right now," the doctor replied. He was on loan from Hygeia as well. Humphreys didn't have an actual physician, just a few med techs. The place had used a civilian doctor, off base, as a consultant, but he'd evacuated with the embassy. "According to the information I got, sometimes the Rossen takes a few hours to get to this point, sometimes a full sevenday. It's been six days now. We're still within tolerance."

Stag leaned on the window. He remembered the Landlord from his brief stint with them. Older. A bit heavier. Obviously burdened. That man on that bed now was just a kid.

"Where are we at with the other issue?" he asked. "The Tok?"

"The one they bagged here? I've got the boys prepping to suction the body, see what we can save."

Cambel was going to love that. If they lost the navigation material. "I need that to be your top priority. Command wants eyes-on at Noqumiut. See what the fuck Lieutenant Chen was talking about." And get the girl back, if she was still alive. What HOMECOM intended to do with her, Stag had no idea.

The historian cleared his throat. "As I'm sure you're aware, sir, uhh, Stag, Command can't make that call."

"No," Stag said, fingers drumming on the glass. "But *he* can."

"Not without a vote from—"

"How long?" Stag asked, cutting that protest off.

The doctor sighed. "I can start sooner, if—"

"If you need a few more hours, take a few more hours. Don't fuck it up trying to rush."

"I appreciate that, sir."

Stag checked his watch. Scat. He had a briefing to go prep. Of course Cambel had stayed up on the *Barachiel*, managing overwatch operations. As second in command, all the administrative bitch work had fallen to Stag. "We've got another status update due to Hygeia at eighteen hundred this evening. Main conference room here. I want you both there."

"His brain waves seem to be normalizing," the doctor said. "He might be awake in…"

Stag tapped the glass again. "In the next couple of minutes, I'm guessing."

The Landlord was moving.

———

FOR THE FIRST time in months, Caleb Ross wasn't in pain.

He noticed that first.

Since his squad's capture, pain had been a constant companion. Everything the whitecoats at the orbital facility had done, they'd done without anesthesia. Nothing as crude as surgery; only the first few of his platoon had undergone any serious dissection. No, whatever chemicals they kept pumping into him burned like fire in his bones, itching in his muscle fibers and between the gaps of his neurons, until simple movement was agony. The bastards even had the gall to apologize for it, promising his men's sacrifices were for the greater good of humanity as they stabbed more needles into his veins, bored into his marrow.

Twelve of them. Whittled down to three.

Two now, probably. They'd dragged the captain out a few nights back. Of all of them, Rallison had gotten off lightest of all. Hardly touched. Until a few nights back. She'd fought; of course she had. Tyr was chained to a bulkhead and Caleb had just spent sixteen hours with blue nightmares dripping into his bloodstream and neither of them had been able to do anything but watch.

The whitecoats had cut the gravity to get her out of the room, tiny spheres of blood hanging in the air currents. She'd bit, kicked, lashed out. She'd screamed.

She'd screamed all the way down the hallway.

The gravity was back on now.

The gravity was on, and he didn't hurt.

But artificial gravity, especially the kind generated by centrifugal motion, had a peculiar quality to it, like being forced down by invisible straps.

Caleb didn't have a sense of that at the moment. Everything felt normal. Or something like normal; he was lighter than he should have been.

Where the fuck was he?

Opening his eyes—and how had he not realized they were closed? —Caleb sat up. Took in the room around him. A simple hospital room, possessing the kind of careless, worn character he normally associated with military installations.

They'd left him some sort of uniform. Looked like an old-school flight suit, all one piece, with a high color and contrast stitching. Gray on the black material. There was some kind of integrated circuitry mesh embedded in the lining.

There were hook-and-loop patches for name tapes, rank badges, but nothing with his name. Cotton underwear, cotton undershirt. Compression socks. Boots, oversized, bulky, knee-high. More of that same circuitry seemed woven through them.

Wasn't anything he normally wore. Probably the only thing they had to give him.

He took his time getting dressed. Movement was difficult. Not painful. More like a soreness that he couldn't quite identify.

There was a mirror in one corner of the room, he noticed, as he was zipping up the one-piece uniform. He stopped, staring at himself.

What he saw made no sense.

He looked…

The whitecoats hadn't fed them well. Hardly enough to stay alive. His body had been wasting from the lack of gravity, the bad nutrition, the drugs.

Now, though, he looked healthy. The right amount of fat. Healthy muscle tone. No stubble. No odd bruises. No missing hair—he remembered his hair falling out in big clumps, the last few weeks.

And his tattoos were all gone.

The chevrons on the back of his hands and lower arms. The unit tag on his shoulder, the row of dots he'd inked on in between two particularly large ilu scars on his right forearm, the names of his sisters, his mom, over his heart. All absent from his skin. As if they had never been.

Crazed whorls of blue ilu scar tissue still littered his chest, back and arms, the legacy of the insanity that had taken his hometown.

Why did those remain, and why was everything else gone?

He wasn't sure how long he'd been staring at himself, trying to figure it out, when the door opened behind him.

"Corporal Caleb Ross?" an unfamiliar man asked. The accent was odd. Wrong. "We need to discuss a few things."

An academic. Caleb recognized the type. He'd killed enough of them over the past few years. Tall, pale, that kind of nervous energy they tended to get when excited. What Caleb didn't recognize were the tattoos on the man's neck, a stylized wing of some kind, feathers spread.

Caleb ignored him. Kept dressing. Undershirt, uniform top. Boots.

"Corporal Ross?" the man was saying, with that strange accent. "My name is Daevid Adair. I'm here to brief you on—"

"Not interested."

The guy, Adair, glanced back. Somebody else was there now too, in a gray uniform similar to the black one Caleb had been given. He had the caduceus of a medical officer on his uniform, and the same neck tattoos as Adair, albeit more complex.

A quick conversation passed between them, something that sounded almost like English but not quite. Caleb thought he caught a few words: *blood, resurrects*.

The boots had connection points, Caleb realized, magnetic contacts for the circuitry in the uniform. They snapped in as he pulled the knee-high things on. "Trying to see if what you did worked out?" he asked.

Adair didn't answer right away. He consulted his tablet instead, a frown on his face. "You aren't on that orbital platform anymore, sir. You're on a military installation in the—"

"My first name's not sir. Who are you?"

Another long pause. No glance at the tablet this time, though. "The lab you were trapped in was experimenting with several different types of life-extension technology. My understanding is that they cycled several thousand test subjects through that facility in the ten years it was operational. Your unit was the last. You, and your dog, were two of the only successes."

"You expect me to believe this shit?"

"It's the truth, Corporal."

"If you were really military, y'all'd kill me. There's a standing execution order, for anybody that gets bio-fucked." Something changed in the uniform as the last connection point secured itself. The fabric had gone taut. The strange sensation of lightness went away. "If you're going to lie to me, get your facts straight."

The door opened again. Instead of the doctor this time, though, it was a different officer. Black uniform, wings terminating just under his jawline. A seriousness in him that was the most familiar thing Caleb had seen yet.

And by his side…

"Tyr," Caleb said, irritated now. "What'd they do to you, boy?"

His dog's heavy, glossy coat had been shorn down near to the skin, and he was wearing an unfamiliar style of harness. But it was him, and he burst forward, away from the strangers, entire body exuberant. He whined, trying to press every inch of himself against Caleb's legs.

Caleb dropped to one knee, scratching that favorite spot behind an ear. That just got Tyr's tail wagging harder. Images, dark and warm and familiar, scattered out of him. It was Tyr's memories of his puppy-hood. He tended to reference those when content.

The others were having another quick conversation in that strange almost-English. Finally, the guy calling himself Adair coughed.

"There's more to it, sir, that we should—"

"Stop calling me sir."

"There's more we need to talk about."

"What's that?" Caleb asked, laying an arm around Tyr's shoulders.

His dog's presence only confirmed they were lying. If something had happened to them in orbit, it was perhaps possible they were keeping Caleb alive for some kind of debrief. But Tyr? Nobody hesitated to shoot a bio-fucked animal.

"The year."

———

WHATEVER WAS BEING SAID between the historian and the Landlord, it clearly wasn't going well. Stag didn't need to understand Silicone English to recognize an argument was forming.

"Let's try something different," Stag said.

Adair tapped his tablet. "There's a script we're supposed to follow."

"Clearly it's not working."

"It has to work. His brain is in the same exact configuration with every wake-up."

Stag ignored that and looked at the young man, sulking on the floor. *If only Mars could see him now*, he thought wryly. The Rossen was larger than life, a man whose legend inspired confidence, pride, even if his continued presence in Arran politics was largely unwelcome. Everyone grew up with the same images of him. In his late fifties, crushing the Civil War. Older still, delivering a speech at the senior enlisted academy or addressing the nation after a Propagation.

"What difference does it make? Let's take him outside." Stag pointed at the door.

"Outside?" he asked, very slowly.

The Landlord looked at him for a moment, then back to Adair. A few traded lines of conversation, and Adair sighed.

"He understood that, sir."

"Good," Stag said. "Let's go."

The Landlord was quiet as they walked to the gatehouse, out through it, into the hangar that adjoined it. Battle damage was still very much evident; Humphreys's personnel had been able to return both facilities to full operational readiness but lacked the resources to make all essential repairs.

The MP manning the place went pale when he saw the Landlord come in. That was to be expected, Stag figured. They'd all known the Rossen before, hadn't they?

The enlisted kid did agree to open the hangar doors for them, though, and in the middle of Adair and the Rossen's continued discussion, the barrier skies appeared.

There, at the base boundary, the atmospheric shields of both the base and the archipelago city descended. Humphreys's sky terminated along a wide, tall perimeter wall, while the Ibbies' touched all the way down to a canal that ran in parallel for a kilometer or so before curving off, except for a small sliver of sky that ran up and over the hangar.

There was a tactical reason for it. To allow Arran air assets access to the city if such things were ever required in a contingency.

But Stag wasn't intending on giving the Landlord a rundown of habitat defense protocols.

The sky over Humphreys was set to mid-afternoon; it was dawn for 4Vesta.

If Stag remembered his history lessons correctly, there had been nothing like this in the Landlord's time.

He said something to the historian.

"Well?" Stag asked.

"He said it's a hell of a thing," Adair translated.

CHAPTER
TWO

CALEB HAD NEVER CONSIDERED himself a particularly noteworthy guy.

The story Adair had been telling him sounded like complete bullshit. Immortality. Absolute power, given to him, a fucking corporal.

He was nothing special. Orphaned at age eleven, one of a handful of children who survived when the Arium Labs turned his town into an experimentation zone. Rescued by the Montana Air Guard, he'd bounced around group homes on military bases until he was old enough to enlist at fourteen.

In the past decade, he'd seen his share of insanity. Whole cities abandoned. People driven insane, starving to death, lost in the beautiful nightmares carried in the plagues. He'd set fire to the Arium Labs and executed the worst of their biological horrors.

Waking up almost eight centuries in the future, in charge of a whole fucking planet, almost seemed sane by comparison.

But he couldn't deny where he was; even the most ambitious void habitats he knew of couldn't boast anything like this. And Tyr kept insisting that this time, this world, was real.

The place he found himself in now looked like every other command staff briefing room he'd ever been in. An attempt at niceness. Hard-worn chairs. Unit patches and command insignia littering the walls. None of those were familiar, but at least he could read them.

They'd given him the chair at the head of the table. Caleb sensed there was something significant in this—symbolism was ground deep into the fabric of the military, any military—but didn't argue it. The space gave Tyr more room to curl up. To his right were a couple of obviously senior officers and, to his left, a chief who'd shaken his hand warmly and said, through Adair, that he was glad to see him alive again.

Caleb understood a fraction of what was being said. Adair, sitting next to him, was attempting to translate. He was stumbling badly, but the corporal appreciated the attempt. The historian had also provided him with a written account of the issue at hand. Partially Adair's summary, partially things pulled from what Adair insisted was some kind of record Caleb had been keeping for centuries.

He'd been going over it while the officers fought.

The leadership in the room was in what sounded like a heated argument with the gray-haired woman on the main screen. A general officer, Adair had told him. The briefing was more for her benefit. Apparently, there were chain-of-command conflicts going on. Picture quality wasn't the best, and there was a distinct lag between when somebody spoke and when she, or one of her staff, answered. It made for a stilted conversation, and everyone seemed irritated.

"We're about fifteen light-seconds away from the Inner Shoals Command HQ at the moment," Adair explained quietly. "Hence the lag."

"What are they arguing about?" he asked. There was a large glass container on the table, in clear view of the camera. "It sounded like *stomach contents*."

"A Nalatok operative—"

"A what?"

"I'm not sure what the equivalent word is. Terrorist, maybe. She hit the base a sevenday ago, blew that hole in the guardhouse. She swallowed something we need in order to get out of that place." He tapped the tablet. "Colonel Cambel thawed her out of stasis today to extract it."

"How'd she die?"

"I was told you executed her."

The woman on screen said something, sharp and direct. Everyone fell silent, including Adair. Caleb looked at him. "Did she just ask if she was boring you?" he asked.

"Close enough," Adair said, and answered her. Some of the words were familiar, but the cadence was strange, Caleb realized. Mostly just the cadence.

The man to Caleb's right leaned forward. His neck tattoos were larger and more elaborate than anyone else's, echoed outlines of wings spreading from the center of his throat to just below his ears. He was also older than the rest, his eyes curiously milky. He made some long comment, then looked at Adair. Onscreen, the older female officer was clearly waiting for it to come through.

"The colonel says it's going to be your call on what we do next," Adair translated. "And he's not moving a fucking centimeter until you say so."

Caleb glanced back down at the written account. "This place, Noqumiut, it's supposed to be some kind of experimental utopia? But everybody's actually dead?"

"Essentially. It's a bit more complicated than—"

"It's never more complicated than that," Caleb said. He didn't understand; this should have been obvious. "What's the issue?"

"It's complicated. There are a lot of politics involved."

"But it's my call, what we do about this now?" He looked at the colonel, unsure if the man could understand him. "I choose the mission parameters?"

It must have been clear enough. The colonel nodded. "Your orders," he said, very clearly.

"That's easy," Caleb said. "We go. We burn out anything that's left intact, and we kill anything that's still alive. Do you have—" He stopped himself, looked at Adair. "Do we have the means to do that?"

"Yes."

"Good."

Another statement from General Cochrane, and Cambel answered immediately. "We have a lieutenant, who went missing out there. We would like to bring her home. This can be justified based on that," Adair translated.

"What the hell was she doing out there?"

Adair asked Cambel, who replied, "You sent her out there."

He'd ordered an officer out to a place like that? Fuck.

Almost a minute later, General Cochrane's next comment came through.

Adair translated.

"She says protocol does demand that we pick up the archaeology team from Mars before—"

"Fuck archaeology," Caleb said. "What part of *burn it out* don't you understand? You don't save anything from these places, nothing. Even the lab notes can be infectious. It all gets destroyed." He realized then that the woman on the screen was watching him intently. He looked straight at the camera. "We go out there, ma'am. Now."

Adair passed that along. It started another argument amongst the officers. Caleb tuned it out and went back to his tablet.

Noqumiut.

Huh.

He knew that word.

———

THEY'D TOLD him he had a barracks room here. After the briefing, the chief, who'd introduced himself as Anders, offered to take him by.

This base, Humphryes, was strange. Unlike any orbital platform he'd ever been on.

Instead, he was out in what looked like a normal surface base, with buildings and roads and landscaping. Which was odd, in and of itself. The sky above them appeared thin, dusty, the kind of sky he associated with high desert. Before the briefing, it had been just descending into a sunset phase. Now, the base had passed into its night phase and the false light had gone dark. In its place, an expanse of burning starfield.

A silhouette was tethered at the edge of the great glistening dome.

"What's that?"

"Deepvoider," Adair supplied. "A, uhh, a spaceship."

The base wasn't large, though, and the barracks weren't far. There was nothing to mark the room as his own, save maybe a number.

"This is your room," the chief told him, via Adair, as he unlocked the door. Caleb forced himself to listen to the chief's voice as well. If he was stuck here, if this wasn't a lie, he needed to learn how these people talked. "We haven't touched it since we got the news."

"Of what?" Caleb asked, more sharply than he meant to. "Me dying?"

"You being the Landlord. Sir."

"I understood that," he told Adair, before the man could translate. Caleb stepped inside the threshold of a dead man's space. His space. "This must be weird for you. We knew each other, right? I was stationed here?"

The chief glanced at Adair, who just shook his head and didn't translate it. "Chief Ross…"

"Corporal," he said absently, taking in the room in front of him.

As far as barracks went, the place was nice. Large. Bed in one corner. Small bookcase. Table and desk, with a pile of tablets and a bulky piece of equipment that looked like some kind of computer. Private bathroom too, which was a luxury Caleb hadn't ever had.

He felt nothing. No hint of familiarity. No sense of home.

"Nothing personal," he commented as he looked around.

Chief Anders, waiting by the doorway, made a comment.

"Wait, don't tell me," Caleb said to Adair, and looked at the chief. "He said I didn't talk about myself much."

"Good ear," Adair said.

Caleb moved over to the bookcase. There was no personal reading material here. Instead, everything seemed to be reference material. Regulation binders, legal texts. On the top shelf sat about a dozen clothbound gray books filled with decent paper and tight handwriting. Leafing through one, he recognized it as his own. "Guess I've been journalling, though."

Adair came over. "We'll need to take these with us when we leave," he said. "Get them archived."

"You archive my journals?"

"For over seven hundred years, Heliosphere standard, yes."

"Heliosphere standard," he grumbled. "That's what, exactly?"

"Earth time," Adair said. "Mars has a six-hundred-day year, and our days are slightly longer. But since none of the other human habitats in the Heliosphere are planet-based, they stayed on Earth time."

Caleb was about to ask how that worked, then noticed a smaller book on his shelf, one he hadn't caught at first glance.

This one was blue, not gray, with thick ink markings on the side. Caleb took this one out gingerly. On the cover, another set of markings, complete with a large glyph-form that he didn't recognize. The writing pulled at something in the back of his mind, a meaning he couldn't quite place.

The writing system he'd seen on his last mission, he realized.

His last mission, the one where his unit had been captured, had been a raid on an unassuming facility out in the middle of the Guatemalan rain forest. His unit had been sent there to deal with a suspected bio-cult.

What they'd found was something else entirely.

Caleb had had a lot of time to think about it. It was as if reality had been split open and stitched back together all wrong.

That place had defied description, something in the facility attempting to rip open the ragged edges of reality. Mapping had been impossible; corridors doubled back on themselves and rooms that should have been in the center of the structure opened out in precipitous mid-air balconies. And everywhere, everywhere were glyphs painted on the walls.

He flipped the notebook open.

Instead of more glyphs, there were neat columns, hand-drawn and carefully divided. Time, date, duration. Words he assumed were locations; he didn't recognize most of them. No descriptions. The paper was yellowed, old. Only three pages had been used.

And then, he had a flash.

… lying on his back, the dark tarmac vanishing off into a low, scrubby landscape, faceup. Mist overhead obscured the sun. Somebody, something, was screaming, a high-pitched sound that cut right to the core of him. He knew, he knew that, he knew…

He had a weapon in his hands, but his fingers wouldn't close. The skin had gone a waxy shade of white. He couldn't move. He could feel his heart pumping, weaker with every beat.

Beside him, Tyr lay totally still, eyes vacant to the sky.

Footsteps.

Caleb reached for his gun, but it was kicked away. Metal skittered across the rough asphalt. He looked up, straight into a barrel.

The shot rang loud in his ears.

An echo that—

"Landlord?" Adair was saying. "Sir, you okay?"

Caleb shook himself. So he'd died before? Many times? Maybe there was more memory there than Adair realized.

He put it aside. Focused.

Task at hand.

"There some kind of process for handling this stuff?" he asked.

Adair hesitated. "You typically review it before handing it over," he said. It sounded like an omission.

"Better take it with us, then," he said, and grabbed a backpack out of the closet.

AFTER A FULL SEVENDAY, Tharsis realized she wasn't hallucinating.

She was in Singapore.

She was on Earth.

Before. Before the genocides. Before the exile. Before.

She'd woken up in a hospital. One so foreign she barely recognized it for what it was. And out of the half dozen or so languages the staff tried with her, she only recognized English. Not well enough to speak it, but the written language hadn't drifted so far.

It took Tharsis a day or so to convince one of the nurses to bring her something to write with. A battered little tablet, a foldout keyboard. Communication got easier after that.

They'd found her in that alley, the nurse told her, naked and unconscious. The police had thought something had happened to her, but there was no sign of violence. Unable to wake her, and with no identity chip to scan, they'd brought her here, to what the nurse called the Anglo hospital. The designation meant nothing to Tharsis, but she suspected it mattered somehow.

Where are you from?

They kept asking. Nurse, other staff. Somebody who called herself a psychologist, and pestered Tharsis every day.

There was no good answer.

What was she supposed to say? Mars?

She didn't even know if settlement had begun out there yet.

She didn't know the date.

It shouldn't have been so difficult to figure out, except the old Christian system had been discarded by the Tenancy, along with the dates of most of Earth's history. Mars had gone to a new calendar almost immediately upon First Landing.

Yet another thing lost to the Euphemism.

Tharsis had no idea what HST date corresponded to the Silicone Age's still running system. Where she was in its cycle.

There was only one point of reference she had.

Exactly one.

Caleb Ross.

While the Euphemism was said to have started decades before, one of the first periods of true horror was said to have passed through his town. Some little ranching community in the mountains of some place called Wyoming. When he was ten, almost eleven.

Not even his age could be entirely relied upon; it was theorized he'd died several times before emigrating to Mars. But it was something. The only thing.

The nurse had showed her how to access the Gig on the tablet, that legendary worldwide information network. One of the great wonders of the Silicone Age.

The Tenancy had banned such things.

These Earthers liked their immersive content, and the Gig was full of it. Almost every hosting location she queried wanted to download information into a VR set for her, create some kind of all-encompassing experience. She couldn't access any of that without an identity chip and wouldn't have been interested anyway.

There were shallows, simple text-based databases, enough for her to check easy things. But it revealed nothing.

Caleb Ross had no presence on the Gig. Nothing she could find anyway, not without a chip.

It was the only lifeline she had.

Considering their last conversation, she considered it ironic.

Wyoming, she finally typed out for the nurse, after she'd exhausted all other avenues of research. Maybe this would yield something new. *I'm from Wyoming.*

She wasn't, of course. Family legend held that the first Chen on Mars had come from the island nation of Hong Kong, his wife from the Gulf States of America. Nobody knew for sure; it scarcely mattered. But Caleb Ross had grown up in Wyoming. Every school child on Mars knew that word.

The nurse cheerfully took down the information. "We'll contact the American embassy for you," she said. "I'll sure they'll want to transfer you to their care."

Tharsis knew that place too. The old republic, sea to shining sea. One of the legendary old countries. One whose flag hung in the Chapel of Memory at the District of Lunae.

It hadn't existed at the time of the Euphemism, if she recalled her history, or at least, didn't exist by the end of it. Torn apart, the coasts claiming the heartlands had rebelled, the heartlands accusing the coasts of the most egregious crimes. Both factions would eventually claim the old nation's name, but neither would keep it after the fracturing. Low-grade civil war was a feature for decades, before the Euphemism wiped petty concerns like politics away. Survival, nothing else, mattered then.

The Gig was able to confirm some of that. After Tharsis made that statement to the nurse, a few additional databases opened up for her. All concerning America. That alone seemed concerning.

And, of course, Wyoming was in the heartlands. Listed officially as a contested state.

She'd heard stories about the security apparatus of the war-torn nation; many of the Founders had written about it extensively during Mars's own early, turbulent period. Corruption was rampant, abuses common.

Tharsis remembered her Academy civics courses. It wasn't a government she felt inclined to trust.

She wasn't about to throw herself on the mercy of that embassy.

She cursed her own stupidity.

Tharsis waited until the late hours of the night, when everything in the hospital quieted to its lowest ebb of activity. She crept from her room, wandering still unfamiliar hallways until she found the staff locker room. There, she grabbed a set of clothes that fit—a dress, leggings—and, after a moment's hesitation, a few hundred in local currency.

Her face was still burning with shame when she slipped out, into the sticky tropical night. Stealing wasn't something she would have normally been okay with.

"One step at a time, Chen," she told herself.

She found an all-night café, ordered something tasteless to eat, and waited until the sun came up to move again.

UNFAMILIAR BACKPACK OVER HIS SHOULDER, Caleb followed the Arrans back to the main gate and its hangar. From there, they told him, they'd get a ride up to that thing they called a deepvoider.

Just as they were entering, the air lock to the city opened, humid air swirling in.

In walked half a dozen men, wearing the same black uniforms Caleb had seen everywhere else but wearing combat kits. Breastplates and shoulder pauldrons of dull gray, helmets, an assortment of weapons. Pistols, a few rifles, one man with something huge hooked into a humming backpack. All of them were bloody. One was leaning heavily on another's shoulder, right arm swathed in what looked like a uniform undershirt.

It was the first thing that felt at all familiar.

The man in the lead said something to Chief Anders before catching sight of Caleb. He smiled broadly then, heedless of the splattered gore on his face, and held out his hand.

"Caleb," he said. "Woke up at last?"

The words still carried that accent, but at least they were all legible.

"This is Sergeant Yerpoli," Adair said. "He's in charge of the *Barachiel's* Marine contingent."

"Call me Yip."

Stag, the officer who was apparently the number two guy around here, asked him something. The sergeant's good humor gave way. He answered in kind, waving his men into the hangar.

"The fuck is going on out there?" Caleb asked.

"On board," Yip said, and pointed up. "We can talk."

———

"IT ISN'T EXACTLY what I would have guessed a spacecraft would look like," Caleb said to the sergeant, searching for anything to break the silence in the small transport craft. "Isn't what they looked like in the movies."

"Oh yeah. I've heard about those. Star Fleet stories," Yip said. "My kids have a couple of picture books."

"What happened to movies?"

The Marine shrugged. "You banned them, sir."

It was simple enough, again, that he could understand it.

"Banned?"

"You agreed to uphold a ban," Adair corrected, giving the sergeant a sharp look. "We didn't elect him as a dictator."

The Marine rolled his eyes and made a comment too quick for Caleb to parse out.

The historian, clearly forgoing translation, went back to addressing Caleb. "Military spacecraft, in your day, were envisioned as battleships in space. But the standard mission sets we deal with are different. We're the only military force in the Heliosphere of any significance. What matters is survivability and longevity. Half that craft isn't fit for human habitation, and that's by design."

Caleb didn't say anything but turned his attention back to the craft rapidly growing in the lander's small window.

The deepvoider resembled nothing so much as some kind of deep-ocean fish. The body formed a rough teardrop, with a spine of antennas running the full length of its back. A trio of stubbed, finlike wings swept out from the front of the craft, along its sides and belly. The lower wing hung like a stabilizing rudder on a sailboat and thickened into a broad hangar at the top. Smaller openings, glowing blue in the darkness, were set in along the sides. The only visible viewing port was set a few levels above that series of apertures. Engine bells flowed out of narrow rear taper.

The oddest thing about it was the surface. Unlike the images Caleb had always seen of metal and glass ships, this was strangely sleek. Dark. Like it was coated in a deep layer of shifting, swimming oil.

"What do you mean? We build ships we can't use?"

"Radiation is a problem. Cooling is a problem. We do have xeno-cyte wrapper shielding, but it's not a guarantee. There's a series of water reservoirs, up to four meters in some places, that encase the crew spaces. Very effective shielding, and an excellent heat sink."

"Also tends to confound idiots who try to cut their way in," Sergeant Yerpoli added.

"These function more like forward operating bases than the carriers of your day."

"Carrier. Single. We're down to just one carrier fleet," Caleb said, and then caught himself. "Or were, I suppose."

"I didn't know that," Adair said, the look on his face making it clear he was eager to ask more.

This was basic. This was essential, in a way, to the war Caleb grew up fighting. Something that he easily could have told them. Why he hadn't, Caleb wasn't sure. And until he figured that out, he resolved to keep his mouth shut.

"It's an ugly bitch, isn't it?" he said instead. "How many of these do we have?"

"Not enough."

Caleb thought about what he'd said so far already. "So there hasn't been any kind of conventional war in centuries? What have you been fighting?"

"A dead woman, apparently."

Caleb settled back in his restraints. "Seems to be a lot of that going around," he muttered to himself.

Ahead of them, the hangar doors slid silently open.

Waiting for them as they landed and disembarked was a younger officer. Caleb hadn't quite gotten the exact marking down, but the meaning was obvious. Neither the chief nor Yip had those throat tattoos. This guy's had a bronze band in the middle of it. Red hair. A serious expression on his face.

"Lieutenant Hans Morray, our comm lead," Adair translated.

The lieutenant held out a small device that looked similar to a glove. He said something to Adair, which sparked off a quick conversation. The historian finally nodded and gestured at it. "He's set up a palm pad for you that will translate for you. He's here to show you how to use it."

Caleb gave the historian a look. "If this has happened so many times, why isn't there a system in place?"

Morray said something, something that got an amused snort from Stag, and then stretched out the fingers on the glove. A tiny web of light between them held a small, tight typeface. *There is a system, just not out here,* it read. He held out the glove again.

Caleb shrugged, and slipped it on, buckling the lower clips around his wrist. "How's it work?"

Morray checked the read-out on his own hand and answered.

"Hold your fingers out taut to keep the projection field active. It'll disengage when closed. The silic"—this didn't translate—*"is housed in the wristband. The translation matrix isn't complicated. Language hasn't drifted that far."*

"Colonel Cambel is wrapping up a few things at the base. Pilot's going to go down and wait," Stag said. *"When he gets back, we'll go. Until then, Morray's going to give you the tour."*

The read-out was fast. Helpful, Caleb decided. Being able to see the words as they were spoken helped him figure out what he was hearing.

He nodded. "Sounds good."

Stag turned to Yip, clearly done with his guest. *"All your fire teams off the 'roid?"*

The reply came almost too fast to read. *"What teams? Half my men are dead and another three are bagged in Medical right now. Doesn't include Nalin and Rich, who aren't deploying again anytime soon. Stefans is probably going to lose his hand no matter what the doc does. Where the fuck are these scat-stains getting their explosives? Where's the fucking Rallarhu?"*

"I heard she's been executing her way through the disloyal local security forces," Morray said.

Yip snorted. *"Like that's going to fucking fix anything. Like I tried to tell Cambel—"*

"*Bitch to me, not the commander,*" Stag said, and glanced back at Caleb. "*Pleasure meeting you, sir. Morray, anything he wants to see. Yip, with me.*"

Morray looked at him. "*You ever been on a warship before?*"

"No."

That didn't need any translation, apparently. "*Great. Let's start with the dive core. It's the most interesting part of the craft anyway.*"

———

THE INTERIOR of the deepvoider craft was as utilitarian, as artless, as its pitted exterior.

Caleb had never been on board a proper military spacecraft before. There were—had been—rumors of such things being built, but most of what they'd used in his time were repurposed civilian vessels.

No polished paneling, no soft lighting. This was a world of painted metal and bare conduit. It did have gravity though, more of a tug at the back of his thoughts than anything else. As if some force were compelling him to keep his feet on the ground. Caleb frowned at the feeling but shoved it aside.

From the hangar level, they took a brief elevator ride upwards. The doors opened out into another air lock, then beyond that, a wide corridor. Rounded, almost three meters high. The space should have felt roomier, Caleb thought, but it was densely packed with pipes, cables, exposed equipment paneling. The corridor was curved, not straight, following what must have been the outer curvature of the hull.

As they walked, Caleb noticed doorways, here and there. All were on the inside curve of the hallway. There were no windows anywhere.

"*We have space for over three hundred men; our crew and two full companies of Marines,*" Morray said as they walked, "*but it's tight when we have that.*"

"What's the normal crew size?"

"*Just under one hundred and twenty,*" Morray replied. "*Six dogs, although we're at half that number right now. Fucking Jovians tend to shoot them first.*"

"Jovians?"

"Citizens of the inwell of Jupiter. A lot of conflict on some of those moons, and the outer Lagrange habitats are cesspits of Polarist sentiment."

Caleb looked to Adair. "Bio-cult," Adair explained. "Largest and most prevalent. There were many during, umm, in your time, yes?"

"Dozens," Caleb replied, thinking again of the jungle. That last mission. "Too many to quantify." He'd never rightly understood it, the intersection of old animism and the transhumanist objectives of groups like the Arium Foundation, but the influence they held—had held—on Earth was well known to anybody who had the wits left to see it.

"We only have the one. Only one to survive the purges."

There was history here he needed to understand, Caleb figured. Time enough for that, once they got that Noqumiut place sorted out.

And maybe there were things they didn't understand. Judging from the way Morray kept looking at his palm pad, or Adair's almost hungry expression, he wasn't telling them something they'd heard before.

Eventually, their small group broke out into a wide atrium, maybe the size of a baseball field. Catwalks ringed the space, four floors high, but Caleb was surprised to see that the place was full of greenery. Grass. Huge shallow pots full of what looked like vegetable crops. Simple creepers that ran up the walls in vertical planters. Diffuse light streamed from the ceiling, the color off somehow. Cooler. Maybe it was what light looked like on Mars.

"Helps with the air supply," Adair explained. "Some water reclamation too."

"It's also nice when you've been out for half a home-year," Morray added.

"How long do you stay out?"

"As long as necessary."

A hatch at the far end of the atrium opened down into a shaft, falling away at an angle into the darkness. Morray ran his hand over a panel. Dim lighting came alive, recessed into grooves along the edge of the floor and wall.

"These were designed as forward operating locations. Drop a few square kilometers of Mars anywhere in the Heliosphere," Adair said. "Capacity isn't the greatest, but for extended campaigns, they'll pull a couple of troop carriers out of deep freeze. Storage orbits, at the

Lagrange point. Then these can be used as command-and-control vessels. But these crews are trained to handle just about anything."

"Sounds like Special Forces."

"Is that what you did?"

"To a lesser degree," he said.

"*This is the most heavily shielded part of the craft. Dead center,*" Morray explained as he waved them in. "*Most stable location. The quant is down here as well.*"

"Quant?"

"Quantum computer," Adair offered.

Morray must have caught that. "*Ours is smaller than what you'd find at Deimos, but it does its job.*"

"Which is what?"

"*Among other things, maintaining the gravity-current simulations for the dive core.*"

That meant nothing to Caleb. He wondered if it was supposed to. But before he could ask, he got a sense of something.

A glimpse. A memory, maybe.

A sunset, the sound of surf, screams rising from…

Caleb…

He stopped.

"Sir?" Morray asked, the word clear.

"What is this thing?' he asked.

"*The divedrive? It's, umm, it's wetware.*"

"Organic?" he asked more sharply. "Human?"

The two men exchanged a look. Adair coughed. "Sir, you need to understand—"

But whatever he was going to say was lost. Something in Morray's uniform buzzed, and he flicked open his hand.

"*Change of plans,*" the comm officer reported. "*Let's head to Ops. You can meet the core later.*"

Whatever was behind the door seemed to whisper to him. Something important. Something…

He felt something, sand perhaps, give way under his feet as he turned.

Definitely human wetware, he thought grimly, and followed the two Arrans up the hall.

CHAPTER
FIVE

MONEY WAS AN ISSUE, as was identification. So many eyes and ears, watching everywhere. Everyone seemed oblivious to it, how tight the surveillance was, how closely every activity was followed.

Tharsis thought it might drive her insane if she couldn't get away from it soon.

Even in shiny, brilliant Singapore, one of the wonders of the age, there was an underground. A parallel economy that supported those who chose not to participate.

A hostel on the edge of the abandoned old Muslim district was happy to give her a room in exchange for work. Straddling the boundary between legitimate and criminal, all sorts of interesting people drifted through the place. Interesting people who had fascinating conversations that, over time, she started to understand.

Tharsis kept her mouth shut and listened.

Many people here wore VR sets, either in the form of wide goggles that completely obscured the face or implants directly into the temples. For those who wore such things, there was a steady stream of information being pumped to them at all times. If she'd had papers, an identity chip, everything from her name to her social postings to her personal history would have been available to anyone at the blink of an eye.

The Scient's bans on brain-linkage technology—hell, the Scient's bans on almost everything—started to make more sense.

Not having a chip wasn't enough to get her flagged or arrested. But

Tharsis still learned to identify the telltale signs of Gig engagement and avoided such people as best she could.

Drugs were another problem. Less easy to identify, but far more difficult to deal with.

Most of the drugs used were things Tharsis didn't recognize. Outside certain Polarist cults, drugs weren't common in the Heliosphere. This time, maybe, had left indelible trauma on the species in that regard. A few names had survived, though, their names legendary. Heroin. Cocaine. Amphetamines.

Ilucoccine.

That last one was the same scat Olin, the Rossen, had ordered her to be injected with. The drug that carried the nightmare of the Wytt.

And it did kill. Sometimes directly from overdose, she was told, but other times users seemed to just stop. They'd sit down and die of dehydration in an alley. Tip off a train platform or blank out behind the wheel of a car.

Singapore had strict laws about such things, but enforcement against certain types was almost impossible. The hostel had rules in place to prevent habitual users from taking up residence there, but no security system was absolute.

As Tharsis had found out firsthand, not long after taking the job.

———

THIS PLACE, unlike Nighttrippers, didn't stay open around the clock. The main doors locked around midnight and didn't open again until six AM. Part of her job, minding the desk, was to make sure that happened.

The battered but comfortable little lobby was barely enclosed. The front of the hostel was more window than cinderblock. Roll-down bars covered the space at night. A veranda lay beyond that, though, separated from the sidewalk with only a low wall. The owner of the place had warned Tharsis it often turned into a hangout spot late at night. The evening before, just before Tharsis had locked the main doors, it had filled with young travelers—not all of them guests—drinking unregulated rice liquor out of cheap plastic cartons. Things had gotten a little wild. She didn't speak any Chinese, and most of them pretended not to speak English, Silicone or otherwise, and so she left them alone.

That night, it was just her and an older couple who were sitting near one of the wire-shielded windows, sharing some kind of fruit and cream dessert, talking quietly to each other.

Tharsis was just about to flip the locks on the front door, lower the metal gate, when a man's hand slapped against it.

The dead bolt didn't catch.

It happened almost before she realized what was going on.

One moment, she was at ease and unconcerned.

The next, she was being shoved backwards, a hand on her throat.

Struggling against the hold, Tharsis found herself staring up into a pair of bloodshot eyes. A small tendril of brilliant blue bled from the skin under his nose, running down his face.

"What are you doing?" he whined in her ear. "Why wouldn't you let me in? Don't you see what's coming for us out there?"

Tharsis could see what he was seeing. Fire. Darkness. Smoke in the air, klaxons out in the streets. Screaming. So much screaming. And a roar, a roar up over the top of it all that shook the foundations of—

Blue staining.

Ilucoccine.

It wasn't real.

Mars gave up dreaming for this, she told herself. *So you can know. It's not real.*

"It's not real," she told him, fighting the tendrils of fear trying to shove their way into her brain. "What you're seeing, it's not real."

He slammed her into the desk. The countertop, some crude stone surface, protruded a few centimeters past the wall. Pain erupted in her shoulders. "You're one of them, aren't you?" he snarled at her. That sick blue was spreading under the skin around his left eye. "High on ilu, can't see the danger right in front of you. People like you are the reason why we're all going to die!"

Scrambling, reaching behind her, Tharsis felt something cold, heavy, that had nothing to do with the nightmare biting at her mind. She grabbed it.

His hand tightened. Her vision grayed.

One chance, Tharsis knew.

She swung as hard as she could one-handed. One of those blows that never would have landed in an out-and-out fight, it caught him square across the temple. He went down like a sack of potatoes.

The cold and the dark cut out. As if somebody had flipped a switch.

The object in her hand—one of the owner's little bronze statues, some Asian deity—was unexpectedly heavy. Tharsis had learned how to move, fight in different gravity than this. The force of her swing dragged her forward. And she might have fallen, if not for the older man catching her.

"You alright, miss?" he asked.

It was the older man, the one who'd been eating dessert with his wife.

"Fine," she said, and nudged the fallen body with her foot. It looked like he was still breathing. She hoped he was.

"Junkie," the old man said, and spat.

There were no police to call, not in this district. At least, not without consequence. The owner had been explicit about that. So Tharsis and the guest moved him outside, out into a nearby alley where he was out of sight of the main street. Somewhere he could wake up unmolested. At least, that's what Tharsis hoped.

He wasn't there in the morning.

Tharsis didn't know what to make of the affair. Drug users were not something she had any experience with. She tried to put it out of her mind.

But the next morning, as she was cleaning up the small breakfast room, it came back up again.

"I didn't get a chance to thank you last night."

It was the woman from the lobby, maybe in her late forties, graying hair pulled back in a ponytail, thick bangs over her forehead. She had the look of somebody who had seen too much.

"What do you mean?"

"You, hitting that man, knocking him out. Stopping the, uhh, well… what I was seeing. That was a thick ilucination that man was stuck in."

"Ilucination?"

"The shit that opens up, the things that come, when you get too deep in the ilu. It's sad, when people go down that road."

That made even less sense, but then Tharsis remembered the Rossen's own history. The Wytt. All the old stories.

She'd always thought of it as akin to any other plague. A force of nature. One that raged out from its origin, killed, and retreated again. Tharsis had never considered the possibility of infection being optional. Intentional.

Recreational.

This is the end of the Silicone Age, she reminded herself. *The start of the Euphemism.*

The older woman obviously took her sudden discomfort at the realization for something else entirely. "I'm sorry to mention it but—"

"I've hit people before," Tharsis said blandly.

"Ah, well. You kept your head, and that's a rare talent these days," the woman told her.

"Your husband saved me."

"Only just, I'm afraid." The woman was silent for a moment. "It's quite terrifying, when somebody's else nightmare leaks out like that."

"I've never seen it before," Tharsis said honestly.

"They say it's just a product of ilucoccine poisoning, the hallucinations, but they've always felt more... real, to me. Who knows?" She was quiet for a moment. "Really, your first time?"

Tharsis didn't know what to say to that. What would have been expected, what was reasonable. "First time somebody's attacked me high like that."

The woman cast an appraising eye over her. "You're military, aren't you?" She smiled a little. Like they were sharing a secret.

Was she? Was she still? Tharsis didn't know. She wasn't military here. But what about if she could find a way home? Would they make her finish out the family commitment? Court-martial her for the Singapore disaster? Would Sergeant Olin, the Rossen, just execute her instead?

"That's an odd thing to ask me," she replied.

The woman brushed back her bangs. The skin of her forehead pulled tight around a livid red scar. A tattoo sat beneath it. *USMC,* in crude, rough letters.

"I was a gunnery sergeant, once upon a time. Infantry." She tapped her forehead. "Got this a few years back. The riots at Annapolis." The smile fell. "Worse than Taipei, that. It was our own we were fighting. Makes it harder to pull the trigger."

Tharsis had no idea about the significance of that event. Didn't know at all what to say. "Was it ilu again?" she asked lamely.

"Worse," the old sergeant told her. "Politics."

———

NOTHING LIKE THAT HAPPENED AGAIN.

Tharsis got good at spotting ilu users in the streets and avoided them like the plague they were.

It all seemed to be voluntary consumption too. But who in their right mind took something that made them see nightmares?

So much about this time made no sense to her.

As the days melted away, Tharsis began to feel desperate. For a direction. For answers.

She needed to get out of this place. Needed to get off this planet. Get home.

Even the Rossen executing her would be better than watching this world die.

Tharsis didn't know what to do, though. The Gig offered her no information about what was happening in the void; no matter how many times she looked, all she found were official government pages containing statements so exaggerated—fatality rates, piracy, deplorable conditions—Tharsis could only conclude it was intentional propaganda. It made no sense to her, either. On fine days, one could see the Malaccan Lift Complex from the southern shore of the city.

It took her a few days to realize those pages weren't Singaporean, but American. It didn't seem to matter what terminal she used, where it was located or if she'd ever accessed it before. Somehow, even without a chip, the Gig was still holding her to that statement from the hospital.

She stopped using it, frustrated.

Where could she go? She shouldn't have been in old Singapore, on old Earth, to begin with. Time travel was impossible. Even if it was, the energy release involved should have been catastrophic.

Beyond that, she should have been dead. The ENEX had been well on its way to killing her. Even if she'd managed to dive herself home—and what arrogance it had been, thinking she could do that—she likely would have died. Only a top-level emergency care unit with void expertise would have saved her. Her body bore no sign of that experience. Her hair was intact, deep and thick and still attached to her head. No radiation damage. No bubbling or warping or melting in her sling. There wasn't a mark on her, except for the burn scars on her neck. For some reason, those had remained.

Besides, her body shouldn't have functioned well here, if at all. Humanity may have evolved on Earth, but the gravity on Mars was three times lighter and the Arran people had adapted to it. Movement should have been painful, if possible at all. But her limbs functioned, her heart pumped, her lungs rose and fell in her chest. Her digestive system worked. Her muscles didn't ache.

It was as if she'd been remade for this place.

Once Tharsis had that thought, it stuck in her brain. Haunted her.

Never mind the how. *Why* was she here?

The implications were disturbing enough that she tried not to think about it. Focus on the task at hand.

How to get off world.

At first, Tharsis thought that perhaps she'd go find Caleb Ross. Get her bearings temporally. But that seemed an impossible task.

Wyoming was half a world away, on a planet where civilization was crumbling. What would she do if she got there? She spoke to a few of the Americans who drifted through the hostel, picking her words very carefully.

None of them had anything good to say about their situation back home.

There was nowhere left on Earth to go, one of them told her one night, up on the hostel's cramped rooftop deck, very drunk. Nowhere anyone could run. Just the void.

Tharsis worked odd jobs while she tried to figure it out. Sometimes at better places of lodging, sometimes for the companies that cleaned the houses of the rich. There were easier ways to raise funds, of course, offers from less scrupulous employers, but Tharsis held on to the memory of Saturn and refused.

She'd compromised too much of herself already.

Never again.

She found a church in the English-speaking sector that she liked. She went every day she was able. It helped her with the nuances of Silicone-Age speech, and it was the only thing in the whole wretched city that felt at all familiar.

The homilies were soft, though, the priests here far too yielding. *In victory we must be gracious*, they said.

No priest in her time would have talked like that.

She found it almost unbelievable that this church, with priests like this, had stood against it at all.

Tharsis longed to go to confession, but there weren't words in this time for what she had seen. What she had done. How could she explain it?

Nothing made sense.

So Tharsis drifted, lost in the ancient sprawl of glass and steel and electrical data, trying to stay out of sight, unsure of where to go or how to proceed.

Until the day she found an answer.

One she didn't like in the least.

CHAPTER
SIX

THE DIVE, Caleb was told, would be instantaneous.

It was not.

One moment, he was in the operations room.

The next, he was lying on his back in a field.

A vast, dark field. Asphalt, he realized. Tyr was nuzzling his side, trying to urge him up.

He sat up, disoriented, bruised. His entire body hurt.

"What the fuck?" He reached a hand out into Tyr's fur.

The dog was gritty. Caleb pulled his hand back. Under his nails, sand. White sand, the fine stuff from a coral beach. One of his fingers wasn't working quite right. His knuckles were raw. Blood was ground into the fine lines of his skin.

Caleb.

Somebody was walking towards him.

Everything was suddenly too bright to look at. He shaded his eyes, tried to see.

Caleb, we need to talk.

Eyes watering in the glare, he blinked.

Then it was over.

Then he was back.

In front of him, through the deep-set viewing window, was the starfield. The starfield, and a great white planet, falling down the screen.

"Location?" Cambel asked. Caleb caught both the word and the tension.

"Distance to sun, confirmed at over 35 AU. Triangulating off pulsar markers," the navigation station replied. "Cross-referencing with known Kuiper Belt object database."

The Void Operations Center was what passed for a bridge on the deepvoider. The central nexus of command and control. The space itself was oblong, with banks of monitoring stations set down on three broad, stepped platforms. They formed two wings, flanking a central aisle where the colonel was now standing. The back half of the space was taken up by a polished glass sphere, a small model of the divedrive held dead center by a slender column. The holographic projection field, they'd told Caleb.

There was apparently no official pilot position. The navigation station took care of general movement, but a small cockpit was available for more specialized maneuvering. It was set out on the surface of the craft in a blister of windows, down a ten-meter hallway that threaded between water shielding, ablative icerock armor plating, and the craft's xenocyte wrapper. Whatever the hell that was.

All Caleb could see of it was a small air lock door, at the front of the operations room, half-hidden behind a wall of flat video monitors.

Stag stepped out beside the commander on the aisle. "Dwarf planet."

"Yes, but which?" Cambel replied, then barked out a rapid-fire series of orders that Caleb only caught on the palm pad. Ship functions.

At his side, Tyr whined.

"*Eris,*" the nav station announced. "*Ninety-nine percent certainty.*"

"*Any sign of life?*"

"*We have a heat signature on the far side. No radio transmissions of any kind.*"

"*The bitch really has gone quiet,*" Stag muttered.

"*It could still be a ploy,*" Cambel replied. "*Distance?*"

"*Eighty-five minutes on the argon-prop to holding distance from the field.*"

"*Good. I want surveillance wasps deployed immediately. The full package.*"

"We aren't going down in person?" Caleb asked.

The translator took a moment to process that, but the colonel's reaction was near instantaneous. *"No sir. We have no idea what's on this rock. And until we do, I'm not risking a single member of my crew. Is that alright with you?"*

It wasn't really a question, despite the phrasing. Even through the lingual drift, Caleb caught that, loud and clear.

"I'm not here to override your authority," Caleb said, feeling awkward.

The colonel just nodded at him and went back to studying the icy landscape beyond the porthole.

"Sir," Stag said, *"if you'd like, you can head down to the Hive hangar to supervise this personally. It's a better field of view down there."*

"Uhh, sure."

FOR ALL CAMBEL'S insistence on holding back on a deployment, the main hangar bay told a different story. Everyone down there was kitted up in void gear; Caleb suspected that once the surveillance drones were able to report in, Cambel intended on sending a team down. Yip had even provided him a suit too, showed him how to pull the thing on. Nowhere near as thick or bulky as the stuff from his own time; Caleb was able to fit the translation palm pad over his fingers.

"Just in case," the Marine said.

That made Caleb feel somewhat better.

Adair had accompanied him down to the hangar, along with an officer Caleb hadn't met yet. He had the basic wing tattoos on his neck, half-hidden behind a white collar, but no rank on his uniform. Nothing but a small gold cross. He had symbols on the back of his hands, in black ink, that Caleb hadn't seen on anyone else yet.

"Padre," Stag said by way of introduction, nodding at the newcomer. "Chaplain Kannik."

The team was rounded out by a dog. A dog in the same gear as everyone else, which had surprised Caleb. Nobody had bothered to explain that yet, other than to tell him they'd need to get Tyr void-qualified on that same survival equipment. She'd exchanged a few sniffs with Tyr, a few growls, bared teeth. None of the Arrans seemed to mind.

Yip tossed Caleb a scabbard after he'd gotten the exogear pulled on. "This is for you," he said. "Favorite blade, right?"

Seax. Fighting length. Nice balance, excellent blade quality, from what he could tell. Must have been something he'd acquired in his previous life. Didn't look much used, though, and Caleb resolved to get the full story out of Adair whenever they were done with this. How did Yip know that about him?

"Yeah," Caleb said, examining it. "What do you think is down there?"

Yip just grunted and wandered off to go deal with his guys.

"Have you ever done any void maneuvers? Any walks in microgravity?"

It was the chaplain, Kannik. His voice was soft, but unlike Yip's clipped attempts at Silicone-Age English, his speech was fluid. It caught Caleb by surprise.

Almost none, Caleb thought wryly. "When do we head down?"

"After the wasps do their job," he said, and pointed at a series of rail launchers along one side of the hangar. A number of small, sleek craft were mounted there, lights flashing, small wisps of smoke escaping from hidden thruster assemblies.

<Wasp squadron set to leave in five minutes,> a voice boomed over the internal speakers. *<You're welcome to stay in here, gentlemen, but you're going to want your hoods up.>*

"What?" Caleb asked.

But even as the word left his mouth, the temperature began dropping precipitously, the air instantaneously painful. Everyone else seemed to be pulling on breathing masks and googles. Like they were going for a fucking scuba dive.

Yip waved at him and demonstrated how to do it. Caleb fumbled through it but got it on. Something in the headgear seemed to seal up as the edges made contact, like the material was merging.

<You getting air? Take a breath,> Yip said over the radio. <Blink three times, fast. You see a screen? Little symbols?>

Caleb thought he caught all that, but checked the palm pad, just in case. <Got it.>

<Everything… everything green?>

<Yes.>

<Blink it off,> Yip replied, and then, louder somehow, said something that contained the words *ready* and *open*.

The hangar doors split open.

The wasps, silent in vacuum, surged off their rails.

In the blue-white glow of their thruster wash, however, was something that shouldn't have been there.

———

STAG PACED the floor in *Barachiel's* VOC, waiting for the wasp video feeds to stabilize. The things were out in the void now, still about a kilometer from the Lighthouse. It was hard to tell. Interference from the Lighthouse was making the images shaky, the data feeds uncertain. Although silent now, the antennas were still bleeding off energy. The further in the wasps went, the more the interference ramped up.

At its present position, the *Barachiel* now held the fleet record for furthest distance from the sun. Stag wasn't convinced the distinction was worth it, no matter how many beers it would win him back at Asaph's Officers' Club. They hadn't had time to complete all repairs, fix the damage done by the mailing's presence. Internal silic-based systems kept displaying new issues.

Most of it was stupid scat, doors malfunctioning or corrupted data files. More critically though, the dive core had failed to transmit the morning status report. And the information flow from HOMECOM had stopped. No new messages in the past three hours. Highly unusual, especially with everything going on.

As soon as the Landlord had left the VOC, Colonel Cambel had gone down to the core to help sort the mess out.

They needed to get back in contact. HOMECOM was pissed about the Landlord's refusal to bring along the archaeological expedition. Both the Scient and the Onias had diverted precious resources to get their people out to Phobos for that deployment. Command had requested the *Barachiel* report back to Asaph.

And whatever the Rossen said, Stag could understand the urgency. The word of Mars's Landlord wasn't going to be enough to assuage the anger building across the Heliosphere. Proof. Proof was essential. The kid didn't understand that.

And yet, his insistence on burning the place out... he had experience none of them had. That had to count for something.

"Weather, anything?" Deepvoiders didn't carry a dedicated scientific research team. When they needed a deeper analysis of something, the task normally fell to whichever ops station specialized in it.

"The Lighthouse is cooling," the sergeant on duty said, and brought up a video feed from one of the wasps on his monitor. "A fraction of a degree since we got here. But it's already colder than it should be, even for a trans-Nep Lighthouse. You can see from the fog that's beginning to swirl over the forest, something's changed."

Stag went over. The image was infrared, color contrast bumped way up. Everything out this far was always so cold. "What does that mean?"

"We stay here long enough, I might be able to calculate the rate of change. But the Lighthouse is going to match ambient temperatures eventually. Eris's orbital path is currently taking it away from perigee, away from the sun. The atmosphere is in the process of freezing back down. Depending on how fast the Lighthouse is losing heat, this entire place could be buried under meters of methane ice in a matter of a few sevendays, maybe a month, two."

Well. That was a problem. "Lighthouses have static membranes for atmosphere retention. It shouldn't mix with the outside air."

"The static membrane takes power, sir. For this kind of cooling to occur..."

"We're talking about power loss." Stag thought about that for a moment. What had that Chen girl done out here? "Hive Head, you on the vox?"

<Listening to every word with bated breath, sir.>

"Primary objective needs to be whatever reactor is powering this thing."

<Roger that, sir. But we might have a problem.>

"What kind of problem?"

———

A FIGURE.

That was what it was.

A human figure.

Standing just beyond the edge of the huge void doors.

At first, it looked as if the figure was wearing exogear similar to their own. Its surface matched: dark, moving like an oil slick. But the similarities ended there, because the figure was quite clearly female. Not a human woman wearing a suit, with all its added bulk, but one who seemed to be made of it.

The face turned to him. The black surface rippled, shuddering as if a breeze were moving across the surface. Shifted.

The black stayed over most of the form. But a face emerged in colors: pale with green eyes, blonde hair slicked back into a bun at the nape of the neck.

It was his captain's face. Rallison's.

She brought her hands up.

=Good to see you again, Caleb,= she signed. =We need to talk.=

Yip recovered from the shock of it first, gun up, trained on it.

=As if that can hurt me. Caleb, tell him to stop being an idiot.=

But Caleb didn't get the chance.

Yip, the hangar, everything, was gone.

He was no longer wearing a void suit, unzipped and dormant. He wasn't wearing a uniform at all. A pair of jeans and a scruffy, heavy jacket.

Rallison was talking.

"We agreed, didn't we, that we wouldn't do this? That you wouldn't bother me?"

He blinked, trying to get his bearings.

It was, of all places, a bookstore. It smelt of coffee and peat and age. They were tucked in a back corner, hidden behind the groaning stacks of old books.

Captain Rallison was leaning against the opposite wall, a Fair Isle-style sweater over her tall, lithe form, short blonde hair pulled back and eyes tired. Suspicious. One hand was mindlessly scratching the soft fur between Tyr's ears.

"You died again, didn't you?"

CHAPTER
SEVEN

ONE OF THARSIS'S favorite places to work was the historic hotel down on Marina Bay.

There used to be more of them, she was told, those hotels. Dozens. Luxury accommodations for the leisure class. Tharsis found the entire concept amazing. There were moneyed families on Mars, of course, but Arran society frowned heavily on sloth. You worked, or you starved. That was the reality of living on a terraformed world. No matter how rich one was, there was always more work to be done.

Singapore had been a financial capital of this world, once. It still hosted a significant amount of Earth's trade and managed the Malaccan Spacelift complex down at the equator. But the last world war, fifteen years past, had hit them hard. Tourism was far more difficult now too, Tharsis had learned. Travel was all but banned.

Most of the luxury hotels had gone out of business.

The lone survivor was a thing of beauty. The hotel boasted a grand lobby, vaulted with curving beams. Whitewashed walls and stone floors channeled in the salty-sweet breeze from the Pacific. It was easy work, waitressing there. Taking drink orders to the bar and bringing them out. Cleaning tables. Straightening things back up after the customers were gone. Tips, an interesting concept, were good when she got them. Time to think.

Pleasant.

Almost enough to make one forget what was coming.

But one of those pleasant afternoons blew up entirely when Tharsis looked up from wiping down a table, just in time to see somebody striding through the grand old space.

Not just anyone.

Peter Donovan.

Tharsis almost dropped her tray.

Younger. No service brand. Face unscarred. No limb wasting. Not yet.

Peter Donovan.

She would have known him anywhere. One of the Founders of Mars. *The* Founder, in many ways. Heir of the company that funded, supported, drove the terraforming. Two of his uncles and one of his older sisters had served on the very first expeditions, working on broad-spectrum biome improvement programs, seeding what thin atmosphere had been coaxed from the melting ice caps with bacteria. His oldest son would be the first Speaker of the House, his only daughter one of the historians who collected the oral accounts of the civil war into books, including *War Dog of Mars*.

As if on autopilot, she set her tray down and followed him.

Clear across the lobby.

All the way to the elevator bank.

Brass doors opened and swallowed him up, Donovan not casting so much as a glance back at her. She hurried, trying to catch the doors before they closed. But somebody stepped out of another elevator with a huge luggage cart, blocking her way. By the time she got around it, he was gone.

Shaken, Tharsis stared at it for a moment, before another guest asked her to move out of his way, and she stepped back.

"Sorry," she said, mind reeling.

She went back to cleaning tables, still trying to work it out. Arran history held that the Donovan family had been the single richest in the Gulf States of America. They'd made their fortune in the energy industry. Hydrocarbons, both terrestrial and Jovian. Early entry into asteroid mining, the development of mig manufacturing. Creating, fueling the engines that had ferried so many from a dying Earth out into the void.

Mars had been their special passion. The family had poured every resource, every last asset, into the terraforming effort on Mars.

At least, that was the story.

Tharsis berated herself, excitement ebbing in her now. What would she accomplish by following him? What had she intended to say to him? *Hi, I'm from Mars.* No, that was insane. Nothing existed on Mars yet.

She didn't exist yet.

Yet.

His family had also run the settlement efforts. The training programs, the void passage.

The exodus craft.

Tharsis thought about the *Padua Anthony*. Its bridge. Its navigation data, blinking at her with the hope of centuries from some half-frozen console.

It was a way home.

Or, at least, could be.

Maybe.

If she could convince him. He was always described as something of a hard-ass. She had nothing to trade. There was nothing important for her to do in this time, nothing critical about her presence here.

There were training camps, though, survival schools, or at least, there would be. Programs that the first wave of pioneers had been, would be, required to attend. Learn those skills for surviving the pressure storms and the agonizingly long winters. Learning to cultivate life from dead soil. How to deliver babies, both animal and human, a thousand miles from the nearest doctor. How to build structures that would withstand the winds.

Some of those skills had been lost, left behind as Mars matured. But its biomes were still young, their shared ecosystems fragile, and children in her own time still learned much of it.

She had skills to offer.

Knowledge couldn't amount to much, could it? Knowledge couldn't change anything.

Maybe she was here, in this time and this place, for exactly this reason.

It was an arrogant thought, and dangerous.

Tharsis tried to set it aside.

She saw him near the end of her shift, the sun setting beyond the grand lobby's wide windows, heading out with somebody else, another man Tharsis didn't immediately recognize.

She took a second shift that night.

Just in case.

Her patience paid off.

Peter Donovan was back by eleven, slightly inebriated. That other guy still with him. Laughing, joking, sauntering off to some of the best seats in the house. Americans were like that, she'd noticed. Always joking.

"I'll take that table," she told the other server, after the woman took their order. Her Silicone-Age English was getting better.

The older woman rolled her eyes and handed her the ticket. "Trust fund babies. Have fun."

Tharsis gave the order to the bar. Coffee, with something mixed in it. Creamy, rich, and sweet. The alcohol was heady. Outside of the few luxury hotels she'd taken contract work in, Tharsis hadn't seen much more than rice liquor and bad whiskey.

The guys, Donovan and whoever he was with, had taken up residence in a pair of thick, deep leather chairs, set in front of the wide-open shutters. Overlooking the lights of the bay. If it hadn't been for the heady night breeze, she would have thought it a night from New Stockholm.

Memories she didn't need.

"Got your coffees," she said as she set the cups down. "Can I get you anything else, sir?"

Donovan was fiddling with his Gig tablet, but the other guy looked up.

Getting a good look at him, like that, she finally recognized who it was.

The Flet. Younger, whole. But him.

He started to say something.

She didn't hear it.

The world slid away.

CHAPTER
EIGHT

"THE GOOD NEWS IS, the core's not dead. The last few dives have proved that."

"At least there's that," Erg said. *"So where the hell are we?"*

The *Barachiel's* navigation officer was obviously irritated by the question. *"I've got the quant working on finding some sort of pattern here. That last dive took us to the very edge of the heliopause. Any further and we'd be out in interstellar space."*

"We don't know if the dive core could survive that," Erg added.

"We don't know if we could have survived that," Aeolis said. *"The magnetics are weird out there."*

"I'm sure Titan will be interested in the data you pulled."

"Titan can go fuck itself. I need to get us back on some kind of course."

The space they were in was tight, spare and sleek as the rest of the deepvoider was crowded, utilitarian.

The core.

The *Barachiel* crew had tried to dive the craft. Six dives in the past two hours.

Nothing seemed to be working. They kept landing in empty space. Which, as the Arrans insisted, wasn't possible.

Caleb kept having flashes. Every time.

The hangar.

The bookstore, Captain Rallison in her sweater, looking defeated.

Sand, underfoot, white in dark rain.

The hangar.

Earth.

He'd finally asked to come down and see what was going on, but it was instantly apparent: he was of no use here.

Three of Erg's maintenance techs were elbows deep in the core's guts, along with two guys pulled from Propulsion. They'd been having a lively fight about automation techniques, until Erg had ordered them to shut up. What his role in all this was, Caleb wasn't sure.

Nobody had acknowledged Caleb yet.

That historian, on the other hand, seemed fascinated by everything.

"How do these things normally work?" Caleb asked Adair now, low so as not to interrupt.

The historian, scribbling in a notebook, started, as if he hadn't expected anybody to speak to him. "A divedrive is designed to follow navigation material back to its source. The shard of the Flet's consciousness it carries reads the worldlines of the atomic particles back to the moment at which they were located at their point of relative origin, then holds on to that idea. The craft pushes down into the penumbra and is snapped back onto the skin of reality, near that location. I don't know all the words for it in Silicone. Quantum… information?" He held his hands out, as if in surrender, "I don't know how to explain it right."

That didn't make anything clearer for Caleb. "Can he, it, go further back in time?"

"In a way. Not to surface, though. …" Adair clearly struggled for a moment, then let it fall. "I don't know the right words to explain."

The core room's door opened behind them.

"Ahh, there you are." It was Stag. *"Commander wants to see you. We need to unfuck this mess with that thing in the hangar bay."*

Caleb cast one glance back at the core, and then nodded. "Okay."

THE THING with Rallison's face was still standing in the void when Caleb came through the air lock and back out into the hangar. Shouldn't have been possible. But there they were.

It didn't have a voice, not out there in vacuum.

The Arrans needed him to translate. That much was obvious. But there was fear there too, fear in the Marines who Yip had posted outside the hangar doors, fear in Cambel's pinched face. Fear Caleb didn't understand.

He put it aside.

Iridescent eyes regarded him, expression cool.

Start with the obvious, he thought.

=What the hell are you?=

=A fragment,= it replied, fingers working through the words. =An axilla, if you will.= That word, it spelled out for him.

=Fragment of what?=

The thing smiled a little. What similarities it held to Rallison vanished; the expression was utterly alien. =They haven't given you the wake-up brief yet, have they?=

He could still hear her screaming. Dragged out of their cell. A few days ago. Centuries. She'd kept her composure for months, all for it to end like that. Like this. =Did anyone else survive?=

=You, her, and Tyr.=

Caleb had never been as fluent with the family sign language as Rallison, but he was conversant. And he didn't miss the way it referred to Rallison in third person.

=There hasn't been time. Something about some crazy-ass white-coat trying to burn down the entire solar system.=

=Yes, the Arcna. She is more than a whitecoat now. More than human. As are we all.=

=She's dead.=

=Yes, that too.= The thing paused. =Your Captain Rallison doesn't exist anymore, not like she was. Things like this are what remain.=

=So you're not her?=

=A derivative. A part of her, broken off and sent to accompany you here.=

=Why?=

=You were coming to Noqumiut. Something the Rallarhu has strictly forbidden in the past. Something she has always forbidden.=

=Why? There's nothing alive there. Why fear it? Why give it any credit?=

=Not everything is dead.=

=Like what?=

=Caleb, you must understand, coming to Noqumiut without unanimous approval of the Tenancy is a violation of international law. It leaves Mars forfeit, open to attack.=

=I thought Mars had the only standing military in the system.=

=Why do you suppose that exists, if there is nothing to fight? Ask them, and they will tell you. Mars is vulnerable. Perhaps more vulnerable than any of them know.=

=What do you want?=

=I need a suit, sealed against this craft's atmosphere,= it said. =And I need to speak with the dive core.=

=Good luck,= he told her. =Damn thing's offline.=

After a short but heated argument over the radio, a suit meeting the axilla's requirements was left for them in the air lock. Designed for internal maintenance efforts in the uninhabitable zones of the craft, or for void walks in protected space, it lacked xenocyte wrapper. Much of the formfitting outer layer was reinforced with some kind of inflexible plate. Like an articulated suit of armor. Or a cockroach, albeit white instead of shit-brown. The hands were bulky, which might limit some of the nuances of the sign language they shared, but it had an integrated radio of some kind. He wasn't sure how the axilla could manipulate that.

He wasn't sure how any of this shit worked.

Caleb watched the thing collapse, the human form melting into an undifferentiated puddle of goo, slithering forward on hundreds of tiny pseudo-feet, climbing its way like a parasite into the suit.

What the hell had happened to his old captain?

What kind of fucked up world had Caleb woken up to?

———

"I DON'T LIKE THIS, SIR," Yip grumbled, outside in the hangar level's main corridor.

"None of us like this," Stag replied. They'd been watching the Landlord's exchange with the axilla. The xenocyte-thing had just sealed itself in the suit, and the Rossen had given the all clear to repressurize the bay.

If it had been up to Stag, he might have just repressurized the bay from the moment the thing set foot on the ship. It was the fucking Rallarhu, after all, or at least, a piece of her. They owed her zero hospitality as far as he was concerned.

"How did it get out here with us?" Cambel asked, neutral.

"It likely came off our hull shielding," and that was Senior Master Sergeant Druz, the maintenance lead, who'd brought the suit down from his shop's storage lockers. "If this thing really is part of the Rallarhu, then it could theoretically attach itself to the hull. Maybe even integrate with our own wrapper."

"That is a myth," Yip said.

"It's supposedly how she took over most of the initial void habitats in the Inner Belt," Druz shot back.

"Great," Stag muttered. "We're going to have to burn the whole fuckin' craft now."

The colonel was stock-still, arms folded, thumb tapping its usual spot on his jaw. It was a pose the entire crew knew well. "Druz, might as well get a team outside, make sure the wrapper's not compromised."

"We'll have to use the rockjump, visual inspection only."

"That's fine. Let's get eyes on the problem before rumors start spreading," Cambel said pointedly. "We've been diving blind anyway. We can afford a few hours for everyone to catch their breaths."

But the Inner Belt's Landlord had other plans.

———

"*UNACCEPTABLE*," the axilla-thing said, signing the word for Caleb at the same time it spoke it through the suit's speaker. "*We must return to the system core immediately. Call for quorum. Do this legally.*"

Colonel Cambel's expression didn't change, but Caleb had the sense the man was seething inside. Yip, beside him, A24 cradled in the crook of his arm, was making no attempt to hide his own hostility.

"*With all respect, you admit you're not the Landlord herself. I'm under no obligation to take your orders.*"

"*This entire vessel is operating in defiance of international law. She knows this. It's why I'm here.*"

Cambel hesitated. *"What do you want?"*

"I want to speak with the core."

"And I told you, it's offline."

"Show me," the axilla repeated, taking a step towards him.

Caleb got between them. "Colonel Cambel, Let me head down there with her. It, whatever. You can't come out of that suit, right? You'll dissolve or something?"

The axilla blinked, those not-eyes vanishing for a merciful moment. *"No, the atmosphere would dissolve this form in a matter of minutes,"* it replied, hands still moving for Caleb's benefit.

"I'll deal with it," Caleb said. "My responsibility."

The colonel was clearly unconvinced but nodded anyway.

———

IF THE CREW had ignored Caleb before, they gave the axilla-thing their full attention.

If it noticed how uncomfortable it made the crew, it gave no sign.

=Do you know who this is?= it asked, tapping the central column in the room. The suit the axilla was puppeting was thick, bulky. Its hand movements were broad. Almost unintelligible.

=Wetware?= he asked. There was no native word for this in the American Sign Language Rallison's family had used; they'd invented it themselves, after it became necessary.

=Yes, indeed.= It patted the column, hand lingering for a moment before pulling back to keep signing. =Very rare wetware, difficult to sustain. But that is a what, not a who.=

=I don't care who the donor is. It's not working right now.=

=The Landlord has seen problems herself. Since you died. Since the lieutenant came out here. Something has destabilized the neural network that keeps these things moving.= It pressed the vox button. *"Sergeant, how long has your core comm been down?"*

"I'm a Marine, ma'am. They don't tell me that sort of thing," Yip drawled.

The officer spoke up. *"It's been buggy for a sevenday at least. Went down completely this morning. We assumed it had something to do with the recent damage we've taken."*

"It is a larger problem. That aligns with the timeline we've observed in the Inner Belt," the axilla agreed, and turned the radio off. It patted the column again. =Do you know who this is?=

=Who?= he asked.

The thing with his captain's face took his hand and pressed it against the column.

All the world vanished, sucked into the white around them.

And in its place was that airfield.

A hangar, open to cold sea air and the far-off cries of birds.

An aircraft.

In front of him was an aircraft.

The wingspan was a hundred and fifty feet at least, from what Caleb could see, the fuselage at least a hundred itself. It was hard to get a good sense of it. Darkness clung to it. The hull was warm to the touch though, a material that didn't quite feel like metal humming against his fingers. It gave the impression of having been grown, not constructed. Organic, but meticulously planned and pruned if so.

Rallison was with him, fine hair pulled back now in a ponytail, loosening in the light breeze.

"One of his," she said, walking the length of the fuselage. "More experimental bullshit. I bet if we cut this, it would bleed." She stopped, looked back at him with those green, green eyes. "How'd you know this was here?"

"Looks like somebody else got here before us," Caleb commented, pointing at one of the wings.

Something dark, oily, not quite synthetic, dripped from it. The entire length was riddled with holes, all of them weeping. Some had gone red, or black. Infected. It stank.

"What happened out here, Caleb?" she asked. "Where is he?"

He stared at the wounds. Bullet holes. Bullet holes, bleeding in the side of a plane. This wasn't something he remembered from before the platform.

Caleb, he heard. Clear as day. Strong as an ocean wind. *Caleb, I need—*

"Who?"

"Dad."

THE GRAND HOTEL around Tharsis was no more.

In its place was a dock.

She was standing on a dock.

A dock. Long. Full of small boats, bobbing at their mooring lines under a sunset so beautiful it could have made her cry.

It took her a moment to realize that the entire thing was built of wood—good, tall, straight wood. Something like that would have been an astronomical luxury back home. Yet here, on Earth, wherever this was, it was almost grungy. Slowly, slowly decaying into the sea.

In front of her was still Peter Donovan. Hair buzzed down to military regulation. A huge ring on his right hand. Old jeans. Alcohol on his breath. "You sure we haven't met before?" he asked, and his speech was slurred.

Tharsis was frozen. Didn't know what to say, didn't know what to do. But then somebody else walked up.

The Flet.

And suddenly, she wasn't on the dock anymore.

Instead, she was on the front prow of what seemed to be a luxury ocean yacht. The one she'd seen in her dream, before waking up in Singapore. White fiberglass and pale wood, aluminum railing and a clear view of the western sky.

Behind them, music rattled a set of tinted, streamlined windows.

How…

She had to grab the railing to steady herself.

"Hey, hey, just take it easy," the Flet said. "You're okay."

He was speaking Silicone English, Tharsis realized.

"What the hell is this?" she asked.

"This boat?"

"This place."

"It's, uhh, a weekend. A weekend out with a friend," the Flet said.

He seemed as confused as she was. But before Tharsis could ask about it, things shifted again.

The sky was darker now, outside tinted windows. Not the same ones she'd seen; these were closer to the waterline. Everything around her was finished with burled wood veneer and huge sections of cream-colored leather.

The Flet handed her a mug. Steaming. She sniffed it. Coffee. "Not just any weekend, Tharsis."

"This is the inside of the boat? The inside, when we were just outside?"

"Exactly."

"Why are we inside the boat?"

"I have slightly more control inside a physical structure." She forced herself to look at him. In the face. Young, younger than made any sense, but his eyes were ancient.

"Right," she muttered. "I was dying on Eris. Dying out there. My hair was falling out. My skin was burning off. You were gone, the divedrive was gone, everything was dead, and then I end up here. Seven hundred fucking years in the past. And then, a moment ago, I was in fucking Singapore, which is also misaligned, because isn't it the middle of the summer in this part of the world?"

"Well, it's February right now…"

"What the fuck is going on?"

The Flet was quiet for a moment. "I have no idea."

"What?"

"You might find this hard to believe, Tharsis, but I was human once. Confined to a body, and," he flexed his hand that wasn't holding a drink, "rather uninteresting to almost everybody."

"All the Landlords were, right?"

"We changed," he said, without agreeing. "I, perhaps, changed the most. But this, this place, remains the same."

"What do you mean?"

"This boat," he said, "teeters on the event horizon."

"The event horizon of what?"

But they were outside again, the shift so sudden Tharsis sloshed hot coffee down her hand.

"I take it you were somewhere else?"

It was the Flet's voice. The Flet watching her. But no longer the Flet's eyes.

It was the young man again.

"We were both somewhere else," she told him.

He sighed and held out his hand. "Tom Donner."

"Excuse me?"

"That's my name. Tom Donner. And you are?"

She dried her hand on the back of her shorts and shook back. "You don't know me?"

"I know something's wrong with you," he said, in a tone that sounded like agreement. "Like you've been pressed out of dust."

"What?"

"I don't know," he said, and, reaching over, tapped her cheek. "Just a thought, girl I don't know, who seems to know me. How does that work?"

"You were just telling me this boat is on the edge of an event horizon," she said, "but you didn't say the edge of what."

He was quiet for a moment. "I, umm, I find myself here. Quite often. This place, this entire evening, is just wrong. I seem to snap back and forth, in and out. Little snippets of this place, then I'm back to where I started. Like my consciousness is flowing loose between my then and now and before, while my body stays fixed in the current of time. Then I end up back here. Nothing changes. Never anything new, though. Not until you."

"I don't know what's significant about—"

"I need your help, Tharsis. I need you to get here, to this night. I need to pass through this thing, find out what's on the other side."

The Flet.

Inside again. Coffee drying on her skin. His own drink barely touched.

"How am I supposed to do that?"

"Don't know yet," he said with a smile.

"Flet, I've done enough," she said. Enough damage. Enough sacrifice.

He smiled at her. Sad. Eternal. "Tharsis, I'm sorry to say, I need you to do more."

The scent of the harbor vanished.

Florals reasserted themselves.

Traffic noise. The chatter of voices.

The hotel.

Singapore.

Donovan was gone. The Flet—Tom Donner, whoever he was—was gone.

She had a tray in her hands, dirty coffee cups perched on it.

Along with a receipt.

Tharsis set the tray down, hands trembling, and sank into the nearest chair. Her heart was racing; she felt faint. What the hell was going on?

What had he said?

Like my consciousness is flowing loose between my then and now and before.

Was that what had just happened to her?

At length, after the shaking had stopped, Tharsis checked that signed receipt.

Donovan had left her a sizable tip. Rich boy guilt, maybe.

———

SHE SAW PETER DONOVAN AGAIN, the next day, this time at dinner in the main restaurant, eating with half a dozen other people who were all older, none of whom she recognized. But again, they tipped outrageously well. It was enough of an excuse for her to ask around about them.

"Big oil and gas family," the manager told her. "Off world too, from what I hear. Can you imagine? Clean fusion powered by the clouds from Jupiter?"

Such engines were hardly ever used planetside, but Tharsis nodded anyway. "Yeah, I can."

"They come down here every year. They've got a stake in the elevators, or so I'm told."

"Really?" She hadn't known that. *How far back did their involvement go?* she wondered.

"That's the rumor anyway. So when they tip you this good, don't worry about it. That family has money to burn."

They wouldn't, Tharsis knew. Not forever. The Donovan family had spent, would spend, every last cent they had, and a great deal more resources beyond that, on the terraforming effort.

And he had fucking known the Flet.

She mulled it over.

The fucking Landlords and their fucking problems; she had no desire to get involved with them again.

But the deep stasis of the exodus craft was her only real chance, however slim, at finding her way home. The ASDF, or the Rossen, or whoever, could make it back out to Noqumiut on the navigation material they'd taken out of her arm. They'd be well-provisioned, their presence sustainable. They'd find the downed craft. They'd find the control room. They'd find the exodus fleet.

How long it would take them to reach those craft, how long to tug them home and thaw out the passengers, if they even could, if anyone could still be brought back after so many centuries, Tharsis didn't know. But it was something, something to go on.

She didn't know what was going on with the Flet. What Peter Donovan might be able to offer her. But Tharsis remembered the lectures, and the homilies, on the nature of space-time. The truths Father Golan had once found.

Our bodies are a temporary configuration in the flow of space-time, that famous quote for the Tri-Testament held, *a consolidation of subatomic particles that, for a brief moment, constitute a physical existence. It's in this way that we know we are more than just matter.*

She had been there, on that boat, that night that was still months in the future. But she hadn't dove there or moved there. That would have taken the energy output of a supernova, maybe more.

There was no such thing as time travel. Not physically, anyway. But if the Flet said his consciousness was knocking around loose, maybe hers was too.

The night on the boat was months away. Months into the future.

It hadn't happened, and yet, she'd been there.

That was where she was going to end up, no matter what she did.

No matter what she did.

Dammit.

It was the only lead she had, though. And hell, if she helped this Tom Donner out, maybe he'd put in a good word for her with Donovan.

CHAPTER
TEN

"WELL, THAT SCAT DIDN'T WORK."

After the last dive, Colonel Cambel had called a meeting up in the VOC's main briefing room.

Let's figure this out, gentlemen.

But twenty minutes into it, nothing had been accomplished.

The crew couldn't find any rhyme or reason to their movements. And from what Caleb could tell, nobody else was experiencing what he was. The flashes of the past.

But a past he couldn't remember.

It wasn't memory.

It was as if he was actually there. On that airfield. Talking to Rallison, before she'd become that oil slick clinging to existence in the void.

If it wasn't memory, if he was experiencing something from the past…

"What if we look for prior locations?" Caleb asked, a thought suddenly occurring to him. Nobody paid it any attention. He raised his voice. "Past locations," he said, trying to imitate the accent as best he could.

It must have been enough, because Aeolis stopped. Looked back at him.

"What do you mean?" the navigation officer asked.

"I mean, what if we are where we are supposed to be, but just minutes or hours or days ago?"

"Time travel..."

"No, I mean, umm, shit." He thought. "What if we're surfacing in the right time but the wrong location? A point that our end destination has already passed through?"

Aeolis shook his head. *"Space and time can't be separated like that. And a divedrive isn't a time machine."*

"I think I know what he's getting at," Erg said. He went for the white-board his guys had brought in. Ignoring their protests, he wiped half their work figures off it and started drawing. *"Space-time's continuous, but location is relative. On Mars, you reckon off the nav constellation, polar stars, the moons, and so on. Out in the greater Heliosphere, we use the sun as a central reference."*

"Go on," Cambel said.

The scribblings got thicker. *"But none of these represent an absolute position. Mars orbits the sun, but the sun is pulled along in the galactic disc by the gravity of Sagittarius A-Star. And our galaxy is constantly being acted upon by the gravity of other galaxies, not to mention the influence of the intergalactic medium. Every second, every body in the Heliosphere is in an entirely different position. Tens of thousands of kilometers pass every single second, everything ever so slightly out of temporal synch with everything else. Space-time is infinitely variable."*

"This is basic," the navigation officer said.

"Yes, but what the Rossen is talking about is possible. If we could model it..."

"We can't." Aeolis sighed. *"There are too many factors to consider. Even with a quant, it's nearly impossible to accurately predict the exact position, given the vast number of variables. You have to be able to ignore those and deal with it in relative terms. That is why we use wetware for this. Literally why the Flet exists."*

"What if the Flet can't do that right now? What if he's accounting for spatial and temporal positioning separately?" Erg countered.

"Why would he do that? How?"

"I don't know." He set down the marker and gestured at Caleb. *"He suggested it."*

"What do you know about the Flet, sir?" Cambel asked.

"Less than you guys do, but something's obviously wrong."

Cambel nodded. *"Aeolis, can you look into that? See if we're in the right orbital path, at least?"*

"I'll see what the boys can come up with. But I can't promise anything." He shot Erg a glare. *"We don't do objective mapping."*

"Make some assumptions."

"About extra-galactic temporal drift? Titan has an entire college dedicated to the subject and still can't—"

"Gentlemen," Cambel interjected, *"how long do you need?"*

"Three, maybe four hours."

But before Cambel could say anything more, a handset in the corner rang. The commander frowned but picked it up.

<We've got a location fix.> It was quiet, only just audible enough for Caleb's palm pad to register.

"Good. Where are we?" Cambel looked over at Aeolis.

<That last dive brought us within range of Pluto. We picked it up on long-range scanners just now.>

"Pluto." The colonel sighed. *"At least there's that. How far?"*

<Four days at full burn. This kind of approach isn't ideal, since we're out of both plane and path, but—>

"Conventional propulsion?"

<Absolutely, sir.>

"Thank fuck for that. Comm, contact Deimos, let them know what's going on. Set course. Let's see if the monastery has any better intel on what the fuck is going on than we do."

He looked over at Caleb. *"Sir, if you and the axilla would like to accompany me, I'm sure the boys would appreciate the extra room in here."*

It was as clear a dismissal as Caleb had ever heard. "Sure. All this shit's over my head anyway."

"Acceptable," the axilla grunted, guttural through the vox emitter, and rose.

"Oh, and Aeolis?"

"Yes sir?" the navigation lead said.

"Take the core offline. I don't want any more accidents like we had back at Eris."

———

ADAIR HAD SET UP A TABLET.

Left it in his small quarters.

Seven hundred years of journal entries.

Caleb wasn't interested in learning what he'd had for lunch a century before. His opinions about the people he served with. His thoughts on a recent political dustup. But that seemed to be what was in those journals as he paged through them.

Curious? He was curious about other things.

Like where that axilla had come from. Why it looked like Captain Rallison. Why in the hell humanity was still using wetware. And he was tired of having to read off everything that everyone was saying.

So he laid the tablet aside and went off in search of Yip.

He tracked the Marine sergeant down to the kennels, where he and two of his troops were cleaning out stalls. The area was larger than Caleb had expected, with a huge training yard. At the far edge lay what looked to be some sort of maze, interconnected rooms opening up in all directions. Three dogs were out there, running. Two of them looked vaguely like Belgian Malinois, but leaner, taller. Gray-white, too, shorn to the skin. One of them was Lua, the dog from the hangar.

Tyr caught his scent, barking happily, and ran over.

"Sergeant, can I talk to you?" Caleb asked, even as his dog nuzzled at his hand.

Yip didn't look up from what he was doing but answered in kind. "What about?"

"I'm tired of this shit," he said. "Reading what everyone's saying."

"Language lessons?"

Caleb nodded.

"You should ask the historian."

"He looks at me like I'm the second coming," he grumbled. "It's irritating."

"You think I can teach you?"

"You taught yourself English from my time, right?"

Yip laughed and clapped him on the back. What he said next, Caleb had to read off his palm. *"I'm not much of a language expert, but you're welcome to hang around and listen. Long as you're willing to work."*

"Work," Caleb said, trying to put the right accent on it, *"is fine."*

Yip laughed again. *"Go talk to Yeti. He'll tell you what he needs help with."*

Tyr head-butted his hip, almost knocking him off balance. Caleb scratched his ears. "How did you learn, umm, Silicone English?"

The sergeant shrugged. *"We don't have much of a library on board these things, but the Rossen's Journal is considered an essential historical record. I've read the whole thing, First Propagation to now, multiple times."*

"Why?"

"I get bored," Yip said.

———

SPACE LIMITED AS IT WAS, the *Barachiel* only had one mess hall for the crew. The officers ate at a different time than most of the enlisted, Caleb discovered that evening.

When he emerged from the food line into the main floor, Colonel Cambel and half a dozen others were clustered around a single table. A flickering holograph field dominated the space between them. Tablets were strewn about.

"Landlord," Stag called, waving him over. *"Pull up a chair."*

The officers were obviously in the middle of some sort of review. Caleb recognized the image as a map of Noqumiut. He sat down, started eating. It was some kind of curry over rice. He didn't recognize the meat, but it tasted fine. He kept his hand open in his lap, reading as he listened. He was catching a lot more of it now.

"This is what we've been able to pull together from Hive mapping," Erg said, stabbing his fork at the projection.

"Looks like a bull ant nest," Morray said.

"Or voider habitat," Stag added.

"It does. You can clearly tell that it was planned, but the shapes suggest growth. Organic. With kinks and turns." Erg pointed one out, the metal of his utensil scattering light as he stabbed it into the field, *"where the pattern deviates. Likely to accommodate structures within the dwarf planet's crust."*

"This is far more extensive than anything I've seen at a Lighthouse," Morray replied.

"It's possible there was tunneling."

"Landlord," said Adair, "any first impressions?"

Caleb frowned, and took one of the tablets, flipping back to the first series of images. It was of a broken-down gate, barely more than a gap in the wall, half-covered with the frozen atmosphere. A sign over it. *Noqumiut.*

His handwriting.

The officers' conversation continued as he flipped through the images. Stills. Some video. A few taken in infrared or other parts of the non-visible spectrum. None of those made sense. Nothing seemed familiar.

Then he reached the facility.

The first antechamber was bare, clean. Pristine. A plinth rose in the exact center of the room, built from the same solid-surface material as the floor. Caleb wondered what it had originally been intended to hold. A statue? A piece of equipment?

Instead, there was a large metal sheet. Flakes of paint still clung to it. Must have been some kind of signpost once.

He couldn't quite see what was on it. But when he zoomed in on it…

… snow, he was standing in snow, walking through snow…

… across the frozen atmosphere here…

… towards a light beyond the trees, its warmth a false promise of…

… fighting through the deep January drifts towards their barn, his youngest sister crying, trying to keep up, their father behind them, roaring like…

He shook himself.

A row of glyph-like symbols ran down the metal, more pictures than words. They bit at him, digging into the back of his mind.

The top symbol, though, he recognized.

It wasn't the same as the others. It was a logo. *That* logo.

A goddamn Arium Consortium facility.

"*What's this?*" Nav said, indicating a large void in the projection field.

Erg shook his head. "*Not sure yet. I haven't received that information from the recon swarm. But it does appear to be something not part of the facility. Buried outside of it in the ice.*"

"*Another facility?*"

"Or a craft, maybe," Adair said quietly. "There was supposed to be a population here. Where could she have gotten them?"

Cambel rubbed his jaw. "Erg, how long will the recon wasps continue to transmit?"

"Batteries have power for a standard month. They'll ice up before then, I'm guessing."

"Orbitals?"

"I put a five-wasp surveillance package out. Data uplinks are functioning perfectly. They'll last for as long as you please."

"Run every scan you can. Keep those wasps moving until they freeze solid. I want every square centimeter of this place mapped and photographed."

Stag glanced at his own tablet. "Have we got the information back on what's powering this place?"

"The wasps down there are still running scans. We should know by this time tomorrow. Whatever it it, it appears to be failing."

The colonel nodded again and fiddled with the controls on the projector. One chamber lit up and gave way to a photograph. Caleb had a hard time telling what it was at first, then realized it was a body. A mummified, mutilated body. "At least we know the Arcna's dead," he said. "That ought to make everyone happy."

"Except the seal-fuckers," Stag said with a shrug.

"Well, that's what the Barachiel is for."

A few of the group chuckled.

"When the archaeology team gets out there, they can carbon-date the remains," Adair said. "Confirm it."

Cambel looked over at Caleb. "Sir, will that be acceptable? For us to pick up the team and head back, when we can get this brick of a craft working again?"

The question caught Caleb by surprise, a glob of food halfway to his mouth. He missed the bite, and it slid off instead, falling into his lap. "Umm," he said, grabbing for a napkin, "I would recommend not touching a damn thing out there. Burn it out or let the methane freeze back over it. Let it die. Ariums are... dangerous. Designed to twist perception, twist reality. Can't trust anything there."

"We can't just forget it," Adair said in Silicone English. "The Heliosphere needs to know she's dead."

"Who is she?"

It was simple enough that most of the table caught it. Based on their reactions, Caleb realized it was the wrong thing to say. The colonel shot Adair a look.

"You haven't told him?"

"There hasn't been time," Adair replied. It sounded pathetic. "Landlord, I should probably get you the wake-up briefing before too much longer."

Caleb looked down at his food. Barely touched. "Why don't we go do it now?" he asked.

"You sure?"

"Yeah," he said, and he shoved back from the table. "I'm sure."

———

STAG WATCHED the Landlord leave the chummer, Adair at his heels. He didn't give voice to what he was thinking—the kid was too young to have the authority the colonel was giving him. Mars had voted for a man with almost sixty years of military and heliopolitical experience, not… this.

"Doesn't know who the Arcna is," Stag grumbled quietly. "What the fuck is that historian doing?"

It got a few huffed agreements from around the table. But the boss took a bite of dessert—some kind of berry cobbler—before responding.

"We haven't had much time for getting him up to speed."

"I'd say that's his fault. What the fuck were we doing out at Noqumiut if—"

"We all had very little notice," Cambel replied, "and don't blame some desk jockey from INSHOALCOM headquarters for not moving faster."

The rebuke was implied; Stag hadn't been talking about the historian, and Cambel knew it. Stag let it go. Later, he could break open a bottle of whiskey in Cambel's office and bitch about the situation all he wanted. Deepvoider crews tended to be less rigid about matters of rank, but there were still conversations one didn't have in front of the junior officers.

"There is one thing I think you should be aware of, boss," Erg said.

"What's that?"

"I do have solid data on the ambient radiation levels."

"Nuclear?"

Morray shook his head. Damn kid was on his second serving of dessert, Stag noticed. "All the Lighthouses have internal nuclear generators. Solar collectors aren't enough."

"Not in the Kuiper," Erg replied. "They were designed to be as maintenance-free as possible. Power sources for the forests themselves are supposed to be organic, sustainable. So tether-lines, radiation collection fields, digestive processes, that sort of thing."

"None of which we observed?" Stag guessed.

Erg shrugged. "It makes sense. To power a static field to fully sustain a pressurized atmosphere capable of supporting human life, the Arcna likely had to bring in a power source."

Cambel finished the last of his cobbler. "So, nuclear. What kind? Fusion?"

"Fission, I'd say. Easier to maintain. Solid fuel. Smaller volume, easier to transport. Consistent with that report Chen sent back, the one about the plutonium."

"Where has this thing been getting fissile material?" Cambel asked.

The chaplain hadn't touched his dinner. He smoothed his mash out with the back of a spoon. "Somebody's been going out there," he said. "Anywhere else, that far from the surface especially, I wouldn't have picked it up. But Eris is so inert, any human presence would of course impress itself deeply into the penumbra. Somebody has been out there. Multiple times."

"What are you saying, Padre?"

"The Naven gave the navigation material to Chen." He nodded at the projection. "Did the Landlord give it to anyone else? Come out here herself? Was the Tenancy sustaining this place, for some reason?"

Stag snorted. "What, like the Rossen—"

"This is all speculation, and dangerous speculation at that," Cambel said quickly, cutting him off. "Padre, you know the penumbra isn't always easy to interpret. And the Naven having some rocks from out there doesn't make this some kind of conspiracy."

"Wasn't trying to imply anything, sir."

"Good." Cambel looked at his officers. "Men, we've got a chance here to potentially end war in the Heliosphere, at least as we know it.

And the Rossen's going to need our help navigating this scat. There's a reason he always comes to the deepvoider fleet when he wakes. He's ours to protect. He's one of us. We don't help him by accusing him of imaginary scat that happened centuries ago. Everybody understand me?"

"Perfectly, sir," Stag said, before anybody else had a chance to start arguing.

"Good. I heard he spent the day down in the kennels with Yip. I see no reason to stop that. He's going to learn contemporary English a lot faster through talking to the crew. Encourage that with your boys." Everyone around the table nodded. The colonel turned his attention back to the central projection. "And Erg? Get me eyes on that thing under the ice."

CHAPTER
ELEVEN

THARSIS HAD little to go on.

Logistics were a nightmare.

Flet hadn't told her where he was; it was entirely possible he didn't know himself. All Tharsis had to go on was the smell of the ocean and the feel of the sky; nothing like back home. The Flet was somewhere tropical. That much, at least, she could determine.

If she needed to check every damned island in the Pacific to find him, she was going to do it.

Routes were tricky. Ferry tickets were hideously expensive. Which would mean getting herself a job shipside, and what could she really do on a terrestrial boat? Tharsis wasn't afraid of hard work, but it still meant finding a ship that would take her.

She drove hard, trying to figure it out. She checked oceanic routes, talked to people at her hostel, at the harbor. Tharsis thought about it until she felt sick from the effort. Until one night, over tea in the hostel's worn lounge, she heard a couple of European travelers talking in hushed tones about their Lift for the next day. What the void would be like. What the new habitats out at Pallas might be like.

It hit her then.

While the historical record was thin for this period of time, there were a few stories that had percolated down through the centuries. Confirmed by the Rossen's Journals and Arran archaeology work on the first settlements. The terraforming effort had been conducted in as much secrecy as possible, but there should have been fingerprints of some kind. The undertaking had been titanic.

There had to be something going on. In progress. Right now. Especially if the Donovan family was poking around in Singapore.

Asking around, and doing a little research on the Gig, she found what she was looking for.

A holding company. New Ocean Initiatives. They had a lovely website, Tharsis noted; people in this time were very fond of their spare, deep graphic design aesthetic. There was no hint of who they were owned by, and only some vague pablum about *being on the cutting edge of oceanic research, to sustain the world's seas for centuries to come.*

No VR engagement.

And all their ships were named after places on Mars. The *Cimmeria Deep.* The *Aeonia Crest.*

Had to be a connection.

According to the Gig, one of the six ships in their Pacific fleet was due into Singapore Harbor in less than a sevenday. The *Vastitas Reach.* Deep-ocean exploration vessel. Some of the crew were doing a presentation at the aquarium there, something that was being heavily advertised on the city's tourism portal. Then another, five months later, in Hawaii.

The ship spent a lot of its time wandering from port to port, all across the Pacific.

The *Vastitas Reach* was still a hunch. Barely a hunch. There were no guarantees they'd let her on. But every day in Singapore was another day of wasted funds, and Tharsis was getting desperate.

The other problem she faced was her complete lack of identification.

For any staff position on any vessel, others on the hostel staff told her, she had to have a scannable identity chip. Damn things were nearly impossible to counterfeit, too.

Where the hell was she going to get that?

Asking around, more circumspect this time, she found Singapore's rather robust black market. Several programmers offered to do her up a counterfeit chip, but all of them sported ilucoccine scars. Who knew what reality their mind was lost in? It took her two days to find somebody who wasn't on drugs, a sober old man who ran his little side business out of his electronics repair shop.

"I'll need an existing set of credentials. Much easier to reassign an identity set than forge a new one," he told her. "Implant included."

Options limited and time ticking away, Tharsis resorted to something she didn't really want to do again: she stole.

Even in highly regimented Singapore, an underground community of desperation and drug use flourished. Whole sections of the city had been abandoned by both polite society and the law. Something like a dozen bodies were scraped off the edges of those no-go zones every night. More, counting people who passed in apartments or hotel rooms. There was often no family to claim the remains. Bodies were incinerated, the ashes dumped unceremoniously in the ocean.

Effects weren't claimed.

Identity chips didn't dissolve.

Tharsis went to the city morgue and volunteered for a job.

Before the events that had led her out to Eris and all its ugly past, Tharsis had never really seen anything. Now, though, she saw it all. Earth was alive, and had been for billions of years, and the penumbra was strong here. The priests back home had always said you couldn't actually see the souls of the dead, and after her introductory walk through the industrial freezer at the morgue, she supposed that was true.

No ghosts. But there were lights. The light left behind was quite real, and almost as frightening. It walked, it sighed, it scattered shadows where none should have been. The echoes of life, fading.

It took her a few more days to find what she needed. A body brought in by the cleaning teams, a young woman about her age, dark hair and similar features. Darker skin, but nothing that Tharsis couldn't explain away in the photo as sunburn. Unlike many of the addicts, she still had a wallet in her purse, one with a serviceable printed ID and just enough cash to round out Tharsis's own little stash. She also had several bank cards, which would require DNA confirmation to access.

Tharsis wondered who the girl was. What she wanted. How she'd ended up here.

It didn't stop the Arran from taking a razor to the girl's wrist.

Harvesting that implanted identity chip, along with enough of a tissue sample for DNA verification.

She barely got her prize tucked away in a pocket before the morgue supervisor came in to check on her.

The dead girl had quite a lot of money, Tharsis found. Some American student, halfway around the world and six months past her last college class. Tharsis wondered how she'd ended up here, how she'd ended up dead, but not for too long.

She paid the old programmer a 50 percent cut of the dead girl's bank account. In exchange, he updated Tharsis's own DNA markers in all the right databases, commercial, government and otherwise. Manipulated the physical identity marker, so it showed Tharsis's own likeness now. Injected a freshly reprogrammed and sterilized chip into the skin of Tharsis's wrist.

Afterward, she could feel the bulk of it, sliding against the tendons.

Damn whatever had landed her in this time.

WITH A STOLEN ID, Tharsis didn't dare return to the hostel. The *Vastitas Reach* was due in the next day anyway. She rented a sound-proof booth in one of the city's ubiquitous all-night VR cafés, down near the harbor, and tried to sleep.

No such luck.

Around midnight came the hands.

Small. Electric. Tugging.

Mylings.

She woke to the sight of one sitting on the arm of her chair. Its eyes, slitted like a cat's and twice the size they should have been, stared at her.

That was when she realized the room was full. Completely full. They were sitting on the furniture. They were sitting on the other stations. Every other living person in the room was asleep.

Panic washed over her. She scrambled back, only to have one of the things crawl into her lap.

Tharsis held her breath.

But the thing didn't try to touch her again.

Instead, it pointed at the door.

They all pointed at the door.

Fighting down the adrenaline spiking through her blood, Tharsis asked, "You want me to come with you?"

It nodded.

They all nodded.

"Where?"

It pointed at the door again.

She was not going to get rid of them, she realized. They were not going to leave her alone.

"Fine," she said. "Let's go."

CHAPTER
TWELVE

THE SILENT LITTLE crowd led her down from the main streets to the harbor.

Companies had their own warehouses, down there on the quay. One stood a fair distance from the others; it was there the mylings took her. Around the back, to a section fenced off by heavy chain-link and razor wire.

PRIVATE PROPERTY, a large sign on the gate read. ARIUM LABO-RATORY CO-OP.

Arium Labs was something Tharsis had heard about in passing. Seen in a few news stories on the Gig. Apparently, they were some kind of consortium that provided generous grants for all manner of research. Much of their research in Singapore, at least in what she'd read, tended to be biomedical of some kind.

There were more mylings inside the fence proper.

Based on those, Tharsis could guess what kind of work was being performed by the researchers here.

The myling that had woken her up tugged again, sending another shock up her leg.

"Yeah, I know," she told it, fear spiking in her blood.

This was the kind of scat, these were the kind of people, that had brought on the Euphemism.

There was no telling what they'd do to her if she got caught inside their facility.

The mylings led her around the perimeter. Towards a back building, smaller than the others and set quite a way apart. INCINERATOR stenciled on its side.

One of them crawled under a loose section of the chain-link fence.

She followed.

By the incinerator, towards the inside of the compound, was a barrel. A big plastic barrel that a lot of families around here seemed to use for water, as tall as her waist. The mylings that had led her here were trying to climb up, misshapen little hands unable to find purchase on the slick material. It stank of bleach and blood.

Steeling herself, she opened the lid.

The sight was grisly. Bodies, little bodies, thrown in unceremoniously, heaped atop each other. Human bodies. Babies. Some still in their birth sacs. Some were small, barely bigger than her hand, while others could have been three or four kilos, wristbands with barcodes looped around their tiny arms. Full term, those. Little fingers curled up or holding on to one another. Not all of them were intact, and blood coated everything.

She couldn't help it. Her stomach turned over. She vomited.

Glaring at the myling, Tharsis tried to clear the taste from her mouth. Hellfire, there were six more barrels like that. "Why'd you bring me here?" she pleaded. "I can't help any of them."

The myling tapped on the barrel again.

She looked back in.

There, under the top layer, there was movement.

Retching a little again, Tharsis forced herself to reach in, move a few of the tiny, broken bodies. They weren't right, she noticed, not normal. One was missing fingers, another lacked feet. The eyes were too large, too far apart. She blocked it out and dug.

And just before she couldn't take anymore, she found the source of the movement.

A little girl, maybe two, two and a half kilos, barely moving. Placenta still attached. Covered in red from the barrel. Her skin was gray, her fingers blue. She was crying, quiet little sobs that Tharsis couldn't hear.

But when Tharsis's hand brushed a chilly little cheek, the newborn's eyes opened.

Red. Red to the lid.

Animal eyes. Rabbit eyes.

The Naven's.

For a moment, Tharsis hesitated. A Landlord. Whatever else the baby was, she was a Landlord. And the Tenancy…

"Buck up, Chen," she muttered to herself, ashamed. It didn't matter. She was here, and so was this little girl, and she couldn't walk away. Not from this.

Taking one last look around, Tharsis stripped off her jacket. She lifted the baby girl clear of the ruin of her siblings, placenta and all. She wasn't sure about that part, but the organ was still warm and she figured better to leave it alone. She laid the baby down in the fleece of her jacket and wrapped her up carefully, using the arms to fashion a makeshift sling wrap for easier carrying.

When she looked back down, the mylings were gone.

She made it out of the compound and away from the quay without incident.

———

THE *VASTITAS REACH* was due in at zero nine hundred that morning and departed the next day. And Tharsis still had to convince them to sign her on as crew. With a baby now.

It was a nightmare.

But she couldn't be mad at the little girl she'd found. It wasn't her fault.

She'd cleaned the newborn up as best she could, made her a temporary sling out of a spare blouse from her meager pack. Tucked in against her chest, the baby slept, little shuddering breaths ghosting across Tharsis's skin.

While her domestic education from her mother, her aunts, and her gran had ended after Brevan's run-in with that damn snow leopard, Tharsis had some experience with babies. Big families were the norm on Mars. Whatever business the family was in, babies went along for the ride, even newborns. Tharsis had never dealt with a baby hatched out of some artificial womb, but she assumed the basic principles would be the same. Warmth was important, nourishment even more so.

A proper kit would be critical.

Most of the things she needed were simple to source. Singapore had a number of large markets open twenty-four hours. It was nearly four AM before Tharsis was able to get to one, but that just meant everything was quiet. Fortunately, a number of places were selling baby items, and she was able to haggle a decent price for almost everything. Cloth diapers. A carry sling that worked with Tharsis's backpack. A few sets of baby clothes, bigger than what she needed. A couple of blankets. Sterilization soap.

But the one thing she needed the most wasn't available at the market. A portable milker.

She'd had to wait until the high-end boutiques on Orchid Street opened.

Tharsis had deep misgivings about that last item. But formula was bulky and expensive, natural breastfeeding obviously not an option, animal milk hardly a guarantee on wherever this journey was going to take her. Them. In the near month Tharsis had been in Singapore, she hadn't seen a single liter of goat or camel milk for sale anywhere. The only place where she'd seen dairy at all was at the grand hotel by the harbor, and that was bovine. Tharsis had no idea where to buy that, much less how to adjust it for an infant's needs.

So, a semi-synthetic mammary milker it was.

They had milkers in her own time, of a better design but similar function, widely used beyond the Arran inwell. A biological digestion and production unit the size of a four-liter thermos dispensed human milk into bottles from the filler at the base. She didn't sprung for the biological nipple attachment; creepy scat. But the silicone bottles were endlessly reusable, and the unit had both pre-set and programmable production settings. The saleswoman assured her that even at the lower price point, she was getting a quality machine, but milk quality was only guaranteed with vitamin packets and the correct food input.

After that expenditure, Tharsis went back to the forger.

It took everything left in the dead American's accounts to get a chip and identification papers for the baby. Birth certificates were, apparently, much easier to acquire, but even then, it still took him most of the day. The old man let Tharsis wait in the back of his shop while he worked, something fond in his creased face when he looked at the baby. He didn't ask where Tharsis had found her, or why she had her.

Perhaps that was the nature of the business.

Tharsis didn't like the implications of it, nonetheless. Were false papers for newborns so common?

After a few hours, the baby sucking down yet another tiny bottle of artificial milk, he came back with a sheaf of paper in his hand.

"I can give you a choice on identity," he told her, "but only if we move quick."

There were dozens of names on his papers. "All of these babies are dead?" she asked, aghast at the number.

"Just pick a name, miss."

It was ghoulish.

Damn this planet.

But one name was familiar, pretty and sweet. Beatrix. Like the old storybooks.

Half an hour later, Tharsis was on her way down to the harbor with a heavy pack, a baby sleeping on her chest, and barely enough money in her pocket to cover dinner.

This had to work.

CHAPTER
THIRTEEN

THE NEXT FEW days passed slowly.

Data trickled in.

Colonel Cambel insisted on Caleb attending every one of his briefings. Shift changeover seemed to be the most useful. Lots of information. Lots of talking.

He was getting better at understanding contemporary speech; what differences there were in the actual language, as opposed to pronunciation or accent, became easier to follow.

Lots of political shit going on, though, more than Caleb could follow. From what he could gather, there was friction between the deepvoider's chain of command and some of the regional commands. Over him, he supposed. He didn't understand this time at all.

Noqumiut, that fucking arium they'd come from, was a different story. The small swarm of wasps left behind were still mapping, still transmitting.

They'd found the remnants of a downed craft, almost a kilometer long, buried in the thick methane ice. That had captured everyone's interest. The morning those images had popped up in the holopit, Adair had spent the day peppering Caleb with questions.

He had no answers to give.

The Arrans told him a story. A dozen different variations, but all with the same general theme. Long-term stasis craft sent out from Earth in the early years of their Euphemism. Set adrift in the Kuiper

Belt. No tracking beacons, except for what was tied into the Lighthouse network. Hundreds of thousands, maybe millions, of people. Waiting to come home. To restore the human genome to its proper state.

It sounded an awful lot like one of the earliest evacuation initiatives he'd heard about. Ark ships. Long-term stasis with the promise of settlement on Mars, or the asteroid belt, once conditions were right planetside or the habitats complete. But there were a lot of rumors in his time, false hope and misdirection seeded by the Labs themselves.

The ships wouldn't have been bound for the Kuiper anyway.

One of the wasps had sent back a few images of a control room, still intact, from the downed ark ship. It had run out of power there, its antennas failed. No more data to be collected. One of the last photographs they had was of a nameplate. USSF PADUA ANTHONY.

They'd asked him if he knew anything about it.

Looking at it, there was something Caleb could almost touch. Some memory, some moment that hadn't come yet, or had been lost. A ship hanging in the void above him, seen through thick glass, a name, a name on the hull, and the feel of it…

"No," Caleb said.

The signals from all the wasps had ceased an hour later.

The more pressing matter, however, seemed to be the reports coming in from Pluto. Thirty-six hours before they were due to reach the tiny dwarf planet, its habitats had come under attack. Short-lived, brought under control quickly. But Cambel mused openly at the evening stand-up that they might best approach the place on a combat footing.

Between all of that, there was Adair.

Caleb spent as much time as he could avoiding the historian. They'd gone over what Adair called *the wake-up brief* first thing on the next morning out from Eris; he wished he'd had the patience to get it sooner. But he had no desire to hear the rest of the story from somebody so removed from events, so eager to pick Caleb's brain for some new tidbit of information.

He'd told them everything he could, or would, in lifetimes past.

Then, he wanted to be alone with it.

What had happened to Captain Rallison, to the entire system, made him sick.

Caleb spent what time he could spare in the craft's small library, reading through as many of his early Journals as he could. His discussion with Yip made more sense: the Journals were written in his speaking voice, in what the Arrans called Silicone English. It made for fast, if painful, reading.

What made no sense to him was why he'd let this entire thing with Noqumiut go. Why he'd shot himself after that first visit. There was a myling out there, for fuck's sake, an active one.

The entire thing made him sick. It seemed the crew felt the same way about him; they were friendly, let him sit at their tables during meals and listen to them bullshit, showed him anything he wanted to see when he wandered into their work spaces, but he could feel them holding back. Holding away.

He didn't blame them for that.

He did find himself wandering, though. Trying to avoid the entire crew, maybe. The axilla had climbed back out on the skin of the craft, once it was decided where they were headed, so at least he didn't have to deal with that thing. Craft regulations held that the K-9 squad had to bunk in the kennel section, something having to do with safety, but the rest of the time, his dog followed him everywhere.

They'd been friends for years.

Centuries.

Nice to know that some things didn't change.

Once Caleb figured out the crew didn't want all that much to do with him, he hung back. Listened a lot. Between the Journals and the palm translator, he found himself hearing more and more of the meaning in the dialect. But then, he'd always been good with languages. It had been a necessity, after things started falling apart. He still didn't feel quite right speaking it. That would come, he supposed. He was stuck here. Had to learn.

He kept dreaming. The moment from before. Rallison. Her Fair Isle sweater, softer than anything he'd seen her in since they were kids. The feel of her was—

He could never quite reach it.

———

THE MORNING they were due into Pluto, Caleb found himself in some auxiliary hangar, tucked into the craft above and behind the main bay where the transport ships were kept. There, he found a bewildering array of flying machines. Stacked in cradles and crates, towering over his head. And in the middle of the mess was Erg.

He was tinkering with one of the machines, soldering gun in hand. He didn't look up.

"Found your way to the Hive hangar, eh, Landlord?"

"Corporal," he corrected, automatic. Tyr bumped his hip and went padding off amongst the crates, sniffing loudly.

"Whatever you say, Corporal. Sir."

Caleb ignored the jab. "What is this, the, uhh, Hive hangar?"

"I take it you can understand more than you can speak right now, eh?" Erg said.

"I can understand most of what you're saying," Caleb told him.

"Your accent is very good," Erg replied. "Considering."

"I was wondering about the, uhh, the stuff we sent down to Eris…"

"Ahh, yes. This. You had swarm technology in your time, right? Small, massed remote air fleets? This is ours." He cast a long-fingered hand around, still working with the other. His limbs were out of proportion, Caleb realized. Too long. Too thin. His eyes had the same milky-white quality as the colonel's. "Weapon, shield, surveillance tools. Very useful. Scalable, too, which is key to the kind of engagements we get in."

"They were," Caleb paused, hoping the words would come out right, "trying to make space lasers, in my time."

Erg laughed at that and set his tool back down in its holder. "We have a few of those, all orbital. But they're ineffective and unnecessary for the battle fleets. Most research efforts now focus on magnetic and kinetic weaponry. Gravitic too, although no proposal for that has gotten past the University of Titan in the past hundred and fifty years, standard."

Caleb could tell Erg's accent was different. Nothing he could put his finger on, though. "Are you Arran?" he asked.

Erg cocked his head. "What do you mean?"

He struggled, trying to find the words. "You don't seem like the others."

"Ah, that." The captain paused, that long-fingered hand resting on the wasp he'd been working on. "Full name's Eanraag Kathalipatr-samit. Naturalized Poseidan."

"What?"

"Don't worry, nobody on the crew can pronounce it either," he said with a smile. "I emigrated from Neptune. A standard century or so ago."

"Adair makes it sound like things are," and Caleb spread his hands, "separate."

"They are. But there's still movement. Some. Coming to Mars is hard, because of the gravity. Most voider immigrants stay out on one of the moons." He smiled. "It's difficult, getting a permanent visa. Citizenship is almost impossible. Not enough space on the moons, you know, and Mars doesn't have civilian orbital habitats. Easier if you sign up with the ASDF."

"Is that why you're here?"

"No." The cheerful cadence flattened. "Seal-fuckers roched our moon, last Propagation. Killed thousands. Most of my family died. My wife and youngest children were on a field trip that sevenday, or I would have lost them too."

"You moved to Mars to escape?"

"I moved to Mars to enlist. Nobody else has any military force of consequence."

Caleb digested that for a moment. The language was getting easier. He barely had to reference the pad for that. "A century ago?"

Erg tapped his temple. "Hive head is a demanding job, and not many can do it. When the ASDF finds a man who qualifies, he gives certain things up. I stay in stasis until the craft needs me. They thawed me out when they had confirmation of a Propagation starting."

"What happened to your family?"

"My boys married into native Arran families, after they served their time. The grandchildren live on the surface now." He went back to tinkering. "They come up to see me when we're at port. I'm quite proud of them."

"Hive head?" Caleb asked.

Erg indicated a patch of skin, right in front of his ear. Discolored, paler. "The wasp Hive has some semi-automated functionality. Like the little ones we left on Eris. But for combat, it requires a human interface." Caleb did have to read most of that on his palm, and the captain waited until he was done. The next words, however, were clear. "How are you doing?"

It was the first time anybody on the *Barachiel* had asked him that. "I should have died," Caleb said, "back on that orbital lab."

By his side, Tyr whined. Caleb got a flash of something warm, furry. Dark and safe. It was Tyr's normal reassurance image, some memory from his puppyhood, before his owner had gone insane and his mother feral. Before Tyr had been the only puppy left from his litter, the only thing in all his world still alive, mewling under a desk in a dead arium.

Caleb scratched the dog's ears.

"We'll be at Pluto in a few hours," Erg said, absorbed back in his work again. "You can feel the craft. Shifted to braking thrusters now."

Shit, Caleb thought. Adair wanted to brief him on something else before they got there. "Thanks."

"We're both men out of time, Caleb. Anytime you'd like to talk."

"Right."

———

CALEB WAS STARTING to hate the historian. Or at least, hate the interminable briefings. Politics. Past histories. He at least had the decency to hold that one in the commander's stateroom, though.

One thing that had struck Caleb about the deepvoider was its lack of windows. Besides the huge, if deep-set, glass circle in Ops and the static fields of the hangar bays, there was no real way to see outside the craft. The mess had a bank of flat screens that were turned on during the evening meal and showed the exterior starfield in extraordinary detail. A few other places on the craft supposedly had access to the same feed. Taken in for the pilot's cockpit, piped throughout the ship. But they were screens, recordings.

The only other true window on the craft was located in the captain's office. His desk sat to the right of the great round oculus, a half meter of high-strength, ultra-clear acrylic set into a meters-deep punch-out within the hull. It was huge, huge enough to provide a decent viewing area.

It was there Caleb observed their approach to Pluto.

At first, it was just a spot in the sky, a point of light in all the black, growing bigger by the second. Then detail came into view. Dirty white, mottled red, just starting to show.

Adair stopped trying to talk as they drew near. As surface structures came into view. Mountains, glaciers.

Having something to focus on let Caleb realize that yes, the craft was decelerating. Like Erg had said.

"What's here again?" he asked.

"The Golanite monastery."

"And they're what?"

"Reunified Catholic monks. There are a few other minor religious communities as well, with a sizable scientific presence. Some of the largest telescopes in the system are here, staffed up largely with Cronuans."

"That doesn't sound like the Heliosphere, the way you've described it."

"It's unusual," Adair admitted. "The monastery's taken on the responsibility of managing the Flet's body. They lease out rights to his neural tissue to a Poseidan shipyard, which constructs both the dive cores and complete vessels, like the one destroyed at Eris."

"And the ASDF."

"Yes."

"Why priests?"

"They were already here," Adair said. "I see that look, Caleb. But we've talked about this. The Republic's not a theocracy, and this is not our territory. Not every monk is even Arran. In coming here, these brothers surrender their citizenship."

"Why?"

"The Tenancy largely suppressed religion in the major inwells. Pluto was originally founded as a refuge from those decrees."

"Except Mars."

"Except Mars."

"Why? How?"

Adair hesitated. "Because you insisted on allowing religion to continue, sir."

There was a knock at the door, and Stag stuck his head in. "We're on final approach. Should be at a docking orbit in less than an hour. If you'd like to head down to the hangar, we'll get the rockjump prepped."

The Rallarhu-thing was waiting for them in the hangar. Along with Chaplain Kannik and that officer from Ops, Stag. Neither Arran seemed pleased with the axilla's presence.

=Miss me, Caleb?=

"Not really," he muttered.

Tyr trotted up after him, up the boarding ramp.

———

"WHAT IS THAT?"

"That," Tharsis said, glancing down at Bea, tucked into her sling, "is a baby."

She had no idea how any of this was supposed to work. Newborns could be so fragile, and yet, back home, it wasn't uncommon to strap one in their sling and go about your daily chores. But children seemed rare in Singapore. And Tharsis supposed that it did make a difference when one was asking for a job on a working vessel.

The *Vastitas Reach* bobbed at anchor, in the vast expanse of Singapore's harbor district. It was hard to get a sense of how big the ship was; at least a hundred meters, she guessed. Some sort of pod-craft sat on the back. Deep-sea diver, maybe.

There were a number of crew out working on the deck, but it was the captain they'd sent out when she stopped by, introduced herself, and asked about a job. She'd been left in the shade of the ship's hull for almost an hour, before he'd come out, a giant water bottle in hand and a look of severe irritation on his face. He was tall for an Earther, skin creased and dark like old leather, dark hair scattered with gray.

She couldn't tell if his skin tone was from a lifetime of sunburn or genetics. His features, otherwise, were something she might have associated with one of the more populous Jovian habitats.

Tharsis still had trouble telling ethnicities apart on this planet; she had no reference points. The void had washed most of the old differences away. Left new ones in their place.

"What job was it that you wanted?"

"Data input," Tharsis replied. They'd given her a list when she inquired; that one seemed like the best choice with little Bea along.

The skipper looked her over. "You don't have a VR rig."

"Who wants that scat in their brain?"

She couldn't be sure that the *Vastitas Reach* was connected to the Donovan family. It was all just an educated guess on her part. It easily could have belonged to the Ariums, or a university, or some other research group. But if it was as she hoped, then she didn't think a little hostility to the planetary status quo would hurt her.

Besides, he didn't have the implants either.

It was the right call, because he chuckled. "We don't have a Gig hookup on this boat at all, actually. So that's not a problem. You willing to work twelve hours or more a day?"

"If I have to."

"With a baby?"

"If I have to."

His expression was still unconvinced.

Tharsis patted the sling. "I'll keep her out of your way. She sleeps with me. She's still so new. She won't bother anyone."

"Okay, but we only have shared cabins here and…"

"She doesn't have vocal cords."

That, finally, seemed to shake the captain out of his casual irritation. He took a sip of his water, obviously considering. "What happened to her?"

"I don't know."

He came over, looked, touched. Bea woke at the unfamiliar contact, blinking those birth-puffy eyes with all the sleepy confusion of any human newborn. If she was human. The red there was almost luminous, even in the bright tropical day. "She's bio-fucked. What is she, one of those animal splices they keep bragging about?"

"I don't know," Tharsis said honestly. "She's seemed pretty normal so far."

"Where'd you get her?"

Tharsis hesitated. "I have her birth certificate, if you'd like to—"

"Now I'm really curious," he said, dark eyes fixing on her. "Don't lie."

Donovan ownership, Tharsis reminded herself. "She, uhh, she's a castoff. From a local Ariums facility."

"Ariums, huh?"

"Yes sir."

"You acquire her legally?"

"I'm not trying to traffic anyone here," Tharsis said, heated. "They threw her away. What was I supposed to do, let her die?"

He thought about that for a moment more, then nodded. "If I can get a blood sample, and you agree to let my staff doctor keep notes on her growth, I think we can accommodate you. If you're willing to work."

"As long as I can keep her with me."

"That's fine. We have a ton of data entry to handle. Drives my crew nuts. They'd be happy to have somebody to take it off their hands." He held a hand out, and she realized he was offering to take her pack. "Come on. We're due to leave in the morning."

She kept her pack. And up they went, into the ship.

The captain passed her off to somebody else, a sunburned blonde woman with an accent Tharsis hadn't heard yet. Later, she'd learn that the woman was from some place called Norway, half a planet away. Marine biologist. She was cheerful enough and cooed over Bea.

"Annaka," she said, by way of introduction.

"Amanda," Tharsis said, using the name off the dead woman's ID. It was close enough to her own.

"We haven't had a dedicated data tech for a few months," the woman told her. "It's hard to screen people. The last we had jumped overboard one night. Ilu, we think. We found syringes in her luggage."

"That's awful."

"Yes, who knows what she was seeing? By the time we realized she was gone..." The woman shrugged. "We looked for two days but never found her. Sad. Druggies. What can you do?"

She led Tharsis through a maze of interior corridors, to one of the cabins the captain had mentioned. "You're welcome to bunk down anywhere you'd like."

The cabin was tight; he hadn't been lying about that. Eight bunks and none of them very big. But for the four female cabins, there were only twenty-six women, and so Tharsis was able to claim a bunk with a little separation from the others. She dumped her pack on the furthest little cubby-bed and straightened. "Do you mind if I, umm, wander around and get a feel for things, or…"

"No, no, come. Skip said I should give you the tour. You and this little cutie here."

———

THE *VASTITAS REACH* wasn't as big as she would have thought. Her guide told her about tonnage and displacement, but Tharsis didn't know what any of that meant and didn't really bother to pay attention. What she did try to keep track of were the hallways, the locations she needed to know. Chummer—they called it "the galley"— and restrooms, restricted areas and her own workspace.

That was a cramped little office deep in the bowels of the ship, with a number of different silic terminals set up. Tharsis was fascinated; this time hadn't had very good quantum computing technology, and their silicone computers were rumored to be more advanced than anything in the contemporary Heliosphere. She had never been the type to take apart old machines as a child, but she had been through quite a bit of training on it as an infrastructure officer. And the history was intriguing.

"This is where you'll work," the Norwegian woman announced, patting the back of a swivel chair, bolted into the deck. In front of it, a curved screen that ran nearly the full length of the desk. "When we get underway and everyone is back on board, Chris'll show you the system. Do you have much experience with database design?"

"A little," Tharsis said. It was all academic. Silic design hadn't changed much from this time period. One of those things that had been frozen by the Tenancy. "I don't know your system though."

"Well, experience would be better, but Skip says you come. They can teach you." Annaka waved her on.

They finished the impromptu tour out on the back deck of the ship. The strange little pods were indeed deep-sea exploration craft, the property of a small, dedicated team that rented the space. A crane, for lowering and recovering them from the water, was bolted nearby. The deck also featured a huge circular marking with an H inside of it. Tharsis wasn't sure what that was for.

"So how did you hear about us?" the Norwegian marine biologist said, after she had pointed out all the different dive craft, their depths and their capabilities.

"I just need a way to get back to America."

The Norwegian woman looked at her. "What do you know about what we do here?"

Tharsis hesitated. She wasn't sure how much she was supposed to know, how much the crew had been told. "Ocean research," she said.

The Norwegian shrugged and waved her on. "Good enough," she said lightly. "Would you like something to drink? We can go back to the galley if so."

Tharsis nodded, then caught a whiff of something. "Can we go back to the cabin?" she asked. "I need to change her diaper."

There were lockers in the female bathroom, more than were needed by the crew. Tharsis grabbed one for Bea's things. Diapers, changing mat, washrags.

"Do you think anybody will mind, if I wash her stuff in here?" Tharsis asked as she methodically worked.

Annaka shrugged. "We have a laundry facility. You can use that."

"It's easier to clean them as I go," Tharsis said. "I don't have very many, and it's going to stink up the place."

"Stink is no good," the Norwegian agreed. "Just don't hang that thing near my towel." And she smiled.

———

THE *VASTITAS* WASN'T due to depart until the next morning. They told her she was welcome to head down into Sydney if she wanted, as long as she was back on board by midnight. But Bea was sleeping, and Tharsis wasn't sure how much she could trust any of them anyway. If that was really the departure time or if they would leave without her. She stayed aboard.

The chummer, the galley, was closed for the evening, but some of the other crew who were still working on one of the submersibles offered to order her something. She told them to get her whatever. What came was some kind of insanely spicy potato curry in coconut milk, something she'd never had before coming to Earth. She sat on the back deck, Bea wriggling her little limbs around with all the wonderment of a new baby, listening to the crew joke with each other as the sun set over the vast island-city.

It was peaceful. Beautiful.

Mars didn't have sunsets like this.

Tharsis barely slept that night. She curled up around the baby, close enough to feel her if she started crying. It seemed to work fine for Bea, who woke up every two or three hours, fists flailing and body shaking until she got one of the tiny newborn bottles from the milker. But the breath kept catching in Bea's little chest, the baby sometimes holding it, sometimes panting, and Tharsis found herself unable to drift off.

If this was the Naven, of course she was going to live.

She still kept a hand on the baby's chest. Listened. All night. Just in case.

CHAPTER
FOURTEEN

THE OCEAN HERE, they told him, was boiling.

Boiling so slowly that only the Flet could properly observe the movement. Some kind of convection caused by a freezing layer of water, kilometers below.

To Caleb Ross, the scene in front of him just looked like the frozen north. Norway, maybe. One of those missions up to Svalbard in the winter, or the lab raid where he'd found Tyr. The far north, under starlight. No aurora, no moonlight.

Beyond the hardened glass windows of the abbot's spare office, glaciers drained out into that frozen sea, nitrogen ice sliding forever into the stillness.

Perched on the edge of Sputnik Planem, the Elysium Monastery clung in thick, stepped segments to the nameless icerock mountains. Living modules, communal gathering areas, chapels, greenhouses, laboratories, linked together with enclosed stairs and bridges. Long legs—in some places, over half a kilometer tall—held the entire thing safely above the frozen surface. Over three hundred degrees below zero.

Insulation and heat exchangers kept the monastery from melting the water-ice, harder than rock, into which it was driven. Satellite facilities were scattered across the entire planet, he'd been told, as well as three of the moons. Fusion generators, tethered at the equator, provided the energy required to keep the network of habitats alive.

Inside, the structure seemed grand, robust, vast. But at least one dome out there had been cracked open, revealed for the fragile thing it was. It resembled a broken snow globe now, its conifer forest flash-frozen by explosive decompression. A swarm of repair wasps, most of them the *Barachiel's*, clustered around it.

"Beautiful, isn't it?"

The Rallarhu's axilla bud had been quiet since their small party had arrived. What it wanted, what it was after, Caleb had no idea. The thing was unreadable in its sealed pressure suit. But it was at least a fragment of a Landlord, and so the monks hadn't questioned its presence.

He ignored it. He wished it would wear any face, any image, besides Rallison's.

"I'm sorry to see the damage here," the deputy commander said. Stag, if Caleb remembered his call sign right. "Last time I was through, the place was beautiful."

"We can rebuild our facilities. I mourn for the lives lost, though."

The man who'd spoken was older, walking up in a hurry. He was rail-thin, the same mig-clouded eyes as the *Barachiel's* Colonel Cambel. Loose robes hung on his wasted frame over some kind of fitted body-suit. He looked much the same as any monk Caleb had encountered so far, except for his age. And despite the low gravity, he walked as though burdened to the very edge of human capacity.

"Abbot," Stag acknowledged.

"Lieutenant Colonel, is it now? It's been a proper few years since you've come through here."

"We have Ops searching for bodies right now," Stag said, intentionally ignoring the pleasantries. "Your people indicated there were several who went floating off into the void when that dome was blown out. If they're still within range, we can get them back for you."

The abbot nodded. "What assistance you can offer, we're grateful for. But don't let our problems guide your decisions." Those milky eyes turned on Caleb. "You must have more important things to do."

"We might not be able to leave. That was one of the things Colonel Cambel wanted me to speak with you about. Every dive core, every comm node, across the entire Heliosphere, is down. We barely made it here," Stag said.

"Yes, so I heard," the abbot said.

"You have any idea what's going on? Does it have anything to do with the attack you suffered? It's an unprecedented situation and if you have any insight on—"

"I doubt it. We've been hit before and have never seen a linkage."

"What do you mean?"

And at that, the abbot truly hesitated. "We've observed events like this before. The Flet's consciousness going missing, brain waves flatlining. Never anything that lasted more than a few minutes, though."

Stag leaned forward. "Why hasn't this been communicated to the ASDF?"

"I'm telling you now," the abbot said, and nodded in Caleb's direction. "Because the Rossen is here."

"What do you mean?"

"The Flet is alive, but rarely conscious. It takes an extreme effort for him to manifest as an apparition. We're not sure why, but he's never done so here. We have a text machine set up for him to communicate with us. He uses it rarely. But when he does, it's almost always followed by one of these absence events. And then, it's always the same phrase." The abbot paused. "'*Caleb, come find me.*'"

Caleb glanced over at the axilla, but the simulacrum of Rallison's face gave nothing away. Why would some wetware ghost be invoking his name? "Then I should probably go talk to him."

"Brother Terzio is waiting outside. He'll show you the way."

———

AFTER BOTH THE Rossen and that Rallarhu-thing had gone, the abbot waved Stag away from the wide windows, over to the corner where his sparse desk was set up.

"The Landlord of Mars," he said, opening a wall compartment to reveal a large pressure kettle inset in an alcove. "Have you ever dealt with him before?"

This was a part of his job Stag wasn't all that comfortable with. Politics. Talking. Playing nice. But politics were a big part of deepvoider operations. Besides, Colonel Cambel was edging close to mig-lock; planets were painful for him to set foot on, even one as small as Pluto. Stag supposed he'd be there himself someday when he made full colonel and had a command of his own. Then he could make his own senior duty officer handle this scat.

Still, he put in the effort.

"For a few sevendays, before he got killed this last time. He seems…" And Stag struggled for the right word. The *political* word. "He's younger."

"Yes, I would think so." The abbot laughed, and handed Stag a small, steaming cup.

Tea. Not Stag's favorite drink, but he accepted it anyway. There was something about Pluto. The cold crept into a man's bones.

"Younger and has no idea what the fuck he's doing."

"Maybe no idea about the Heliosphere, but he was a soldier from a young age. He understands the nature of our common enemy. Existential as it may appear to us sometimes, it's very real," the abbot said. "Don't mistake his behavior for the ignorance of youth."

Stag looked out the thick glass curve of the abbot's office wall, towards the shattered remains of the environmental dome. It had been one of Elysium's main environmental parks, part of the life-support system. The loss of both its atmosphere and water would be a rough blow to the entire monastery. "Doesn't seem so existential right now, Father."

"Indeed," the abbot said, and sipped at his tea. "Now come, tell me, what does Ignace want to ask me? He wouldn't have sent you in person if there wasn't some pressing need."

Stag set his tea aside. "We're missing a lieutenant. Lost out at Noqumiut. Command wants her found, but it's like she vanished. No body, and the divedrive she took out to that fuckin' place appears to have been destroyed there."

"Ahh," the abbot said. "The young lady who ended the Propagation. I was quite fascinated by her broadcast."

"Doesn't look like everybody here was," Stag observed.

"Proving their paradise dead won't stop people from believing in it." He turned to the window. Sipped his tea. "You're asking about skin diving. If she moved herself off Noqumiut."

Stag frowned. "I've heard about it, but—"

"It's not a story or metaphor. Every brother here has done it. At least once." The abbot smiled. "For most of us, only once."

"I've always heard it really has nothing to do with faith in—"

"It doesn't, although that's a common misconception amongst the voider nations. One of the more pernicious legacies of the Euphemism was the repeated attempt to blur these lines. Father Golan's great insight, one of them, was illuminating the distinction between the spiritual realm and the penumbra. As members of his order, we undertake this as a means of comprehending the difference." The abbot ran a thoughtful finger around the rim of his pressure mug. "That is why our order cares for the Flet. Why we host such a large scientific community here. He is… the secular understanding."

"So what's that got to do with Lieutenant Chen?" Stag asked. "Could she have done it?"

The abbot breathed out, obviously considering the idea carefully. "Anyone is theoretically capable of it. But it's an incredible act of—"

"Will?"

The abbot shook his head. "If it was just that, we wouldn't need void craft. But we do. As I said, it's a very rare feat. Often it takes years of preparation."

"So…"

"If she had accomplished it, she would most likely be here. And unfortunately for her, she is not."

"What do you mean, here?"

"As you know, in the Silicone Age, it was thought that space-time was akin to a smooth sheet. We understand the nature of things a bit more completely now. Space-time is more like an ocean. It has depth, and when we push down into it, the nature of reality tends to shove us back up. We can't exist anywhere but the surface. It's the nature of reality. God's order."

Stag really, really hated this part of the job. "I know, but—"

"There are currents. One of these, the surface current, we experience as the flow of time. But there are others that flow in other directions, under the surface. Most aren't well understood, but we do know there is a significant one that flows here. To the Flet."

"So what, the Flet has some kind of gravity that pulls people in?"

"Our metaphors are clashing now, of course, but yes, something like that." The abbot paused. "As I said, it's not well understood. The person best suited for studying it is the Flet himself, but he is disinclined to do so."

"So where could she be?"

"Quite likely, somewhere he is."

"But he's here."

"Yes," the abbot agreed serenely, and would say no more about it.

————

"WE HAVE the most comprehensive suite of deep-space telescopes in the Heliosphere today," one of the monks told him as they floated along what seemed an endless corridor of glass. "Most of them remain in orbit over the planet, for maneuverability purposes, but we have a few on the surface, anchored to one of the rare hard—"

"I don't care," Caleb interrupted. "What does this have to do with the Flet?"

"Saturn wasn't the only haven for research and scientific exploration founded in the early days of the exodus from Earth," the monk told him. "There were a number of parallel efforts, to save scholarship from the insanity."

"News to me," Caleb replied. "I remember a lot of scientists going absolutely bug-fuck nuts."

The monk gave him a look, and Caleb belatedly realized that phrase probably didn't make any sense. "The records we have indicated serious disagreement within the academic community. Not everybody wanted to see the species made extinct."

Below them, the glaciers were running up into jagged peaks. "So they came all the way out here? That's a hell of a trip."

"This facility was sponsored by a religious consortium. Similar to Mars, in some ways, but with a much different focus and more signatories. The original settlers came out here on a massive colony ship, much larger than most things built today. The bones of that provided the bulk of the original facility. As we grew, as more people came to join in our mission, our settlement grew with it." The monk gestured ahead of them, towards an air lock just visible along the curve of the space walk. "The Flet provided both the bridge and gate for those later generations. Not many children are born here, although it's not strictly proscribed. Most people come for a few years or a decade, to perform research or contemplate God in solitude, and return home. In the early centuries, these halls would have been awash in dozens of languages, many faith traditions. But so much of that has been swept away by war or privation now. Our records now are what remains of the vastness that was once humanity's rich religious diversity."

"Smaller colonies couldn't compete?"

"Smaller colonies couldn't always survive, although a few have defied the odds. Even many of the larger ones have failed. Humanity is a guttering candle in the darkness, Landlord. You can see what damage a handful of saboteurs have inflicted here. Many here believe we would not have survived another Propagation."

"What do you think?"

"I think peace may prove equally destructive, if we do not approach it the right way." They had reached the air lock, and the monk slid easily out of the gravity sled towards the control panel. Handprint and retinal scan. "I believe this is why the Flet has gone silent. To give us the time we need to figure out how not to destroy ourselves."

"Lovely theory," the axilla said, through the suit.

Caleb ignored it.

The door slid open.

Caleb hadn't really known what to expect. A sterile white room, maybe, with a big fish tank in the middle. Something medical, like an operating room.

Nothing like that lay beyond.

Salt hung in the chill air, stark as the landscape behind them.

Tyr had his nose to the breeze. The hair was rising on the ridge of his back.

It was the hangar. The plane. Rallison, walking around it.

"Jesus," she said. "What was he working on?"

Caleb was about to answer when something else caught his eye.

A small, boxy structure jutted out from the back wall of the hangar, windows grimy with dust.

"Smell anything alive, besides us?" he asked Tyr.

The dog huffed and trotted on. Caleb followed. Into that office.

The eeriness of the place only grew. Bookcases, a worn-out sofa stuffed in a corner next to some kind of 3-D printing cabinet. There was something in the way things were arranged, the careless order of it. Something felt very familiar.

Sitting on one of the desks was a notebook. A cheap one, pages yellowed with age and crooked from use, no larger than the palm of his hand. A single large image was stamped on the front in black, a logo maybe. Caleb flipped it open.

Arranged on the first page was a series of neat columns, DEPARTED and ARRIVED written on the headers in distinctive handwriting. The columns contained timestamps in military format, along with a series of numbers that looked like GPS positional data.

Every page was the same, some entries containing additional notes on events or places that didn't quite make sense.

Caleb knew that handwriting. He knew it.

And on the last page were two words.

FIND US.

Rallison took the notebook from him.

"Was she with him, Caleb? Bea?"

The scream rose in his mind again.

The illusion, memory, vision of the past, shattered under the force of it.

Caleb stumbled, Tyr catching him.

Ahead of him, the monk and the Rallarhu-thing paused.

"You alright, Landlord?" the monk asked.

"Fine," he lied.

"Many of our number experience interesting effects in this chamber," the monk said, spreading his arms. "Some see the past. Some see deeper into the penumbra. The ocean of time crashes heavily here."

"Because of him?" the axilla asked.

They'll never stop, they'll keep coming, always coming.

"Because of him."

For all the buildup, there wasn't much to the room. A round chamber, domed and dark. More for effect than any real purpose, Caleb thought. And perhaps it was the monk's words, but he thought he could hear the surf, waves breaking on some rocky shore.

Orbits decay, Caleb. I can't hold this position.

In the center, slightly awry, was a tank. A large tank, glowing softly with some kind of internal light. Walking up to it, Caleb could see a form inside. Roughly human, but a human surrounded by something that looked like roots, branching out in all directions. The shape was an illusion. Spun from naked, raw tendrils of neural matter.

"Wetware," Caleb muttered, reaching out.

Caleb, you have to—

"There wasn't much left of him, after his mission on the *Undine Glory*," the monk explained, coming up alongside Caleb. "What remained came here, and we have cared for him ever since."

"And made a pretty penny off selling bits of his brain to the divedrive shipwrights," the axilla said. The radio voice betrayed no emotion.

"That too was his choice. Look at what's happening right now, with the dive networks offline. We need his talents."

I can't hold this forever. It's time, it's time, it's time to go, I have to make…

"What do you mean, the network?" Caleb asked. "I thought we were just having issues with the *Barachiel*."

"Your *Barachiel* is the only dive-enabled craft that seems to be working at all," the monk said. "We saw a spike in neural activity from him over four days ago, and since then, nothing."

The scent of the ocean was back. The chill of the air.

Rallison was bent over a computer terminal, set into a small bank of monitors. It was the airfield security station, although Caleb wasn't sure how he knew that. A security video was playing. A man, clearly unconscious, being carried off. A girl, barely into her teen years, screaming, struggling, as somebody threw her over his shoulder.

"If we do this," Rallison said, "we do it for her. Not him."

But even as she spoke, she was fading. Away from him. Back into the white.

Caleb laid his other hand on the tank. "He's not here."

"What do you mean?"

"Would you believe me if I said I wasn't sure?"

Behind him, the radio emitter scratched out a foul sound. Arhythmic. Unpleasant.

He realized the axilla was laughing.

CHAPTER
FIFTEEN

DESPITE ANOTHER HALF hour in the Flet's chamber, they learned nothing more. Caleb saw nothing else. The monk eventually suggested they needed to leave, to avoid stressing the life-support system in the chamber.

On the way back across the bridge to the main body of the monastery, Caleb mulled it over.

Wetware was a contentious topic in his time. Organic computers, human derived. Proponents of the technology insisted that tissue was taken only from dead donors, but in Caleb's experience, they were either grown from fetal tissue or distilled out of young children. The younger, the better, it seemed. Ugly, nasty, but capable of things that even quantum computers couldn't emulate.

They produced mylings, though. Phantom figures, children, pulled and warped.

He hadn't seen a myling from whatever was in that tank.

He wasn't sure what that meant.

The abbot himself was waiting for them inside the main air lock, hands tucked into wide sleeves.

"Did you find what you were looking for?" he asked. His Silicone English was perfect.

"I saw something in the Flet's chamber. Felt like a memory, but not something I remember from before. It was Earth."

The abbot nodded. "The Flet is an interesting man. His movement through the depths of space-time is not well understood, but we know he can at least perceive events that we might consider in the past."

"Might consider?" Caleb asked.

"The now, what has passed, and what will come are interlinked." And the abbot wove his fingers together. "What will exist, has always existed."

"Doesn't that violate the concept of free will? I seem to remember that from Sunday school."

If the abbot was offended, he didn't show it. "I am not talking about fate. I am talking about the inevitability of who each of us is. We choose, but there is only ever one choice we might make."

That didn't make much sense to Caleb. He wasn't sure if it was his own lack of understanding, or if it was some kind of translation error. "So he can time travel?"

"No. He can see through the past. Can even take us along sometimes, but such things are very dangerous." The abbot nodded. "We experience time as a flow, steady, continuous. But this is a matter of perception. Causality is not always a straight line. It may be that the solution to the Flet's problem will not be found now, but then."

The abbot left them outside the hangar complex, citing the recent attack.

Caleb thanked him for his time.

The axilla said nothing until he was gone.

"Golanites," it said, derisive.

"Why are you here, anyway?" Caleb asked. "Here, wearing her face?"

"It is her face, and I'm a part of her."

"Do you have her memories?"

"Some. Since taking stewardship of the Inner Belt, the Rallarhu's consciousness has become fragmented. Disparate. Spread out." The suit arms stretched wide. "Too much space to cover. Too much for one mind. The Flet is similar. It takes a powerful mind to deal with the dissection of its brain."

He wanted to ask what the difference was, but felt like that was bait, somehow. "Who is he?" he asked instead. "What's the connection here, him and you and me?"

"The Flet, Caleb, is her father." It touched the suit. "Dad."

Caleb groaned, the pieces clicking into place. Bea. Rallison. The airfield. "Holy shit."

"You went to work for him, private security, after the military realized something had happened to you in orbit," the axilla told him.

"I was wondering why they hadn't executed me."

"They tried. Many times." It brushed that aside. "Caleb, whatever the Arrans have told you, the Rallarhu is not your enemy. It is in everyone's interest to get the Flet back."

"What are you proposing?"

"Something very, very simple."

———

YET THE ARRANS didn't seem to appreciate the logic when Caleb presented it to them, a few hours later.

A few members of the command staff, most of whom Caleb still didn't know, were clustered in the main briefing room when Caleb had gotten back up to the *Barachiel*. Waiting on him, perhaps, but already talking. They all ignored the axilla, which had come up with him.

"Obviously we have an issue with troop movement," Cambel was saying, as Caleb and Tyr entered. He waved Caleb forward, gesturing at the seat at the head of the table. The axilla likewise took another unoccupied seat. "But Home Command is right. We have more pressing concerns right now, and we're not entirely dependent on divedrives for—"

"It's more than that," Adair interrupted, a few seats down. "Maneuverability isn't the primary concern here."

Stag made a derisive little noise deep in his throat. Cambel held up a hand.

"Then what, Mr. Adair?"

"Political response. If one of the Landlords is missing, there can't be a quorum."

"I thought that dead bitch we found in the radio room was supposed to be a Landlord," Caleb commented, breaking in. "How has she been participating?"

For a moment, nobody spoke.

"I can't explain that," Adair finally said. "We lack insight into some of the Tenancy's inner workings. My understanding is that things normally have to be conducted in person. Without a functional dive core, the Landlords will be dependent on conventional propulsion." He followed up with the same brief sentences in contemporary English.

"Even our best fusion drives would take a while to get out to Uranus or Neptune," one of the officers, the guy Caleb had seen at the navigation station, said. "Months, maybe years."

"That's obviously untenable," Cambel said, and looked to Caleb. "Sir, did you learn anything down there?"

"Not much." He thought about the fragment of the past from the life-support room. "I think he wanted us to come here. Wanted me to come here. And he was obviously able to get us here."

"Barely," the nav officer said.

"There has to be something there to work with, right?"

"We have a missing lieutenant who must have attempted a skin dive," Erg said, quiet until now. "We have a missing Landlord, one whose specific talent involves manipulation of reality."

"What are you saying?" Stag asked.

"The two things seem related to me," Erg said.

"The abbot assured me they're not."

"How can he be sure? How can we?"

"I don't want to risk another dive blind," Aeolis said.

"The abbot said there's a kind of current that flows in the penumbra to where the Flet is," Stag said slowly. "Could we use that at all?"

"Sure. If you can get the quant to model it, which it can't. It's incapable of the intuition leaps required to—"

Colonel Cambel rapped the table.

"Boys, I enjoy discussions about theoretical metaphysics as much as the next man, but we have a real mess on our hands. How do we fix this?"

"We need to find him," Caleb said.

"How?"

Caleb flailed for a moment. "I've had encounters with mylings, wetware consciousnesses. More than I'd like. They're always bound to what's left of their bodies. The Flet's like that, isn't he?"

"Little pieces of him are scattered everywhere," Morray said. "There must be a good hundred or more dive cores across the Heliosphere."

"I'd guess he'll be somewhere where there is a significant amount of him left. More substantial than what is integrated into the dive cores. If there's a current, won't it flow there?" Caleb held out his hands. "I'm guessing here. You know this world way better than me. Is there anything left of him elsewhere?"

Adair tapped a pen against his notebook. "The only thing that would have a significant amount of his neural tissue, beyond what an average dive craft has, is the *Undine Glory*."

"Isn't that in a museum in the Venus inwell?" Stag asked.

Aeolis groaned. "How do you propose we get to Venus from here? And don't anybody give me that current scat again. The dive core's offline, even with a full fusion burn it would still take years to—"

"The Rossen's proposal is sound. The Flet's neural tissue here is alive, capable of doing its job, and it will listen to me. I can pilot it," the axilla interjected. "All I need is access."

"What kind of access?"

"Full."

Stag snorted. "You want us to depressurize the core room so you can, what, ooze all over the place? No."

"I'd have to concur," Cambel said mildly. "We're not doing that."

"Caleb's already agreed," it said. "So I suggest you start working on it. Now."

"I don't take orders from you," Colonel Cambel replied, more forceful this time, and looked to Caleb. "Sir, we may be able to perform a quick action to temporarily drop the atmo in there, but I do not have unlimited storage capacity. Draining a space of that size will stress our tanks."

"How long can you live in the air outside of that thing?" Caleb asked.

That simulacrum of Rallison's eyes, unblinking, dead, fixed on him. "Maybe two minutes. And I will require rest, much rest, outside the hull afterward. A drop in pressure would be helpful."

The colonel was clearly bristling at the very suggestion but made a show of looking over to Caleb. "Sir, what would your recommendation be?"

"We go after him."

Inside the helmet, Rallison's face was smiling.

"I'll see what Life Support can do," Cambel agreed, grudging.

———

THE PROCESS TOOK AN HOUR. It also required them to be in the room; there was no air lock, and the colonel couldn't guarantee that air wouldn't leak back in. Caleb was wearing the same type of pressure suit that the axilla was. Designed for internal repairs or shielded void dock space walks, the suit was more similar to the ones he'd known in his own time. No skin-eating wrapper.

<Whatever you're planning on doing, be quick,> the watch supervisor messaged through the internal vox. A light coating of frost had crept over many of the surfaces inside the core. <That's as empty as we can get it.>

Caleb glanced over at the puppet.

The axilla shed the void suit like a snake shedding its skin. The figure that emerged was human-shaped, female-figured, but indistinct. A woman dipped in a thick oil slick, it seemed, liquid forced into an impossible shape by some unseen force. It hissed, light flaring along its surface.

And then, as if with a great force of will, the shifting stopped.

A simulacrum of skin, hair, eyes, nails, emerged. Bare hands. A face —Captain Rallison's face. But the rest of her form was obscured, as if she were wearing an oily, formfitting jumpsuit.

There was no air, so there was no sound.

That was fine. Caleb wasn't keen on hearing his officer's voice from this bio-fucked creature anyway.

The axilla was already moving, over to a central column, hand out. It gestured to him, and he followed.

It laid its hand on the smooth, seamless white surface.

False eyes closed.

"Thank god he keeps the controls the same."

The past rippled out.

Rallison, in a pilot's chair, framed by a halo of thick glass windows, smudged with fog. A heater had been turned on; the chill of the day was at war with the blast of warmth from vents around Caleb's ankles.

"You'd know better than me."

She snorted. "Dad's little copilot. Up until he fucked everything." She had a checklist spread out in her lap, running procedures one by one. Flipping switches. Checking gauges. "Up until he betrayed everybody."

"What'd he do?"

Rallison snorted and pointed. "Come on, don't tell me you didn't see that."

Off to the side of the cramped cockpit, set deep into a small alcove, was a sphere. A sphere of glass, filled with a greenish-white liquid. Inside was a fist-sized nodule of neural tissue.

Wetware.

"I'm doing this for the kid," she said. "Let's see if this piece of shit machine can get its ass in the air for us."

Beneath them, engines rumbled to life.

The sound of a buckle closing behind him made him turn.

The void suit was closing itself up again.

Gone was the field of toggles and switches. No more were the cockpit windows, looking out over a mournful expanse of mist-obscured rock.

Instead, there was white. White that burnt the eyes. Lights dancing in every panel.

Back in the core.

<Whatever you two did, it worked,> Ops said. <Location confirmed. >

Caleb looked over at the axilla. He thought about asking it, seeing if it remembered that conversation.

It's not her, he told himself.

=I require void access,= the axilla signed. The movement seemed slower. The inside of the helmet was beginning to fog. =There is still atmo in this suit.=

=I'll walk you there.=

CHAPTER
SIXTEEN

BREAKFAST OFFICIALLY OPENED at zero five hundred, with a morning briefing by the captain at zero six-thirty. Tharsis found out later that was a daily occurrence, open to anybody who wanted to attend. Annaka and the other women in her cabin seemed cheerfully annoyed by it but told Tharsis she had to attend. They dragged her, half-asleep, out of bed and down to the galley.

Tharsis filled a tray, Bea sleeping against her chest, and found a place to sit.

That first day as they were headed out of port, nearly the entire population of the ship was there. Being a research vessel, there apparently wasn't much distinction between those who saw to the ship's operations and those who paid for lab space or passage somewhere.

The briefing was far from military standard. It lacked the formality that even Major Lanin always observed. Instead, the tone was laid back, setting casual. Interruptions happened without warning. Laughter was frequent.

There were a few different bridge crew who spoke: navigation, weather, security. The ship's drug policy was read out loud. The head of the kitchen gave a quick talk about dietary options. Somebody who was referred to as the scheduler, in charge of managing resource requests, reviewed the next four days' worth of allocations.

Their route for the next two sevendays, the helmsman said, would take them down through an island nation called Indonesia, down through the coastal waters of eastern Australia, then out to the east. A huge map dominated one of the galley's walls, and somebody had marked out a meandering route that the *Vastitas*, apparently, was meant to follow over the next six months.

Tharsis found it overwhelming. The distances were staggering, the number of islands immense. How was she supposed to find anybody in all of that blue?

She was still pondering the immensity of the Pacific when the captain took his place up at the makeshift podium.

"We have a couple new crew members who joined us in Singapore," Skip said. "Amanda, you want to get up and tell us a little about yourself?"

It startled her out of her reverie.

Amanda. That was her.

"Not really," she called back.

Laughter ensued.

"Okay, that's fine," Skip continued. "Amanda and Bea are here for the next few months. She's back-filling for Lily but she's new here, so be kind. Bea's an orphan in Amanda's care, nonvocal. Please extend some hospitality to both."

The briefing concluded not long after that. Tharsis didn't have to report to her new position for another thirty minutes and took the time to get another bowl of oatmeal and some of that Earth coffee.

She'd had coffee before but wasn't sure if she'd be able to go back to the orbital-raised stuff when she got home. Mars's climate was too cold for the original plants and the best attempts at genetic adaptation had all failed. Coffee was instead grown largely on orbital agriculture platforms, but the taste wasn't the same. There was something about the Earth sunlight, the Earth soil, that was unique.

Another thing humanity had lost to the void, she found herself thinking, and bounced Bea in the crook of her free arm. Fortunately, the newborn seemed to be tolerating the sling well, but Tharsis didn't want to keep her wrapped up all the time.

She was just finishing when somebody set their own cup down on her table.

"Cute," he said. "Did you pattern her?"

Tharsis looked down at Bea, and then back up at the young man who'd spoken. Somebody new. Sunburned. Brown hair flopping over his forehead. The hands too many men had in this age, thumbs warped in from too many hours on a keyboard. A kind of earnest expression on his thin face.

A lanyard around his neck held an identification badge. ARIUM LABORATORY CO-OP.

Tharsis was instantly wary.

"What do you mean?"

"You know, her DNA." He leaned forward. "Those are very interesting eyes."

"No," she said. "I'm just her, uhh, caretaker."

"Right, right," he nodded. "I'm not into the biology end of things myself, but it is fascinating what they can do."

Tharsis fought the sudden flare of temper down. The way he was looking at her reminded her, for one terrible moment, of tDaer. Of her own mistakes, mistaking obsession for interest. "Who are you, again?"

"Oh, sorry, I'm, umm, Wyatt Blalock. Just wanted to say hello."

"Amanda," she said, curt. She was not going to repeat those old mistakes. "I really should get her a bottle before I go to my shift, Wyatt."

She thought it was enough of a dismissal, but apparently, he didn't know how to take a hint. "I'm one of the long-term guys here. If you need anything or have any questions about the ship, I'm happy to help."

"Thank you," she said in the same flat tone, and very deliberately patted Bea on the back as she stood. "Let's go get you fed, little one. Shall we?"

He picked up his coffee cup.

"Well, uhh, nice meeting you."

She just nodded at him and walked away.

The anxiety she'd felt at his presence faded almost as soon as she left the galley.

Strange.

———

THARSIS STOPPED BACK by her cabin to grab the milker and a few clean bottles for the day, and reported to the man she was told was in charge of the data center.

He was older, maybe in his late fifties, and had a distinctive drawl to his words. He introduced himself as Chris from Louisiana. He had kind of an expectant look on his face when he said it, and Tharsis realized too late that it was another one of those things she should have recognized.

She needed to brush up on her geography.

Still, he seemed friendly enough, waving an arm around the space where she'd be working. It looked like every other data center she'd ever been in: a small room with a few desks and terminals in it. A thick interior door with a handprint lock hummed. A white-blue fog seemed to be vibrating out of it.

It took Tharsis a moment to realize it was something in the penumbra. Something she was seeing for the first time.

Mercifully, there were no mylings.

And interestingly, there was a mobile playpen in the work space.

"That?" he said when she asked, glancing at it. "Got it out of storage. Takes up a hell of a lot of room, but you'll need your hands free from time to time."

"Do you have children?" she asked him.

But he didn't answer that. "Let's get you spun up on what we do down here."

A little bit of everything, it turned out. The *Vastitas Reach* was open to almost any manner of proposal but focused primarily on deep-sea research and exploration. Time could be reserved on the submersibles, but the real sought-after resource was a series of holding tanks in the lower levels of the ship.

Empty now, her new supervisor said. By the time they returned to Singapore in eight months, the holds would be full. Sand samples full of bacteria, scavenger fish, a vast array of invertebrates. High-pressure tanks in the ship's hold simulated conditions of the abyssal plain. Most of the life brought up was kept alive.

"There's a team handling all of that," he said. "It's their big ongoing project. Been with us for the past four seasons. They're our biggest data hogs, next to the post-doc student who's studying surface-to-floor currents and keeps wanting to run his simulations on my mainframe. I've told him that's what the quant's for, but he won't buy the time on it."

Tharsis wanted to ask. She really did. Especially after seeing that particular team's database. The amount of information collected was staggering. Terabytes, monthly. And they were in charge of managing it all.

Depth, water temperature, soil composition, life-form groupings, and a thousand other variables were all tracked. Every specimen tagged. Every dive meticulously mapped.

It had to be about terraforming. Mars's ecosystem, all its various biomes, had been built organism by organism, year by year, especially in those early decades. All of the information being collected would be needed in order to maintain balance. The smallest detail overlooked could have led to disaster, so the early terraforming researchers were said to have cast a wide, wide net.

"Does every user on the system have a setup this complicated?" she asked instead.

"Most are much more straightforward," he told her. "Some of them don't trust me at all and manage everything on their own machines. One guy we have doesn't even use a computer and keeps everything in notebooks in his lab space. Technically they're not supposed to do that, but as long as they're paying their rent and don't cause trouble, Skip has us leave them alone."

"What trouble could come from writing?"

"Plenty," the old computer expert told her.

A walkthrough of the data system only took an hour or so; nothing much ever happened on the sail out from harbor, he told her, and he released her for the day. Tharsis picked up a fresh bottle for Bea and headed out to a place she remembered from yesterday's tour.

There were some deck chairs and recliners set up on one of the forward decks. A few other people were up there when Tharsis found it, working on portable terminals or tablets, a few just reading.

Her entire situation was overwhelming. Trapped sometime in the Euphemism. Out of time. A place she never should have been. Stuck now with a baby. But the equatorial waters were a blue Tharsis had never seen before her in life, and the jungle island was unlike anything that Mars could boast, and it was Earth. Earth.

Despite herself, Tharsis still felt a swell of excitement in her heart for it.

The baby in her arms couldn't have cared less about the view, little body moving in tight, jerky movements. One little yawn.

"What am I going to do with you?" Tharsis asked her softly.

One thick, tiny hand relaxed against Tharsis's arm. Those huge red eyes were shut.

Tharsis held the sleeping baby and watched the Pacific roll by.

———

ONE UNEXPECTED ADVANTAGE of the ship, Tharsis learned over the next few days, was that the movement of the waves helped lull the baby. But she was still a newborn, and so her sleep was predictably unpredictable.

The last time Tharsis had been so tired was the sevenday after the Koronis scenario, back on the *Centrifuge*. What the other girls in her squadron would think of her now, she had no idea. Family, children, those weren't things any of them had ever planned on having. And this was a baby spit out of a Euphemism bio-lab, not even a normal human. Tharsis couldn't be sure she even was the Naven.

But at the same time, what was she supposed to do? Leave her, abandon her? The Naven had seemed human, all things considered. Had certainly behaved the most human of any of the Landlords. This baby seemed much like every other newborn Tharsis had ever encountered back home. Whatever else she was, she deserved a chance.

Another bonus of the ship was the scenery. She could have sat out on deck and watched the ocean, its islands, roll by all day. If she hadn't had to work. But the workload was still light at the moment, or else Chris was taking mercy on her; Tharsis only spent a few hours a day down in the server room.

Night was dark, though, and night was when the baby was active. Tharsis decided if she was going to keep both of them safe, she needed something to occupy her mind. Help her stay awake during those hour-long feeding sessions, when she drew their bunk's blackout curtains and tried not to wake the other women.

Tharsis found herself in the ship's small library more than once in those first few days, the baby cuddled close in her sling while she perused the sparse shelves. The place was peaceful, done up in warm polished wood that would have cost a fortune back home. It was also the first written media she'd seen.

Books were ubiquitous on Mars. Every family, no matter how poor, had a bookshelf or two. And there was almost no one who didn't possess a copy of the Tri-Testament Bible.

There was no copy of the Bible to be found here, though, which seemed a melancholy thing. But then, the Silicone Age had been the start of the secularism that now reigned in so much of the Heliosphere.

So Tharsis settled for reading something at random every few nights, marveling at some of the story lines or places. Earth was a huge planet, with centuries and millennia of cultures all piled on top of one another, and it was almost too much to take in.

She read, and listened to Bea sleep, and dreamed of the Flet's yacht.

CHAPTER
SEVENTEEN

THE DIVE into the Venus inwell may have been less than a heartbeat, but the trip into orbit was significantly longer.

Caleb had asked about it in Ops.

"It's about gravity distortion," Aeolis had told him from the nav station. "What we think of as the observable universe, the skin of space-time, isn't flat. Every object in the solar system impresses into it, distorts it, and of course, those distortions affect each other, deepening or canceling out. Like waves on the surface of the ocean. The divedrive fleet's learned how to model it over the centuries."

"I thought this thing just popped up where it wanted."

"The key factor is for time to align properly. We can't arrive at a point before we leave, or vice versa. Gravity bends time, so surfacing too close to a major celestial body can cause such a phenomenon. There's a standoff distance we have to respect."

"How do you keep track of it?"

"We don't," he said. "The quant is running a continuous simulation, but even that's been known to be inaccurate. That's where the wetware comes in. We need the intuition that the Flet's brain provides. He corrects any issues in the nav sims."

For Venus, in that moment, that distance was a full day's burn. How far that was in kilometer, Caleb wasn't sure. Half of it was acceleration, the other half braking. That was as much as Aeolis had volunteered. Caleb hadn't pressed.

Instead, he'd come down here.

The weapons range.

The range sat at the very back of the craft, a narrow space wrapped in half a foot of steel on all five sides. The sixth was a set of double void doors, set forty yards back from the firing line, that opened at a ninety-degree angle to the engines. Target drones could be deployed up to a kilometer from the outer skin of the hull. The range manager, during the in-brief, had stressed to Caleb that the radiation risk meant that void target practice was strictly controlled, for everyone's safety.

Apparently, most deepvoider combat actions were close quarters anyway. Distance was hardly ever a factor.

"Caleb!" It was Yip, striding across the floor. "Finally found you. I thought I told the boys I want Tyr down on the mig field, teach him how to move."

"He doesn't have great memories of being in free fall," Caleb replied, and kept loading ammo.

"So you just ignored me? Don't you ever want to take him on a mission?"

"We'll figure it out."

"Great attitude when neither of you can die."

Caleb rolled his eyes. "I don't need a fucking lecture on combat discipline, Sergeant."

A fresh ammo can hit the table beside him. "You're exactly the way I remember you."

Caleb paused, thumb on a round that he was jamming into a magazine. "What?"

He had selected what the range manager called an A24, a compact, fully automatic rifle that reminded him strongly of the gear he'd trained on as a kid. Thirty-round magazines. Recoil compensators in the butt. Momentum like that could be deadly in zero-G, he figured.

"You're exactly the way I remember you," Yip repeated, and picked up one of the empty magazines. Started loading it with practiced, efficient movements. "Pissed at everything, but especially us. I didn't understand it at the time, of course. Most of the boys who come out to the fleet want to be here, and those that don't? We all grow up knowing we're going to serve our time. There's no point in having an attitude about it."

"Sergeant, I don't have an attitude."

"Sure you do. You think it's all spiderscat, and guess what? I agree with you. Your position, fuck, your existence is an affront to the Republic."

Caleb set the magazine down. "Is there a point to this?"

"Yeah. The colonel won't say it to you, but he's got politics to play. I don't. So I'm saying it. Nobody wants you here."

Caleb stared at the pile of bullets in front of him, spilled out of their metal containment. He was seven, eight hundred years in the future. Earth was gone. His unit, everyone he'd ever served with, was long dead. If he didn't belong here, where was he supposed to go?

"Yeah?"

"Yeah," Yip repeated. He laid a finished magazine down and picked up another. "Yeah, you see it's my fault that the *Barachiel* got involved. We knew each other, kept in touch over the years. When you had an issue you needed help with out at Humphryes, you called me. I convinced the colonel we had to go. He had to call off support for another situation out in the Greeks, but we made it out."

"You can't hate the Landlord thing that much if you were willing to do that."

"I didn't do it for the Landlord. I did it because Master Sergeant Caleb Olin was a stand-up guy, and my friend." Yip tapped a bullet against the padded table. "That's what you've got to understand, Corporal Petrison," he said, and pushed a calloused finger against the name tape on his uniform. "The Landlord can go fuck himself. But this guy, this name you're wearing? He can be worth it. Once you get the fuck over whatever it is that's bothering you."

"Like waking up eight hundred years in the future and finding out we didn't stop jack shit? Like that?"

"Mars exists. That's something."

"Yeah, a planet I'm not allowed to set foot on."

"That scat," Yip said. He got up. Headed back to the armory. "That's the scat I'm talking about right there."

"They should have dropped me down a volcano," Caleb muttered.

"We should be glad they didn't," Yip replied. He had another A24 in hand, breech locked open. "Otherwise it'd be that bitch Rallison running Mars. Whatever set her off that day on Ceres, whatever she was pissed about, it could have been our planet instead. You think that axilla-thing is bad, try dealing with the whole package in the Rallarhu."

Adair had told him about that. On the way back from Pluto to the *Barachiel*. Probably some attempt to get him to rescind his permission for the axilla to do what it did.

Rallison, the Rallarhu, opening up the sky, breaking the sea ice. Killing the entire population.

It didn't seem right. Didn't seem like something Rallison would have done, no matter what was going on. But then, they'd both gotten bio-fucked. Who knew what had happened to her mind?

"You think she was pissed about something?"

"Yeah, I do. I think she was throwing a bitch-fit about something out at Noqumiut." Yip shrugged.

"I don't remember her being particularly emotional." The *particularly* came out in Caleb's own Silicone English, different enough to get an eyebrow raise from the older sergeant. He corrected himself, answered in modern cadence. "You couldn't afford to be, back then."

"Never underestimate a woman's anger," Yip told him, and started loading another magazine. "Now, I seem to remember you being pretty good with a slug-thrower."

"Hunting was one of the main ways we fed ourselves when I was a kid," he said, and paused. "I haven't changed?"

"No. Not even a little. It's kind of freaky, actually."

"So how'd I get over my shit before?"

"We beat the scat out of each other a few times," Yip said with a smile, and got serious again. "And then there was the mission out on Ariel. You were, are, one of us. You'll figure that out. Now, are we going to shoot something or sit here and talk all day?"

"Shooting something sounds great."

"Wonderful," Yip said, and punched a control panel in the table.

The range doors slid open to the void, the shimmer of a static field all that was standing against them and the killing void.

Between them, they went through a full ammo can before Caleb called it quits.

He took Tyr down to the training fields when they were done.

Yip was right. He did want his dog along with him on whatever they were walking into next.

———

THAT NIGHT, Caleb dreamed.

One of those dreams that didn't feel like dreams.

He was standing by a plane, on the edge of its dying wing. Bea was up there. Bea, in a pair of oil-stained coveralls that were far too big for her tiny frame. Bea, gray-white hair pulled back in its usual thin ponytail. Bea, smaller than she should have been.

"What're you doing up there?" Rallison called.

=Trying to save the plane,= Bea replied, exaggerating her hand movements a bit for better visibility as they approached. =I was going to find a way out of here.=

"Why?" Rallison called back. "This is home."

=Didn't you see the sky?=

Time skipped.

Bea, on the ground, fourteen and defiant and desperately glad to see them both, throwing her arms around them.

All of them, in the back of the hangar, drinking terrible coffee and watching her explain.

=He's missing,= her hands said, =they left me here and they took him. I don't know why.=

Outside again, under blinding desert light. The sand, the buildings, the dead reservoir just visible to the north. Long gone now, a ruined canyon left behind.

Caleb knew this place.

Northern Arizona. Page. The town where he'd grown up for a few years, after Wyoming. Where they'd all grown up.

Once, when they were kids, this had been a thriving, if small, operation. It had been the closest operational airport to both Sedona and the Grand Canyon, for those who could afford the trip, who could secure the travel permits. A sign had once hung in the terminal: *Welcome to Your Desert Adventure.*

Now, it was empty, vacant, a husk of a place, mummifying in the high desert temperatures and dry, dry air. Or at least, it had been, last time he could remember being through.

Things had changed.

They were standing at the gates. Simple chain-link, but somehow a barrier against what was outside.

Caleb knew those streets, these homes and businesses. It was all wrong. Instead of the small, stubborn, proud community he remembered from his last visit here, rot had set in. Weeds grew up from cracks in the roads. Buildings had fallen apart, many looking as if they'd been torn apart by some kind of bomb blast.

Cars littered the street, obviously abandoned. But it looked as if they'd been there for a long, long time, windows busted out, tires collapsed, chassis rusting. Even the seats were decaying.

A blood red sun bathed everything in unearthly light.

Caleb shaded his eyes. "How long has it been like this?"

=Two days.=

It was wrong. It felt wrong, at some deep, visceral level.

"How the hell does this happen in two days?"

=Probably some kind of shared ilucination= Bea replied.

"We shouldn't be seeing it, if it's ilu-induced," Caleb said. "We've all had the inoculations."

Bea pointed to a series of huge banners, strung from the roadside lighting posts. They had writing on them, glyphs. Like Tikal. Like Noqumiut. =Maybe from that? Could be amplification of some kind.=

"I miss when things weren't fucked up," Eliza said, close by now. Her thin T-shirt clung to her in all the right places. Caleb looked away. Whatever might have happened between them in this time, there was no happy ending for them. Not with what she was. Caleb didn't want to think about it.

=When was that?= Bea replied.

"There's no way this happened in two days," Eliza muttered. "I don't like this at all. Bea, are you sure about the timeframe?"

=They dropped me here around two AM. Everything was fine. I noticed it the next morning.=

Tyr growled.

Caleb turned.

A solitary figure was coming towards them, out of one of the hangars. Hunched, dressed mostly in rags held together, it seemed, with rawhide straps. Twitching, jerking as it walked.

Caleb had no sooner seen it than he heard a soft explosion.

Pressurized air.

Tranq gun.

Rallison held the pistol steady. "What?" she asked, when Caleb looked over at her.

Feathered round stuck in its neck, the figure didn't stop its advance. It was close enough now for them to hear it moaning. It sounded female, but these days, who knew?

"Dead rounds?" he asked.

"Shouldn't be," Rallsin said, voice flat. Angry. She shot the figure again.

For a moment, the figure wavered. Only for a moment. Then it fell like a puppet with its strings cut.

"Not a dead round," Caleb said, going over to checked the woman's pulse. It was too weak; she wasn't going to make it.

No blue stained her skin.

Rallison knelt down next to him. "This isn't ilu," she said.

Tyr started howling in earnest.

Time shifted.

Caleb was hauling Rallison up the tongue of Donner's experimental aircraft. One hand around her waist, the other free, holding his AK. Footfalls behind him, running fast. Bea was ahead, practically throwing herself at the stairs to the cockpit.

Broken fingernails dug into his free arm.

Sparing one look at his old captain, he dropped her on the cargo floor and tore his knife loose from its sheath.

There was an entire mob in front of him, or at least, that's how it seemed. Rags and raw leather, bloodshot eyes and ruined teeth. They grabbed for him with bare hands, biting, scratching, driving him back. There were too many to fight, too many to shoot, one figure bleeding into the next until there was nothing but a wall of flesh around him. Rallison's body disappeared.

Tyr saved him. The huge dog tore back in, all teeth and rage, jaws locking around the bicep of the closest monstrosity and wrestling it away. The space was all Caleb needed to get the seax up.

He pushed it straight through the first man's throat.

Blood fountained, arteries severed. The body fell, life fled.

The mob around him fell apart. Like sand drifting down through water.

Just gone. Like they'd never been there at all.

The plane was moving.

The tongue rose slowly, blocking out the airfield and Page's bloody sky.

In the last of the daylight, before the lights flickered on in the bay, he saw Rallison. Collapsed on the floor.

Her right arm was torn open. Clean through, wrist to elbow.

She wasn't bleeding.

Black ooze seeped from the space, smoking in the air.

He woke up.

CHAPTER
EIGHTEEN

IT WOULD HAVE BEEN easy to sink into the rhythm of the *Vastitas Reach*. To stay there, and never leave. Chris worked her, true, but most days, it wasn't particularly difficult. Nobody would tell her exactly what they were doing, and Tharsis had no idea what she was looking at at first. She didn't press him. She appreciated the quiet.

Tharsis hadn't had much of a chance to breathe lately. Since arriving at Earth. Since Major Lanin left.

She wondered how he was doing sometimes. If he'd settled into his cushy planetside assignment at District of Lunae, taking a dirigible out on the weekends to visit his family. Then she would remember: he wasn't born yet. Nobody she'd known existed yet.

Except for the Rossen. Maybe.

Most days, she tried not to think about it. Him. The Euphemism.

Tharsis had been moving for so long, it was nice to have a place to sit still. Nice to be somewhere without any expectations, without the responsibility of her rank, her enlisted guys looking to her for direction. To just be for a little while. Even if it was with a stolen baby and a stolen name.

About a sevenday into the cruise, just as they were rounding the northern edge of Australia, she got called up to the skipper's private office.

Unlike many a commander's space she had seen over the years, Skip's office was as unremarkable as the rest of the ship. Huge maps, rolled tight, stood in a rack near the edge of a bolted-down metal desk. A round porthole, thick with anti-corrosion paint, looked out over the back submersible staging area. A bank of filing cabinets overflowed onto the floor.

"They finished Bea's gene panel this morning," the skipper told her, waving her in. He had a folder in hand. "I found it fascinating."

He passed it over. Tharsis wanted to protest, to say that she had no experience reading genetic information, but maybe this was another of those things she was expected to know. She opened the folder in silence. Inside were a number of large prints on flimsy plastic sheets, lined and labeled.

Certain aspects of the baby's physiology had been clearly circled, marked out in pen.

Other than that, she couldn't make sense of it.

"What am I looking at?" Tharsis finally asked.

"That is a recognizably human genome," the skipper said, and gestured for her to give him back the folder. He indicated the circled areas with a pen. "Indeterminate ethnicity, which is interesting, but the donor gametes were probably East or Southeast Asian. They've clearly screwed with a few things, her height, hair and eye color, reproductive system. Although we're not sure what's going on there. We'd need a hell of a lot more data to model that. And notably, she seemed to be lacking a few key genes that might explain why she doesn't have a larynx."

"So...?"

"There doesn't appear to be nonhuman RNA in any of her tissue samples, which the folks down in the lab checked as well." He sat back in his chair. "She's a counterfeit hybrid, so to speak."

Tharsis patted Bea, sleeping in her sling against her chest. The baby still spent most of her day sleeping or eating. "She's human?"

"We'd need to run this through a medical quant to get a model of how she's going to mature, but it appears that whatever was done to her was superficial at best."

Something occurred to her. "Wait. They intentionally took her voice away, what, to make it seem...?"

"Like she's some kind of splice. Rabbit, I think, is what they were going for. There are, well, rumors." He looked disturbed. "I don't know what's worse, actually doing it or faking it for funding. Makes me wonder, what other false answers are being cooked up in the Arium Labs?"

"I know this probably isn't what you wanted to find," Tharsis said.

"On the contrary, it's fascinating." He shrugged. "How's she doing?"

"Sleepy."

———

SKIP KEPT the gene panel results in his office. Tharsis didn't tell anybody about what he had found. There seemed to be factions on the ship, undercurrents of tension between some of the personnel.

"Whitecoats," Annaka told Tharsis one evening, after the two of them witnessed a particularly nasty argument in the middle of the galley. Bea, cuddled in Tharsis's arms, was half-asleep, greedily sucking down a bottle. "What can you do with them but ignore them?"

"Whitecoats?" Tharsis asked.

"You know, the ones who are working on the so-called big question." It was one of the other women, Maria, a chemical engineer whose area of study was deep-sea hydrothermal vents, and who was part of some team out of a place called Guam. While some of the researchers had private cabins, most officially had a bunk in the shared crew cabins.

"Thank god Skip didn't put one of those bitches in our cabin," Annaka said. "I wouldn't stand for it. I can barely look at them."

"They're just trying to save the planet."

"From what? With what? Animism and voluntary extinction?"

"If it's voluntary, what does it matter to you or me?"

"Death mandates never stay voluntary," Annaka shot back.

"I get enough of this discussion down in the kitchens," one of the other women said, quite deliberately brandishing a set of headphones. She'd only come on board at the last port of call, two days before, and Tharsis didn't know her name yet. Her accent was North American. "Can you two knock it off?"

"Amanda asked me a question, and I answered."

"She's First Nations, isn't she? She knows what whitecoats are.

Leave it alone."

Bea was still fussing. Tharsis fetched her another bottle from the milker. She needed to up the thing's production. The baby was going through a growth spurt.

First Nations. She had no idea what that meant.

There was so much about this world she didn't understand.

But if the conversation left Tharsis with more questions than answers, all became clear the next day, when one of the Arium grant-holders came down to talk to the data center about some adjustment to his file structure.

Two ghostly little child-figures in tow.

Mylings.

Exactly when, and how, humanity had discovered mylings, nobody in Tharsis's time knew. The Rossen never spoke about it.

She hadn't noticed the little things when she first came aboard. Whether that was because the penumbra here on Earth was different, or if they'd been hiding from her, she didn't know. But after a day or two, she'd started catching glimpses of them.

What you acknowledge, you'll see more of, Gran had always told her. *When you see them, they see you.*

Tharsis couldn't not see the mylings.

She had, however, been wondering where they came from. There was no wetware in the data center.

Personal lab spaces, then.

Mylings weren't quite real, in any sense of the word. But then, they were still animated by that *other* quality that Father Golan talked about. Energy from under the surface of space-time wrapped around them. They could be quite dangerous, if they felt like it. Tharsis couldn't tell if anybody else saw them. Their presence did make her suspicious about who—what—the whitecoats were.

A suspicion that was confirmed, solidly, a few days later, when Wyatt Blalock interrupted yet another meal.

———

DESPITE HER SIX YEARS, HST, at the Arran Military Academy, Tharsis had little experience with others showing interest in her. A few experimental fumbles back at school barely counted for anything, and that situation with tDaer hadn't been much better.

Wyatt seemed determined to not leave her alone.

Interested, maybe, and Tharsis had no idea what to do about it.

He made her nervous, for reasons she couldn't quite define.

His personal myling, maybe. It was the only ne on the ship that truly scared her.

It was distinctive. Unlike most of them, it had normal proportions, normal features. Almost completely human, but for the ridge of little triangular spikes that ran forehead to tailbone. Its scale was hard to figure out, too. The nearest she could figure, it was somehow one-fifth of the height of whatever room it was in. Out on the deck, it was monstrously tall.

It was also the only one that didn't try to interact with her.

Tharsis wasn't sure what that meant. It made her skin crawl.

Wyatt's enthusiasm was undiminished though, no matter what she said or did to try to get him off her back. He often tried to sit with her at meals. Annaka had intercepted him several times, but a few nights before they were due into Sydney Harbour, he caught her alone.

But the offer that came wasn't anything she'd been expecting.

"Hi again," he said, sliding into the seat across from hers. "I know I keep bothering you, but—"

"You are," she said. The myling was looking at Bea, head cocked over at a disturbing angle. The baby seemed heedless though.

"I was, ahh, hoping I could get your opinion on something."

Maybe that interest wasn't sexual after all. *Fuck, tDaer made you paranoid,* Tharsis told herself. Maybe if she talked to him, he'd back off.

"What's that?"

———

TURNED OUT, he wanted to show her his lab space.

Most of the private spaces rented out on the *Vastitas Reach* were on decks three and four, inward facing with doors that led in off the outer hallway. Wyatt must have had some decent funding, because his was situated in the very back, with a wide bank of windows overlooking the ocean, the ship's churning white wake. He had books, too, professionally printed books, piles of them. Something Tharsis found to be quite rare these days. She glanced at a few of the titles piled up on his desk. *Collected Oceana Folklore. Oral Traditions of Australia. The Secret Teachings of All Ages.*

A sign hung over the door. The Arium logo, circles within circles. A single line of text.

THE GREATEST QUESTION HUMANITY WILL EVER SOLVE IS ITSELF

She wondered if that was what Annaka had been talking about.

Bea had gotten fussy on the way down here, wanting out of her sling. That was happening more now. Tharsis had the fabric looped around her shoulders now, holding the little girl instead. Having her hands full made it easier not to interact with the space, with Wyatt.

The myling had taken up position under the desk, watching her.

"Where are you headed?" she asked, moving over to a notebook, open-faced next to the pile. There was something about the symbols there that reminded her of the ones she'd seen in Noqumiut. Not quite visible, she could only see them out of the corner of her eye. Looking straight at them made them vanish, somehow.

"Oh, this has been my work space for a couple of years now."

"You're not researching the ocean, though."

"I'm researching the islands," he said. "Or the cultures there, I guess you could say. Their stories, their myths."

Once, she might have asked. Once, she might have been curious. That was before. Before Noqumiut. Before the Scient. Before tDaer. Her silence seemed to make him nervous, and he fiddled with one of the stacks of books. Kept talking.

"I am working on getting a space at one of the land-based ariums. Japan. Which would be amazing if I could get it. Their written language is fascinating. Layers upon layers of adaptation. Of course, China would be better, but considering what a mess that place is…"

"What are these?" she asked, shifting Bea's weight into one arm to tap the notebook. The baby squirmed but didn't wake.

"Umm, I don't quite have a name for it yet. A language that's beyond language, I guess you could say."

"That doesn't make any sense."

Deflated but undeterred, he handed her a few more sheets. "It's, umm… One of the biggest failures we have, humans, is this inability to understand each other. That leads to all kinds of terrible things. War, poverty, the very notion of right and wrong…"

"Wait, you think evil's caused by misunderstandings?"

"Well, evil is a relative term, not all that useful in the actual evaluation of people. But things have been falling apart for a century, longer, and people still don't listen. They don't listen to what they're being told. Our parents' generation tried reordering society with AI but that didn't work. Artificial intelligence was too far from us for it to truly comprehend our problems, or for us to comprehend its solutions. So humans have to fix themselves, but language itself becomes a barrier. If we can solve that problem, if we can close that understanding gap, make it impossible to not see, maybe, maybe we could fix… I don't know, everything."

"It's a nice thought," Tharsis said without conviction. Bea squirmed in her arms, but she wasn't about to set the baby down. Something was wrong with the space. There was a hum in the penumbra here, a murmuring discordance that her brain couldn't unscramble. Painful.

"Here, I'll prove it." He dug another notebook out of his backpack and flipped it open to the first page. "What is this?"

There was an image on the page, a single figure. She had to force her brain to focus on it. Something in the penumbra whispered. "I don't know, an animal?"

"Yeah," he said. "That's the primordial symbol for animal. Everyone I've shown it to has said the same thing."

"How could it not be an animal?" she asked. "You drew a picture of one. It's got legs and a head and ears."

"Here, I'll show you another one." He flipped to a different page. "What's that?"

Tharsis frowned. It felt familiar, the meaning just outside of her grasp. The whisper grew. The answer hit her. "Happiness."

He smiled, turned the page over. That was the word, written there.

"That doesn't prove anything."

"This is another one that tests with a 98 percent accuracy rate, across all cultures. I've got dozens of them now, but I want to figure out the rest. All of them."

"What constitutes all?"

"Every thing, every action, every state of being or piece of knowledge one can hold. Imagine what we could do as a species if language was no longer an obstacle. If total understanding could be established, based on unambiguous communication. If you could simply write a few glyphs and the other person couldn't help but know exactly what you were trying to tell them." He flipped the notebook closed. "So, what do you think?"

Tharsis didn't respond. She didn't trust herself. Everything suddenly was blindingly clear.

Whitecoats. The Ariums.

This was where it had started. How. The Euphemism.

Seven billion people. Seven billion people were going to die for this hubris. Would that matter to him, if she said anything? But then, what did it matter at all? She'd never heard of him, or this writing system. Just another ridiculous transhumanist fantasy.

That myling was smiling at her.

Where had the damn thing come from?

"I think the ship needs an exorcism," she said, and dropped the paper back on the desk. "You might need to consider it too."

He laughed. "I haven't heard that one before. That's funny."

The flippancy made her angrier.

"I think you're ignoring something kind of important."

"Yeah, like what?"

"What if people understand exactly what you're saying, and they just don't want it?"

A look of confusion crossed his face. "We're trying to heal the world, end war, end poverty, end all of this negative shit we've been dealing with for so long. Who wouldn't want that?"

A line from *War Dog of Mars* came to Tharsis's mind then.

War is in you

War is in all living things

It is the nature of nature

"I don't think you understand people as much as you think you do," she said.

He cocked his head. "I guess I choose to be an optimist."

"AHH YES, that one. Paranoid. He's the guy on board who won't let us store his work. I don't know what he thinks I'm going to do with it."

That was what Chris told her, when Tharsis asked him about Wyatt Blalock the next day.

"It should all be deleted," she grumbled. Her hands were starting to cramp from too many hours at the keyboard.

"A lot of whitecoats come through here. Some just want a ride somewhere, others are trying to stay off the grid as much as they can. They can be a secretive lot."

"I just can't figure out what the hell he wants from me."

Chris snorted. "Well, you're Navajo, aren't you? That was probably it."

There it was again. That reference to something—ethnicity, nationality?—that Tharsis didn't understand. She had to figure it out. To cover up her unease, she reached down to give Bea a pat, napping in the playpen. "Why does that matter?"

"From what I can gather, and I've been watching these kids a long time, there's an unspoken belief amongst many of the whitecoats that Western scientific traditions have taken us away from deeper truths about, I don't know, the planet or nature or reality. That in moving away from it, we've become so detached that we can't understand that we're killing it. So, if we return to the oldest belief systems, we'll gain insights we've lost."

It sounded a lot like some of the conversations she'd had with Ang, back in her own time. Polarist scat. "What's that got to do with me?"

"Probably thinks you can help him with his research. He spends a lot of time with tribal organizations when we're at port."

"I'm Catholic," she said derisively.

Chris laughed.

Tharsis didn't think it was funny at all.

She had bigger problems than Wyatt to deal with, though.

So far, the *Vastitas Reach* had only been to a few places. None of them looked, smelled, or felt like the place where she'd encountered the Flet. Chris said that was going to change after Sydney, their next port of call. After that, they'd head out from the shallow barrier waters into the deep blue depths of the Pacific proper. He said they normally stopped somewhere at least once every sevenday, but the schedule was always subject to change. Politics, or money, drove the choice of everything from open-ocean dive sites to morale stops. Chris wasn't sure how exactly those decisions got made and didn't seem to care much.

Tharsis needed to find the Flet's event horizon.

Time didn't seem to be flowing right. Instead of one nice smooth progression of moment to moment, day to day, her sense of its passage came in fits and starts. Without the little baby to ground her in the here and now, Tharsis was worried that she might float away entirely. The currents of time carrying her somewhere else were equally undesirable.

She dreamed of the yacht sometimes. Not every night, but it was the only dream she had. The deck, the failing light. Sometimes she heard single words in a conversation, old as the sun.

What had happened there, she couldn't see.

She hadn't gotten there yet.

Tharsis wasn't sure if it was a problem with her perception, or if she was destabilizing something. She wasn't supposed to be here; she didn't belong. She could feel it in her bones.

If she was gone, though, who was going to take care of Bea?

She wasn't too proud to admit to herself that she was growing attached to the baby.

Nobody else was there for her. Nobody else was going to take care of her. Who would tell her stories? Who would clean that last little bit of spittle off her face in the bath? Who would carry her outside on those sleepless nights and point out the stars and tell her about all the magnificent things that awaited her out there?

Who would care for her?

And there were times—little hands grabbing hers, the first little smile on that tiny face—that Tharsis could have let herself melt.

But she couldn't be this little girl's mother.

The Naven would die because of her.

She tried not to think about it.

A hard task, most days. The guilt ate at her.

She couldn't shake the memory. Couldn't forget the trust in that little face, even as that temporal misalignment tore everything apart. And she really couldn't shake the thought that maybe the Naven's trust in her had started here. That the Naven had done what she'd done because of what Tharsis was doing now, in the past.

———

ALMOST TWO SEVENDAYS into the cruise, they put into Sydney Harbour. Sydney was a glorious mess. Huge gleaming towers, wide streets, too many people. Messy, loud, and brash. Like a voider habitat.

Exhausting.

At least, that's how it seemed as they sailed into the harbor.

The *Vastitas Reach* was going to be in port there for a few days, and the entire ship's complement was making plans. Annaka was organizing something she called a pub crawl, and the deep-ocean team had been working with Tharsis on data pulls for some kind of lecture they were giving at the aquarium. Wyatt had asked her to join him for coffee shoreside, and maybe a conversation he'd set up with some local Aboriginal leaders. She begged out of all of that.

Tharsis had no plans to do anything out in the city. She was looking forward to getting some rest in, taking a few well-deserved naps in her bunk with Bea when she could.

But Chris, of all people, managed to get her off the boat.

One of the odder features on the *Vastitas Reach* was a small hydroponics bay set up in one of the upper decks. The place had a hundred and eighty degrees of glass all around and looked more like some kind of captain's lounge than lab. But if it had ever served such a purpose, any niceties had long since been stripped away. The floor was the same bare, painted metal as the rest of the ship's work spaces, and a complex series of piping delivered desalinated water to all manner of plants.

Since Tharsis had been aboard, the galley was the primary customer, growing lettuces and radishes and things like that for the salad bar. But anybody could plant stuff here.

Chris had had her doing crop inventory. The kitchen staff that tended the place kept everything written down on a damp clipboard near the entrance, but the ship's logistics officer made his purchases through some kind of Gig-enabled system. Once a sevenday, Tharsis had to go up there and manually transfer the clipboard's contents into the *Vastitas Reach's* inventory.

This, Chris said, was crucial when they were in a port as large as Sydney. Stocking the correct type and quantity of perishable food was apparently quite important.

Tharsis was yawning her way through the task at the bay's small desk when she overheard talking.

"It's a three-hundred-day growing season. If we—"

"Three hundred days, followed by winters that might end up being harsher than here. How the fuck do you keep perennials alive in that?"

"We're talking about corn, not fruit trees."

"So what, fuck apples? We don't get apples on Mars?"

Tharsis looked up from her work. It was one of the submersible mechanics, a man she recognized but barely knew. She was surprised to see him in the hydroponics bay at all. And somebody else, somebody with a different accent, although she was still terrible at identifying regional differences. Must have been somebody new to the boat; she couldn't place his face at all.

"Greenhouses," she said, without really thinking about it. Vast structures pulled over the fields back home in the autumn months. Mars, with its three-hundred-day winters, would have never survived without them. Seemed such commonplace logic, she wondered why they didn't know about it.

"Come again?" the newcomer asked.

"Greenhouses," she repeated. "Heated through a combination of passive solar and active methane or fusion heaters, although you need a pretty large setup for fusion to make sense. Communities share that resource."

"We'd be talking about entire fields, though," the newcomer said.

Tharsis shrugged. "Demountable solid panels for areas with larger snow loads, roll-out flexible plastics for areas with milder climates."

"You can't tent every tree in an orchard. Or a forest."

Laying her tablet aside, Tharsis said, "Things adapt, quicker than we give them credit for. But biomes are going to settle where they settle. Not everything will take root. It'll work itself out. Might take a few generations, or some basic gene editing, but it will work out." She realized how she sounded. Faltered. "Or would, I suppose."

The newcomer looked amused. "Greenhouses, huh?"

"You can't grow anything in the snow," she replied.

"What if the winters are particularly nasty?"

"Ranching makes more sense than broad agricultural activity in those types of places. You use the arable land for hay production and build bigger barns. But for the more temperate regions," and she picked her tablet back up, "greenhouses."

The mechanic looked amused. "Hypothetically," he said.

"Hypothetically, of course," Tharsis said.

And she didn't think much of the conversation after that. Went back to a blissfully empty cabin, laid Bea down on their bunk, and curled up around her for a nap. It wasn't until later that evening, headed to the shower room to give the baby a good scrub, that the topic came up again.

When she ran into Chris.

"What schoolhouse are you out of?"

"Excuse me?"

"You're from northern Arizona, right? That's high desert, isn't it? Altitude, cold winters. I imagine the regional coaches talk a lot about that sort of thing with y'all." He shook his head. "Why didn't you tell me you were connected to the Ark Project?"

Tharsis had no idea what he was referring to. Not directly. Not by name. But there were those stories, the stories from back home, some of the whispers she'd heard since arriving here. The hope she was banking on, trying to help the Flet with whatever the hell it was that he wanted her help for.

It might have been a stretch, but she was almost certain Chris was taking about the old training programs. The survival schools. The ones the early Arran pioneers committed to, before they left Earth.

Before they arrived at Mars.

It was, potentially, another connection. Another little thread she could pull on. To get herself that berth off world.

"There are whitecoats on board, aren't there?"

Chris visibly relaxed. "I thought you knew more than you were saying," he said. "Look, Assam—"

"Who?"

"The man you spoke to earlier today, about greenhouses, he's the regional training guy for East Oz. One thing they can't simulate for the folks here are cold-weather issues. He was trying to cycle everyone through the training grounds at Kathmandu for that, but with the recent unpleasantness up there, it's too much of a risk. And New Zealand, obviously, is fucked."

"Of course," Tharsis said, completely lost.

"There's a meeting tomorrow. He asked me if I could ask you to come."

A meeting? With a first group of settlers?

"I wouldn't miss that for the world."

———

IT TOOK Tharsis and Chris almost the entire morning to get out to the location for the meeting. She didn't find it the easiest trip; doubt plagued her. It could have been a trap. It could have been a setup.

Chris didn't say much. He was taking just as much of a risk as she was, Tharsis figured, and didn't press him for details.

They took the train. First, one of the big metropolitan lines. Then, a smaller one that led out of the city proper into the more forested areas beyond. The windows on that train were open, the breeze that swirled through the cars laden with humidity. Dry eucalyptus groves rustled around them. Bea slept in her sling.

But eventually, they reached a stop, just outside a huge park, where the trees retreated and acres of manicured grass asserted themselves.

There seemed to be some kind of youth ball game going on that morning, and the place was packed. Not rugby, which was by far the most popular sport on Mars, but something played mostly with the feet. There were more children than Tharsis had yet seen together on Earth, too. More children than adults, by far. They walked through the crowd, Tharsis fascinated, and then pulled the coordinates back up.

Chris indicated a meandering path. A kilometer and a half, it ran. Through the dry forest, the smell of it stinging in her nose. In the shade of the bigger trees stood lopsided dirt mounds. Termites, Chris explained when she asked.

Tharsis barely noticed the distance.

There was nothing like this on Mars.

After a thoroughly sweaty walk, she heard voices off the path. A few dozen meters more, and the two of them emerged into a clearing. Natural, this time.

Packed with people.

"Ahh, you did make it. We were about to begin."

Tharsis looked around. Adults, mostly, quite a few teenagers as well.

"Sorry if we're late," Chris said gruffly, walking over to somebody at the center of the throng. An older woman, long hair braided and thrown over one shoulder, the brunette ends fading up to white, face creased from a life outdoors.

"Don't worry about it," she said in that local accent. "I was just excited to learn you had somebody who had some idea about cold-weather survival."

The ball game at the front of the park was a blind, Tharsis realized. A ruse. An excuse for this gathering. That's why there were so few adults down at the pitch. They were up here.

"What would you like me to talk about?" she asked the pair.

"Winters," the woman said.

"Winters on Mars?"

The older woman chuckled. "I reckon that's some extrapolation, but sure. On Mars."

How much could she say? How much should she? Tharsis

wondered about that. But then, if what the Golanites held was true, if everything that happened already had, there was no changing things.

She had always come to this clearing.

She had always spoken to these people about winter.

Her people. Her ancestors.

"Okay," Tharsis said.

The older woman—clearly some kind of organizer—called for silence.

Tharsis began.

"Mars, once the ocean returns and the magnetic constellation secures the sky, is a world that will evolve," she began. "What you'll find there isn't what your grandchildren will have. But the climate is largely determined by orbital path and sunlight. When it stabilizes, the climate's going to resemble the higher latitudes of this world. Alpine forests, taiga, that sort of thing. Winter survival becomes critical..."

Tharsis wasn't sure how long she spoke. An hour, maybe two. She talked about the first snows and the early pressure storms, of traditional sealed dwellings and community shelters. She talked about lost herds and failed crops, about the struggle to get barns heated and fields lit in winters made harsh as weather patterns stabilized. She talked about snow in the towering pines. That legendary first real Christmas, fifteen years after the first forests were planted. She talked about waning root cellar stocks and the fear and the way communities banded together to keep children fed.

She talked until she had nothing more she could say. When the words ran out, and she had nothing more to offer. When Chris clapped her on the shoulder and asked for a round of applause and announced it was time for lunch.

Over barbecue down at the pitch, more people came up to her, asked her questions in low voices, the same question, over and over.

Is it worth it?

She couldn't tell them the truth. Not all of it. Not what was coming. That so many would try to flee and so few would make it. That Mars itself would be a struggle, titanic, for that first century. That civil war and storms and crop failures would come for the first generations of the planet-born and would make it seem hopeless.

That the First Propagation would wipe away so, so many hopes.

But they'd built a world for themselves.

They always would.

They always had.

"Yeah," she kept saying. "It's worth it."

———

CHRIS WAS quiet on the way back from the park.

Quiet, for most of the journey.

"Bea reminds me of our youngest granddaughter," he said, when they were almost back to the marina. "Minus the red eyes, of course. She was just about this age."

The words took Tharsis by surprise. Chris had been pretty tight-lipped about anything but work, up to this point. "What happened?"

"My daughter's husband drove the entire family off the road a few years ago. Straight off Highway One, down into the ocean. Ilu, according to the autopsy. God only knows what he was seeing," he said bitterly. "Government keeps refusing to ban the shit, though. I was at a hearing for it, after the accident. Some of the things the officials said… that's when I realized, they're in on it. Or they don't care if we die. It all amounts to the same thing."

Tharsis glanced down at Bea. The baby was awake, blinking up at her with those huge red eyes, just starting to gnaw on her little fist. She'd need a bottle when they got back onboard.

What would it be like, Tharsis wondered, to lose her?

But then, she would, wouldn't she?

"You okay?" Chris asked.

Her eyes were watering. Hell. Tharsis wiped her face on her sleeve. "We've all lost somebody," she said.

"We have. And we're going to keep losing, until there's nothing left. That's why we have to. There's no future for us here. The white-coats are already changing their tune. When I was younger, it was 'leave a smaller footprint.' Now, it's just 'leave.'"

"What are they worried about?" she asked. She'd always wondered about this; everyone back home wondered about this. "Jovian H-Three is endless clean energy. Zero-G manufacturing can move most damaging industry off planet. The technology's there to—"

"It's the technology that's the problem," he said. "They tried AI. Doesn't work the way they wanted it to. So now they've moved on. Biological engineering. But even that's not really the point, I don't think."

Bea, in her sling around Tharsis's chest, yawned.

"What do you mean?"

"They can't seem to give up this idea that we're a virus on this planet. That we don't deserve to exist, that the only way we can atone is by ridding the universe of humanity. Remaking it, or wiping it out. It's like a sickness with some of these whitecoats."

She thought about Ang. About tDaer. "Or a religion," she said softly.

"Let's hope it doesn't go that far," he said.

They were within range of the ship now, close enough to hear the maintenance guys on the back deck joking as they worked on one of the submersibles.

They never talked about Mars again. But things had changed between them. Tharsis never could figure out just how much Chris risked, taking her to that meeting, but it seemed to be a significant extension of trust. He was less gruff, after that, kinder. And if he offered, from time to time, to give Bea her bottle or rock her back to sleep, Tharsis let him.

He was Arran, after all. In his own way.

The next day, the *Vastitas Reach* left Sydney Harbor and the azure waters of the inner reef. Headed out into the dark black of the open Pacific.

BOOK TWO

ABYSSAL

"SO WHAT, again, do I need to know about this thing we're going to see?"

"The Dena?" Adair turned to Colonel Cambel. "How would you describe her, sir?"

"Insane." That was Yip. "She's out-of-her-fucking-skull insane."

"Sergeant," Cambel warned.

"What? She's nuts and everybody knows it."

"Seems to be a running theme with the Landlords," Caleb replied.

The pressurization controls in the air lock beeped.

Colonel Cambel straightened his uniform. The entire contingent from the *Barachiel* was in formal service dress. Even Yip, although he still had his A24 on its shoulder sling, unapologetically wrinkling his navy-blue jacket. Caleb wouldn't have bothered anyway, but they didn't have dress grav-boots for him. That seemed a reasonable enough reason to stay in the nondescript black uniform he'd been wearing since he'd woken up in this place. He had his seax strapped to his thigh.

Cambel was along as a matter of propriety, some political thing. Adair had begged his way onto the landing. Yip had insisted on coming. Morray and one of his enlisted guys, Haas, rounded out the party.

The axilla had shown up at the ramp of the rockjump before departure.

Caleb couldn't get the image of Rallison out of his head.

Bleeding black, arm smoking.

Passing out of the air lock, the *Barachiel* crew stepped into parkland. Of all things.

Tyr lifted his blunt muzzle, sniffing.

The Venus Sanctums had been planned as a series of luxurious accommodations, Adair had told Caleb on the flight over here. No expense had been spared in their initial construction. The idea was to provide the well-heeled of Earth a comfortable exile from the home-world. Most labor functions had initially been either contracted to free-lancers from other colonies, with strict limits on their movement within the Sanctums themselves, or automated with sophisticated silic-guided machinery.

The upper atmosphere of Venus was the Heliosphere's best source of engine-critical argon gas, as well as easy access to a few other choice chemicals. No radiation, no magnetics to deal with.

For a while, it had been one of the wealthiest places in the Heliosphere.

Until it became the primary target of the Second Propagation. Several entire habitat platforms had been fully vented to the void, others heavily sabotaged. The populace had been unable to fight back in any effective manner. By the time security drones put down the coordinated worker riots, an estimated 90 percent of the original popu-lation was dead.

By HS0300, there were no permanent human inhabitants left.

Unlike many colonies, these hadn't passed into ruin. The argon mines had been hardened, too important a resource to lose. A few of the main habitats had been rebuilt. It was not without a human popu-lation, albeit a highly mobile one. The ASDF maintained a dry dock complex in Venus's orbit, and the habitats were popular locations for shore leave. Leisure tourism was more selective but steady, Adair had said, drawn in by the grand architecture, vast museums, ambitious garden-ecologies.

From the air lock, the group from the *Barachiel* passed out onto a wide platform, raised five meters or so above the surrounding land-scape. Below them, a thick carpet of wildflowers obscured the ground, blooms in every shade and color imaginable. Beyond, pleasant trees rose a hundred feet or more, broad leaves stretched to the light of the false sky. Signs, wrought from iron and vibrantly painted, along with a dual set of tracks, indicated the place was a train station. A clock on a central pillar ticked away the time.

An attendant in a waistcoat and sleeve guards came out of a booth on the far end of the station, trundling towards them. As the figure got closer, Caleb realized it wasn't a human at all. He had to grab Tyr's harness to keep the dog from lunging at it. Clearly some clockwork construct. Gears that served no purpose whirled in the face beneath a transparent glass skin.

"Greetings, esteemed guests and Landlord," it said, voice mellifluous despite its obvious artificial nature. "The Dena humbly welcomes you to her abode."

"Humble, my ass," Yip muttered.

"Transport shall be here in a few minutes. If there is anything you require, refreshment or—"

"We're fine," Colonel Cambel replied, tense. "Leave us alone."

The thing bowed again. "As commanded," it half sang, and retreated to its booth.

"I hate those things," Cambel muttered.

It was the first real emotion Caleb had seen from the old officer.

The train, when it came, was in the same vein as its station: over-wrought, over-detailed, colorful. The benches in the passenger car were deeply padded, upholstered in velvet, and the thing actually steamed as it pulled out of the station.

Low rolling hills, covered with a thick wildflower meadow, gave way almost immediately to the forest, a broad tunnel of trees.

"The outer ring of all these habitats is like this," Cambel explained, as they passed into the thick forest. "A full kilometer deep."

"What's the purpose?"

"Atmosphere regulation. Plants still do a better job of managing the air than machinery alone."

Caleb lifted a hand. "Gravity seems to be what it is on the ship."

"It used to be heavier, actually, Earth-normal," Adair said. "Mars lowered it to Arran standard when we took stewardship of the place."

"I thought this place had its own Landlord."

"We have a mutual protection treaty with the Dena."

"Mutual? What does this place provide?"

"Wasps," Morray replied. "This is where our wasps are built."

———

TEN MINUTES LATER, the train rumbled into another station, this one even more lavish and ridiculous than the first.

"Not exactly the sort of thing I'd expect from the rich on Earth," Caleb commented to Adair as they disembarked. "A little gaudy."

Adair nodded. "There were dozens of individual habitats originally. Some were meant as primary dwellings, others, as entertainment or leisure venues. The primary habitats were targeted first."

"So what, this was some kind of theme park?"

"As I understand it. There were also some historical buildings and landmarks they brought out here with them. There's one built completely around those. I think there are a few such places here as well."

Another mechanical messenger was waiting for them, a little further into the colonnades of the travel hall.

The thing was vaguely human-shaped, but any resemblance to a real person ended with its silhouette. It was an assemblage of brass cogs and polished glass, bits of old-style police accoutrements clinging to its chassis. Blue eyes stared at them, still, inhuman behind the gilded mask. It was, Caleb realized, supposed to be female.

Tyr growled at it.

"You're up, sir," Colonel Cambel said in a low voice.

"Welcome, soldiers. Welcome, honored Landlord." Its voice sounded like bells ringing. "Welcome to the Venus Sanctum of the Endless Ironlight."

Yeah, Caleb thought, *insane*.

"Where's the Dena?" Caleb asked. "Orbital Control informed us she was on this habitat."

"All official business is required to register at the Hall of Visitation," the clockwork-thing continued. "You will follow me to begin processing."

"We don't have that kind of time," Caleb said.

Be as direct and severe as possible. Both Adair and Cambel had been emphatic on this point. They'd be here for a sevenday or longer just dealing with bureaucratic niceties if Caleb didn't aggressively push back.

"It is standard for—"

"As a member of the Tenancy, I claim my right to speak directly to my peerage, without delay," Caleb said, remembering the script Adair had handed him. It would have been embarrassing if it hadn't been so deadly serious. "Failure to do so will result in a violation of Accords section one-point-three-point-six, subsection B."

"It is standard for—"

"Sergeant Yerpoli?"

"Yes sir?"

"If you shoot this thing, will it shut up?"

"I don't know," Yip said with a smile, and unslung his rifle. "Let's find out."

But before the big Marine got a chance to squeeze off a round, an entire bevy of security drones had surrounded them, weapons drawn.

"It is standard for you to begin your visit at the Hall of Visitation," the messenger automata repeated.

"Is the Dena there?" Caleb asked again.

The robot was silent for a moment. "No."

"Then, citing my authority under the Tenancy Accords, I order you take us to where she is."

Cogs whirred in the thing's head. Contacting the Dena via wireless, maybe, or cogitating its options. Adair had been emphatic on this as well; most of these things lacked any true autonomy. What wasn't directly controlled was specifically programmed for function. "Agreed."

———

THE MESSENGER LED them down into the streets of the habitat, wordless.

Caleb tried to take it all in.

The streets were paved with cobblestone, smooth and level, almost polished from centuries of care. Buildings rose in a meandering grid, brick and bright wood, handblown glass windows and wrought iron.

Walking through the place, Caleb was reminded of old family trips to the mountains, to places like Jackson Hole or Steamboat Springs. Everything looked bespoke, belabored. As if the work of lifetimes had gone into crafting the finest facsimile of Victorian detail. It felt too clean, too polished.

It felt fake.

"Like you said, it was a theme park," Adair said, when Caleb asked.

Morray butted in. "What's a *theme park*?" He used the correct Silicone accent for the last two words. Caleb hadn't realized how foreign it sounded to them.

"Don't you have places of fun, game booths and rides and over-priced food?"

"What, like a parish harvest fair?" the comm officer replied.

"Maybe? But with permanent buildings and a deeply immersive feel to it."

"I don't think I'd want to be deeply immersed in the harvest fair," Morray laughed. "Way too much goat scat."

Yip smiled. "I personally prefer the beach habitat. Or that one where it's tucked into those crazy pines, with the fake hot springs."

"What, Nippon? That's because the brothels are there," Morray said.

"Like I'd touch those robot hookers." He snorted. "No, it's the food. They've got real fish there. Most of the meat here's vat-grown unless you rent out a kitchen and bring over your own stores."

"We should do that again, Colonel," Morray said. "That was great, last time we were in."

"One thing at a time, gentlemen," Cambel said. Of all of them, he seemed the most on edge. "Let's deal with the Dena first."

"We need access to the museum complex," Adair reminded Caleb.

"Museums?"

Yip smiled. "What do they call that habitat? The Halls of Ancient Knowledge? Something ridiculous."

"The Halls of Boundless Ancient Wisdom," Adair said. "My wife and I spent a month out there once. Didn't see half of it."

"What is it?"

"Supposedly, a collection of the greatest museums from all over the

Earth. Moved up here, artifact by artifact, brick by brick, before the Euphemism could destroy it all."

"What, like the entire Louvre?"

"Possibly. What was the Louvre?"

There were a few people here and there, most of them flesh and blood, a few as false as their messenger. Most were in costumes appropriate to the scenery, embellished and heavy. Some were clearly tourists, in styles that Caleb didn't recognize at all.

Their number increased as they walked. Moving towards the center of the city, Caleb supposed. But he could see the curved dome of the sky rearing up, closer now, and realized they'd passed through the main body of the town, right out to the other edge.

The buildings fell away. They passed through a gatehouse set into a low wall.

Out into a wide lawn, stretched a quarter kilometer towards a grand manor house, built in something like a French country style.

"Oh, you've got to be kidding me," Caleb muttered under his breath.

"Welcome to the Dena's private hunting lodge," the automata announced.

"What does she hunt?" asked Yip. "The contract labor?"

"Sergeant Yerpoli," Cambel snapped, "show some decorum."

"My apologies, sir," he said, totally insincere. "I must be overwhelmed by the extravagance on display."

If the messenger registered the insult, it didn't show. "This way, gentlemen," it said, and led on, up the grand sweep of the gray stairs and into the house itself.

———

"HEY, Stag? We're getting something on the omni."

The deputy commander pulled himself away from the news feed. Nothing new. The same spiderscat. Increased Tok activity. More suicides in the Jovian Lagrange habitats. Another angry message from HOMECOM, political scat the boss was going to have to take care of. "What kind of something?" he asked.

The on-shift sensor threw his screen into the three-dimensional holopit that dominated the back of Ops. "Not sure yet. Take a look."

Stag stepped down onto the observation ledge, walking around. The *Barachiel* had a number of different sensor arrays, some omnidirectional and some very narrow. Those tended to give better readings, but the field of view was much tighter. The omni gave a 360-degree view, but at the expense of clarity.

For ease of interpretation, there was a small model of the deep-voider held up on a slender rod in the center of the pit, and the array in question would light up in relation to its position on and around the craft. The sensor was referencing the omnidirectional radar at the moment, and so the entire sphere of the pit was lit up.

Venus itself was too far away to be represented by the set scale, but the nearest Sanctum was clearly represented at the edge of the field. Threads of light traced point paths through the space around it.

"Looks like space debris. There's a ton of it up here. Hard to differentiate..."

Using a handheld laser pointer, Stag indicated the area around the Sanctum. "What's the average size of this scat?"

"Two meters, give or take."

"Big enough for a swarm," Erg said. Stag started; the lanky Hive head was right next to him.

"The Sanctum's? One of the transport craft that bring in new workers?"

"Doubtful," the sensor operator said. "We're not getting any identifier transmission."

"Their IFF beacon could be malfunctioning," Stag mused.

"Can you switch to narrow beam?" Erg said, and indicated another area, about a kilometer away from the Sanctum's planet-facing edge. "What's down here, where the concentration of debris is greater?"

"Hang on." It took an agonizing thirty seconds to switch the sensors, longer to consolidate the feed for viewing.

Stag folded his arms, waiting. Erg leaned forward on the railing.

"What are you thinking?"

"Maybe some kind of mobile command craft," Erg said, "or you know how voiders are awful fond of slapping engines on—"

"Asteroids," Stag finished, as a small cone of light illuminated in the pit. "Oh, would you look at that?"

"Initial readings consistent with an arrogate asteroid," the sensor said. "Not big, maybe two, three hundred meters long, half that wide."

"What the fuck is it doing here? How'd it get past orbital defenses?"

"Iron ball paint, most likely," Erg said. "Scat's easy to manufacture in any of the low-altitude platforms on Jupiter."

"This isn't a transport," Stag muttered. A flat screen projected at the edge of the pit, technical details scrolling across it. If it was iron ball radar shielding, the arrogate was likely far larger than it appeared. "Comm, notify the colonel."

"Recommend pulling back," Aeolis said. "If the thing decides to ram us…"

"No. We're better being close in that case. It's synched to the Sanctum's orbital speed. It'll need to fire its engines up to come after us. The less distance they have, the better."

"They aren't here for us. Arrogates don't move fast," Erg said. "This has been a decades-long project, maybe, for whoever's in that thing. Nalatok scat, more than likely. Parked out in the Aphroditan Lagrange point, waiting for the Arcna to start talking."

"What is it with you voiders and that crazy bitch?"

"I don't know." And Erg smiled. "We say we're atheist, but we do things like this."

"We don't know anything yet," Stag said. "But get the myrmid wasps out anyway. And the relays. Just in case."

The comm station chimed up. "Colonel's not responding, sir. I think we're being jammed."

"By who, the voiders?"

"I think it's the Sanctum itself."

"Great," he muttered, then louder, "Contact Orbital Control. Let them know what we're seeing. Get an accurate read on that mod out there. And put the Marines on alert. If this scat goes sideways, I wanna be ready."

Stag leaned against the rail, listening to the chatter in Ops pick up. He'd seen many a Tok arrogate incursion before. Never routine, those events, but there did tend to be a rhythm to it. Whatever was going on, the *Barachiel* would deal with it.

CHAPTER
TWENTY-ONE

THE MESSENGER MADE the Arrans wait in some antechamber. Opulent, almost revoltingly so. More clockwork automata had emerged from nooks in the walls, bearing food or flagons of something cold and sweating, every one professing its desire to make the visiting military men feel right at home.

Cambel had rolled his eyes, accepted a beer, and told Caleb to make it as quick as he could.

He and the Rallarhu-thing had been shown into a chamber that reminded him of the Flet's. But where that one had been stark, unadorned, this one was dripping with ornamentation. Marble fretwork screens lined the walls, so translucent that the blinking lights of mechanical equipment showed through, hidden in alcoves beyond. Geometric mosaics covered the floor. Distant windows, set into a high dome, shone with broken light. Darkness clung to every surface.

At odds with the vintage facade was the cylindrical tank at the dead center of the space. It glowed with pale green light, subtle movement of fluid within casting ripples across the floor.

Beside the tank was what looked like a dress form, hung with a sickening amount of silk, bunched and gathered and smoothed. Headless.

"What is this?" Caleb asked the messenger automata.

"Her place of repose," came the answer. The thing bowed, then retreated, leaving them alone once again.

As soon as the automata was completely gone, a series of mechanical arms rose from the base of the tank. Brass and rivet construction belied the smoothness of their movements, as they unfolded broad, many-fingered hands. Delicately, they reached into the tank.

Light flared.

Caleb could have sworn he heard music.

When the arms re-emerged, a wet, pulsating object came with them.

Another set of arms was working on some type of casing, setting it in place on the form's neck. A filigreed mask covered the eyes and delineated a nose. Its lips were a perfect, unmoving curve. A head, Caleb realized, and the tank object was slipped inside.

"Horrific," the axilla said. Even through the flat vocals of the suit's radio, it sounded contemptuous.

"An interesting sentiment, coming from you," another disembodied voice replied.

Caleb scrubbed a hand over his face. "Great," he muttered. "Another one."

"I am nothing like that thing," the other voice replied. It was coming from speakers built into the body's neck, Caleb realized. "I retain my human form."

"We're both occupying machinery right now," the axilla said.

"Yes, but I can still exist within baseline atmosphere." Lights flicked on and off down the mannikin's body, and one hand twitched. Experimental, its movements. "Ahh. Connection."

"You're a brain in a jar," Caleb observed.

"If I had kept my body through plastic surgery, enhancements, would I be any less false?" the Dena asked, and stepped free of her platform. The dress rustled around her, the low gravity allowing the structured material to flow as if underwater. "It is easier to sustain neural tissue alone, outside of all else."

"We had a word for this in my day. Bio-fucked."

"A term that applies doubly to you." The Dena gestured to them, bidding them follow, as she piloted the impossibly graceful robot body towards a doorway. "Now, why are you here?"

"Surely you noticed the divedrive network is offline." The axilla seemed different. Its speech was smoother. More conversational. "This is a critical resource for the Heliosphere."

"Your concern, not mine," the Dena countered. "My trade routes are reliable as a pulsar and my communication needs are minimal. I conduct no critical business over the dive lines."

"Your tourism industry is wholly dependent on it. How many well-heeled voiders do you have in orbit right now, unable to return home?"

"Nepos seldom cause real trouble."

"Seldom is not never."

"This is a civilized place. I run civilized habitats. There is no threat of terrorism here." The doorway led out to a wide veranda, curved colonnades overlooking the parkland they saw when they first came in. "Mine is an inwell of calm."

Tyr, still padding along at Caleb's side, sniffed the air. He sent Caleb a sense-impression; the scent of cordite, the distant sound of something exploding.

"Then why is there gunfire right now?" he asked.

"I hear nothing."

"He hears everything," Caleb said, and patted Tyr's head. "And he hears guns."

The Dena's glass mask turned to the dog. "Another worker riot, I would assume. There has been some unrest amongst the workers since the Propagation failed. Some are calling it an omen."

"The woman y'all call the Arcna ate herself, as she lied to the entire Heliosphere about some beautiful utopia she created," Caleb said. "What possible omen is that?"

"Belief, Caleb, is a powerful thing. It is not based on logic, so how can it be disproven? Noqumiut is heaven incarnate to them, and the loss of the Arcna's voice is a terrible thing indeed." The Dena made a clicking sound. "And to think, we've tried so hard to shepherd them."

"Shepherd who?" Caleb asked. "All your people are dead."

The lights along the Dena's visible body flared. "How dare you speak of it, when Mars did not save us!"

"Lady, I don't know what kind of interactions we've had in the past, but I have to tell you, I don't see much here worth saving."

The Dena looked to the axilla. "He died in one of your asteroid seas, did he not? Where were you?"

It didn't answer.

"We're here because we need access to something you have. The divedrives aren't working because the," and Caleb stumbled, "the governing consciousness seems to be missing."

"What do you mean? Is the Flet dead?"

"No, but brain activity at his tank on Pluto indicates he's being… occupied elsewhere."

"Where?"

"We need access to the *Undine Glory*."

"Why would he be there? The place is a mausoleum."

"Your entire inwell is a mausoleum that serves up whores and ice cream to bored Nepos from Themisto," the axilla snapped. "You are going to provide us with the keys to the living sections of the *Undine Glory*, or I will strip every square centimeter of xenocyte from your hulls and leave you at the mercy of the solar wind."

"Threats? What else to expect from you?" The Dena made a little show of checking the glittering fingernails on her fake hands. "But the craft is not located in this Sanctum."

"It's in the Halls of Boundless Ancient Wisdom, isn't it?" the axilla asked.

"What's there, in the Museum of Aerial Antiquities, is a replica. The actual craft remains in the void. It may take Orbital Control a few hours to locate it." The Dena laughed, a terrible sound. "That should give you Arrans time to get the current situation well under control."

"Your worker riot? Why is that our problem?" Caleb asked.

"Acceptable," the axilla said, and stormed away, back into the depths of the chateau.

A mechanical hand caught Caleb's arm before he could follow. Crushing force in the fingers, barely held back.

"It's not her, you know. No matter what that thing is programmed to say, how like her it's tuned to appear, it's not your captain."

"I've seen it out of that suit, ma'am. I get it."

"You have not been awake in this time long enough to truly understand. Mars and the Inner Belt have maintained an uneasy alliance, thanks to your shared history. But you must keep in mind what she is, and what she is not."

He shrugged the false hand off. "From what I can tell, none of you Landlords are human anymore."

"You should perhaps consider what that means for yourself," the Dena said, and then visibly jerked. "But we have more immediate problems."

"Like what?"

"Like the Nalatok vessel that just rammed through three levels of my manufacturing complex." She waved him away, silk lace fluttering against the cold surface of her body's hand. "Now, the sooner you deal with it, the sooner you may seek out the *Undine Glory*."

———

STAG PACED the floor in Ops, attention divided between the holopit and the flat monitor displays for the damage report.

One of them was a text feed of the Aeneas Orbital Control radio chatter. Piping in the voice was possible, but half the stations in Ops were already communicating with their counterparts over there. Stag didn't want to add to the din.

His own handset rang.

<*Barachiel*, are you reading what we're reading here?>

"Yes, unfortunately," he said, eyes back on the holopit even as he spoke.

<We can't get a size estimate on this thing.>

"Our sensor grid is having the same problem. We need a closer visual. Where's your swarm?"

The radio crackled, canceling out the reply.

"Can you repeat, Aeneas?"

<They knew where to hit, or they got lucky. The arrogate impacted our swarm hangar. Damage estimates pending.>

Fuck. That was going to add to the response time. More time for the 'roid to disgorge combatants into the Sanctum's guts. Stag scanned the text feed; whoever was on the line with him was giving him summary information; the details were much worse.

"We'll deploy," he said, nodding to the Hive station tech, who immediately went to work. "Can you patch me through to Colonel Cambel?"

A long pause. More chatter on the text. "They're still with the Dena. I'll do what I can."

———

CALEB FOUND the group from the *Barachiel* waiting on the front stairs of the Dena's insane little hunting lodge.

Colonel Cambel, locked in furious conversation with one of those clockwork attendants.

"What do you mean," he was demanding, as Caleb and Tyr walked up, "the air lock's closed?"

"Sir, please remain calm," the thing told him in its dead voice. "The Dena wishes all to achieve harmony in her w—"

"The Sanctum's been rammed," the Dena said, coming out behind Caleb. The silk of her overwrought dress rustled in the false afternoon. "Looks like some Toks are having a spot of fun."

"You sure it's Toks?" Cambel asked.

"I am," and the mechanical body shuddered slightly, "suppressing their broadcast of the Second Propagation recordings. And they are killing their way through my menial and manufacturing levels."

"I hope they don't find your wine cellars," Yip replied sarcastically.

Cambel cleared his throat. Loudly. "I need to contact the *Barachiel*, ma'am. Do you have a command post where we might…"

"Oh, indeed not." And she laughed. Tapped her bronze cranium. "Why experience things in such a crude way when it's entirely unnecessary?"

Sensing the commander's irritation, Caleb stepped in. "Set something up for us."

"Well, I suppose we could let you use the comm room. But it is not at all in keeping with the aesthetic I cultivate here and—"

"That's fine, ma'am," Cambel said. "I just need a radio."

TEN DAYS OUT FROM AUSTRALIA, the morning briefing was somber.

"We'll be performing our annual pass by New Zealand," Skip announced, rain beating against the windows and the ocean gray outside. "We'll have the rad counters out on every deck, but you never know what can happen out around here. Stay on alert. I want decontamination kit set up for the submersibles."

The crew present took the news with a kind of sorrowful seriousness.

It was another one of those things, Tharsis knew, that she was likely expected to know. Something anybody from this time would have been aware of.

So much history had been lost.

"After that, ahh, series of incidents about a decade ago, New Zealand's been a no-go zone," Chris told her when she asked. "Data's been hard to get on it. It's not that far of a detour from our route, so we drop down here once a year to sample the radiation levels. So far, the damage seems land-based. We haven't detected anything serious in the currents."

Tharsis looked it up later when he wasn't paying attention. There had been a catastrophic series of meltdowns in a chain of new small-cell modular nuclear plants. Installed only a few months previously, every one had gone reactor critical. The entire country had been poisoned beyond human tolerance. Sabotage had been suspected, but there was no official culprit.

Sounded like Tok scat to her. Modular reactors were incredibly stable. In almost eight hundred years, HST, there had only been a handful of incidents with that technology on Mars, and all but one had been successfully contained to the facility itself.

New Zealand rolled by over the next few days, a land of towering mountains and deep pine forests. The ticking of the rad alarms, out on deck, was both reassuring and intimidating, but they never hit a serious pocket of radiation. The *Vastitas Reach* came in close to the shore in a few places, usually near towns. Harbors sat abandoned, buildings crumbling.

A few of her cabinmates got in an argument over it on the first night. Whether that was a fluke, or if every city, everywhere on Earth, was going to look like that eventually.

Tharsis didn't have the heart to tell them who was right.

AFTER NEW ZEALAND, the *Vastitas Reach* wandered in the deep blue for a good long while, well over a month. The submersibles were in the water almost as much as they were on the deck. The sheer amount of data flowing in from the deep-water teams kept Tharsis busy, often well into the evening, Bea cuddled into her shoulder as she fixed some fuckup in this or that database.

Wyatt left her alone.

As did the mylings. For some reason, none of them liked the background hum of the silic mainframes.

At night, Tharsis collapsed into her bunk, too exhausted to care about the bitching from the other women about these long stretches at sea.

She dreamed of the yacht, of the sunset and the rain that came after, of a dark ocean beating fast against a speeding hull. Of a glow beyond the edge of dark headlands.

Tom's event horizon.

The place Tharsis wasn't going to find, not this way.

Finally, Skip announced they were headed into a port of call. Some island called Niue, smaller even than most single-family 'roid settlements. No real reason for the stop, Chris told her later, other than the fact it was along their route and it was good for morale.

If nothing else, it was a day without work.

But the women in Tharsis's cabin invited her along on a dive trip, quite insistent on the entire thing.

She balked. The last time she'd gone out on an excursion with somebody she thought she could trust, it hadn't ended well.

"I can't leave her," Tharsis insisted that morning, pointing at Bea, batting at a toy on their bunk

"Didn't Chris offer to watch her?" Annaka said pointedly.

"Yes, but…"

"She is going to be safe and sound all day with Mister Grandpa, and you are allowed to take a break."

They were insistent, to the point where Tharsis realized she was doing herself more harm than good by not accepting. She grudgingly passed Bea off to Chris, donned a swimsuit that was loaned to her by one of the other women, and headed out with the group.

A small boat was waiting for them in a different part of the marina. They all clambered in, sipping water and chatting happily about nothing. Tharsis tuned it out.

The island rolled by, low white cliffs carved into almost organic shapes by eons of wave action, crystal clear waters caught in bowls between them. Vegetation so green it hurt the eye crowned the hilltops, and everywhere was the sound of gentle lapping waves.

Tharsis balked again when the suits and air tanks came out. Wet suits, the leather-skinned boat operator told her, scuba gear. Tharsis didn't care what it was called. Her skin prickled just looking at it.

Instead, she spent the morning just swimming. The boat had a nice selection of wide watertight masks and something the operator called snorkels. Good enough for viewing the reefs below.

Back home, the ocean was too cold for shallow-water corals. Seagrass, kelp forests, dominated much of the coastline. There were some deeper water species that had apparently taken root quite well, but those were visited sparingly, and then only by the marine biology teams that monitored the fragile, still evolving balance of the northern sea.

There was nothing like this. Nothing like the teeming shoals of fish with their riots of color, sparkling in the sun. Nothing like the deep nooks and crannies where eels lurked and octopi slept. Nothing like the vast spread of corals, tiny animals building their grand structures in the silence.

Even the unnerving sensation of weightlessness couldn't dampen the excitement of it.

Tharsis was so engrossed in it all that she didn't pay much attention to how far she'd drifted from the boat. Not until there was a touch on her arm, causing her to startle quite badly.

"Time for food," the boat operator told her, and pointed out from the island. "And you're starting to head out to sea."

Still trying to calm her heart, she looked.

Out that way, closer than she'd realized, dark blue water loomed.

"Thank you."

They ate lunch that day on a wide sandy beach. Finer and whiter than anything back home on Mars, Tharsis understood it had once been coral. Like the island itself had once been coral. She ate her fish, staring out over the ocean. On a boat, it was easy to see only the similarities with home. But Earth's biosphere was unspeakably old and had clearly left its mark on the planet in ways that Tharsis had never imagined possible before.

Mars, at the time of the first stirrings of settlement, had been a largely abiotic world. While very simple bacteria had been found in frozen caves deep within the crust, there was nothing even approaching the density of life found in the most barren of dirt there on Earth. The entire ecosphere had had to be built from raw sand up. Although the forests, both terrestrial and maritime, were centuries old in Tharsis's time, they were incredibly young compared to Niue.

"So, why no wet suit?" one of the younger women asked, when Tharsis headed back to the main tent for her second drink of the meal. They'd brought an insulated chest full of it with them. Water, beer, cider. She pulled a freezing cold bottle from the icy slush. Truthfully, she preferred Sabaean apples for cider over whatever they used here, but the buzz felt good. They definitely brewed the stuff stronger on Earth.

More of the women were looking at her.

"Come on, Rachel, not everybody likes scuba diving."

"Yeah, but we talked about it this morning, and—"

"I had a, uhh, a couple of accidents not too long ago," Tharsis said. The mere thought of putting a suit with an air tank on it, surrendering her ability to breathe to the environment, made her hands go clammy all over again. "Almost died up there."

"Up where?"

She probably wouldn't have done it if she hadn't been out in the sun all day, if she didn't have two ciders' worth of alcohol in her bloodstream. But it had also been months. Months of lying. Months of pretending. Even before she'd woken up in that hospital.

Tharsis pointed a finger straight up.

It set off a flurry of questions from all of them, wanting to know where she had been and what she had seen. If she had actually been out to the Inner Belt or Mars—Tharsis found out later there had had been quite a bit of speculation about this amongst the *Vastitas* crew. What it was like.

But all she had room for in her thoughts at the moment was the reef.

"What we have to do to survive out there… I don't think it's worth it. Wasn't worth this," and she waved her bottle at the water. "It's not worth losing this."

Maria smiled at her. "When we leave Earth, we're going to take this with us. All of it."

Tharsis didn't bother to argue. To tell her the truth. There was nothing like this out there. Their efforts would help make Mars habitable, though, even if not every biome could be replicated. Some of what couldn't survive on Mars had found homes in other habitats, early on. But as humanity drifted from what it had been, they abandoned such reminders of the home world. The void carved away what little bits and pieces of Earth they'd saved, until nothing at all was left.

They headed back to the *Vastitas Reach* not too long after that. The rest of the women headed back out to town, but Tharsis headed right for Bea.

Her baby was safe, unharmed, as promised. Chris had been reading to her, her tiny body cuddled in his arms. A smile spread out on her face, though, when she saw Tharsis.

The Arran's back was horribly sunburned—another thing that was a complete novelty—and one of her cabinmates had to help her slather on some kind of lotion that was supposed to help. Tharsis felt feverish all night, and Bea woke up more than normal, crying her soft little cries. But when she slept, she had the rare pleasure of a dream. Floating over the reef. At peace.

Tharsis got more questions after that. More interest. About the void. She said what she thought she could.

At every port of call from there on out, she went snorkeling.

It was a way to look for the Flet, she told herself. Get a feel for the landscape, see if the local harbor matched the one she saw from the deck of that yacht.

Wasn't selfish at all.

CHAPTER
TWENTY-THREE

A SWARM DEPLOYMENT was always an interesting thing to watch.

In a long-range deployment, with anything beyond half a light-second from the hull, or in an environment that could screw with communications, a specially designed command craft could be sent out, Erg safely ensconced in an acceleration couch.

Most of the *Barachiel's* actions were close quarters though. Or what passed for close in the void.

That day would be no exception.

Indicator lights, round pinpricks in the holopit's foggy interior, started spreading out from the central point of the *Barachiel*. The Sanctum lay just within the sphere of view, scaled accurately. The piece of scat just off its hull was of indeterminate size still.

"Get me eyes on that thing," Stag ordered, but at this point, it was an unnecessary command. Everyone knew the order of battle this early on, and Ops was humming along. "Aeneas Orbital, give me an update."

Text scrolled, fast and furious, across the radio transcript scene. It took a few moments for the controller on the other end to answer.

<Unchanged from last transmission,> came the response. Arran accent this time. Probably a contractor. <Reports from inside the Sanctum are conflicted. Enemy forces estimated in the high hundreds.>

"Intel?" Stag asked, turning to his own station.

That answer was more immediate. "Given standard life-support equipment for one of these things, I'd estimate a two-kilometer length."

<Pushing recon wasps as hard as I can,> Erg reported, unprompted. <Estimate another twenty-eight seconds to reliable visual contact.>

"Aeneas Orbital, are we clear to destroy this thing?"

<Negative, *Barachiel*. The Dena wants it parked.>

Of course she did, Stag thought bitterly. Made this all that much harder.

"Erg?"

<Heard and received,> the Hive head replied. His voice boomed over the vox. He always sounded different when he was inside his machines. <Changing weaponry configuration on myrmid units now.>

"Sir!" the comm station called. "I have contact with the colonel."

"About fucking time," Stag grumbled. "Put him on vox."

———

AFTER ALL THE AFFECTATION, the cold utility of the comm room was a pleasant break.

One of the Dena's robots took them back into the lodge, into the east wing of the place. From the outside, it had looked no different than the rest of the place, grand windows looking in on marble floors and wide, sunny halls. That was largely an illusion. The inner wall ended barely two meters back from the windows, accessible through one set of wide double doors.

Instead of opening into some grand ballroom or salon, though, they had found themselves in a stark white space, humming loudly with the sound of thousands of silicone processors set in oddly familiar tower-racks, lights in a rainbow of colors blinking as they passed. The floor didn't feel right; raised, Caleb guessed. It was cold; pipes marked with the symbol for nitrogen snaked through the racks.

"Looks like something from my own time," Caleb grumbled, but not even Adair, a few paces to his left, seemed to hear him. The noise was intense.

Morray seemed fascinated by it, though, and Yip had to grab him more than once. Stop him from touching something.

A small glass room stood in the center of the space. Inside was silence, along with a few computer terminals set into dull green consoles. A flick of a switch by the robot, and one of the glass walls turned into a giant monitor. A glowing black background held spirals and loops and balls of color, squares of text superimposed in the margins, which Cambel instantly began studying.

"Pardon the crudeness of this setup," the robot said with a bow. "I have piped in one of the feeds from Aeneas Orbital Command. It is not three-dimensional, but—"

"This is fine," Cambel said, distracted. "Radio?"

"Patching," the robot said. Its head jerked a bit, then its mouth fell open. Body still.

Cambel watched it in disgust, but huffed out a breath and asked, "*Barachiel*, can you hear me?"

A static crackle issued forth from the robot's mouth. Then, a familiar voice. <Loud and clear, Colonel. How is it in paradise?>

"Remind me to book my next vacation here," he said. He turned his attention back to the wall of light. "Get me up to speed. What's the situation?"

———

THE ONLY THING the Silicone Age had gotten right about void combat, Stag found himself thinking, even as he briefed the commander, was how tedious it could be.

Stag had started his career as an intelligence officer, but when the opportunity had come up to cross-train into a command pipeline, he had taken it. Meant an Arran year spent out in the Hungaria sector of the Inner Belt, out at the Void Operations schoolhouse. That training had made the *Centrifuge* run from the Academy look like child's play. But he'd passed near the top of his class, and gotten picked up as a shift commander on the Barachiel. Been working his way up since then.

He may not have had a voider's feel for three-dimensional combat, certainly not like Erg did, but he knew how to process large quantities of information swiftly. Extract meaning from it. Find the right answer.

<You've got command of this,> Cambel told him, after he finished bringing the man up to speed.

"You sure, sir?"

<We don't have a good setup over here. Just keep the vox on for me.>

"Roger that, sir." Stag watched the swarm drift towards the modified asteroid. Serene points of light, color-coded by purpose and position. Command units in purple, myrmids in blue, tugs orange. Even in the relatively small holographic field, it felt slow.

Per the history courses from the schoolhouse, spaceships had once been envisioned by humanity as gigantic weapon platforms, replete with massive crew complements and energy shielding. Battleships in space, powered by fusion instead of wind. Hell, Stag's boys back home loved those old stories, had little toys of some of those ships.

Completely impractical, of course.

The romantic notions of Silicone Age theorists and storytellers hadn't survived actual first contact with void warfare.

There had been experimental combat-capable craft built by half a dozen of the old global powers, in those uncertain days of the Silicone Age's twilight. After the third major planetary war, before the Euphemism had begun in earnest. The last reliable records from that period.

But spacecraft of the day were too delicate to withstand much of anything. There was no need for advanced weaponry; simple space debris or a concentrated burst of charged particles was enough to kill a crew. Kinetic attack worked almost too well, likely to destroy the aggressor right along with the victim. Old treaties forbidding the weaponization of space were therefore publicly adhered to.

Directed energy weaponry research had been pursued, but at great expense and with little need. Even with the best of fusion reactors, laughable amounts of precious craftside real estate were required for proper beam focus. Pressurization was required; the finicky equipment had been in need of constant maintenance and repair. Laser cannons that spanned half a kilometer of precious atmo-space were a ridiculous expenditure of resources when a handful of spare bolts could often achieve the same objective.

But perhaps most importantly, the need had never come. Not then, not when the next war was one of extermination, not politics or land or resources. The mass of humanity that was lucky enough to escape into the void cared little for fighting each other. The Heliosphere, at the time, had seemed big enough for everyone. Besides, the struggle for survival had been total. Nobody had had the energy, the resources, the will, for war.

Laser technology was largely relegated to more mundane applications: mining, micrometeor defense for habitats. Miniaturized and fitted onto wasps.

Then, heavy ablative rock-crust was developed for mining rigs. The xenocyte wrapper was discovered in the tholin fields of Saturn's moons. And with the end of the Euphemism, the ratification of the Tenancy Accords, the only standing military left was Mars.

And their enemies tended to skip the concept of craft-mounted weaponry entirely.

Perhaps, if humanity ever had the misfortune of dealing with some alien race, they'd find themselves needing battleships again.

Until then, humanity fought with the craft themselves.

What good was weaponry when the entire environment was murderous?

On the holopit, the majority of the blue lights had broken off, headed back for the *Barachiel*. Yellow dominated the field of view.

———

"IT SEEMS like this is taking a really long time," Caleb said. The axilla, of all things, had been pointing out some of the salient data on the black screen.

Adair was taking notes, and Yip had gotten himself a second radio line set up, listening in on what was going on in the lower levels. Morray and Haas were in some kind of quiet argument about the exact nature of the supercomputing silic in the room beyond them and why the Dena didn't have her mental backbone on a quant. Something to do with quantum data being unsustainable and irreplaceable.

"Chemical propulsion can be a marvel, but it does have its limits," the axilla said, pulling Caleb's attention back. "And, of course, there's only so fast a wasp can go if you want it to complete a task at the end of its flight. Braking is just as critical."

"It would be quicker," Adair said, "if we were allowed to miniaturize fusion drives."

"Maybe you should take that up with the University of Titan, Doctor," Yip drawled. "You know how all that works, right?"

"Quiet," Cambel ordered, and gestured at one of the clumps of light. "Deceleration. The swarm's setting up for its run."

———

<SWARM RECONFIGURED,> Erg confirmed. <Ninety percent of tug assets voidside. Myrmids being recalled from full assault. Setting up for a run on the engine bells.>

"Confirmed, Hive," Stag said. They'd scrape the thing free. Like popping a tick off a dog's soft underbelly. Hardly the first time the *Barachiel* had performed this maneuver. "Aeneas Orbital, what's going on over at the Sanctum? Are the lower levels depressurized? Do we need to be worried when we snap this thing off?"

<Any active fighting has moved to the upper levels of the underbelly. Air locks sealed in between decks.>

"Any wrapper merging reported?"

<Negative, *Barachiel*. Sanctum wrapper not affected.>

"That means the lower levels were abandoned, sir," the intel station offered.

"Agreed," Stag grunted. Probably with everyone on them too. Pragmatism was the rule of the day in the void, but no Arran-run craft would have allowed civilians to be vented to space like that. Even with hull penetrations like that, wrapper merging could offer some evacuation time. Fucking Dena. Had to have ordered the wrapper pulled back from the affected section when the impact became unavoidable. "Less to worry about, at least. Hive?"

<Setting up attack run now.>

"Sensor, magnify in the pit."

The myrmids out in the void sent out a hail of solid-round fire into the engine bells of the modified 'roid. It was exceptionally difficult, not destroying these things. Voiders tended to just slap scat onto the surface, or just under it, with little thought for protection. An unpredicted explosion in even one of the external chemical tanks could throw the thing so violently off course that planetary reentry became inevitable. There was a precise order to how and where one could be hit.

Erg, however, was good at what he did.

Ten seconds after the myrmids swept the length of the arrogate, the engine bells were ruins. Tugs were already clamped on, stabilizing the thing.

"Colonel Cambel, are you seeing this?" Stag asked, switching his radio channel.

<Confirmed. Looks like a clean strafing run. Good job, men.>

"Not done yet," Stag said loudly. "Erg?"

<Engaging tug wasps now.>

Without prompting, Sensors changed the holopit display, widening the field to the outer envelope of Venus's deadly atmosphere. Scale drastically changed; the Sanctum appeared as a marble-sized icon off the *Barachiel's* hull, planetside. The swarm indicators remained large enough to be viewed.

The oversized chem-props on the intercept wasps flared to life. Yellow vector lines on the holopit, threads of blue void-fire outside Ops's window.

<I have positive control of the 'roid,> Erg reported. His voice was strained. <Beginning orbital maneuvers now.>

Ops fell silent as the wasps did their work.

Nudging the modified asteroid away from the Sanctum, gentle as tugboats in the Bay of Chryse.

Pushing it down, down, down.

Disengaging at a precisely timed moment.

Venus's gravity caught the rock a few minutes later.

<All tugs away,> Erg said.

"Low orbit achieved," Navigation announced.

"Aeneas Orbital, can you confirm?"

<Correct parking orbit confirmed. Thank you for your help, *Barachiel*. Launching recovery craft now.>

<Good job, gentlemen,> Cambel said. <Now get somebody at Aeneas to pass us the location of the fucking *Undine Glory*. We're headed to the port. Over and out here.>

"Acknowledged." Stag switched the vox off, letting himself sag back against the holopit railing for a moment, the rest of Ops running system checks and post-op checklists. The chatter from Aeneas was still scrolling across the monitors. The lights of the swarm were slowly streaming back to the *Barachiel*. Suddenly very tired, Stag checked their relative orbital speed.

The wasps would be fueled for more distance than they'd flown on this, though. And any they didn't recover, which always seemed to happen, they could pick up on their next orbit.

"Should have roched it," the lieutenant at Propulsion grumbled.

"Stow that scat," Stag snapped, still watching orbital path calculations unspool in the holopit. "We could have local ASDF forces still in that thing. Wouldn't want to kill our own guys."

That little fact notwithstanding, however, he agreed. God only knew what the Dena was going to do with the thing. Smash it apart for any useful minerals. Cull the population of any real troublemakers, fit the rest with control harnesses and put them to work. Probably with the same mining rig. Would have been more merciful to disintegrate the entire thing in orbit.

The Dena had a sick sense of entitlement.

Nobody in the void service liked being stationed there at Aeneas.

What had the colonel asked for? The location of the *Undine Glory*? Wasn't that what they'd gone over there to figure out? Stag silently chastised himself for not getting clarification.

But then, if that was the only thing he'd fucked up over the past half hour, it was still a win.

Taking one last look at the returning swarm, the tumbling asteroid, Stag pushed off the railing and went back to his station. Picked up the handset. Time to deal with the next task.

CHAPTER
TWENTY-FOUR

THE REMAINS of the *Undine Glory* were larger than Caleb had expected it to be.

"The habitable section of the craft was small, barely sixty meters in diameter," Adair told him on the rockjump, as they burned towards it. "A bottle habitat, the kind that maintains gravity through centrifugal force."

"It's huge, though," Caleb said, looking at it through the bubble canopy of the cockpit. The habitat section looked like a bead strung halfway down a thick, long bundle of cords. "That's got to be miles long."

"The entire craft was almost fifteen kilometers from end to end." Adair sounded distracted. "God, that's a pretty sight."

Caleb didn't agree.

Despite the sound of sporadic gunfire, they'd made it back to the port just fine. The train was apparently shut down for security purposes, until the fighting was entirely extinguished, but the Dena had offered them a ground car. Like everything else in that place, it had been almost comedically ornamental. Gaudy was too polite a word for the place.

They'd reached the *Barachiel* a half hour later. Stopped just long enough to pick up Padre and a couple of Marines and drop off the lieutenants.

Then they were back out in the void.

177

Hurtling towards a spacecraft that made little visual sense.

"Energetic stabilization array," Morray added, as Caleb moved back to his seat. The comm officer was along to see what could be raised from the neural tissue. "Moving the amount of water required was an incredibly taxing event for the Flet. As we saw on Earth recently, even the smallest misalignment in space-time between the dive core's physical location and the objective can result in a misalignment of matter during transference. The craft was positioned as close to the center of the Heliosphere as possible, both to provide him a temporal baseline and an energy sink in case something slipped out of its place in the gradient flow. He was able to keep things mostly in place, but there were a few accidents."

"You said it destroyed a city on Earth, right? When something like that happened?"

"And that was a relatively small rock. This was billions of tons of water that he had to locate and yank out of the outer solar system."

"Ceres has water, doesn't it? Other moons and bodies?"

"By the time this occurred, almost all major water-bearing bodies were claimed," Adair said. "Reaching further out was the only option."

"The official story is that he used the solar wind to help him locate water out in trans-Nep space. Followed it out and pulled it back where and when he could," Morray said, "but nobody's really sure how he did it. Since then, he's needed hard, physical material as a reference point for movement. But even with the insane amount of wetware processing power backing up his consciousness, the effort was almost too much for him. It's amazing he lived through it. Every single one of those tendrils was strung through with cultured neural tissue. Let him vent any energy discharges directly out into the sun's corona."

"The hull looked burned."

"Apparently the crew had a couple of close calls in the two years they were out."

"Two years? On that thing? Shit."

"Worth it, though. We remember them, on Vastitas Day."

"But nobody remembers who the Flet is?"

Morray shook his head.

"Why not just ask him?"

"He's not what he was," Adair said. "That's what you say, when pressed for it. And he doesn't say anything."

Caleb made a mental note of that. He had no idea why this was a secret, but he was determined to keep his mouth shut until he figured it out. It wasn't as if Tom Donner had been an important figure of any kind. Just a rank-and-file flight officer, until he'd gotten caught moonlighting with that Arium grant a few years back.

Centuries ago.

"What do you think we're going to find over here, sir?"

"I have no idea." He turned to Adair. "Is that map of yours going to work?"

The historian looked sheepish. "I downloaded it from the National Science Academy database. It's the projection they distribute for classroom instruction."

"So it's kid scat?" Yip asked.

"It should be accurate. It's a compilation of everything we know about the *Undine Glory*."

"Kid scat," Yip repeated. "Lovely."

Everyone fell silent after that. The only sound in the hold was Padre, clicking rosary beads together. What he was praying for, Caleb had no idea. He settled back in his harness and tried to relax.

The deployment, when it came, was similar to the one over Eris. Hold depressurized, back doors opened. There was no place to set the rockjump down here, so the pilot said he would settle into a holding orbit around the station. The rest of them fired suit thrusters towards the ruin of the station.

<The outer layers of the craft are open to the void,> Yip said. <Orbital was able to tell us that much.>

<And then?> Padre asked.

<And then, they were vague. Said the Dena comes over here every once in a while, fuck knows why.>

The small team touched down, immediately inside what remained of the air lock. Nobody took their helmets off; there was no breathable air here.

One of those metal signs was bolted to the bulkhead. The glyphs. Scratched deep and stained with something dark.

Caleb tapped it. <Is this supposed to be here?> he asked over the team radio channel.

Adair flicked on his wrist projector. A small image popped up, cast from the optical emitters in his ENEX's fingertips. <No,> he said after a moment.

<Tok activity out here too, then,> Yip said, and flicked the charge switch on his boarding-action shotgun. <Be ready.>

Morray shook his head. <There's no reason for them to be out here, though.>

<Considering what's going on over at the Sanctum, sir, I vote for not taking chances.>

<Agreed. Let's be careful, gentlemen,> Padre said, and unslung his own shotgun from his shoulder. His was a lower charge than what the rest of them had been issued, he'd explained to Caleb. It could temporarily paralyze somebody, overload their nervous system, but it wouldn't kill them. Odd to see a chaplain armed at all. *We have to be practical out here*, he'd said.

<Where are we going, Adair?>

The historian pointed. <That way.>

———

ANY GRAVITY the *Undine Glory* had once possessed was long gone, the spin of its habitat area no longer enabled by power or mechanics. The place had been decommissioned though, not abandoned, and large sections of the bottle habitat had obviously been intentionally dismantled. Anything usable had clearly been stripped out. Even some of the internal bulkheads were gone. Some of the space was still segmented into rooms, hallways, but much of it was just open space.

More signs, Caleb noticed. More signs, everywhere.

The team split up. Caleb, following those signs. Everyone else, sticking with Yip and the map Adair had.

<What are you expecting to find?>

<Not sure.>

<Caleb, I can't begin to understand what you're going through. I know we're all strangers to you. But we're your people.>

Caleb wondered if the chaplain had planned this conversation, and he didn't care. It wasn't something he wanted to deal with. Not after the mindfuck that had been the Dena's little clockwork kingdom. <I'm guessing we should head to the hub.>

<You're going to have to trust us sooner or later,> the chaplain said.

<It's not about any of you,> Caleb said. <It's not about trust.>

<Then what?>

The chaplain had definitely planned this, Caleb thought, somewhat irritated by that realization. <There are a number of things that I would have expected to be common knowledge, easy shit for me to have passed along. Except I haven't. Why not?>

Padre nodded. <You want to know why you've been keeping secrets from us?>

<There's obviously a reason for those omissions.> Or, Caleb thought to himself, they've been removed from the record. He didn't know if something like that was legal or even possible, but then, there was always somebody who didn't care. For whatever reason.

They reached the entrance for the hub in silence and pushed up it. The trip was quiet, Caleb alone with the sound of his own breathing echoing in his ears.

The hatch that greeted them at the end of the passage had clearly been tampered with. The metal handle was twisted, the door dented. Caleb wished he could have brought Tyr. He always felt better when his dog was with him. But Yip hadn't cleared the dog for a full mig deployment yet.

Touching it, the chaplain pulled back as if burned.

<Do you know how a man qualifies to serve in my position out here in the deep void?> he asked, shaking his hand.

<No.>

<Heightened sensitivity to the penumbra. You'll get a different answer from everyone about what it is, of course, but we all feel it. There's something wrong here, something that doesn't belong.>

<Can I shoot it?>

<Usually not.> But the chaplain pushed open the hatch door anyway.

And the bottle habitat was gone.

Bea was sitting cross-legged on the cargo bay floor, an aluminum tumbler of water in her hands. Small as she was, it looked huge.

Beyond her, framed by the arch of the plane's back opening, dusty mountains rose on the edge of a wide plain. Dark and stubborn. Thunderheads building over them. Outside, the day was roaring hot.

=Stop pacing and wait,= Bea signed at him. =Eliza will be back when she's back.=

These slips were getting easier to handle. Caleb took it in stride. "Where are we?"

=Tucson.=

That explained the emptiness.

Tucson, like most human inhabitation in the American Southwest, was broken.

Most of the city had been dismantled. Wall by wall, brick by brick. Only a few false mountains, rising from the desert valley's floor, gave testament to that. Torn down, but not moved; there was no place to take it. The ruins of hundreds of thousands of buildings remained.

Caleb couldn't see how that was really any better than just leaving the buildings in place. But nothing could live in them now but pack rats and scorpions, and he supposed that's what they'd really been going for.

What remained—if he recalled correctly—was the base, and a small community of civilians. Too stubborn or too stupid to leave.

=Why?=

=She wanted to check in with her unit.=

That, at least, Caleb was familiar with. He'd been through that place more than once. Before. A sprawling place, filled with the flags of a dozen different nations, a hundred different units. Most of all that had been breaking down; Europe especially had fragmented into smaller states a decade or more ago. In other parts of the world, the concept of the nation-state had proved fragile. Like so much else of the old world order, it hadn't survived the relentless extermination campaigns being run by organizations like Ariums.

Many nations, reduced to something more akin to ethnic or tribal groups, were pouring what resources they could into escape planning. Void habitat construction was a multitrillion-dollar business, the space lift practically the last major industry left on Earth. Other regions already established, like Jupiter or the asteroid colonies of the Inner Belt, were rushing to house the waves of refugees.

And Mars, Caleb supposed. There had been rumors about Mars for as long as he could remember. Rumors that obviously had quite a bit of truth to them. The *Barachiel* couldn't have existed otherwise.

But in this time, this world, for every human who left the surface, it seemed that whitecoats became just that more desperate to keep them there. Spread out across the vastness of the system, the galaxy, humanity would multiply and threaten any nascent life, any alien cultures, they said. To them, it seemed that humanity was a plague to be wiped out, before it caused any more damage. Anything, anything was justified to stop it. Humanity couldn't be allowed to exist, not as they were. Not without deep change.

So remnants of the old militaries stayed. To guard the retreat. To stop what they could.

That, too, must have had some success.

=You doing okay?= Bea asked, coming over to sit next to him. =You can talk to me about it.=

He sighed. "You're fourteen."

=Not really.=

Maybe that was true. None of them were what they were supposed to be. "I'm… slipping around," he said. The truth, but not all of it. "Like time moves on without me."

=That sounds like what Dad experiences,= Bea said.

"Could be," Caleb said, and wondered how that might work.

=We need to get him back.= She hunched over her water. Even in the shade, they were both sweating. =I have to get him back.=

"What's so important about that?"

=We had a flight plan. One Dad told me was very important, the most important thing he's ever done or ever will. We're supposed to be in Singapore,= and it took her a little longer to spell that out, like she wasn't quite sure of the word, =by next Monday. Five days left.=

"And a whole planet to search," Caleb mused. "Did he tell you why, why Singapore?"

=No. but he told me it was important. Told me to do anything to get him there by next Monday.= She looked out over the desert, expression serious. =Eliza better get back soon. We're losing time.=

Caleb felt himself pitch forward. It was only the chaplain grabbing his backpack that prevented him from tumbling headfirst into the void.

Beyond the door was open space.

<Fuck,> he muttered.

<Did you just see something?> Padre asked.

<I don't know what you're talking about.>

<Because I did.> And the chaplain leaned heavily back against the nearest bulkhead, grabbing on for a better hold. Through the private radio channel, Caleb could hear him breathing hard, deep.

<What difference would it make if I had?>

The chaplain was unreadable behind his ENEX's goggles. <The Golanites mentioned currents leading back to the Flet. If you were looking for him in the past…>

<You saw that?>

<You were talking to the Naven, weren't you?>

Caleb felt cold. He didn't know what was more disturbing, that the priest had been pulled wherever he was pulled, or that the priest knew who that was. <That's not how I knew her.>

<Who was she?>

Eliza Rallison's foster sister, he almost said, but that connection seemed not to be known either. He hesitated.

Over the radio, he could hear Kannik's sigh.

<You are going to have to trust us,> the priest told him, <if you're going to lead us.>

<Padre, no offense, but I didn't ask for this job.>

<Actually, Caleb, you volunteered for it,> Padre told him, and then fell silent. Completely silent; he'd shut the private channel.

The rest of the team caught up with them in short order.

<The Flet's section is supposed to be here,> Adair said, pointing to the now closed door.

<There's nothing there,> Caleb said. <Just empty space.> He noticed a glyph, cut into the metal. He traced it with his fingertips. It looked familiar, this one. <There's nothing here.>

<So where the hell is it?>

CHAPTER
TWENTY-FIVE

THE *VASTITAS REACH* cut a meandering path, working its way up north from the southern Pacific through a dozen island chains, each stranger than the one before. Samoa, Marshall, Micronesia, Palau. Sometimes, they'd stop at an atoll—more of those islands built from lava and bones—for a few days. Sometimes, they'd be out at sea for a sevenday or more. The ship had to detour more than once to avoid bad weather, or sailed through it. On those days, Tharsis would strap into her bunk with Bea and pray.

The little girl wasn't going to die, though.

That was a certainty Tharsis clung to.

Bea wasn't going to die.

Not until Tharsis met her for the first time, centuries from now.

The dreams still came. The Flet. The yacht. The harbor. But she couldn't find the place. Some of the islands they stopped at looked similar. But nothing was right.

She was no closer to finding the Flet than when she started.

———

"NEXT STOP," Wyatt told her excitedly one morning, almost four months into the cruise, "is Kyushu."

Tharsis had long since stopped trying to dodge the linguist. The *Vastitas Reach* wasn't large enough to hide from him. And Chris had asked if she maybe couldn't drop in from time to time, get some intelligence on what he was working on.

Since Australia, the data center tech had been much friendlier with her. Secrets once uttered, she supposed, brought people together. They rarely talked about Mars; she avoided any mention of the void at all. Chris was too old now to make the trip himself, something he openly acknowledged, but he had family, nieces and nephews with children of their own, whom he desperately wished to save. His work would secure them berths out. Or at least, that was his hope.

What his exact role was, how connected he was and to whom, she wasn't sure. The sense Tharsis had gotten from the meeting in Australia was that pioneer groups were as isolated as Tok cells, and for the same reasons. Harder to track. Impossible to use one to find another. Even in this age of constant oversight, there were still ways to hide. But whatever Chris knew or didn't, Tharsis could see the logic in having the chief data engineer on the *Vastitas Reach* engaged in information collection.

He had access to everyone's files. Everyone's research.

Except Wyatt's.

So despite her misgivings about the man, Tharsis let him eat breakfast with her. Almost daily now.

"What's significant about Kyushu?" she asked, sipping her coffee.

"Other than the fact I'm still trying to get my request for research space approved? One of the big annual Arium conferences is held there. Top secret location, of course," he said, and winked.

She rolled her eyes. "Of course."

"I'm kidding." And she hated this about him. All this earnest humor. Like he wasn't receiving grant funding from an organization that was trying to wipe out the species. "It's a fun event. A lot of us are signed up for it." He took a bite of one of the synthetic meat patties he seemed to favor. "You want to come with me?"

His myling, that creepy little myling, tried to touch Bea. Tharsis swatted it away.

"What?"

"Fly."

She had no interest in attending any Arium event. Ever. She'd had enough of the whitecoats on board without putting up with hundreds of them, in one place, for days on end. But when she mentioned it to Chris, his eyes lit up.

Nothing would change, but maybe it mattered that she went.

"I'm in," she told Wyatt the next morning. "What do I need to do?"

———

OVER THE PAST FEW MONTHS, Tharsis had heard much from various people about the scale of environmental degradation in the Pacific. Either it was looming, or upon them already; one of the Arium-funded marine biologists onboard was in a near constant state of panic about it. Nothing could stop the damage now, they claimed. Not fuel restrictions nor travel bans. Not capping agricultural yields nor international treaties throttling fishing. Not reproductive limitations.

Too late, they all said, much too late.

The Arran wasn't sure. She had no frame of reference for what Earth's waters should have looked like, but from what she could tell, they seemed healthy.

What had bothered her was the grinding poverty so many people seemed trapped in. Amid the riches of the tropics, people starved. Villages lay abandoned. Entire islands emptied. Humanity was being squeezed out.

It didn't seem justified. The ocean she'd seen so far was vast, almost beyond comprehension, and even then, it was only a part of a much larger whole. Surely, there had been a place for them to stay on their birth world.

It wasn't until they reached the Ariums's island that she witnessed anything like the disaster so many of the whitecoats bemoaned.

"Once," Wyatt told her up on deck, as they drank coffee and watched Yakushima's port come into view, "cedar forests covered the entire island. Ancient forests, trees hundreds of years old. It was beautiful."

It was November now, and the *Vastitas Reach* was the furthest north it had been yet. There was a chill in the air.

"What happened?" Tharsis asked. The granite mountainsides they were passing were bare to the elements, scrubby with young foliage poking out of the bare rock.

"Strip mining," he told her.

"The Battle for Tanegashima during the last war didn't help either," Annaka said, a little way down the rail. Like Wyatt, though, her expression was pinched. Flat. Angry. "A goddamn year, the Chinese and Americans spent fighting over that spaceport. It's amazing anything in this region is still standing."

"The Chinese were at this place long before that," Wyatt shot back.

Annaka nodded at the mountain; a long, deep valley was just coming into view. Under the low clouds, a deep green clung to it. "They didn't get everything," she said. "And the Ariums are replanting, aren't they?"

"You've seen the East China Sea, haven't you?" he retorted. When she didn't answer, he turned his attention back to Tharsis. "The Ariums bought the island from the Japanese government a decade or so ago, after the war ended."

"Yes, when the Japanese were starving," Annaka replied, and pushed away from the rail, coming over. "You can pretend your consortium has the moral high ground in all things, but the truth is, they're as opportunistic as anyone."

"Don't you want to see things like this fixed?" he asked, almost plaintive.

Annaka didn't answer. Just shook her head and walked back inside.

"I don't understand the reluctance," Wyatt said to Tharsis then, like he was confiding in her. Like he could; like she understood.

It made her angry.

"I need to go find my boss," she told him.

Chris had offered to watch Bea for the day. Tharsis was grateful for the offer. She had no desire to drag her little, red-eyed baby into whatever awaited them on the shore.

ACCORDING TO WYATT, most of the original structures on the island had either been destroyed in the previous decade's war or torn down by the Ariums in their enthusiasm to put things to right. The town that remained reminded Tharsis of the tourist books from the Venus Sanctum of Cedar Honor. Her father had brought one home after his stint on that mining craft; he had raved about the beauty of the place.

She wondered if this island was the place that had inspired that habitat.

The town was small, its buildings scaled oddly. Angular structures of raw block and bare wood stood along narrow streets; curved roofs capped the buildings off. There were no personal vehicles anywhere, but many bicycles. Dyed linen fluttered in open windows.

Nothing was in want, Tharsis noticed as she walked through the town. The taps poured clean water. The restaurants in town boasted real meat and fresh wheat bread. The little bars were stocked to the gills with a dizzying array of liquors. And everywhere, there was a sense of abundance.

It was almost obscene how different it was from most of the other places she'd visited so far.

But as they made their way through the town, out into the open country of the island, everything changed.

A grand old hotel stood apart on the rise of the hill, clearly distinct from the rougher construction. That, apparently, was where the conference was.

It should have been beautiful.

It was crawling with umbran.

THE MAIN EVENT, Wyatt told her, was that evening.

That wasn't quite how anyone phrased it. Keynote speaker, main presentation. Those phrases came up a lot. But the atmosphere that morning was one of a group anticipating some kind of circus.

Tharsis would have gladly been just about anywhere else in the Heliosphere.

Instead, she spent the day wandering. Observing, taking notes, collecting business card, flyers, presentation hand-outs. Trying to pick up on something, anything, that might help Chris.

In another situation, she might have been able to enjoy herself. The conference was lavish to the extreme. The food was luscious, almost all of it naturally grown, beautifully prepared, and so generously portioned out. Fresh water flowed, liquor was poured, everyone enjoying, laughing, the sounds of a dozen languages and dozens more accents mingling into a mélange of sound that would have been unthinkable anywhere else but Earth.

Only here, in these times, could people be like this together.

Since this moment, things had diverged. Humanity had diverged. As black as their purposes were, here was a unity, a comradeship, that was physically impossible in her own time.

Tharsis couldn't relax, though. These weren't just people, and this hotel wasn't just some beautiful place. They were whitecoats. This was an Ariums conference.

She got a glimpse of the team that would be presenting. They had a crowd of umbran following them. Too far removed from a human form to be proper mylings, Tharsis still found them unnerving. None was larger than a foot tall. One-eyed. Pale. Three-fingered hands, swollen to distressing proportions, clung to small glass spheres or glowing camp lanterns.

What that symbolized to them, Tharsis had no idea. But there were dozens of the little shades, and that meaning, at least, was obvious.

Whatever else the presentation team was attempting, they had wetware they were keeping alive. Somewhere. Dozens of individual little systems.

The event featured a sit-down meal, one that might have been pleasant under different circumstances. The group from the *Vastitas Reach* had a whole table to themselves. Despite herself, Tharsis had never really been able to hate any of them. Most of them were friendly enough. Nice. Even Wyatt, with his puppy-dog eagerness, was like that.

But then, she'd thought tDaer was a friend.

Tharsis wasn't especially hungry. And any appetite she might have had vanished when the main course was brought around. Round, perfectly uniform tenderloins. Liveried waitstaff. Silver trays. Like it was worth something, the synthetic flesh on offer.

Her obvious refusal to touch the vat-grown scat made the rest of the table uncomfortable. *Fuck them*, she thought savagely, and picked at her salad. The vegetables tasted as if they'd been grown in real soil.

The whitecoats argued. Friendly arguments, friendlier than on the boat. Academic discussions.

Tharsis thought about the static field on Iapetus. The Scient. That jovial, smug manner of his.

"You know," one of them said, still eating, "this is tasty, but I do wonder about these sorts of projects."

"I agree." Wyatt nodded, hair flopping. "This is a fun distraction, but it's not the way we're going to fix anything. The way to solve the question is not through genetic reductionism, but mental perfection. Humanity possesses what it needs to overcome these failings of ours, but it needs the proper guidance to do so."

"Your language, no doubt," one of the others said.

Wyatt nodded over a mouthful of food, swallowing before he could answer. "Well, yeah, I think we all think we've found the solution, right?" he said.

"Don't be modest," another said. "That collaboration we're working on shows some really interesting possibilities."

"Oh, what's that?"

"Ilucoccine can be guided, it seems, by that language Wyatt's developing. We can tell somebody what they're going to see. If a hallucination can be guided, shaped, utilized for such great ends, can one truly say it's all merely chemical? Ayahuasca ceremonies, or other such rituals from animistic religions hold that—"

"A drug-induced stupor is just that," Tharsis interjected. "It's not a gateway to anything but the inside of your own mind."

"And yet, the human mind is so much greater than we give it credit for. Do you know that, even now, we're discovering individuals who can reshape reality with thought alone? Who can warp it as they please? Imagine what we could do if we could guide that process? Perfectly?"

"We don't have that power," she said.

"That's a very Catholic kind of answer, isn't it? But doesn't even theoretical physics allow for the power of perception to be able to—"

"The structure of the universe isn't subject to human whims," Tharsis objected.

Wyatt smiled. "We can shape clay, move water, manipulate metal.

What is that, but humanity reshaping the universe for our own designs?"

"All I'm saying," the first whitecoat said, jumping back in, "is if the idea behind this project is to ensure the absolute optimal protein for human consumption, there's no real reason for it. Beans exist. We don't need synthetic flesh."

"Yeah, but like you said, it's tasty. It's also easier to grow off world than—"

But before he could finish his sentence, a bell rang out in the ballroom.

Somebody at the head table, set up on the main hall's low-slung stage, got a microphone and began speaking. The lights came down. Projected images materialized in a pair of holopit's smoke fields. A lecture, she realized. A talk, much like she remembered from her biology classes at the Academy.

Instead of somebody outlining the mistakes of the Euphemism, however, the speaker was extolling them.

Much of it was very technical, and she couldn't quite catch all the terms. The umbran were on the temporary stage too, staring out into the audience in the most unnerving fashion.

The presentation went on.

One sentence caught her attention.

"Now, one of the intentions behind this project was to ensure the absolute optimal proteins for human consumption."

Then Tharsis realized where the umbran had come from.

Approximations of human life. Life that couldn't live. Life that wasn't allowed to be.

They had created an approximation of human flesh. Synthetic, of course, patterned in a lab from bare base pairs, no doubt with the help of a quant or something of the sort. But patterned from real tissue samples, real human tissue.

That was what was on their plates.

Not even the most debased of the Jovian moons went that far with their nutrient manufacturing.

Tharsis grudgingly sat through the rest of the presentation, picking at her salad. Grateful that she'd left Bea with Chris for the day. The little umbran were moving between the tables, pausing every now and then to look at somebody. Maybe somebody sensitive. Maybe somebody they'd taken a dislike to. Tharsis wasn't sure. Seeing them wasn't the same as understanding.

One stopped near her, eyes like those of some deep-sea fish cast up at her. A few years ago, it would have likely had her gibbering in terror.

"I'm sorry," she whispered to it, and wished she'd brought a few of Bea's books along.

"Amanda, who are you talking to?" Wyatt asked.

She turned her attention back to the table, spearing a small greenhouse tomato off her half-eaten salad plate. "That list of places that need an exorcism is growing."

———

LATER, when she was finally able to extricate herself, Tharsis headed down the hall towards the toilets.

Entering, she heard somebody throwing up.

An older woman, it turned out, with darker skin that marked an ethnicity Tharsis was unfamiliar with. The void had long erased the old Earth distinctions; she still hadn't picked up the knack of identifying them. Her eyes were haunted.

"Do you see them?" she asked in a whisper, voice shaking.

There were five of them. One had a distended hand wrapped in the woman's skirt. The rest were pressed incredibly close.

Tharsis sighed. "Tell them a story or something. Apologize, maybe. They can't really hurt you like this."

"What are they?"

"Dinner," Tharsis said.

The umbran wrapped up in the woman's skirt touched her leg. She screamed as if she'd been burned.

Tharsis left her to them.

Any sympathy she might have had vanished with those platters.

One of them was waiting outside for her.

You can't change anything, Tharsis reminded herself.

But maybe what she did mattered.

"Where are you?" she asked it. Those eyes just kept staring at her. "Show me."

———

THE LITTLE THING led her to a pair of huge, refrigerated shipping containers down by the docks, off to themselves in the vast expanse of old concrete. It was dark by this point, almost midnight, and there was a chill in the air that made the entire thing worse, somehow. She walked towards them, drawn in by the light within. The penumbra was glowing here; there was something alive behind the metal and insulation of the walls.

There was no lock on either set.

Hand trembling, the crowd of umbran growing, Tharsis pushed one of the container doors open.

Inside was an abattoir.

A white-walled, spotless, bloodless abattoir.

The slaughterhouse feel of the place had nothing to do with appearance. It was quite neat inside, like any of the labs back aboard the *Vastitas*. Neat rows of tanks held chunks of synthetic meat, cradled in the bioeletrical harnesses and nutrient tubing. Fat smeared the red tissue's surfaces. A few were empty, or else held musculature not yet mature enough to fill out the initial webbing. Much like the technology from her own time, it appeared that seed cells were being injected into an initial ligament and blood vessel matrix, then grown into fully developed muscle.

The back showed signs of processing. Industrial steel tables, wiped down now, a row of knives magnetically held against a rack of cutting boards. A prep sink with water and waste barrels underneath. Trays.

There shouldn't have been mylings here. It shouldn't have felt like death. But those lights were rising, the ones from the morgue at Singapore, from Ceres.

This meat was human somehow, or human enough.

She had always heard that neural tissue had to be involved to produce mylings. She saw no sign of it, though. *You're not a biologist,* she told herself, but thought about Father Golan's writings once again.

The second trailer was much like the first, except here, most of the tanks still contained just the growth matrices and instead of a kitchen, there was a small, compact data center. She wondered if it held the whole of their research.

The little ghosts of children-who-weren't were clustered around the doors as she came back out. She had thought them umbran, but they could have been myling. Human. She couldn't be sure. And even then, this still would have been necessary. There was nothing to save. There was nothing she could do.

"I'm sorry," she told them again.

The *Vastitas Reach* was at anchor only a fifteen-minute walk away. As she headed back through the November darkness, every step seemed heavier than the last. Guilt spiked. Was she really just going to leave that mundane horror to its own devices? For the whitecoats who'd built it? So they could pack it up and take it somewhere else?

Keep doing what they were doing?

"Dammit," she muttered, the gangplank of the research vessel in view.

This time of night, with the *Vastitas Reach* docked, everyone would either be asleep or out partying in town; she'd seen that pattern repeated over a dozen ports of call.

The back deck, with its submersibles and all the associated accoutrements, was deserted.

It took Tharsis almost no time to find what she needed and get back to the containers. Or maybe that was just her perception misaligning again. She didn't much care just then.

External hard drive. Sample jar.

Ten gallons of biodiesel.

Tharsis tried accessing the little data center in the second container; the password protection wasn't much of a problem, but she didn't have the skill to bypass the biometric reader. Instead, she settled for yanking a couple of the data cores.

Choking down her own disgust, she cut a tissue sample out of one of the vats, sealing it carefully in the jar.

She had no idea if Chris, or his superiors, were curious about such things as this. Seemed like the thing to do, though.

Then, she set the whole thing on fire.

Flames licked out of the metal shells as she took the now empty fuel cans and headed back to the ship. The mylings walked with her, for a way, until they faded away.

Gone.

Chris took both the sample jar and drives with a neutral expression when she stopped by his cabin. "Have fun?" he yawned.

"Why do they do this scat?" Tharsis asked him. "Why do any of it?"

He yawned again. "She woke up twice for a bottle. I think she missed you. Let me get her for you."

Maybe there were no answers, Tharsis thought, as she carried her sleeping baby back to their own bunk.

———

BREAKFAST WITH WYATT, the next morning, was beyond awkward.

"You okay?" he finally asked, after she'd almost finished, his own meal untouched.

"Why should I be?" she snapped.

For a moment, the linguist seemed lost. "We're all after the same thing," he said, clearly gathering himself back up. "Trying to solve the same problem. But I don't think this is the answer, this kind of extreme genetic manipulation. That's why our research is so important."

"Yeah. You're a real humanitarian," she said.

TWENTY-SIX

THE SECOND TRIP through the Sanctum was significantly more eventful than the first.

Void dominance may have been secured by the *Barachiel*, and the modified asteroid effectively neutralized, but a significant amount of its passenger load had managed to flood over into the Sanctum through the torn lower hull.

"I need access," Caleb said, depressing the talk button on the cockpit radio. "Immediately."

<That's a negative, *Barachiel*. Everything is locked up tighter than a nun's—>

"I need to talk to the Dena again," Caleb said, cutting off the controller at Aeneas Orbital. "Get her on the line or get me inside."

<The Dena's left strict orders to not disturb her for the duration of the riot.>

"Is that normal?"

<She's disconnected her radio features, sir. And all air locks are closed for security purposes.> There was a long, long pause. <Precaution, sir, against further intrusions.>

Caleb started to make a snide remark when Stag's voice cut in on the line. <What kind of intrusions?> the ops officer asked in a neutral voice. <We parked the arrogate. Thing's way outside suit thruster range now.>

<There were a few Toks who must have taken sleds over to the

hull. They're actually putting up quite the firefight down at the tertiary freight loading bay. Manually overrode the air lock down there.>

<That's a shame.>

<Hell of a thing. We've got security wasps headed down now. Should be buttoned up within the hour.>

<Keep us posted on what kind of support we can offer,> Stag said, and dropped off the line.

"Let me guess," Caleb said. "That was a hint?"

"As much help as they could offer over an open line like that," Yip replied.

"You give the orders around here, sir." The rockjump pilot changed vectors, the yellow-brown of Venus's poisoned cloud layers rotating back into view. "If you want to go, it'll take twenty minutes to get there," he said. "Tight, but we can manage."

They made the freight hangar just in time to see a pair of myrmid wasps dropping the last of the Tok intruders. Caleb and Yip and a couple of the Marines jumped out, the station's artificial gravity carrying them to the hangar floor as the rockjump peeled away, just barely making it out the air lock before it slammed shut again.

The damage to the bodies, as they passed, was immense.

<Everybody's been telling me about that disassociation thing with wrapper. How it works like a kind of armor,> Caleb said.

<It's true to an extent. But wrapper's affected by all kinds of things. Mass of the projectile, thickness of the xenocyte layer, a bunch of other stuff you need to be a biologist to understand.> Yip nudged one of the still forms. <DE pulse cannon, wasp-mounted. Overloads the mechanical components of a suit, blows the O2 tanks. Scatting unpleasant way to die.>

<Your guys told me we don't have laser weapons.>

<Not for craft-on-craft combat. But they are effective for antipersonnel actions. Come on. Let's find the atmo.>

When the Arrans had told him there was rioting ongoing, Caleb had expected something more intense. Instead, they wound their way up through several levels of manufacturing floors without encountering anything more than a few myrmids on patrol. The wasps scanned them, blinked green, and let them proceed unimpeded. Bodies were scattered about, some showing clear signs of battle damage, burns and hollow-point strikes. Others, Yip said, were depressurization fatalities.

<We're inside the habitat, aren't we?>

<The Sanctums were constructed in multiple layers, separated by air locks. Standard for the better void habitats,> Yip told him. <If one area suffers some kind of system failure, it's easier to isolate it.>

<She did it with her people still inside?>

<Looks like.> Yip sounded tense. <Abandoned the manufacturing complex and everyone inside.>

The air lock up into the main habitat lay up a long shaft, marked with the same long grooves that served as foot- or handholds for more efficient movement. Gravity tugged at them as they got closer.

Caleb fell the last three meters, impacting the ground hard.

<Fuck,> he groaned over the radio.

Yip was climbing down, rifle slung over his shoulders. <Sorry about that,> he said, in a tone that indicated no such thing. He made for a panel, recessed into the wall above the air lock doors. <It's the gravity paneling on the floor above us. Security should let us through.>

Mars-normal gravity, Caleb told himself. He lay on his back, staring up at the shaft they'd just descended. Had he just fallen *up*?

<Don't think about it too much,> Yip added. <You'll get void-sick.>

A few minutes later, they were buzzed in. Jumping down through an air lock, falling on the interior door, and then having to crawl up and around it when it finally opened made Caleb's stomach turn.

Fighting had spilled out into the uppermost level of the Sanctum, the main area with the parkland and the false Victorian town. They encountered surprisingly little of it, although Yip's Marines did have to clear a few of the streets as they went.

"The security wasps are doing their job," Yip observed. "The heaviest fighting's over by now."

"You call this a riot?" Yeti sniffed. "I've seen more energy from starving adlets."

"Yeah well, the protein overload tends to fuck with their brains," Ninden said.

The Marines' conversation was at odds with their movement. Tight, terse.

They made it back up to the hunting lodge without incident.

———

CALEB LEFT THE MARINES OUTSIDE, ignored both the chittering drones and clamoring automata, and headed straight for the Dena's chamber.

The brain wasn't in its tank.

Instead, the Dena was out on the lawn that lay between the estate and the forest. A small table had been set up under a brightly colored pavilion canopy, Oriental-style rugs strewn across the grass. An ancient-looking phonograph with a curved brass bell stood on a stand nearby. Venus's Landlord had exchanged the complicated dress for a khaki getup of belted jacket and jodhpurs. The clockwork body was sipping tea from exquisite porcelain.

It was like something out of his granddad's old movies about the British Raj.

Except instead of irritating music, the phonograph was playing what must have been the main command network. Grainy voices exchanged life-support status updates, wasp positions, insurgent movements.

"Ah, Caleb," the Dena said, and waved a hand at the empty chair. "So good of you to join me. Please, sit."

"How could I refuse such a civilized offer?" He pulled the chair out and sat down in it backwards. The serving automata made an unhappy noise but poured him a cup of tea regardless. Caleb squinted at it, as it was held out to him on a small silver tray. "What is this?"

"Earl Grey, our own local blend," the Dena said. "Most visitors to our inwell only see my Sanctums, but I assure you, our agriculture platforms are the finest in the Heliosphere."

"I don't really care," he said, and set the tea aside. "Where's the *Undine Glory's* cockpit?"

"Pardon?"

"We went over there. Searched the entire facility. But the section, the segment that contained the Flet, it wasn't there."

"I have no idea," the Dena said.

"I'm getting real sick of this shit," Caleb replied. "All of it. I don't appreciate being lied to."

"Caleb, I am not lying to you. The command section should be with the rest of the craft." But the Dena paused. "Unless..."

"Unless what?"

"We have seen some odd behavior with certain assets," she said. "Things moving out of their orbital paths, voids opening where voids should not be. One of my harvester platforms ended up on the other side of the planet from where it was supposed to be, torn apart. We had an incident, about a sevenday ago now, where one of the intraorbital supply transports turned out into deep space, thinking it was headed in the right direction."

"I don't understand."

"Surely you must remember those years on Earth. When things started falling apart. When nightmares began walking."

... rain, falling around him, a soft pitter-patter. On the leaves. On the smooth concrete walkway. Rain, dripping down through his hair, running off his nose.

He couldn't wipe it off. There was a weight on him, on his shoulder, in his arm. A body, carried between him and behind them, screaming, screaming that would never...

... Rallison was crouched next to him, binoculars held to her face. The jungle around them bore down on them, as if trying to listen to their heartbeats, their breath. Plotting a way to steal it.

"It's not much of an arium, I know," she was saying, "but we've got reason to believe what's being cooked up here is next-level nasty."

"Convenient you got my platoon," Caleb heard his own voice say.

"I requested you," Rallison replied. "Only person I..."

... a snowfield that stretched to the eternity of the void, cold starlight the only illumination and yet somehow glowing...

<No welcoming committee,> Rallison was saying, and her voice was...

... rain, falling here, falling forever, a curtain of water, an ocean cast up in the vertical, cutting off that which lay beyond from...

"It's only ever symbolic," an all-too-familiar voice said, the man against his shoulder, the weight in his arms. "Seeing the totality of it would wreck your mind."

Donner.

But before Caleb could ask, he was gone again.

Caleb grabbed the chair to steady himself. The Dena was staring at him, that mask cocked at an inhuman angle.

"What are you implying?" he asked, brusque, forcing himself to stay in the moment.

"It's happening again, Caleb. Somehow, somebody has found a way to resurrect some old horror. Which one, which one? There were so many." She tapped a false, glittering fingernail against the cup. It seemed a gentle movement, but the delicate porcelain cracked. "Perhaps they'll bring it all back. Wouldn't that be fascinating?"

He didn't want to think about the implications of that. "Doesn't answer where the command section's gotten off to."

"If the Flet's alive, and I have no reason to believe that he's not, then he may be attempting to retreat from this. Or he may have unconsciously snapped back to somewhere he was previously."

"What makes you think that?"

"Caleb, my darling, do you really believe any of us want to see things twisted away from what they are now? We all stand in opposition to those old goals. The Arcna was an abomination. It gladdens me to know she has been dead for this long. We have found our own answers. We don't need hers."

"Where's the Flet?"

"If he dove away, he could be anywhere."

———

THE LANDLORD WAS in a black mood when he stormed back into Ops, almost an hour later.

Adair heard the conversation from the commander's briefing room: loud, insistent, angry. The Landlord's English had improved significantly over the past sevenday, but he clearly still had an accent. One that was thicker now than it had been.

The conversation was getting strident now, though. The Landlord was leaning back on the holopit's railing, arms crossed, body language as coxed as it came. Colonel Cambel was impassive.

Stag was clearly pissed.

"This is a wild goose chase, pointless," he was saying. "Where else are we supposed to go?"

"Where was the *Undine Glory* deployed?" the Landlord replied. "Where was it built? If it's gone back to some other previous location…"

"Then it could be out in the middle of fucking interstellar space," Stag snapped. "How are we supposed to find it?"

"Where was it?" he asked again, emphasizing every syllable.

"Mercury," Adair supplied without really thinking about it. All eyes turned to him. Cambel was frowning. Well, scat. He pressed. "The basic components were manufactured mostly in the Earth inwell, but the sensitive material, the neural network, was grown on Mercury."

Cambel shook his head and paced back to the holopit. "Aeolis, where's Mercury right now?"

An orbital map came up, paths and locations of the inner planets highlighted in the smoky projection field. "Not that far. A complicated approach but not impossible with the fusion drive. We could probably reach it in a few days, honestly, if I execute a gravity slingshot. Just past aphelion, as you can see. Lower risk to the *Barachiel*, sir. Relatively speaking, if we make sure to stay in the shadow."

"We could dive again," the Landlord said.

"We will if we have to. I'd prefer to not have that thing touching my dive core again, and a dive that close to the sun is risky under the best of circumstances. That alright with you, sir?"

"As long as we get there, Colonel, I don't really care."

THE *VASTITAS REACH* MOVED ON.

Southeast from the broken nation of Japan, down through another series of atolls and reefs, meandering.

There was time without landfall. Time for reflection.

But whether it was the sameness of the ocean or something else, Tharsis barely noticed the passage of time. The longer she was on the *Vastitas*, the more it caught up with her.

Time slipped through her fingers. Or maybe, she slipped through it. Lost her sense of it. There were days when she could clearly recall waking up, eating breakfast, going down to the data center, but no sooner had she sat down than it seemed time to get dinner. But when she asked Chris if there was an issue, he'd just shrug and say she was doing good work.

It could have been the sea.

Every day was much like the one before it: the weather had little variation and much of the time, they were out at sea. The baby was her only true indication of change. Bea ate, slept, and changed at a prodigious rate. No different than any other baby, Tharsis supposed, but it was the first time she'd ever seen the process as an adult.

There was something fascinating about watching her grow.

Tharsis had never given much thought to her future. It had been set from the moment her brother lost his leg. As a child, growing up, at the Academy, she'd never given it much thought. Her service clock had started at Humphryes. Six years standard, three Arran. It seemed an endless period of time, plenty of space to figure out what came next.

But looking ahead had always been painful. What was she supposed to do? Go back to Mars, work her parents' ranch, help her sisters and brother raise their own children? Or go to District of Lunae and be one of those career females, working some contracting or government job? Or just stay in the military and make a life out of it, like the INSHOALCOM commander infamously had?

Marriage hadn't been something she'd ever considered a possibility, much less a family of her own. Children had never entered into the equation.

But now, she watched Bea roll around in her playpen, grabbing her toes with fat little hands, and wondered.

———

DESPITE THE WEATHER, it was winter in the northern hemisphere and with it, the holiday season. There was something called Thanksgiving that the North Americans on the crew insisted on celebrating. Some kind of harvest festival. One of the guys from the maintenance crew smoked half a dozen turkeys, which had apparently been socked away in the freezers for exactly this occasion. The galley churned out potatoes and beans and savory bread puddings and pumpkin pie, all of which had likewise been saved for the holiday.

Tharsis hated the way most food tasted these days. She wasn't sure if it was her, or another something wrong with her body. Everything was engineered to fuck now, staples like wheat, rice, corn, tightly controlled. But that pie had been made with what tasted like good Sabaean winter wheat, with home-canned pumpkin. Tharsis shamelessly ate three slices.

Although none of the heavy traditional dishes fit the climate, it came with a full day off, anchored near a nameless atoll with an untouched reef. It was a day of drinking and eating and swimming beneath a flawless sky. As night fell, crew gathered back on the decks. The North Americans told stories about their families, their holidays, from earlier times. Everything had a wistful quality to it, as if describing a world already lost.

Christmas came a short month later. Tharsis was disappointed there was no mass said for it; even the most rudimentary of Arran outposts or ships would have marked the day thusly. Instead, there was more eating, more drinking, more swimming.

Bea received a prodigious number of presents from the crew, or at least, it seemed like it. She was still too young to properly understand what was going on and had a full-blown meltdown halfway through the day, eventually sobbing herself to sleep in Tharsis's arms.

Tharsis received one gift.

From Chris.

"It's an older tablet. Bought it at the last port and refurbished it for you," he said as he gave it to her, "and you can't connect out to the Gig, but that doesn't strike me as something you care about."

"What's it for?"

"I loaded a sign language program. American. For both of you."

There was a whole language with hand gestures, Tharsis learned that night, when she had a chance to go through it properly. Something she could teach to Bea, something the little girl could talk with. She'd been trying so hard to coo, to babble, to communicate.

The sign language program would help her learn how to do that.

It was a humbling gift. Chris's thoughfulness. The responsibility that came with it.

———

THE DREAMS GOT VIVID.

No longer just impressions.

A few sevendays after Christmas, when Bea had finally started sleeping longer stretches, the night before they were due into the Hawaiian Islands, Tharsis closed her eyes, only to find herself walking up that dock again.

Walking.

No.

Standing. On the yacht's deck. Sun setting in front of her.

"Good to see you again," the Flet said.

"Where are you?" she asked.

The deck fled.

In its place, a beach stretched out around her, tight and circular in a punch bowl of dark lava rock. It was just beginning to rain. There was a dog, howling.

She was on the deck, a pause in the snow revealing the inky black sky above.

Tharsis closed her eyes, willing the slips to stop.

The sound of the crashing surf was closer. She wondered if it was a storm, if the *Vastitas Reach* was sailing into rough seas again. She desperately tried to wake herself up.

The Flet, Tom, standing against the sunset, just smiled at her. Apologetic.

"I can't control it," he said. "That's the entire problem."

"So what the hell am I supposed to do about it?" she snapped back. "Tell me where you are, and I'll get there."

Ignoring the question, he nodded across the dark waters of the bay. "Do you hear it?" he asked. "The screaming?"

The next thing that made any sense was breakfast.

Bea, whining for her bottle.

Hash browns, growing cold on the table in front of her.

She was in the galley. And she had no idea how she'd gotten there.

Tharsis held on to the baby and clamped a hand over her heart. Anxiety was beating at her ribs. Anxiety, and fear, and not a little anger.

Unlike a Jovian, Tharsis hadn't been raised to consider the members of Tenancy as demigods. Unlike a Cronuan, she hadn't been raised to respect them. If anything, it was an Arran privilege to hate them.

Fucking Landlords.

But the Flet had saved her life. More than once, maybe.

After getting her bearings back, Bea in her arms, Tharsis walked up to the giant map of the ocean, plastered to the galley wall. Their route out of Singapore was mapped out there, little pins with paper flags attached to them, designating islands or important dive sites, the dates they were there. The last had just been put up this morning. *December whalefall.*

Between their present location and Hawaii, three weeks hence, there was almost nothing. A few volcanic islands. Something indicated as the *Great Plastic Float*. But not much beside that. And after Hawaii, she understood, their route would take them to the western shores of North America. Nothing at all between Hawaii and there.

She was running out of ocean, and she was running out of time.

It was beyond frustrating. Why wouldn't the Flet just tell her where he was?

Bea made one of those soft little grunting noises of hers and settled into Tharsis's shoulder. One little hand grabbed at the short hairs on the back of the Arran's neck. It was sweet, artless.

Tharsis patted the girl's back, swaying a little, eyes on the map.

A dangerous thought forming.

All of this, all of it, she was doing on the thin hope that somehow, the connection between the Flet and Peter Donovan would get her a berth on one of the exodus craft. Get her off world. See her into stasis out beyond the orbit of Neptune and maybe, maybe waking up in her own time.

At least, that was what she kept telling herself.

But that was only what she wanted, wasn't it?

Tharsis had gone into the ASDF out of a sense of duty. Of necessity. Deep-rooted obligation had defined her entire adult life.

But more than that, she'd done it because she had needed the purpose.

Purpose.

What purpose would she serve, back home? What was so important about getting back there?

If she left Earth now, who would take care of Bea?

He saved your life, she reminded herself. *You owe him.*

After, though.

The *after* was hers to decide.

"WE'VE LOCATED HEAT SIGNATURES, SIR."

"Not surprising."

"In Prokofiev Crater, in the shadow."

"Gloaming Station," a radio-enhanced voice explained, cutting in. "It was where they assembled the *Undine Glory's* more esoteric components."

Nobody had seen the Rallarhu-thing enter Ops, and the Arrans were clearly put out that it was there. Caleb would have thought they'd have gotten used to it by now. Instead, it seemed to be making everyone more uncomfortable with every appearance.

"So what does that mean?" Caleb asked.

The sensor operator spoke up. "High probability that something's alive down there, sir."

"But there's no Landlord here, correct?"

"Not anymore, no."

The Hermian terminator was coming into view through the *Barachiel's* limited window, a thin strip of twilight encircling the blasted little planet. There was nothing alive here, they had reassured him. How any part of the Flet still existed here, they had no idea.

Caleb didn't find any of that comforting.

The trip to Mercury had taken a little more than three days, not counting a half-day gravitation maneuver that had apparently helped with velocity. Aeneas was mopping up what remained of the Tok incursion back at Venus. Not their problem anymore.

Too bad, Caleb thought idly. Seemed like a much more straightforward mission.

"Who's down there?" he asked.

"We're going to find out, sir," Cambel said, and thought for a moment. "Stag, how do you feel about a broad deployment?"

"I'm sure everybody would love a chance to go get a little sun."

"Stag."

"I'll go get it put together. I'm guessing we can expect more of what we saw at Venus."

"Or some poor maintenance workers who got caught when the Flet dove," Cambel said. "I want nonlethal rounds issued, just in case."

"What if they're Toks?"

"Do what you have to do, obviously. But it wouldn't be terrible to have somebody to interrogate." Cambel nodded. "When will we be in range?"

"A few hours."

———

THE TRIP out hadn't been the easiest. Caleb hadn't slept well; the past plagued his dreams. What had the Dena said? Nightmares walking? Oh yes, he remembered that well.

It had always come from a predictable source. Traceable. Ilucoccine. Sometimes predictable. Almost always individualized.

But since he had died, things had changed. Somewhere, things had changed.

Things had changed.

"What do you think it is?" he'd asked Bea, a few nights before, as they waited in the back of Donner's plane, monsoon rain pummeling the desert outside.

It had taken another thirty-six hours to get her answer.

The slip came to Caleb down in the kennels, Tyr running the mig obstacle course again. The scent of piss and disinfectant had vanished, washed away by wet creosote, mesquite. The silence after a storm.

A bag dropped on the metal floor.

"That was interesting," Rallison said, and laid down next to her bag. "Fuck, it's hot outside."

She had a hand over her eyes.

She was sitting in one of the jump seats, eating something red and chunky out of a pouch.

A thunderstorm cell was passing outside, a cool breeze blowing stray mist through the back of the plane.

=This is it?= Bea asked. She picked up a gray folder, waggling it.

"That's it. That's what the intelligence shop was willing to give me, and then only after I told them I was down here officially from Keflavik."

=These have all been altered.=

"Apparently that's the only way they're safe to look at."

=How dangerous is it?=

Caleb walked over, peering over Bea's shoulder. In the folder was a thin stack of paper, printed reports that each seemed to profile one glyph or set of glyphs. Bea was right: they had all been altered, obviously crossed through with heavy marker, or covered with stickers applied in some attempt to add voids to the shapes. Like that, they all seemed mundane. Somebody's ridiculous idea of some ancient language.

He saw the header on one and pulled it free. TIKAL. The arium where they'd been captured. Dated six months before that ill-fated mission. It raised questions he didn't want to ask, not even himself. "They've been aware of this for a while."

Rallison swallowed her bite of food without chewing. "A few years, but there's been no recorded effects like this until the last week or so."

"What happened in Page took longer than a week."

"Apparently not."

=It started when Dad went missing.=

Rallison speared another chunk. "You think Dad has something to do with this?"

=He has been working on something recently.=

"That mass transfer thing?"

=Right.=

"He's been working on that since we were kids. It's never gone anywhere. It's never worked."

"It will," Caleb said, thinking of the *Undine Glory*.

=Which, if it does, brings into question the nature of space-time…

=

Rallison cut that off with a wave of her fork. "What does this have to do with the glyphs?"

=There's uncertainty in what he does.=

"That's not an answer."

Bea was clearly struggling. =When he does what he does…=

"What he's trying to do," Rallison corrected.

=He's forcing himself into a state of quantum uncertainty. More than one outcome is possible, until it's over. Until he decides.=

"So you're saying that you think whoever took him is weaponizing his, what, perspective? To what, reshape reality?"

=Yes. To force impossibilities out into reality. Or make little pocket universes, where such things can exist. Or…= Her fingers wavered for a moment, half-formed words dying at their tips. =I don't know. He doesn't perceive space-time the way we do. And the timing is right. It has to mean something.=

"If there is a connection," Caleb said, "we need to find him. But we're looking for him anyway. Nothing about what we're doing changes. Were there any leads at all?"

"There's no pattern in the places this is happening. No pattern, no regional grouping, no similarities shared by more than two locations…"

A rap on one of the folded jump seats.

=I know this guy.=

Bea held up another sheet from the file. A photograph. Obviously taken at long range. A group of whitecoats on some boat dock somewhere.

"Who is he?"

=A linguist.=

Caleb hadn't gotten the chance to ask her any more than that.

The kennels had returned too soon.

Now, with the transport cessna hurtling down to Mercury's sun-blasted surface, Caleb wasn't so sure about Bea's analysis. He couldn't discount it, either.

Something new then, perhaps, but now, very old.

What the fuck had happened during what the Arrans called the Euphemism?

Not even Adair seemed to know.

Records lost or destroyed. Never written at all, maybe.

Caleb knew there were plenty of things he wished he could forget.

Padre was with them again, as was Yip. But instead of the small Marine contingent, there were thirty men along for this. Most of them Ops crew. Caleb had asked about this; everyone, it seemed, was trained to the same standard.

Most were enlisted. Some of them Caleb knew and some of them had names he didn't recognize. Aeolis was along, as was the comm officer, Morray. Neither one of them was expendable. Caleb was confused by their inclusion, but he hadn't overridden the colonel on it. He was pissing off the man enough as it was.

"What do you expect to find down there, sir?"

Morray. "No idea," Caleb replied, startled out of his thoughts. "Something weird."

"That's almost a guarantee," Morray laughed. Of all of them, he seemed the most at ease.

Everyone's backpacks contained a modular heater, threaded into the interior layers of their suits and hooked into the contents of the pack. Mercury was cold where they were going.

<On final approach,> the pilot said. <Want to come take a look, Landlord?>

Unclipping himself from his seat harness, Caleb floated up and forward, up to the cockpit door.

They were approaching the shaded edge of a massive crater. Details were hard to make out. The *Barachiel's* heavy transport boasted a far smaller amount of viewing glass in its cockpit than the rockjumps did but held far more people for these mass deployments.

The pilot pointed. Down, about five o'clock. "There it is."

At first glance, Gloaming Station was nothing much to look at. It seemed a collection of beer cans had been spilled out across the floor of the crater, clinging to the shaded side of the walls. Small tunnels, of metal and rock, ran between them. Most of the cans were broken, clearly open to the void and whatever stray radiation reached past the glare of the sun.

A few were whole. And in these, lights gleamed.

"Those supposed to be on?" Caleb asked, but the pilot was already on the radio.

"Ops, Ops, we have activity on the surface. Requesting void support now."

<We have a shield swarm headed out. Should rendezvous in two minutes.>

"Roger that," the pilot muttered tersely, and looked back at Caleb. "Precaution only, of course, sir. If we're lucky… fuck." He grabbed for the intercom. "Brace, brace!"

Through the cockpit windows, Caleb saw something hurtling towards them through the void. Some kind of missile, he assumed, although it was rounded, without any visible means of propulsion. A giant chunk of rock, he realized.

It hit the transport below them. It slid between them, a ghostly outline, a phantom of rock almost a meter in diameter. Caleb had the strangest chill pass through him, as if his cells themselves were being frozen, and then it was gone.

The craft bucked.

He looked up. The chunk of rock was flying away from them. Velocity unchanged.

"What the fuck was that?" he demanded.

The pilot was flipping toggles with one hand, his other clearly braced on the stick. He didn't answer.

Aeolis, drawn by the commotion, pushed his way into the cockpit. "What's going on?"

"Both of you, strap in," the pilot snapped.

The nav officer took a seat immediately. "What are they throwing at us?"

"Kinetic scat, slingshot," came the terse reply. The transport bucked again. Another rock floated through the cabin.

"If they had any sense, they'd hit us with a scatter field," Aeolis said, and Caleb realized the officer was talking to him. "Sling up a whole scat-ton of material. Wrapper's good but on a craft this size it can be overwhelmed pretty easily with—"

"Shut up, Aeolis, or get the fuck out of my space," the pilot snapped, and flipped the radio back on. "Ops, I need that support."

<Should be seeing it now.>

Alongside, out the windows, one of the little wasp-craft pulled up alongside. Unlike the ones Caleb had seen Erg working on in the cargo bay, sleek and streamlined, this one had a wide, blunt body.

"They take the hits for us," Aeolis explained. "The shrapnel's annoying but not nearly as problematic."

More rocks, spinning towards them.

The pilot hit the radio button again. "Ops, can you do anything about this? This scat's coming from somewhere."

<Negative, negative, the colonel doesn't want to risk damage if the command module is down there.>

"Great," the pilot muttered. "We're going to have to put down short of the target. Landlord, you good with a little space walk?"

"What do you mean?" Caleb asked.

CHAPTER
TWENTY-NINE

DESPITE FURTHER IMPACTS, the transport was able to touch down and disgorge its passenger load safely. As Caleb was disembarking, the ENEX squeezed to his face. The wrapper waking up, Aeolis had warned him. He didn't like the sensation.

The axilla had made the ride on the outside of the transport itself, half-merged with the wrapper there. Caleb saw something dark ooze off the hull as he passed down the craft's open tongue. Like liquid dripping from a surface, the axilla dropped to the surface of Mercury. It rose a moment later, still that parody of a human figure.

=Fun ride,= it signed to him.

Caleb ignored it and looked ahead to a small depression where the team had gathered. Aeolis had helped him set the gravity circuits in his boots; unlike the deepvoider, this was apparently purely mechanical in nature. The field generated was restricted to the suit's internal circuitry and wouldn't extend more than a fraction of an inch from its surface. This could apparently be a problem on smaller bodies, but Aeolis had assured Caleb he would be able to move naturally.

He wasn't sure about that. It felt like walking through thick mud.

The axilla walked beside him, wearing Rallison's face once more, her facsimile of blonde hair pulled back into a bun.

Yip had been given tactical control of the insertion portion of this mission, and he was at the center of the small huddle. Caleb waited on the edge as the Marine sergeant started talking.

<Fan out,> Yip said. <We've got a kilometer of ground to cover, and we don't know what they've got out here. Wasps don't always read everything.>

Caleb suspected it was for his benefit; everyone else was already moving like they knew what to do. Once again, Adair stuck close.

Despite the initial shelling, they encountered no resistance on their way into Gloaming Station.

Caleb did determine, however, that he hated space walks. The silence was immense, the absence of atmosphere and the isolation of the suit almost overwhelming.

<Something's not right here,> Padre said as they came within sight of the half-ruined station. Private channel. Caleb was getting used to the different quality of sound between that and the main vox line.

<What do you mean?>

<The penumbra's twisted,> he said. <Waves in the ocean. Big ones.>

<I don't understand.>

<Neither do I.> Chaplain Kannik switched to the main vox. <Be on alert. Things may not be right here.>

<Roger that, Padre,> Yip said, and something beeped on the line. <Go ahead.>

<Contact spotted, seven o'clock,> one of the Marines called.

Yip hesitated for just a moment, then the radio clicked again. Caleb recognized that noise now: it was the sound of the vox turning on.

<This is the Arran Self-Defense Force. We are here investigating an international security matter. Walk forward with your hands up and identify yourself. Any violent action will be met with—>

A coughing sound echoed on the vox, like somebody had just gotten the breath knocked out of them.

<Ninden?> Yip asked.

<Rock shot, Sergeant. ENEX holding.>

Yip repeated the hail.

More rocks started falling down amongst them. Everyone moved to take shelter.

<Ops, any confirmation that this is Tenancy activity?> Yip asked.

<Negative. Landlord appears to still be in stasis. Habitat in Laxness Crater still not responding to hails.>

Yip looked at Caleb for a moment, goggles blank. Then he keyed up the vox again. <Cease kinetic assault immediately and lay down your weapons.>

The response was a huge chunk of rock digging into the ground not two meters from them.

<Right,> Yip muttered, the word almost lost in the static. He flipped a couple of switches on the butt of the large, cumbersome-looking rifle he was holding. <Landlord, stay here with the good doctor. *Barachiel* crew, wide advance.>

———

NOBODY HESITATED. With a steadiness that seemed foolhardy, the line of Arrans advanced, stride unbroken. More rocks, big chunks of frozen mantle, were flung at them, at what seemed to be impossible speeds. Not exactly shrugged off, but they did pass through the Arran line. Passed right through the Arrans who were hit.

Fifty meters out, the line started running.

Twenty meters out, the shooting began.

A series of clicks on the radio, and the entire line fired at once. The initial effect was like a sheet of light, burning through the freezing void towards the dark facility. It came in bursts after that, blast after blast of shining, glowing hail. It was unnerving in its silence.

Fifteen seconds after it began, it was over. A dozen black-wrapped bodies lay where they had collapsed on the ancient dust, or spun away towards the stars, never to be retrieved. A couple of the Marines paced through the prone forms, shaking out bulky handcuffs with some kind of integrated rock spike. Driving that deep into the ground, the person inside was locked in place.

Everyone else was moving inside.

<Kinetic rounds alone will disassociate right through wrapper,> Yip told Caleb as he and Adair walked up, as if reading his thoughts. <It can be overwhelmed but I'm guessing they didn't have the means to build larger slingshots for that.>

<What'd you shoot them with?>

<Electric charges. They'll still pass through, but even then, the energy transfers. Usually more than enough to overwhelm suit

mechanics, interrupt airflow, knock somebody out or at least immobilize them for a while.> He paused. One of his guys, still kneeling by a body, gave him an exaggerated thumbs-up sign. <Good, a few of them are alive. We'll collect them on the way back.>

<What about inside?>

<In atmo, these rounds will stop your heart, but won't puncture walls,> he said, and patted the butt of his shock rifle. <It's best not to take chances.>

A click on the line. <Sergeant?>

<Go.>

<We're not finding atmo.>

<It's there, even if it's just survival tents. No way these guys would still be alive if it isn't. Keep looking.>

THE ONLY THING remarkable about the facility was the state of ruin it seemed to be in. Metal walls were torn open, twisted as if from the inside. Dust had settled in the corners, clogging old equipment and half covering signs of life. The axilla seemed quite interested in all of it, inspecting every little corner with silent intensity. It had made no more attempts to communicate with Caleb, which he was grateful for.

<There's no wind here, right?> Caleb asked.

<You're asking about the damage here, right?> Adair asked.

<Yeah.>

<That was us, centuries ago.> Yip's voice darkened. <After the damn place went adlet.>

<Adlet?>

Yip ignored him.

<Feral, eating itself,> Adair replied, and left it at that.

More calls in. Nobody was finding anything. Until Padre came on.

<I think I've found what we're looking for, boys.>

Yip stretched his palm pad out between his fingers. <Anything alive?>

<Not anymore.>

<I've got your position,> he said, and nodded to Caleb. <Sir, if you'll follow.>

And deeper into the ancient facility's guts they went.

———

PADRE, along with a couple others, was waiting for them at the threshold of a broken habitat dome. He was just inside what remained of a covered walkway, the curve of it so low Caleb could have brushed it with his hand.

<What is it?> Yip asked. He'd slung his shock rifle back across his chest, and one hand tapped on the butt.

Padre gestured at the air lock. <Can any of you see that?>

Caleb looked. Stepped forward.

The air lock was clean, burnished. Lights blinking in its control panel. And around it…

Caleb's fingers brushed the glyph, fresh-carved in the metal.

For a moment, he had the impression of a full glass arch above him, around him. Of warm air on his skin. Solid insulated decking underfoot. And beyond that air lock, beyond, inside…

Fog swirled against the windows before diving back between the boles of huge trees, casting strange shapes through the dark woods. Rain was falling, soft and endless.

Caleb had the strangest sense that the forest was watching him.

"Bea, there's nothing here."

He turned back around. Bea and Rallison were standing in the middle of a wide space. Desks ringed walls made mostly of glass, while the center of the space was dominated by a series of rolling blackboards.

Every single one was blank.

=This is his space, the last place I heard of him working,= Bea insisted. =This is an Arium facility, isn't it?"

Caleb tore himself away from the contemplation of the forest, walking back over. "This is the guy who developed that glyph language?"

=Yes.=

"Why this lab?" Rallison asked. "Why did he come down here to the ass end of Japan?"

=I don't know.=

Landlord? somebody called. *Landlord?*

And touched his shoulder.

Caleb sucked air, the cold of his ENEX's pressurized oxygen a shock to his lungs after the warm, muggy air of that forest.

He was back. In the dust, in the ruin.

<Everything alright?>

Yip. Padre. The *Barachiel* crew.

He shook himself.

<There's a glyph there,> Caleb said, and turned away. <Anybody else see it?>

<I do now,> Adair said, walking up. His hand was out. He sounded fascinated.

Padre grabbed his arm. <We haven't been inside yet. We don't know what they were trying to do.>

<No time like the present,> Yip said, and punched the entry control switch.

The air lock slid open.

Warm atmo blew out.

Sea air.

"Why is it that this thing's here?"

They were standing on the edge of a harbor, concrete forms like giant jacks piled up high to make a breakwater. Down a causeway was an oversized seaplane. Bobbing softly on its pontoons. Japanese signage featured prominently in the town behind them.

"Why is it that all of these assets seem to be staged where we need them?" Rallison was asking. "This plane, the depressurization chamber on the last one, the stuff in Page…"

=Maybe Dad knew that we'd need it here,= Bea said.

"How?"

=He doesn't view space like we do. So maybe he doesn't view time the same way either.=

Both of them were looking at him. "What do you mean?" Rallison asked.

=I'm not sure,= Bea said. =We've been moving things into various positions for about a year now. He never told me why, just said it was necessary.=

"If he knew we needed this stuff, wouldn't he know where he is? Wouldn't he have left a big note saying, 'Hey, pick me up here'?"

"Maybe he doesn't understand it himself," Caleb muttered. "Because none of this shit should be happening."

He didn't get to hear their answers.

The dock was gone.

Mercury was back.

In front of him was a vast hangar. Sterile white. Whole. Perfect.

Except for a dark, rocky monolith, right at its heart.

Voiders—pale, slender, tall, scarred with radiation burns—stared back at them. Maybe half a dozen. Gear, empty ration cases, were scattered everywhere.

For a moment, they stared at each other.

For a moment.

Then the hangar doors were broken, the air lock dead. Dust piled up around their feet.

The atmo was gone.

And the voiders, the voiders rushed at them. ENEXes sealing up even as their skin began to blister, their bodies' moisture boiling away.

The ensuing firefight was brief but brutal. Nothing fair about it, just like the assault on the approach in. One disciplined round of fire from the team, and it was over.

Yip began barking orders to his men: *take inventory, what did they have here, report any equipment damage immediately*. But even Caleb could see the age on the cases scattered about.

It made no sense, no sense at all.

And, of course, there was that strange monolith in the center of the hangar space.

He walked up to it, fingers brushing the hull.

We're running out of time.

A whisper. Centuries past. Echoing in real time around him.

That was it. That was the still beating heart of the *Undine Glory*.

———

UNLIKE THE EARTH-BOUND aircraft he associated with Donner, or the crisp white blankness of the *Barachiel's* dive core, the

Undine Glory's command module was a beast of a thing. A great curving mass of pitted gray rock, only the shape of it giving any indication it was man-made. The surface was not uniformly cratered; it had geometric shapes underneath it, as if the outer mantle had been laid over a substructure ringed with pipes, conduits, nodules. A colossal monument, taken from its Neolithic resting site and forgotten in some warehouse.

The module was roughly ovoid, thicker in the middle and tapering off on either end. Walking around it, it must have been sixty, seventy meters long. In the butt ends were the first outward signs of human craftsmanship. Embedded metal, sheared off as if under great force. An air lock, its oculus-style door still sealed tightly shut.

A door that was a good five meters off the ground.

<I'm going to need help up,> Caleb said on the open line, to nobody in particular.

Yip clicked on. <Turn down the gravity in your boots. You should be able to jump it with no issues.>

<Right,> Caleb muttered, somewhat embarrassed he hadn't thought of that himself.

The leap wasn't hard. Catching himself at the top proved to be a greater challenge. He timed it wrong, and almost went bouncing away to the roof of the hangar.

As soon as he settled, though, the door unscrewed, opening into the dimly lit lock.

He felt a vibration next to him.

The axilla.

=This is interesting,= it commented. Out of the suit, its movements were fluid, fingers almost flowing through each other, in and out of its hands, rather than holding their own integrity.

=If there's air in here, you can't come,= he told it.

It nodded. =I await your report.=

There was no control panel, nothing to interact with. But once he stepped inside the air lock proper, it closed behind him.

He waited for a rush of air. For the sensors in his suit controls to start chiming their way across his goggles.

Nothing like that came.

Instead, Caleb found himself deck of a boat.

The living components of his ENEX had pulled back automatically, and he scraped hood and goggles from his head. He still had the A24, though. Why did he still have that?

A woman, he realized, was out in front of him. Motionless at the railing of the ship, staring off across the ocean. There was nothing but water in all directions. She had a baby, asleep in her arms.

But then she turned. Saw him. Went gray. "You shouldn't be here," she said.

"Why not?" he asked.

"Fucking Landlords won't leave me alone," she grumbled, and glanced down at the baby, bouncing it a little. "But I guess I shouldn't be here either, eh?"

From behind her, the wind washed across them, laden with moisture. Salt. Hot and sickly sweet. The sound of rain came with it, and suddenly, instead of the endless blue, there were mountains. Volcanic, steep and green.

Screams. He could hear screams. A hellish cacophony.

And on a whim, not understanding why, he asked her. "Where's Tom Donner?"

"I don't know," she told him. In that moment, she looked ancient. Weary beyond measure. "I've had enough of this horror to last me a lifetime."

He took a step forward, hand out, but the only thing he contacted was the interior door of the air lock.

<Pressurization cycle interrupted,> a cheerful voice chimed.

Behind him, the doors slid open. Back into the hangar.

The chill of his bottle oxygen bit at his throat.

Adair, Yip, Padre.

<Sir, thought we might join you,> the chaplain said.

<Mr. Adair here wants to do a little tomb raiding,> Yip added.

<If there's anything historically significant, I need to—>

<No, it's alright,> Caleb said, and looked around. <How do we get this thing to work?>

Yip touched something in the wall. The doors slid shut behind them. Even through the goggles, Caleb could see his wink.

He sighed.

The trip through the command module was shorter than he'd

imagined. Despite the size of the thing, the actual accessible space was quite tight. A hallway that led deep into the interior, intersecting with an oblong circular route. The design there was more familiar, the same white surface as the dive core's interior, the hallway shaped with a circular cross section. The surface was dimpled at routine intervals. Handholds, Yip explained. The gravity in their boots failed the second the air lock opened.

There was light enough, and atmo. After Yip was satisfied nothing was going to poison them, they all took their hoods off.

"All of these would have held neural matter," Adair explained as they pulled themselves through the space, indicating sections of the hallway's bulkheads that protruded out slightly from the walls. "The processing power required to locate, track, and fix water molecules through the outer system was vast. The sheer volume of space is unimaginably huge."

"So what happened exactly?"

"He reached out and pulled in an ocean," Yip said.

"I thought he needed navigation material to move things."

"He does," Padre said, catching himself and killing his momentum to touch one of the protrusions before moving on. "Now. The effort of the ocean transfer almost killed him. The story goes that he let his consciousness ride the solar wind out into the Kuiper, and beyond into the Oort, to locate what we needed."

"That sounds a little…"

"Unscientific?" Padre finished with a half smile. "It was far more complex than that. But it is essentially what he did. And ice clump by ice clump, he built our ocean and gave us the hydro cycle that Mars relies on for life and breathable air."

Yip nodded. "I heard he also pulled quite a bit of nitrogen back."

"Yes," Adair said, "some of it was locked up in deposits, but obviously the early terraforming project needed far more to—"

"Here," Padre said, and stopped at a panel. His finger traced something Caleb couldn't see. "This is the door."

Another oculus opened in the wall.

A rush of cooler air came out.

Another long passage led into a small spherical space barely four meters in diameter. Wiring ringed the endless wall, feeding in through the smooth surface. These were coiled, no, stowed neatly, but even a cursory glance showed that they must have been long enough to reach the center.

Or the bottom, depending.

A deep layer of sand had been set in the sphere. Red, almost painfully so in the white space. A few grains floated above the mass, but most seemed under the influence of some form of gravity. Adair said as much, musing even as he frantically scribbled notes in his book.

"The planet's?" Yip mused.

"Or the craft itself," Padre said.

Caleb had a flash.

An image.

Rain, falling on sand. White sand, stained dark, washing away.

Caleb…

He blinked, and it was gone.

"Landlord?" Padre asked.

Yip shrugged. "As amazing as this is, I don't think there are any answers here."

The rain was falling again. Moving the red-stained sand. Moving…

Caleb, I can't hold this much longer. You need to…

There were no handholds in the room, nothing to grab onto. But Caleb saw the corner of something sticking out of that sand pit and managed to maneuver himself just far enough to grab it. Both Padre and Adair protested, reaching for him, but he caught it. Plunged his hand in and pulled out a notebook.

A simple, unremarkable little notebook.

Sand spiraled up, swimming through the room.

The Arrans were all staring at him, he realized, as he unzipped his ENEX and stuffed the little thing in a uniform chest pocket. "Let's go," he said.

CHAPTER
THIRTY

MAUI, when it came, was a welcome stop.

January in the Hawaiian Islands had once been peak tourism season, some of the other women told Tharsis. It was the time of year when winter weather was at its roughest elsewhere in the Northern Hemisphere. The vast migration of humpback whales had been, once, a huge draw as well.

Now, nobody but the researchers followed the whales. Civilian observation from boats had been strictly banned decades before. Most of the waters around the islands were now classified as highly protected marine preserves. The economy was fueled largely by research groups; some international astronomy association, the Arium Consortium.

They owned yet another island here. Apparently.

The *Vastitas Reach* was scheduled for a full two weeks in port. Almost every researcher on board had something planned for their time.

For the paid crew, it was a nice holiday.

Tharsis had no idea what to do with herself. Chris warned her that it would be nonstop work for them on the last leg of the journey, into North America.

"Everyone's going to come back with a ton of data and conflicting service requests for us," he told her. "Go enjoy yourself for a while. Take a break."

It seemed like good advice. She'd had a nightmare about the Rossen a few nights before. Last time she'd seen him, he was threatening to execute her. She couldn't shake the funk from it.

Tharsis ended up buying a bus ticket from the port up to the only town of any size. The bus came only twice a day; she got in around sunset.

Lahanai was a pleasant little town. Whitewashed and salt-nipped, low buildings rose between the orderly guidance of narrow streets. Some opened into gardens or had storm shutters pulled back to take advantage of the cooling air. Art galleries spilled brilliant color out onto the sidewalks. Birds sang in the trees. The warring scents of fruit and damp rot filled the air. Somewhere in the distance, rhythmic drums and rising voices marked some kind of celebration. Tourists—the rare breed who could afford the astronomical travel costs—meandered through it, the sounds of a dozen different languages clearly audible.

The dark remnants of an ancient volcano rose against the falling night in the east. Soft waves on a narrow beach and high-piled lava rock broke to the west, scattering light from the falling sun. In front of her, a gigantic tree tangled through the air, supported by dozens of wooden posts, roots and branches almost indistinguishable. A banyan tree, a bronze plaque nearby read. She'd never seen anything like it.

"Look at that, Bea," she murmured to her baby, half-asleep in her sling. "There's a new wonder, everywhere."

Tharsis splurged on a decent hotel that night and fell quickly asleep, the baby curled against her.

In her dreams that night, she watched the sun set from the deck of that yacht again.

The Flet was talking to her.

"You have no idea how critical it is that I regain freedom of movement."

"Why?"

"How are they supposed to find the exodus craft if they can't reach Noqumiut?"

"Wait, this is affecting my time?"

"Tharsis, time is an ocean. There is no your time, my time. If it will exist, it already does."

She wanted to ask him. What he meant. What any of this was.

There was nobody at all there but her.

Tharsis enjoyed the peace of it all for a while, until she wondered where Bea was and woke in a panic.

———

THERE WAS something about the island across the channel, she thought the next morning. The hotel sat on the edge of the water, a white sand coral beach reaching for a kilometer or more south of a huge volcanic outcropping. Somebody had told her that once, there had been dozens of hotels along the stretch. Now, there was just the one.

Earth was already tearing itself apart.

Tharsis had picked up breakfast from a little outside cabana and taken both Bea and their food down to the water.

There was definitely something about the island across the channel.

Bea was more concerned about getting to the applesauce.

Tharsis fed the baby mechanically. Her unease lingered.

Of anywhere she'd been, Hawaii seemed to be the best candidate for the landscape she'd seen around the yacht. The peaceful emptiness of Maui was at odds with the bustling metropolis she'd glimpsed beyond the yacht, but Tharsis still went looking. She thought that perhaps the bay was here.

She found a bus schedule and circled the island more than once, taking a few days just to search every nook and cranny. A few sections of the island were extremely difficult to reach, and those areas, she had to hike into on foot. The jungle landscape was miserable, though, and uncomfortable for Bea, so she did what she could, hoping it would be enough.

After a few days of that, though, Tharsis realized she hadn't seen the bay from the land. It was a poor perspective to take. She talked Annaka—who had a charter boat—into taking her on a trip around the island, fully circumnavigating the entire thing over a two-day period. They saw whales and sea turtles and dolphins, but nothing that resembled what Tharsis had seen in her dreams.

If they were dreams at all.

WYATT INVITED Tharsis along to a meeting he'd set up with some local shaman. Tharsis found the entire thing somewhat embarrassing. He peppered the woman with questions about creation myths, language nuances, gods and monsters. About eschatology, which was a subject the tribal elder clearly did not want to discuss.

That damn myling came with them too.

While exposure had inured Tharsis to the presence of most, that one still made her uneasy. There was something wrong about it, wrong in a way she still couldn't define, and it seemed particularly fascinated with Bea. Constantly trying to touch her, poke her, make her cry. The Arran wished she knew where it was coming from. That was one wetware node she would have gladly cast into the sea with no regrets. But even after months on a ship with him, she'd never seen Wyatt use anything other than paper notebooks for his work.

At one point, when Wyatt stepped away to use the bathroom, the elder turned to Tharsis.

"What are you doing with these people?" the old woman asked.

"What do you mean?" Tharsis was wary. Wyatt had introduced her —yet again—as Navajo. She'd had time to look this up. They were a tribe who had arrived in the North American continent before the Europeans, much like the shaman's people had settled in Hawaii. Civilizations that predated the Age of Navigation. The First Nations. Tharsis still couldn't quite fathom Wyatt's fixation on it, on her.

The old cultures had originally been animist, though. Maybe that was why.

But the old shaman made no mention of any kind of supposed ethnic connection between them. "You can see them," she said instead.

It wasn't a question. "See what?"

"The children who come from the ariums, the ones that follow these whitecoats around, the ones that never lived."

"They're alive," Tharsis said softly, and shooed Wyatt's myling away from Bea again. "That's the worst part about it."

"Some might be," the shaman said, and glared at the myling. "This one is different."

"What is it, then?"

But the other woman wouldn't tell her, and Wyatt came back soon after, and the awkward conversation resumed.

———

THE NIGHT before the *Vastitas Reach* was scheduled to leave, the entire crew was invited to something called a luau, held on the sands of the only remaining tourist resort. Chris gave up his spot to watch Bea, so Tharsis could attend. It was a grand affair of drums and fire, dancing and feasting, long into the night.

Tharsis ate her coconut pudding, and watched smoke rise into the night sky, and wondered, not for the first time, why they'd ever agreed to leave this world.

CHAPTER
THIRTY-ONE

COLONEL CAMBEL MET them down in the hangar, upon their return from Gloaming Station. Equipment was handed off, the Rallarhu-thing slithered back outside the ship, refueling began.

"Are we clear to head back to Mars, sir?" the colonel had asked.

Adair hadn't been long in the military, but he knew that tone. It wasn't somebody asking for permission.

The Landlord must have clearly caught it too. "Yeah, I've got what we came for."

"Good," the colonel told him.

"Is there any place I can go and maybe look through the archives? Of my, umm, journals?"

Cambel nodded. "We've got a comprehensive set of them in the main library. I can have somebody show you where it is."

"That'd be helpful," the Rossen said, and looked over at Adair. "Do you have some time?"

"At your disposal, sir."

————

THE *BARACHIEL'S* library turned out to be a small space squeezed along the main atrium. There wasn't much there: a few desks, a dozen or so bookcases, a terminal for displaying whatever digital media the craft's silic held. Adair guessed it was used largely for recreational reading, as well as a few professional courses that crewmen took from time to time. Especially with the distances involved, correspondence courses were likely the only way many of them could stay up on their ASDF-mandated training. Hygeia had a small education office, but most void bases weren't so lucky.

The place was empty when they arrived, but between Tyr's massive bulk and the Rossen's irritation, it was suddenly full to bursting.

"Do you know what this is?" the Rossen asked, pulling an object out of an inner uniform pocket. It was the thing he'd taken from the *Undine Glory's* command module. A few grains of red sand scattered across the library's single group study table.

"It looks like a notebook, sir," Adair said. "One of the ones from your barracks room, right?"

Laying it down on the small table, the Landlord creased it open to the first page. Rows of numbers, neatly organized, ran across it. "Yeah, it does, doesn't it?" He placed the other beside it, flipping open to the second page. "Same figures in it."

"Different handwriting," Adair observed, and got his own notepad out.

"I know. It's hers."

"Who?"

"The, uhh, you call her the Naven. If I pronounced that right."

"You did." Adair stared at the notebook, not quite believing what he was hearing. "You knew her?"

"The Flet and I both."

And there was a revelation. "You knew the Flet before the Tenancy?"

"I knew him on Earth."

"Who was he?" Adair asked, intensely curious now.

"I don't know why I haven't told you all certain things. But considering what happened down there on Mercury, I don't think now is the best time to start offering that up."

His contemporary English really was getting better.

"Can you tell me anything? Anything that might help?"

The Landlord was silent for a good two minutes. "When I first met him, he was flying aircraft for the Air Force. Our country's military. What was left of it, anyway."

Military pilot. Adair wrote that down. Seemed significant.

"Like I said, I want to be sure about what's going on before we start talking about this in depth."

The Landlord's eyes were on his notepad, Adair realized. He shut it. Clicked his pen shut. "I understand taking precautions."

"Based on how shocked you all were by that shit down in Prokofiev, I doubt it." The Landlord stifled a yawn in his shoulder. "That? That was something that would have happened during the Euphemism."

"I've never seen anything like this, in any record we have from or about you," Adair agreed. He tapped the table beside the notebook. "What is this?"

"I have no idea," the Landlord said, giving the bookshelves a weary look. "Hopefully, it's the answer for where the Flet is. The answer to what's going on. But I'll be honest, Adair, I am shit with this sort of thing."

"Would you be willing to let me ask around for you in the morning? I know you probably want to look into this yourself, but honestly, sir, there's nothing you're going to find in the public Journals archive. I've never heard of anything like this being mentioned in connection with you."

"I was hoping you would," the Rossen said with a bitter smile, and yawned. "See what you can figure out."

"Do you mind if I show this to—"

"Anybody you want," he said, and yawned again.

———

FOR AS CONFINED as the crew spaces were on the *Barachiel*, it still took Adair the better part of the next morning to track down the first person he wanted to talk to. And then, he only found the man because of daily mass.

Chaplain Kannik, prepping the small craftside chapel, had had no feedback on the notebook itself, but he did have a few insights on the events at Gloaming Station.

"I spent the night in Medical," he told Adair, when the historian finally caught up with him. "Their life-support shop has been busy. Rebuilding our ENEXes."

"Rebuilding? Why?"

"Everyone who was there in the hangar sustained damage," the chaplain said. "Wrapper damage."

"I don't—"

"It was dying, Daevid. Our ENEXes were dying in the presence of that atmosphere. Atmosphere that should not have been there. Medical observed similar issues for the voiders' gear, the ones who were killed."

"How did that even happen, the atmo being there?"

"It wasn't just atmo. It was an entirely different place. Or rather, the same place but a different point in time maybe."

"Time travel's impossible," Adair replied, almost automatically. It was an axiom, one that any first-year physics student knew. "Worldline folding is impossible."

"It wasn't that," Kannik mused. "It was as if…" and he trailed off. "It was as if we were within the penumbra. Underneath, in a bubble."

"That doesn't make any sense, Father."

"Oh, I know." He looked pensive. "I've sent a request to both my own order, back at Orcus, and the Golanites out at Pluto. I don't expect to hear back before we make the Mars inwell. But it bears further investigation, once the divedrive fleet is functional again."

"What do you suppose is going on?"

"My guess is that it's linked to the Flet." He stared off for a moment. "And the Rossen. He knows something, or at least, he suspects something."

"Why do you say that?"

"The penumbran energy I saw down in that crater matches what I see around him."

But what that meant, Kannik wouldn't say.

———

ADAIR MADE the rounds with the crew after that. He started with the transport pilots, figuring that if anybody knew anything about antique pilot-talk, it would be them.

But in the middle of their conversation, somebody else offered an answer.

"What is that?"

It was one of the sergeants, somebody Adair had seen at the nav station over the past few sevendays. Night shift crew, probably.

"Something the Landlord asked me to decode for him," Adair said, and held up the book.

The sergeant took it, shifting the weight of his dinner tray into one hand in the process. Gravy splashed over the edge, hitting the guy behind him.

"Hey!"

"You'll live," the nav sergeant said, and sat down next to Adair. "Okay, I might be wrong about this, but it looks like a space-time position record."

"What do you mean?"

"This is definitely a time code," he said, pointing to the last set of numbers in the first row, "and this duration. A few seconds. HST. These, right here, are orbital positioning coordinates, like we'd get from the satellite net on Mars."

"Okay, but the Landlord hasn't been on Mars in decades."

"I can't help you there. And this, oh, this is probably pulsar map data." He tapped the last first set of numbers. "Pulsar map. We use it out here. Better accuracy than triangulating position off the sun and planet set, but the format's weird. Those coordinates..." He frowned. "We shouldn't have this much movement."

Adair thought of something. "Maybe it's absolute shift."

"What do you mean?"

"Do you think Major Gallin is awake?"

"Aeolis? He's on shift right now. You want to go talk to him?"

———

THE *BARACHIEL'S* head navigation officer was more than happy to hand his station off to his sergeant and join Adair in the ops briefing room. He took his time studying the notebook, which Adair appreciated, before echoing much of what his sergeant had said. But he had more to say about it.

"This column is weird," he said, indicating the same set of numbers his sergeant had. "Terrier was right. There's way too much spatial movement in this."

"So what does that mean?"

"My first instinct would be that the Landlord's got some other means of tracking location. Not pulsar triangulation, not satellite coordinates," Aeolis said. "But why is he tracking anything at all?"

"I'm not sure he knows."

"That's convenient, isn't it?" He tapped the notebook again. "But me saying that doesn't address the most glaring issue here."

"Which is?"

"There are two sets of timestamps. And one of them is centuries in the past."

Adair thought about that attempted dive to Pluto. Gloaming Station. The *Undine Glory's* hangar.

Bubbles in the underbelly of space-time. Currents.

"What if that's where the coordinates are coming from?"

Aeolis just stared at him. "That sounds like time travel, college man. And we all know time travel's not possible."

"I think it's time the Rossen told us what the hell is going on with him," Adair replied.

———

DOWN IN THE CHUMMER, the Landlord didn't look up from his goat stew. "What is it?" It didn't look like he'd slept the night before.

"If we're going to decode this, we need to understand a little bit more about what's going on," Adair said.

He paused, a loaded fork halfway to his mouth. "Like what?"

"Maybe start with why there are dates in here that seem to be from seven, eight centuries ago," Aeolis said.

He did look up at that. Set his fork down. Waved at the empty seats around him. "Okay, let's talk."

Adair began. "What's been going on with you?"

"What do you mean?"

"Your wake-up was different this time," the historian said. "That's never happened. You've evidently been seeing things…"

"There's definitely been some sort of odd penumbra activity lately," Padre added.

"And we have no records of anything like that happening either."

"Then there's this," Aeolis added, brandishing the notebook.

The Landlord reached over to scratch his dog's ears. "I, umm, I have been seeing things. Moments from the past. Things I don't remember, things that… happened after I died for the first time, I think. Real enough to feel like I'm there."

"Maybe you are," the chaplain said.

"Is that possible?" Aeolis said.

"Maybe you're aligning with yourself, consciousness being shoved back into a previous iteration." Padre held up his hands. "I don't know how. The Flet's never gone AWOL before. We're in uncharted territory."

"What is your connection with him?" Adair asked.

"Or the Rallarhu's?" Aeolis asked. "I have never heard of anybody manually diving a core."

At that, the Landlord did hesitate. "He, uhh, he and his wife fostered me for a few years, after my own family—" He stopped. "After that, and before I enlisted."

"And the Rallarhu?"

"Her dad."

Adair was shocked. Judging from the reactions from Padre and Aeolis, so were they. Padre recovered his composure the fastest.

"Well, that's a hell of a coincidence," the priest said drily.

The Landlord reached for his coffee. "I'm starting to think that maybe it wasn't. Maybe Rallison had something in her, something from him, that they knew they could exploit. Maybe it was dumb chance. But I think he must have known about me. He was like that sometimes, knowing things that hadn't happened yet, or forgetting things that were. Like time was different for him."

"As far as we know, it is now. Maybe it was then too," Padre said.

Adair was still trying to process that.

"So why the time stamps in the past?" Aeolis asked and shoved the notebook back over.

"That's Greenwich Mean Time," the Landlord said, glancing at it. "Umm, what we used on Earth. I recognize that. Standard military time code."

"That would indicate to me you are indeed moving. Slipping back through your own timeline, maybe."

"Look, I don't know how any of this works," he said. "You all are the experts, not me. But I assume I've had this happen to me before, these slips. It seems pretty intense right now, and I apparently worked for Donner…"

"Who?"

"The Flet."

"When?"

"Soldiers who got bio-fucked got executed. It was policy," the Rossen said. Flat. Matter of fact. "I assume they tried that with me. Somehow, I either got out or they let me go. I don't have any details on that. He gave me a job, working security for him."

"Security for what?"

"His arium."

Adair blinked, and pulled out his notepad, flipping back through the last few sevendays' worth of notes. "I thought you said that organization was aligned with—"

"He must have been working on the *Undine Glory* at the time, or whatever underlying technology was in it. Like I said, I don't know." The Rossen gestured at the notebook and went back to his eggs. "He told me something. Maybe it was a dream, I don't fucking know. He said something about an orbit that was decaying."

"Maybe you're being pulled along in his wake," Padre mused.

"Or maybe he's doing it on purpose. He's asking for help. I think whatever happened, though, it started back then. In the time I can't remember." He ate another bite of breakfast, chewing thoughtfully and washing it down with more coffee before asking, "Has this ever happened to me before?"

"Only one way to know for sure."

"What's that?"

"Check the private archive," Aeolis said, and Adair shot him a glare. He held up his hands, mock-innocent. "What? It's an open secret that he has a vault on Deimos, and you know it."

"Sounds good," the Landlord said, and handed the notebook back to Aeolis. "Anything you can do with this, sir?"

The nav officer shrugged. "Maybe. I'll see. We've got a few more days before we're into port. It'll give the boys something to do, at least."

"I'd like to keep all this quiet, until we know more. That okay?"

"Perfectly fine."

Adair folded his hands on the tabletop. "About the glyphs, sir…"

"That is some Euphemism fuckery," the Landlord said, and went back to his meal. "It should have died on Earth. We're not dragging it out into the void now."

———

WHEN ADAIR GOT BACK to his own borrowed quarters, there were a number of urgent messages sitting in his comm account. From his boss. From General Cochrane. From the Historians' Office on Deimos. Everyone demanding updates. Status. On the situation, on the Rossen.

He spent an hour and a half drafting replies. Deleting them. Drafting again. Editing down.

There was nothing to report, though. Not really. Not yet.

Not until the Rossen released him to talk.

There was one message, different than the rest. His wife.

I've been reading the daily reports, Daevid. Are you doing okay?

That one, he replied to. She'd probably talk to Cochrane about it, and even if she didn't, the comm boys on Hygeia would scrape the message anyway. So he kept it short, succinct.

The Rossen's taking us on a hunting trip, he told her. *It's a fascinating thing to witness.*

CHAPTER
THIRTY-TWO

THE LAST LEG of the *Vastitas Reach's* trans-Pacific cruise between Hawaii and North America was about to start. Tharsis felt panicked. She still hadn't found the Flet. But after they left Maui, they had one more stop.

Another island. Some city called Honolulu.

The cruise only took a few hours, the research vessel sliding carefully through inter-island channels, a shallow route that took them past migrating humpbacks. Many of the crew, everyone who could spare the time, hung out on the outer decks, hoping for a glimpse. Tharsis found herself and Bea a good spot in the shade and pointed the giant sea mammals out to the baby as they swam by.

"Pretty amazing, huh?" she said softly.

The terraforming teams had tried to introduce as wide a variety of fauna as possible. They'd found, however, that the larger the animal, the more difficult the adaptation to Mars's lower gravity. Brought over as either babies or raw gametes, and raised on nursery spin-craft, some species had gone through multiple generations, many opportunities for subtle genetic tweaking, before transferring to the surface. Whales had been brought over in full family pods, however, towards the very end of the Euphemism, without any such gene manipulation at all.

The only whales that had successfully colonized Mars's ocean waters were smaller, cold-water species. Belugas, orcas, narwhal. Dolphins. Anything larger, like the humpbacks, hadn't taken.

Tharsis found them a wonder. Like seeing dinosaurs, maybe.

The baby, seated in Tharsis's lap, clapped her little hands every time a pod of dolphins jumped between the waves, or a humpback breached in one of their amazing mating displays. She was constantly trying to mimic Tharsis's movements now.

Since receiving the sign language videos for Christmas, the Arran lieutenant had tried to practice as much as she could. Talk to Bea as much as she could, fingers and hands and wrists. It was tricky, but she was getting the hang of it. And Bea seemed excited about it.

Tharsis let the little girl have her fun.

Worried about her next move.

After Honolulu, the *Vastitas* was scheduled to head to North America. Then up the coast, into more frigid waters. Places that wouldn't hold the rain-drenched tropical night of the Flet's event horizon.

Tharsis had a decision to make.

She'd seen dozens of islands, all across the ocean, and none of them had been right. None a match. She'd exhausted every avenue of investigation the *Vastitas Reach* could give her. She had nothing to go on.

No details.

No guarantees.

The vagueness of it all was beyond frustrating.

But then, there was Bea. Solid, present, real. Almost six months old. Rolling over. Reaching for bites of food. Trying to talk, in that new way Chris had given them.

Growing up.

Tharsis had been working her way across the planet for that yacht, that night. For whatever it was the Flet needed help with. For passage off world, and maybe a wake-up in her own time.

But if she did that, who was going to take care of Bea? Who would raise her? Who would be there to hug her when she cried, feed her in the middle of the night when she woke up hungry? Who would teach her how to speak and eat and walk? Who would tell her stories? Who would clean that last little bit of spittle off her face in the bath? Who would carry her outside on those sleepless nights and point out the stars and tell her about all the magnificent things that awaited her out there?

If Tharsis left her behind, would she end up back at some arium? In a box, a cage?

Tharsis had no desire to watch Earth die. She'd seen too many beautiful things already, met good people, marveled at what humanity had accomplished here, the history and the hope. If she stayed, she'd have to watch it all end.

And yet.

Time was what it was.

Wouldn't she find herself there, on that yacht, in that moment, no matter what she did? Or more accurately, could she even choose to do something else?

The entire thing was maddening, and she had no idea what to do.

Keep looking, keep moving, or find a safe place to hunker down with her baby and hide?

She was still trying to figure it out when Wyatt invited her out for the day.

———

"I JUST GOT SOME UNDERGRADS. Fresh out of Stanford. I want to break them in."

"I don't know, Wyatt."

"Come on, it'll be fun. Walk around Waikiki, get dinner, nothing to it. Leave Bea with Chris and come out with us."

"Chris is doing a data purge today, and—"

"You really want to just sit on the ship all day? Come on, it's Honolulu!"

His myling was watching her, its eyes far too big. Too eager. Just like its owner. Tharsis wanted nothing to do with either of them. There was no intelligence to be gathered on a pub crawl. But Chris had nothing for her to do, and she was driving herself crazy, thinking about her next step.

Remember the last time you thought no harm would come of it? she asked herself.

Still.

"Sure, okay," she said. "Why not?"

She left Bea with Chris and grudgingly headed out.

Tourism elsewhere in Hawaii may have been restricted to only the ultra-rich, but Oahu still boasted a bustling metropolis, far larger than any other island city the *Vastitas Reach* had visited thus far. Much like Sydney, though, the city was a faded jewel. At the height of its glory, the Silicone Age was said to have built grand skyscrapers, glass and steel towers that reached into the heavens and shook with the winds. Abstract geometry had been the height of fashion, and countries had vied for ever more impressive structures. Honolulu had a few such examples, huge towers that were all the more impressive for the gravity they had to withstand.

Few such structures were built on Mars. Not so high, not so flashy. Arran architecture was meant to endure, to inspire, and to guard.

But Honolulu, while boasting its few examples of past grandeur, already showed the cracks of the coming Euphemism. Ragged tents clustered thick on the sidewalks, trash everywhere. Barefooted children, malnourished and dirty, looked at them with huge eyes, while adults lounged in drug-induced stupors, propped up against walls or sprawled flat on old asphalt.

Wyatt's little group of young college students chattered and laughed, moving through those streets seemingly untroubled. West they headed, towards a row of massive hotels fronting onto a sandy beach, milky-white waves beyond.

Their first stop on the sands, a booth with a palm-thatched roof and dark-polished wood beams out front, looked like any number of local structures Tharsis had seen throughout the Pacific. But inside, the place had the sterile appearance of a medical facility, spare, modern, with glass-fronted cabinets displaying vials. Backlit in neon blue.

"What is this?" Tharsis asked Wyatt quietly.

He looked at her like she had just asked what the ocean was. "It's the enhancement center," he said, confused.

"Excuse me?"

"This is where we get the local enhancement strain. I want to run a little experiment with the kids. I want to see what they'll see."

Enhancement strain? she wanted to ask.

The answer became apparent almost immediately, though.

Scattered around the floor were couches, sparse leather furniture barely recognizable as such. A few held bodies, still, perhaps asleep.

Tharsis walked around one, curious.

The man had an injection mark in his arm. Blue patterns spreading out around it.

"I wouldn't recommend that level of depth for you," a voice said behind her. A girl, dressed in some barely there flower-print dress. Smiling. Salesclerk, Tharsis realized. "Not if you're new to the blue. But we do have quite a few shallower enhancements that are well worth exploring."

"What do you mean?"

The salesgirl looked confused. "What better way to experience all that the quarter has to offer than one of our designer ilu impressions?"

"Can we get seven vials?" one of Wyatt's new students asked, coming over.

"Six," Tharsis told the salesgirl.

The other whitecoat looked at Wyatt. "I thought you said she was cool."

"Cultural objection," Tharsis said. The whitecoats all seemed to back down when she said something like that.

"It's fine, Perez," Wyatt said with a shake of his head. "She's Navajo. Remember I told you about that?"

"Six vials it is, then," the salesgirl said cheerfully.

The whitecoats all carried their own injectors, it seemed, the vials clicking in and needles sinking deep with very little effort. Tharsis watched the whole affair, doing her best to keep her disgust down.

If he'd mentioned anything like this, she wouldn't have come.

Since when was Wyatt into drugs, anyway?

———

WYATT DID INDEED SEEM to be running some kind of experiment. Out of the half dozen students, he handed three of them a couple of cards. Glyphs, that writing system he was working on so diligently. She'd seen bits and pieces of his work over the previous months; the symbols, the entire concept, made her uncomfortable.

Wyatt chatted with them as they walked, a small digital voice recorder in his hand catching the entire conversation. The ones who had the glyph cards seemed to be having a deeper experience than the others. Different. They spoke of some old-world glory: an empty beach, surfers on wooden boards, nothing but jungle. The ones without the cards seemed to just describe a heightened version of what was actually there. The modern architecture. The crowds.

They wandered around the beach district, in and out of the grand hotel lobbies, cavernous spaces filled with the sound of fountains and thick with the sweet scent of flowers. It should have been beautiful.

All it did was make her more uneasy.

The stories from the undergrads changed as they passed through those. Wyatt handed out more cards.

Every once in a while, Tharsis caught a glimpse of what the others were seeing. It was subtly different for all of them, but after a few flashes of it, she realized it could all likely be described in much the same way. Impressions. Shadows. Details. The feel of things.

She wasn't sure how. That natural immunity of hers should have cancelled it all out. Or so she would have thought; other than the incident with the junkie in Singapore, she hadn't been bothered by ilu much during her time on Earth. Something deeper was going on. Something more… external.

Maybe it was the cards.

What had he said about it? Finding the language under language?

Some way to hack the human brain?

Wyatt had, apparently, ordered a fairly low dose for everyone, and after about ninety minutes, it started to wear off. By that point, it was late enough for an early dinner, and the group settled into some little café situated right on the beach. Everyone kicked their shoes off, dug their toes in the sand, laughed about nonsensical things until the first round of drinks came.

Then, things got a bit more academic. What they saw, what it could have meant. All the students were very curious now.

Alcohol, apparently, killed the stuff in the bloodstream. Chris had told her that at one point.

Tharsis tuned out the chatter. Ate her fish tacos slowly and kept her eyes to the beach.

She watched the sun set over the vast, shallow bay.

The water was wrong, but the light was right.

Was the yacht—was the Flet—here?

"What did you see?"

It was one of the students. Tharsis started. "What do you mean?"

"It's a good question," Wyatt asked. He'd had three drinks by then, blue and slushy. But he still had one of his ubiquitous notebooks out, and his handwriting was steady as ever. "What do you see, Amanda?"

His myling was out beyond the line of tables, playing in the water. Outdoors like this, the damn thing seemed as large as the mountains.

What was it doing? Where was it coming from?

"Not much."

<hr>

AFTER DINNER, they meandered back to the *Vastitas*. A few of the group purchased more ilucoccine shots. At other booths scattered around the beach. At the harbor on the way back onto the ship. Tharsis wasn't sure why. If the effects wore off that quickly, or if they were just enjoying it. It seemed a foolish thing to do. One of Skip's ironclad rules was no drugs shipside.

Drinking was allowed though, and Wyatt had had more than a few beers on the way.

He still insisted on walking her back to her cabin.

"See, I told you it'd be fun," he said, words slurring a little as she unlocked her door.

"It was interesting," she agreed, without really agreeing. There was liquor on his breath, sharp, unpleasant. "The whole thing with the ilucoccine shots…"

"I should have warned you. I remember you telling me you aren't interested in any of that," he said. "But you really should try it some-time because it works. Tonight was proof, proof of a concept I've been working on for a long time. The glyphs make the visions more real. Like anything's possible. Which it is." Wyatt smiled, and leaned in against the jam, waggling his notebook. "We should be celebrating this. Through this could lie the answer to the question." He slapped his notebook against her shoulder. "You should read it sometime."

"Right," Tharsis said, and took the book away from his alcohol-limp fingers, sliding it into her pocket without thinking, "your Ariums's question."

She tried to shut the door, but he slapped a hand against it, holding it open. "I looked you up, you know."

Heart picking up speed, Tharsis forced her voice to stay neutral. "What do you mean?"

"I looked you up. Amanda Redhorse. Navajo Nation, last registered address in northern Arizona. One of the separatist states." He shook his head, movement unsteady. "You're not in the Ariums's directory. Which I find strange, considering the splice you travel with."

Fuck. Fuck fuck fuck. "I'm a courier," she lied, thinking fast.

"From where? Singapore?" he asked, more pointed now. "The arium there had a break-in a few months ago. Right around the time we got into port."

His fingers drummed on the door, arhythmic. Still nervous, she realized, and wondered what he was trying to prove here. What he was trying to get out of her.

How drunk he was.

His myling, tiny again, tugged at her skirt, reaching up underneath. Trying to get to the pocket, she realized. Its fingers burned.

None of the other women were back from their own shore excursions yet. The hallway was deserted. Wyatt wasn't a particularly large man, but he had a few kilos on her, and she didn't trust her limited self-defense skills in Earth's heavier gravity.

Michael, she thought silently, *get me through this.*

"Well?" Wyatt asked and touched her shoulder. "Care to explain? Or should I go talk to our head Arium rep on board?"

Tharsis choked her rising anxiety down and went on the offensive.

"What are you trying to do here, Wyatt? The hell do you want out of me?"

"I..."

"'Cause I think you've got too much scat in your bloodstream right now to realize what you're saying. Are you trying to threaten me, hold something over me, so I'll what, suck your dick?"

The researcher blinked, and then looked at his hand, like he hadn't realized where it was. "I... I wasn't..."

"Move your hand," she hissed at him.

He actually took a step back. "Amanda, I wasn't trying to—"

"I have no idea what's running through your head right now, but my business is my business and where I'm taking my little girl has fuck-all to do with you," Tharsis snapped.

"I just wanted to ask—"

"The answer to that question is no."

He stood there for a moment, looking tired, used up. Around his mouth, trailing out from a corner of his lips, was a thin, meandering line of blue. Then he shook himself. "I'm sorry, that isn't… that isn't how I meant for that to go."

Tharsis wasn't sure if she believed that or not. She still wasn't sure what he wanted out of her, truly wanted. If she was just sensitive because of everything that had happened with tDaer. But that myling was leaving fiery scratches on her leg now, and Wyatt had lied to her about his intentions once already that day. She didn't particularly care about sparing his feelings. "Dinner was good, Wyatt."

"Yeah, it was."

"I need to go get Bea," Tharsis said.

Slammed the door in his face.

She waited a few agonizing minutes, long enough for him to retreat, and then started running.

DISEMBARKING EARLY the next morning was tough.

The *Vastitas Reach* had become, in its own strange way, home. Bea's home, and Tharsis was ripping her away from it.

It wasn't that Tharsis wanted to go. Not at all. But she was traveling with a stolen identity, one with a nationality that most of the whitecoats seemed fairly emotional about, and she wasn't sure what would happen if she got exposed as a fraud. She wasn't sure how far Wyatt was willing to take things; he threw himself into everything zealously.

She had thought maybe, maybe, she could stay. Keep sailing. Keep working. Let Bea grow up here, at least for a while longer.

Wasn't a choice she could make now.

The baby was wide awake as Tharsis carried her and their pack down the gangplank. The Arran had taken as many of the little toys and trinkets from the crew as she could, but the playpen, however portable, was too bulky to take along. The other large items they'd been given, along with most of the books, she'd likewise had to leave behind. Tharsis felt guilty about that.

"I'm sorry to see you go," Chris told her. "I was hoping you could stick around for a while."

"Me too," she said honestly.

"I've got some contacts in the local pioneer group. I can put you in touch if you'd like."

It was an honest offer.

There was so much she could have told him. About Earth's future. About what was coming. But most of all, she wished she could tell him that his efforts wouldn't be in vain. Mars would have an ocean, a living ocean, a living ecosphere, again. Soon. A mere handful of decades. How many, she still didn't know.

Thanks to people like him, scientists and sailors and technical minds she'd never heard of.

Tharsis promised herself, if she ever made it home, she'd tell their story. Tell everyone. For as basic as their work seemed, it was essential to creating the world where she'd grown up. Its sky and its air and its water.

"I'd appreciate that," she said. There was no other gratitude she could express.

He held out a small envelope. "It's not much, but it's good currency once you get away from the coast. Hang on to that."

"Skip paid me."

"You've got the little one. Take care of her."

She looked at it for a moment, then decided she didn't care what the fuck happened. What changed. She looked back up at him. "Tell your family, if any of them are offered a berth on a, umm, a spacecraft with long-term stasis, called the *Padua Anthony*, don't take it."

"Can you tell me why?"

"Probably shouldn't."

He nodded, expression grown serious. "I don't know what you are, Amanda, but it's more than you claim. Wherever you're going with that little girl of ours, you take care of her."

Tharsis bounced Bea in her sling. The baby giggled her wheezing little giggle and clapped her hands happily. "Don't worry about her," she said. "This kiddo's going to outlive us all."

"Good to hear," he said.

He gave her a hug before she left. Fatherly and warm.

She realized, as she was walking away from the ship, it was the first time anybody besides Bea had touched her in months.

Tharsis wiped her eyes and didn't look back.

———

THANKS TO CHRIS'S offer of help, Tharsis found a small guesthouse on the edge of some old residential neighborhood that took her and Bea, no questions asked. It was old but pleasant enough, with a proprietor who always looked as if she'd just stepped out of a wind tunnel. Genial, though, and quite taken with little Bea, saying the baby reminded her of her own grandchildren. She even gave Tharsis a discount.

It took Tharsis only half a day to find work.

It was a neighborhood agricultural center, something ubiquitous on Mars. Back home, such places existed more out of tradition than anything else; self-sufficiency was a quality strongly valued in Arran culture. In urban areas where families didn't have space for a proper production garden, a few dedicated acres with small, high-density crop beds and wintertime greenhouses for rent was an ideal solution.

Here, though, it seemed that the community gardens were kept for other reasons. Subsistence for one, profit another; excess food was allowed to be sold. A whole network of gardens kept the better hotels downtown with a constant stream of sun-grown produce. Judging from the gaunt faces of some of the children in the area, though, Tharsis wondered how much of what was sold was truly extra, beyond the needs of the local community.

She couldn't judge it too harshly. The entire archipelago nation, outside of the glittering resorts and state-of-the-art research facilities, seemed desperately poor. They'd once been part of America, or so she'd heard, rich and prosperous. But the last war had left North America exhausted, even before civil unrest had begun in earnest, and after gaining their independence, this was what Hawaii had sunk to.

At least, that's what she could gather. Even now, there seemed to be competing narratives on what had truly happened.

Tharsis didn't recognize most of the crops. Many were tropical in nature, things that would never have survived on Mars. Others were more familiar. Squash, peppers, tomatoes, corn, strange varieties of potatoes and greens. Beans too, lots of beans. A small orchard that was mostly citrus, something she'd only seen in specialized greenhouses before.

There were animals too, in some quantity. Goats, sheep. Chickens, which seemed surprising; most people kept their own on Mars. Even a few huge animals that Tharsis only recognized from history books, like cows. Brahmans, she was told, as she walked around the facility with the manager.

"I have experience with everything but the cows," she told him. "I'm willing to do anything, but the baby stays with me."

"If you're willing to actually pick up chicken shit and stay off the ilu when you're on shift, you have yourself a deal," he replied.

The pay was decent, and Bea could stay with her.

She took it.

———

TUCKED INTO AN UNFAMILIAR BED, Bea asleep in her arms, Tharsis dreamed that night. She dreamed again. Of the divedrive, exploding. tDaer dying. That endless walk back to Noqumiut.

The yacht and the darkness and the rain after.

The Flet, next to her. Not the cadet, not Tom Donner. The Flet. Limbs missing, nondescript flight suit. Exactly the same as she'd seen him in the Arran embassy, all those months ago. Standing in front of her, sunlight streaming through his indistinct form.

It wasn't right, that light.

Sunset.

It was sunset.

But not the right sunset.

Not sunset on the yacht-that-was. The marina-that-had-been. There was no dock. There was the sound of the surf and faint outlines on the shore behind her, beneath low, creeping brush, delineating where buildings had once been.

But even that wasn't right. Everything was blurred, indistinct. Like looking up through shallow water.

Below her feet was nothing.

"This is an oob," she said.

The Flet sat down. On what, she couldn't properly see. The yacht deck, perhaps. Nothing made any sense. "Of sorts."

"Is this my time?" she asked, spreading her hands.

"Would you like it to be?"

Tharsis wasn't sure what to say to that, and judging from his sad smile, he knew what she was thinking.

"I don't know how to get you home, Ambera. I don't know how you ended up here in the first place."

It was frustratingly obtuse. Where was here? "I don't know if going home is really the right call anymore," she admitted.

"Ah. Bea. My little navigator." Tharsis looked at him sharply. His smile got a little less sad, just for a moment. "Don't worry about her."

"Before, before Noqumiut, you told me I would see her again," she said. "Did you know about this?"

"Did I? A moment I haven't reached yet, perhaps."

"Why am I here?" she asked, tired. "I dragged myself halfway across this planet, for this. Why?"

"There's something waiting out there in the night. A room," he said, "and in that room is my body. What happens from there, once you're inside, I don't know. I can't see it. I can't touch this place. Hence…" and he gestured, as if that single motion was some kind of explanation. "We're so close to the edge now. Any moment, we'll tip off."

"Into what?"

He was quiet for a moment. "An arium. An experiment, perhaps, a proof-of-concept test. Unmoored from where it should be, plunged deep beneath the surface currents of time, maybe. Nothing is flowing right around it anymore."

"This doesn't make any sense," she pleaded.

"Get me out, Ambera, before anything else collapses into their nightmares."

She woke sweating, guilty.

———

IT WAS LATE JANUARY NOW, February only a few days away. Time moved fast on Earth. Tharsis marveled at it; on Mars, with its longer years, the seasons lingered.

Tharsis often found her early days taken up with collecting eggs, spreading feed, or mucking out pens. The manager had a dog who kept ferals away from the chickens and birds out of the grain beds.

Tharsis tried to talk with her on several occasions, but she was a herder and not all that interested in conversations with humans. Sometimes, the manager had her do simple data entry, or working small tasks. Checking the crops, rotating things in the greenhouse. It was a concept that was being tested out in a few places, she was told.

A way around a lot of the harsh agricultural restrictions in place in the Islands.

Most mornings, if she got up early enough, she would have an hour or two for herself before she had to head to the ag center and start work. Usually, she spent that time feeding Bea, and letting the baby have some free time on a blanket on the floor. Let her play a little bit, stretch her tiny arms and legs out, before going in the sling for the day.

But sometimes, she'd take her coffee and watch the sun rise to the east, over the distant ocean. A brilliant display of golds and pinks. The sun was larger in the sky than back home, and its rising and setting always seemed like grand events. Whatever was coming, she was still grateful for the chance to see the sun over Earth.

Why humanity had given this up, she couldn't understand.

Despite being in the middle of a city, it was peaceful. Bea had some routine in her day, and Tharsis had enough time in the afternoons to walk them both to the library. Look at the books, see the other little kids playing. Bea wasn't anywhere near the point where she could join in, but Tharsis figured it was good for her anyway. Her chubby little hands, becoming more articulate by the day, always clapped with excitement.

Back home, nobody did this alone. Family would come in if they could, or friends from the parish would stop by. Almost everyone had big families, and yet, everybody made time to help each other. Those were habits ground deep into the Arran soul. Few communities would have made it through the winters of the early settlement days without some such spirit.

There were no winters here in Hawaii, though.

Tharsis longed to see snow.

———

DESPITE HERSELF, Tharsis still found herself looking for the Flet. The island seemed right. Its sunsets. The easterly mountains. The smell of rainfall, when it came.

When Bea wasn't at the library or napping, when Tharsis wasn't working, she looked.

She checked every civilian harbor, all along the western edge of the island. None seemed right. None were a match for the place she'd seen.

One Sunday, in frustration, she returned to Waikiki and the little café where everything had started going so wrong with Wyatt. The food had been good, and it had seemed like a peaceful place to think.

But as she was waiting for her lunch, Bea playing in the sand by her feet, she saw something unexpected.

Across the water, to the north, a gigantic gray airplane was taking off.

Tharsis watched it for a moment, fascinated. Fixed-wing atmospheric craft were rare on Mars, and she hadn't seen one so large, so close, at all on Earth.

There were markings on its tail, faint but still legible at this distance.

USAF.

Some kind of patch.

Military.

Military.

Hadn't both the Flet and Peter Donovan had those haircuts?

"Excuse me," she asked the waiter, when the man came back to fill up her water glass, "but is there a military base here?"

"Yeah, I'd say so," he chuckled.

CHAPTER
THIRTY-FOUR

ASAPH BASE WAS the most lively place Caleb had been yet.

At least it wasn't under attack. That was new.

It had taken the *Barachiel* a few hours to reach the place once they'd entered the Arran inwell. Caleb had found an empty station in Ops, and just listened. They'd been given priority clearance through the magnetosphere, but it had still taken almost two hours to maneuver into their anchor position in the moon's orbital path. From there, more priority clearance was requested and eventually rewarded, to send the rockjump down to the base's main port. The craft's larger personnel transport was a few hours behind.

Caleb was glad for the change of spacecraft. The rockjump had a far better view than anything else on the *Barachiel*.

Adair, Aeolis, and Morray, along with two of his sergeants, came with him.

Deimos wasn't a huge moon, far too small to have crushed itself into a sphere. The crew had told Caleb that it was barely even visible from the surface of Mars. Over the centuries, the ASDF had crafted it into the largest military base in the Heliosphere, and it was here, he was told, that he normally woke up after dying.

Asaph Base took up most of its surface, with only a few square kilometers left open as training grounds or standoff distance from the Lighthouse facility. Far from the glittering spires of New Stockholm, or the open plans of Gloaming Station or the Elysium Monastery, Asaph resembled some metallic coral reef, structures built on top of each other, expanding or merging almost without plan.

Both Aeolis and Morray pointed out major areas on the surface. Maintenance facilities, atmo-controlled training fields, the Command headquarters. One area, slightly removed from the rest, boasted glass domes, interlocked.

"That's the rest and recovery resort," Morray said, when asked.

"The what?"

"Anybody who spends more than a home-year out on void duty has a mandatory quarantine period before he can head down to the surface."

"Void exposure does all sorts of weird things to the human body," Aeolis added. "The lack of gravity alone…"

"But there's gravity on the *Barachiel*."

"Only because of the dive core. And even then," Morray said with a shrug, "it's not really the same."

"You'd think we could have figured this out by now," Caleb said.

Aeolis shrugged. "We have."

———

A REPRESENTATIVE from the Historian's Office met the rockjump at the landing pad.

It was more of a reception than Caleb had been expecting. He hadn't thought they'd send anyone.

It was an older woman, with the same milky eyes that Colonel Cambel had, body wisp-thin from too many years in mig. Braces ran from her waist down to her legs and white hair clung to her temples.

"Caleb," she said as he and Adair neared, "it's so good to see you again." She extended a hand. It trembled.

Nobody had been that familiar with him yet, and he gave Adair a questioning look, even as he shook back. "I don't remember you."

"Of course not, you never do. I was the lead on your last regeneration, twenty years ago, and a team member on the one before that, almost forty."

"I die that often?"

She laughed. "They like to keep you out in the fleet. They aren't exactly safe postings. I was hoping I would see you once. Not like this, though."

"I appreciate that," he said, not sure what else to offer her, and rolled a shoulder blade under his backpack. "I'm told I can access my private library here."

"Yes, yes, of course. But we have some procedures…"

"I don't have time for that right now, ma'am," he told her.

"We've got a tight agenda for this visit," Aeolis added.

She glanced at him, like she hadn't noticed him before. "What kind of agenda? We weren't informed."

That had been at the colonel's recommendation. Asaph was, apparently, a hotbed of politics, and he'd suggested avoiding all that by not releasing a schedule.

"May I ask what you're looking for?"

"No."

She sighed. "And what can we do for you boys?" That was directed at the *Barachiel* personnel.

"Quant time," Morray said, "and access to one of the big holopits."

"Let me see what I can do."

———

WHAT SHE COULD DO TURNED out to be quite a bit. Within the hour, she'd arranged for all of it, and came to fetch Caleb from the officers' lounge attached to the DV hangar.

"The facility location is a bit of an open secret," the historian told him, as she led him to another hangar, one where she promised the ground vehicles were kept, "but there are a few of those out here, so we don't worry about that too much. Access is limited to just you, key-coded to your DNA."

"Nobody's ever accessed it?"

"And survived? No."

"What," he asked, smiling a little, "there some kind of *Indiana Jones* temple guardian thing?"

"There's no breathable atmo in the facility, but enough xenon to kill an ENEX. Static fields deactivate conventional pressure suits and gear. You'll have to rely on one of the facility's bottled air breathers, and that storage container can only be opened with your palm print. The security system constantly monitors respiration for trace DNA. Somebody can fake a sample, maybe even fake a few breaths, but longer than that? It's no good."

"What if somebody brings their own air? Mechanical only, no circuits to screw with."

"There's atmo there, but not much. You'll have fifteen seconds to strip off any void gear you're wearing and reach the cabinet with the bottles. Then, the lock gets flooded with the same xenon air mix as the rest of the facility."

"What if you bring your own bottles?"

"Inadvisable. Without confirmation that it is the Landlord breathing into one of the bottles, the entire place will depressurize."

He thought about that for a minute. Jesus fuck. What the hell was hiding in there? "Did I install it?"

"Every modification has been made with your oversight, yes." It was her turn to smile. "Nobody understands the programming language you used. You normally pay the place a visit every few Heliosphere-standard years, make sure everything's operational."

"Drop off a new notebook?"

"I don't know, sir. Restricted Journal entries are supposed to be rare." She eyed him. "We don't see you that often."

"Some of the guys have told me Mars doesn't like having you around."

"We Arrans have a complicated relationship with the Tenancy."

"The Tenancy seems like a load of bullshit."

"It's meant to keep us safe from the old ways, the ways that led to the Euphemism." They were in front of another air lock. She paused at the door, checking something on the control panel. "The hangar should be cleared for you, sir."

"From what I can tell, the shit you call the Euphemism never ended," he told her. "Not with Noqumiut still around."

The old woman blinked, cloudy eyes sad. "Yours is the six-wheeler that's powered up, sir. Ground control will walk you through the exit."

"You're not coming?"

She held out a sealed file. "No sir, this is your domain. Be careful."

THE SECURITY MEASURES were what the old historian had described. Perfectly.

Moving through it all was a bit nerve-wracking. He had left himself enough time to manage it without a huge time crunch. That surprised him a little.

As did what he walked into, when he opened the inner air lock door.

Fog.

Fog and mist and rain.

It was the arium, he realized. The same one he'd seen in the Undine Glory. The place where the glyph-language had been born.

Bea and Rallison were arguing about something, their gestures swift, Rallison's short and biting, Bea's exaggerated. He didn't bother trying to figure out what it was about. This was the first time he'd slipped back to the same place twice.

Had to be significant.

"Ladies," he said, and whistled for Tyr. "Let's figure out why the hell we're here, okay?"

Between the four of them, it only took about fifteen minutes to explore the entire place. If it was an arium, it was a small one. It lacked the expansive nature that many of these places did. One lab space, the place where all boards were set up. A bathroom with a shower stall and a bank of small lockers. A small kitchen and dining area. Upstairs, a few bedrooms with Western furniture and tatami mat floors. Everything smelled of dry grass. Even Tyr couldn't sniff out anything significant.

"There are clothes up there, personal effects," Rallison observed, after they regrouped in what had to be the dining area. There were a few floor tables scattered around the floor mats. "Things are put away. I'd guess whoever lives here is coming back. That Wyatt guy Bea was talking about."

Tyr sent an impression to Caleb. Flowers fading, grass growing. "Dog says he's been gone a few days," Caleb interpreted.

Bea came in and tossed something down on the table between them. =Found something,= she announced.

A flyer, written in both Japanese and English.

=It's one of their annual symposiums,= she said. =They host a few of these every year. Showcase new developments, networking, that sort of thing.=

=It's dated for this week. Already started.=

"And?"

=Wyatt Blalock's the keynote speaker,= she said.

But as Caleb tried to reach for it, the entire world dissolved.

His own private library reasserted itself.

No answers to be found.

———

FOR SOMETHING with so much buildup, so much reverence, with so much security, it seemed too small. Too tight a space to carry such weight.

Hexagonal, six meters to a side. One bookcase stood at the far end of the room, ancient wood obviously oiled and cared for. A writing desk of the same wood. An armchair of unfamiliar design was positioned in the center. Bolted to the floor. All else was matte-gray metal. A fan whirred quietly overhead.

He was getting sick of this world, this Heliosphere, with its secrets and its mausoleums and the death of all they had hoped for. Caleb had been young when the plague came to his town, young when he'd enlisted. He'd still had hope. Too many things had been buried, though.

How was he supposed to find answers like this?

The bookcase was mostly empty. Notebooks ran across one shelf.

A tablet sat on the writing desk. A note, taped to it. *Watch me first.*

It was Caleb's own handwriting.

"Interesting that doesn't change," he muttered to himself, and powered the thing up.

Command line prompts led him to a video. A single video. The only file contained on the tablet, from what he could tell.

"Caleb, wish I could say it's good to talk to you."

It was his voice, his face. Impossibly aged. A nasty scar ran temple to chin on the left side of his face, and his white hair was buzzed short. His voice was still strong, though.

"It means that I died again, though, and I can't say I'm looking forward to that. How many times it'll be, when you're watching this, who the hell knows." His older self scrubbed a hand across his shorn scalp. "You might be wondering what this place is. You're probably wondering what this whole fucking thing is about. It's about Mars, my friend. They may not seem like your people right now, but you're the reason they're here. They know that. We, I, did a lot for them in this life. I'm proud of what we've made of this place. I'm proud of them."

Caleb paused it and glanced back at the bookshelf again. Six books. All of this, for six books? He hit play again.

"Why this place? Our war for Earth, it's being forgotten. It's passing out of living memory, Caleb. When the last of this generation is gone, nobody will remember it. But it's not over. Maybe it never will be. In fact, I've got to go deal with it again now. Some nonsense on Europa." The image turned, and Caleb realized it had been taken in this exact room. The bookcase was there, but only one book was on the shelf. "There are things they're already forgetting. There are things we have to let them forget. Some things need to pass away. You know why. But some things you're going to need to know. You have to carry it for them, Caleb."

"So why didn't I carry that shit out at Noqumiut?" he muttered into his breathing mask, but the recording couldn't answer.

"Besides, there's a little project we started, back after we died that last time on Earth. Donner's slips. They drag me along sometimes, maybe once every few years or so. I write it down because Bea always did. She always said it was important." The old man on the screen shifted. "I've never talked about it before, so fucking respect that, okay? And recopy it from time to time, so the pages don't dissolve from age."

That was why it looked different, then.

"Take care of them, Caleb. They'll need you, even if they don't realize it."

The tablet went dark, and Caleb laid it aside.

The books on the shelf contained the same columns, the same type of alphanumeric annotations, as what he'd taken from his barracks room. From the sand of the *Undine Glory*.

He just hoped Morray and Aeolis could make some sense out of it.

"Why couldn't you fuckers have left me some directions?" he asked.

But like so many things in this time, there was no answer forthcoming.

CHAPTER
THIRTY-FIVE

DESPITE THE INFORMATION retrieved by the Landlord, Morray didn't have a whole lot to go on.

"Not many instances here," he'd said, when the Rossen had handed him another small notebook. "Maybe two dozen? I don't know if that's going to be enough."

"It's all I could find. Maybe there were more I didn't write down."

"Or maybe this is a very rare occurrence," Aeolis had said.

"Either way, I need you guys to start working on it for me." The Landlord had looked uncomfortable. "I have a few stops I need to make, planetside. How long do you think it'll take?"

"Sir—"

"I know, nobody wants me down there. But nobody's made any kind of notifications to a couple of these families, and I thought I should take care of that."

"Nobody on the crew's died since…"

"Major Lanin, the Humphryes base commander. I, uhh, I understand he was trying to save me. I owe his family… something." He'd sighed. "And that lieutenant, Chen, is missing. Nobody's told her family shit. Thought I should."

That had been yesterday.

Morray and two of his best techs had been eyeballs deep in data manipulation since then. A number of the Headquarters's quant specialists had volunteered their days off to help work on the problem. A good challenge was always irresistible.

And the Rossen's data was a challenge.

It had taken the team ten hours to crack the second set of positioning coordinates. It was formatted like pulsar location data, but most of the stars being referenced weren't located in the Milky Way. That little breakthrough had come from another sheet, tucked in near the back of one of the Rossen's more recent Journals. Once they had that, things went a little easier.

Quantum computers were always a challenge. The *Barachiel*'s was mostly used for Heliosphere weather prediction and navigation, continuously running a best-guess model of conditions anywhere in the entire system. Down under the surface of space-time, right into the penumbra. The core didn't necessarily need that, but it helped maximize efficiency on dives if they knew exactly what the gravitational currents looked like.

There were a breathtaking number of variables to consider, and any small fluctuation in the input data from one of half a dozen craftside functions could send it into a tailspin. Their quant was scaled to the divedrive's needs and ran new programs only with the utmost reluctance. Morray wasn't an expert himself, but three of his techs had been through the grueling quant course. Useless for anything with the silics, but experts on that crazy little black box humming away in the bowels of the *Barachiel*. But even they couldn't set up a proper simulation.

They'd needed the functionality of the Deimos navigation quant. Bigger and better. A thousand operating simulations they could tap into for reference at need.

It had taken another few hours to find, locate, and tap into the correct star maps, but with the help of the local team, they'd managed.

Now, they were close.

Very close.

Morray was still working on programming the Landlord's space-time coordinates into the quant simulation when the team from the Homeworld Command Council showed up.

"Who's running this little project?"

The other comm officer gave Morray a shrug, barely glancing up from his terminal. Morray sighed. Technically, the other guy outranked him, but the Landlord had left him in charge. And this was a HOMECOM colonel glaring at them right now. No headquarters junior staff officer was going to stick his neck out in front of that.

Morray hooked a thumb through the waist strap of his uniform, trying to stay calm. "What can I do for you, sir?"

The colonel's expression didn't change. "I need you to pack up your team and head back to the *Barachiel*."

"Sir, with all respect, we're working on—"

"Something for the Landlord, yes, I've been told." At that, the colonel's face did twitch a bit. "But this is diverting critical resources from other HOMECOM initiatives."

"What's more critical than the Landlord's orders?"

"The *Barachiel* has a functioning quant."

"Sir, a myling nearly fucked it to hell a few sevendays ago."

"I've read that report, yes."

"Then you won't mind if I continue doing what the Landlord's told me to do."

"Lieutenant, you and your men are to stop working and vacate this position immediately."

"On whose orders?"

The colonel was definitely getting irate now. "HOMECOM operations commander, General O'Bryn. He reports directly to General Scrivner. You may have heard of him."

Scat, Morray thought. "I need to talk to my commander first."

"I'm right here, Hans," Colonel Cambel said, coming up behind the HOMECOM team.

"Sir, you understand I can't transfer this data, and I can't replicate it craftside," Morray protested, waving a hand back at the monolith in the center of the room. "If I stop, we lose it. I lose the model."

"What exactly are you trying to model?" the other colonel asked.

"I'm not sure if the Landlord—"

"Tell him, Hans," Cambel said.

Morray still hesitated. He wasn't sure himself what they were looking at.

The other officer, the guy in charge who'd volunteered to stay and do this, spoke up. "Space-time is ripping, Colonel Nelssen. Or compressing. I'm not quite sure how to describe it. Like a string in a dog's guts, bunching everything up together, wrapping it in on itself."

"And?"

"We're trying to find the string."

"So the Landlord can un-fuck it," Morray added.

The colonel stared at him. *Right*, Morray reminded himself, *don't curse around headquarters staff officers.* It was easy to get inured to rank out on the *Barachiel*, but things worked differently back home. "Does this have anything to do with some of the stranger things we're hearing about out in the Jovian inwell?"

Morray could have died from relief. "We know it has to do with the Flet and the inoperability of the dive core network. If there are other effects being felt elsewhere…"

"There are." The colonel, Nelssen, clearly looked torn. "You boys have keyed this into General O'Bryn's favorite holopit."

"It's the best suited for displaying the final data set," the other comm officer said. "I offered it. It's my responsibility."

"I don't need you falling on a sword for this."

"I really did offer it, sir."

"We have a scat-ton of movement right now, and we're going to need this prepped for tomorrow afternoon's strategic briefing. Prep starts at fifteen hundred hours. You understand?"

"We can be done by then."

Cambel clapped the other colonel on the shoulder. "Mads, come on. The boys have this well under control. We'll meet the commander's intent, keep the Landlord happy, and maybe keep the Heliosphere from ripping apart in the process," and he smiled with a very obvious forced mirth. "Now, you promised me a trip to that new officers' club they opened out on the edge of the training wastes. You can see the aurora out there, right?"

"Ignace, don't fuck me on this."

"If my boys say they can do it, they can do it," Cambel said, and gave Morray a look. "We'll talk about this later, Hans."

Morray nodded. Once. Tight. "As long as we can finish this up."

After Cambel finally talked the other colonel out of the room, the other comm officer collapsed, falling into a cross-legged position on the floor. "Scat, that was close."

"Man seems like a hard-ass."

"You have no idea." He ran a hand back through his hair. "We gotta get this done by tomorrow morning, or we are fucked. General O'Bryn is an absolute monster when it comes to his briefings."

"Why use this room then?"

"Nothing was on the schedule." He shook himself and pushed back up. "Come on, let's finish that data set."

Just about then, Aeolis came back with a stack of insulated meal containers. He'd volunteered to hit up the chummer, as nobody else was in a position to leave. "What'd I miss?"

"Lieutenant Morray told a colonel to go fuck himself," one of the techs said with a laugh.

"That is not what I said."

"Don't swear at senior officers, Hans," Aeolis said with a sigh. He set the food down. "All they had left were pasties. Hope everybody's okay with that. Now seriously, where are we at?"

———

"DO THEY ALWAYS LEAVE SNACKS OUT?" Caleb asked and popped another handful of dried cranberries in his mouth. He had no idea what they'd been candied in, but they were good.

"Only when distinguished visitors are in town," Cambel replied.

"That would be you," Stag added. He'd helped himself to a drink from the minibar, some amber-colored liquid that smelled similar to whiskey.

"Ahh." Caleb chewed slower. Tyr pawed at his leg, and he tossed one of the berries to the dog. Tyr sniffed it, and went back to pawing at his leg, the half-formed image of meat coming unbidden into Caleb's mind. Maybe they could get him some jerky. "I thought I wasn't popular around here."

"Protocol is what it is."

His trip to the surface had been strange. Another ASDF representative—Senior DeLaCroix, some kind of protocol sergeant—had met him at the Lift base with a small flyer that looked similar to the rockjump, stubby wings and all. It didn't seem like something that should have stayed in the air, but it got them to his two stops fast.

Lanin's wife had cried. Hugged him.

Chen's mother had invited him in for lunch.

Both lived in more rural conditions than he'd expected. Ranching families, like his own had been, except that cows seemed to have never made it off Earth and the fields were dotted with the cloudy fleeces of horned sheep. The planet, or at least what he'd seen of it, had reminded him of home. The mountains. The rugged terrain, geography naked beneath a thin veneer of vegetation. Dirt in the creases of people's hands.

It wasn't home, though. Not even in this time. DeLaCroix, despite her formal service dress and polite words, had clearly been uncomfortable with his presence. Possibly angry about it. He'd gotten her smiling at least, by the end of the little trip, but he'd been glad to get back on the Lift.

How was he supposed to take care of these people? Lead them?

"Sir?" Morray stuck his head into the small room. "We're ready."

The room beyond the DV lounge was perfectly spherical, ringed about the center with a catwalk of some dark-coated metal. The coating seemed to absorb sound, and nobody's footfalls registered in the space. Lights set into the edge of the catwalk provided the only illumination. A small console was half-extruded from the wall opposite the door, a terminal of some kind clearly built into it.

"Looks like a planetarium," Caleb said, thinking about the field trip his third grade class had had to Cheyenne once. Before the world went to hell.

"We normally use this for leadership briefings, fleet movement analysis, that sort of thing," an officer said, coming out of some door near the console. "In fact, when it's not in use, you can come in here and watch every object in the Heliosphere in real time, if that's what you want."

"Real time?"

"It's a model, constantly corrected against both surveillance and Lighthouse space-time telemetry," he said. "I appreciate you coming down here this early in the morning. It's going to take me a while to get that simulation set back up for the general's briefing this afternoon."

"Sorry about the inconvenience," Cambel said.

"It's alright. Looking at your data, sir, I think we have a sizable problem on our hands."

"What kind of problem?" Caleb asked.

"Let's get into it," the officer said, and the room went dark.

"We had a bit of an argument over how best to represent this data set. There are three ways of looking at this. First, we view it from your perspective."

A trail lit up through the holopit, bright gold snaking through the solar system, out and back, with occasional loops back towards the rocky worlds.

"That's just the route we've been traveling for the past few weeks," Caleb said.

"Exactly, that's why we didn't bother running a deeper analysis on that." The view shifted. "This is what we get if we run the data against the second possible perspective, which is time-indexed to the experiences in the past."

The room filled with a massive series of overlapping spirals.

"This implies movement," Cambel said. "Dives are instantaneous."

"Yes and no. Space-time warps, ever so slightly, around the gravity wells of every large body in the Heliosphere. That's why achieving a safe distance from gravitational influence is so important when executing dives," Aeolis said. "But Caleb's been moving back and forth between Earth and whatever our location was at the time, including inwells. That implies a temporal dimension to his movement. Plus, we have to account for the duration of time that he has moved out. It's not a one-for-one time swap, indicating, again, a temporal dimension."

"This is useless," Caleb said. "There's no pattern here."

"I agree," the quant specialist agreed. "Which is why we ran it from—"

=A third perspective,= Bea signed.

Caleb blinked.

The three of them were standing in the back of the experimental craft, a Pacific sunset glowing on the horizon beyond them. In a bottle projection field, a simulacrum of Earth rotated.

=We have to time what you've seen against what's happened because of it.=

"Sir?"

Asaph. The holopit. The briefing. Caleb shook himself. "Got another one for you," he said, and Morray silently held out a napkin and pen for him. "But let me guess, you attempted to model it based on causality?"

The officer blinked as Caleb started scribbling the time down.

"No, actually, we were trying to model the Flet's perspective if—"

"The Flet's mind is so shattered I doubt his perspective is even possible to simulate," Caleb said, and passed over the napkin. "Model it on causality."

"How is that represented in the data?"

"At least since I woke up, things seem to be happening mostly in sequence. Except for the first two data points, which seem to be later." He shook his head. "Can you group them together by Earth location? I'd assume that'd get us close."

"Earth location?"

"Yeah, didn't you use the GPS coordinates?" They were staring at him. "I've been slipping back to Earth, not Mars. Is that what you used?"

"Holy hell, I was wondering why things looked so weird," the officer muttered.

"Can we pull that information from anywhere?" Cambel asked.

"I'll call the Historian's Office."

An hour later, the old woman with the milky eyes was back, a small disk in hand.

"This is silic data," the officer groaned.

"You boys are clever enough for that, aren't you?" she countered.

Another half hour of work, and the data coalesced.

The simulation began.

A path started to trace.

Again, looping. But instead of a spiral spinning off into the galaxy, it started tracing the outline of some spherical volume.

"It's an orbit," Aeolis said.

"What?"

"Look at it. It's an orbit."

"An orbit of what?"

"A moment," Caleb said, the realization hitting him. "A single point in space-time."

"What's at the center of this?" Cambel asked.

"It's focused on Earth," the quant tech said, "but off-kilter."

"It won't be focused on the center of it," Caleb said. "It's got to be somewhere on the surface, right? Somewhere he, I, would have been."

"Calculating," the tech said, and a moment later, "here."

A red point lit up on the hologram of Earth.

"That's the big ocean," Morray said.

"Pacific, the Pacific Ocean," Caleb replied, and scanned it. "Do you have a better resolution map? This shit might as well have sea monsters drawn on it."

"No sir. This projection system's built for fleet movements, macro stuff. I don't have a detailed file of Earth to even load."

"Best guess then," Caleb muttered, and breathed deep.

He could taste the sea in the back of his throat. The scent of sun-warmed sand, just surrendering to the evening. Wind in the trees. The threat of rain in the air.

Screaming.

Wherever it was, he was there. Maybe he'd always been there, in that moment, waiting for whatever the hell had happened to happen.

His fingers touched the flyer Bea was holding.

A glimpse, a glance.

The Hawaiian national flag.

Where the symposium was.

"We're going," he said, and pulled away from it.

"Wait, what? Going where?"

"Earth. The Pacific. Its most isolated land mass." He jabbed a finger at the map. "Hawaii. That's where the Flet is."

"Sir, there's hardly anything left on that planet. The odds that something of him could have survived all this time, uncared for—"

"It's not about what's there now. I thought that was the whole point of this little exercise. We're going."

CHAPTER
THIRTY-SIX

PEARL HARBOR. That's what it was. Pearl Harbor.

Even in her time, history remembered that place.

The name filled Tharsis with dread. Supposedly, one of the very first Euphemism die-offs had started there. But nothing had happened yet. That event could have been years off. She had no way of knowing, and so, tried to put it out of her mind.

It had a small marina in it, apparently. She thought about chartering a boat, sailing around through the Oahu shallows to reach it. But it hosted both air and sea assets, and she had no doubt that the waters would be patrolled. Heavily, if the main gates were anything to judge by.

Controlled. Locked down.

How was she supposed to get in?

Tharsis contemplated just waiting, finding the Flet when he was off base. But then, that wasn't how the moment went.

She had to get inside.

To the dock. To the yacht.

She had to.

The holiday he'd mentioned was that coming weekend; she'd checked the library's Gig about it. Not an event recognized in Hawaii, but certainly something that the Americans who owned the installation would have celebrated.

It wasn't that Tharsis was particularly eager to walk into whatever awaited after that moment. What lay within the Flet's event horizon. If she would survive it. If she could justify taking Bea into it.

That was what worried her the most.

Bea.

But even if she didn't ask for anything in return, if she eschewed her original notion of asking for a stasis pod, Tharsis knew.

There was no avoiding it.

She'd found herself here, hadn't she?

No, she had to see it through.

Bea would survive.

Bea would be fine.

The handful of days she had remaining to her wasn't nearly enough to plan out anything complex. Falsify documents or make contacts that might sneak her in.

But Tharsis had one tool, exactly one, that she thought might work.

Wyatt's notebook.

She wasn't sure why she'd kept it. Maybe to spite that myling; the little thing's fingers had left burns on her outer thigh, where they had scratched her. Maybe because there had been no good way to give it back to Wyatt. Drunk or not, his mask had slipped that night and she hadn't liked what was underneath.

Tharsis only hoped the glyphs worked on people who weren't high on ilu. She couldn't imagine the military permitted recreational drug consumption.

The night before the holiday, after Bea was fed and asleep, she forced herself to look through it. There were maybe a dozen or so glyphs, some doodled multiple times before a final version was traced over with solid pen, approved in a side note. Some were obvious nonsense. Others shifted on the page, fading out of sight, only visible out of the corner of the eye. All had extensive annotations attached.

Beyond the little drawings, however, the notebook was a collection of written ramblings, things that reminded her of some of the Polarist scat from back home, run-on paragraphs of musings about human nature and reality and fixing the way people saw things.

Perception begins and ends with language, he'd written over and over, neat lines of script that eventually fell off the page.

Tharsis didn't enjoy looking through it. Didn't enjoy the idea of using something, anything, that may have contributed to the Euphemism. But all the glyphs here were tightly focused on guiding what people saw, and she found one she thought she could use.

It had to work.

It was going to work.

She had already stood on that dock.

She would stand on it tomorrow.

Tharsis traced the right symbol onto a fresh bit of card, cut to the same size as all the other little identification documents that people used around here, and prayed that this would work.

Then she packed up her kit, kissed her baby goodnight, and tried to sleep.

It was afternoon the next day before she worked up the courage to head down to Pearl Harbor.

THE BASE HAD a number of large gates. Most for vehicle traffic, but one was accessible to the island's large tram network. It was here that Tharsis stopped.

Bea, facing out in her sling, made a few little babbling hand movements.

"That's right, baby girl," Tharsis replied, signing the words back, slowly but surely. "We're going to go find our boat."

The card she'd drawn got her in. No questions. Even with Bea riding on her chest and her obvious, bulky backpack.

What the guard had seen in the glyph, she didn't know.

It was disquieting, how easy it was to get through. They even swiped the card through a silic terminal reader; the screen came up flashing, but the guard didn't seem to notice.

The base had a tram, the guard at the gatehouse told her. She waited for it outside, in a small pavilion where a couple of local enlisted boys were laughing and sharing some kind of pipe. The blue smoke was a dead giveaway: more ilucoccine.

What the hell was the military thinking, allowing that?

It had been over half a Heliosphere-standard year since Tharsis had burned her rank tattoos off. They weren't wearing her uniform, not even close. But she still felt an unexpected pang, watching them. Nostalgia, maybe, or guilt.

She bounced Bea a little, breathing in the humid noon air. It stank of jet fuel.

This wasn't the ASDF. Not her people, not her time.

The tram eventually showed up, and despite the crowd on it, Tharsis was able to get a seat by a window. She held Bea in her lap, talking to her with still uncertain movements.

———

A SMALL MARINA pulled into view, full of boats. Almost all were small, obviously unsuitable for anything but trips around the island or single-day fishing expeditions. Most had a uniform, worn appearance, the look Tharsis had come to associate with charter craft. But one, anchored at the farthest point of the longest wharf, was different.

At least twenty-five meters long, sleek and aerodynamic. Expensive.

A name, *Pride of Isidis*, covered the back.

She stopped for a moment, looking at it. Isidis was an Arran place. That had to be it, didn't it?

A woman, no older than Tharsis and possibly younger, passed by her. Swimsuit top and shorts, cloth grocery bags in hand. Sunglasses pushed up into shoulder-length blonde hair. Tharsis had to do a double take. For a moment, the woman looked almost exactly like one of the portraits that hung in District of Lunae's Hall of Remembrance. The painting of—

"Can I help you?" the woman asked, casting an eye at Bea, who giggled silently as she passed.

Holy fuck, Tharsis thought, and fought to keep her composure. It couldn't be her. Not a chance. She had been a contemporary of Caleb Ross. Younger, at least at first, if the old stories were true. And even with all she'd seen, Tharsis had no reason to believe she was that deep in the Euphemism.

It wasn't Eliza Rallison. It couldn't be.

Coincidence wouldn't be that cruel.

"I'm looking for Tom Donner," she said. "I heard he was here."

BOOK THREE
HADAL

CHAPTER

THIRTY-SEVEN

NANUK relaxed against the interior of the shipping container.

He could feel the deceleration sequence beginning. A subtle tremor in the heavy transport's decking. A shift when the braking thrusters started to fire.

Everything was proceeding on schedule. To plan.

Over two sevendays now without hearing from Riqan; he doubted his kinsman was still alive. The last few messages he'd gotten from him had been fragmented, like something had been scrambled in the signal. Dive comms were normally so reliable. No matter.

It made the Nepo extremely curious about what was actually out at Noqumiut. But that didn't matter either.

Nor did it matter what any of the rabble in the other containers thought. They'd been told what they needed to hear. A chance to strike back. An opportunity to serve She Who Brings the Light, or whatever this particular sect of Polarists fancied the Arcna to be.

The Arcna was dead. That much had come through from Riqan. A desiccated corpse, a fool who'd died eating herself. Why had she done that, he wondered, so she could keep talking right to the end? What had been the point of it?

Landlords and their secrets.

It'd be the death of them all.

Nanuk hadn't been compatible with the Onias's true gifts. Unlike Riqan, however, Nanuk had no issue with that. He'd never had much desire to be a political meat-puppet, a vessel for centuries of memory, responsibility. He was quite happy to be what he was. He was quite happy to be doing what he was doing.

Especially with the promises of his current patron.

Another rumble. Docking engines engaging.

It wouldn't be long now at all.

———

"SO THIS IS OFFICER LAND?"

"This is general officer land. Look at this scat. Is this real wood?"

The half-eaten remains of dinner were still strewn about. Caleb, and the rest of the crew who'd come over, had been waiting for what felt like hours. There were worse places to be stuck than the GO section's private bar, at least. The place was a world away from the bare steel utility of the base. Wood paneling on the walls, stone floors, a carved bar with a brass draft beer system, polished to a mirror finish. Small pub tables, made of the same wood as the walls, waxed and inlaid with mosaics of stars.

Nice.

The kind of nice that only came with rank. Rank and peace. Any luxuries, military or otherwise, in his own time had been relics of the past.

At his feet, Tyr growled softly. The rep had brought the dog a massive lamb shank, which he'd proceeded to flense with glee. His teeth were making scraping noises on the bone.

"How long did they say this was going to take?" Caleb asked, turning to the protocol rep who'd shown up with dinner, half an hour ago. A very junior lieutenant, he hadn't said much, and the *Barachiel* crew were clearly ignoring him.

"I don't know, sir," he said. The words were clipped. Short. "General Westland didn't give me his itinerary."

"They're trying to figure out whether or not they can take your order," Morray said. He'd helped himself to a beer from the taps in the corner. The other lieutenant had raised an eyebrow but hadn't attempted to stop him. "At least, that'd be my guess."

"Idle speculation, El-Tee," Aeolis said with yawn.

"Doesn't seem so idle, sir." Sergeant Haas, the more senior of the pair from the *Barachiel*. He was studying the patch wall, a vast expanse of unit and mission insignias that almost covered one entire wall. *Historic and contemporary,* he'd told Caleb when Caleb had asked. A few of the patches were framed, with little brass plaques giving tight, military-speak versions of events from long ago. "Why else would they have made all of us, including the Landlord, stay behind?"

"Generals doing general things," Aeolis said with a shrug.

"My point exactly," Morray replied.

Confused, Caleb tapped the table. "What order?"

"The order to go to Earth."

Caleb frowned. "I didn't order…"

"This really is complete spider-scat." That was the youngest of the *Barachiel's* crew present, a quant specialist named Dinar. Caleb hadn't gotten to know him very well yet, but it seemed like they were about the same age. "Normally, they let the crew disembark, have a little fun. Maybe catch the transport over to Phobos for a little bit of R&R at the casinos. But not this time."

Morray nodded. "Which makes me wonder, what kind of hell are the brass-inkers putting the colonel through?"

"Why?" Caleb asked. "He hasn't done anything wrong."

The effect on the crew was subtle, but there. Morray shook his head, went back to his beer. The enlisted guys exchanged a look. Aeolis finally sighed. "Look, sir—"

He shrugged. "You all outrank me. Except the kid over there."

"Hey!" Dinar objected.

"Call him Petrison," Haas said. "It's what's on his uniform."

Aeolis came over and sat down across from him at the small table. "Okay, well, Petrison, what you might not be aware of is that HOMECOM has been screaming at Colonel Cambel to get the *Barachiel* back here. He obviously hasn't complied."

"Because of me?"

"Because of you, yeah."

Caleb huffed out a breath. "So what does that mean?"

"DEEPCOM is headquartered here too," Dinar said, as if this carried some great importance.

Morray brushed it off. "They don't have the upper hand here."

"They've usually got the ear of Congress, don't they?"

Aeolis shrugged. "I am not an expert on whatever fucking politics are running amok in this place right now. But HOMECOM's going to try to keep you here."

"What, like guilt me into it?"

"Or threaten the boss into ignoring you," Morray said. "That'd be my guess."

"It's all speculation though," Haas replied, and poked at one of the patches. "Are these replicas? They're in really good condition."

Tyr's ears perked up, twitching a little, until his entire head came up.

"What is it, boy?" Caleb asked.

The dog didn't have a chance to answer. Not before klaxons started wailing.

"THIS IS NOT A DRILL, I REPEAT, THIS IS NOT A DRILL. ALL PERSONNEL ARE TO SEEK SHELTER IMMEDIATELY. ATMO BREACH REPORTED IN MAIN LOGISTICS WAREHOUSE. THIS IS NOT A DRILL."

"Huh," Haas said.

The lieutenant was on his feet, at the handset in the corner, clearly trying to get through to somebody. But it was wasted effort; a moment later and the main door was thrown open. A pair of security troops, wearing the same body armor Caleb had seen Yip in, back on New Stockholm. Looking grim.

"Landlord, we've been asked to move you to a more secure location."

"What's going on?"

"Tell you on the way, sir."

———

NANUK LET the last body hit the ground. *Should have brought a bigger security detail,* he thought with a smile, and wiped his knife clean.

The explosion, half a kilometer away, had been perfectly timed.

He hoped she would appreciate just how much effort had gone into this, and at the last minute too. Pulling together a raid on Asaph Base in less than a sevenday wasn't exactly an easy task.

"Where now?" one of his own men asked, falling in next to him.

"The main objective," he said quietly, and looked around. "Let the rabble play where they will."

Amid the chaos unleashed by the four dozen voider Toks, Nanuk and his small team slipped away. Into the base's heart.

———

BLOOD.

Caleb stopped, looking at Tyr. The dog had his nose to the air, all casual ease from the bar wiped away now. Hunting mode.

"What did he just say?" the MP asked.

"You can hear him?" Caleb asked. He didn't know what the current word was for it; Tyr didn't so much speak as throw images, impressions.

"We all got that," Aeolis said. "Where, boy?"

Tyr growled but could only gesture with his muzzle in the correct direction. Down one of the branching hallways.

"Do you hear that?" Haas asked.

"Gunfire."

"They're shooting solid slugs in a void habitat?" Morray demanded.

"Toks, Hans, they're all insane," Aeolis replied.

The lights flickered.

"We need to keep moving," one of the MPs said. The group picked up the pace.

The other put his hand to his ear. "Enemy contact confirmed," he said. "Moving towards the, uhh, scat, that doesn't make any sense." He looked at his counterpart. "They're moving towards the records dome."

The first began to answer. "The rec—"

He didn't get any further than that.

A fist-sized globule of red and gray gore punched out the back of his head.

Everything started happening very quickly.

Aeolis grabbed the protocol lieutenant—the kid was standing there in shock—and thrust him back, into the nearest doorway, even as the rest of the crew scrambled back. Caleb dove for the MP's fallen weapon, hand closing on it a second earlier than Haas's. One glare from him, and Haas just nodded, retreating.

"Sir," the remaining MP began.

"What's going on?" Caleb asked. The hallway in front of them was empty.

The security sergeant tapped his earpiece, listening to whatever radio feed he was getting. "Command Post doesn't know. Everything's fucked."

The lights flickered again. This time, they went out. Emergency lighting, dim and red, came on a moment later.

In its glow, movement.

Half a dozen forms, maybe more.

A round hit the wall beside them. Then another.

"Don't place any shots lower than shoulder-height," Caleb told him.

"What do you mean?"

But Tyr was already off, huge frame carrying him forward at break-neck speed. He was on the voiders before they knew what hit them, massive jaws closing hard around a shoulder and shaking as hard as he could. In the low artificial gravity of the moon, the effect was devastating. The unfortunate assailant's body was thrown across the hall-way, crashing with a wet thud into a wall. Tyr howled and went for another. They scattered.

The dog's size alone, in Caleb's experience, was threat enough. When his blood got up, he was terrifying.

Caleb took advantage of the lull to strip anything useful off the dead MP. In addition to the rifle he'd already grabbed, the body had a pistol-like sidearm and something that resembled a thick cattle prod. Done with that, he glanced up.

Tyr was shaking the second body. Clearly dead.

"Off!" Caleb barked.

The dog growled.

"Now, Tyr!" he yelled.

Grudgingly, the dog released the body and came trotting back over to them. Blood was smeared across his teeth, the fur of his lower muzzle.

"Come on," Caleb said, and dragged the sergeant back into the room.

It was some sort of office space, desks and terminals and a huge window that looked out on Mars beyond. Haas and Morray were busy working on a barricade, while Aeolis and Dinar were working on that protocol lieutenant. Aeolis, trying to talk to him, and Dinar, trying to get something pulled up on the terminal with his input.

"Let me," the MP said, and slid in next to Dinar, access card in hand.

Tyr went to join the two men at the door. Caleb paused to hand them the weapons, then went over to where the captain was.

"What's wrong with him?" Caleb asked Aeolis.

The nav officer shrugged. "You tell me."

Caleb gave the lieutenant a once-over. The kid was clearly going into shock. *From seeing one headshot?* he wondered, and then reminded himself that this time had largely been at peace. Probably wasn't all that usual right now.

"We don't have time for this," he grumbled, and, considering his options, very deliberately slapped him.

It took two more hits, but the lieutenant finally put a shaking hand up. "I'm, I'm alright."

"Where are we?" Aeolis said. "Where were we headed?"

"There are a couple of bunkers set throughout the station," the MP said. He had a two-dimensional map pulled up on the screen. "We were going to take you to this one. But it looks like it's reached capacity already."

"What capacity?" Caleb asked.

"Atmo, sir."

"So what's our next best option?" Aeolis asked.

The MP indicated on the map. "Here, but that's a half kilometer away."

"What are these?" Caleb asked, pointing at dots, moving through the hallways.

"Blue's us. The red is whoever broke in." The MP shook his head. "The silic's processing video data, so it might not be exact."

"There's no pattern here. Except for this group. It looks like they're heading here," Aeolis said. He touched the screen, leaving a fingerprint over a cluster of five red lights. "What is this?"

"It's the records dome," the MP said. "But there's nothing there to hit. The main archives, the station library…"

"The Historian's Office?" Aeolis said, and looked at the lieutenant, who nodded. "That's where the boss is right now. Having their little General Officer shindig."

"How would they know that?" Dinar asked.

"Doesn't matter how they know, or if they know," Caleb said, something niggling at the back of his mind. "What matters is that they're headed there."

"You want to go there?" the MP asked.

"It's closer than the shelter," Caleb said.

"I'm inclined to get the boss back," said Morray. "Captain?"

Aeolis noddd, terse. "It's the Landlord's call."

"We're going."

THIRTY-EIGHT

TOM WAS NOT HAVING a good day.

Everything had seemed so promising, too.

Don was in country. With his dad's private yacht, nonetheless. How he'd convinced his father to let him borrow it, Tom had no idea. Much less how he'd gotten permission from his command to sail out to Hawaii from his own home station of San Diego. They'd both only had their commissions for less than a year. He shouldn't have had enough leave saved up for the trip.

But that was Don, and always had been.

The guy always had some way of getting what he wanted.

It was good to see him, though. That graduation trip out to Singapore was the last time they'd been together in person, over seven months ago now. Tom hadn't made many friends at the Academy, in his time there, but his roommate had always hung with him, no matter how strange things had gotten.

They'd gotten each other through that last terrible week, too. When the school had come under literal siege. Protest, the news had called it. Which had been bullshit from the start. Cadets had died. More than one of Tom's friends.

Bonds like that didn't break, though.

It was good to see him.

His face brand hadn't healed up any better than Tom's had. Almost everyone in their class had them, though; if anything, it was seen as a point of pride. Surviving that week.

Don had shown up this morning. Not totally unannounced, but close enough to it. Called Tom up at his base apartment and asked if he wanted to do a little sunset cruise. So Tom had asked his wife, who'd rolled her eyes but agreed to go out.

Doing anything with Don was always a treat.

The guy had been an enigma for as long as Tom had known him. He came from money, his grandfather one of the early pioneers of asteroid mining and with a long family history in the energy industry before that. Tom had been invited along on several of his summer vacations. In a world where everything seemed to be falling apart, Don had given him glimpses into how luxurious things still were at the top. Still, Don didn't have a rich-boy attitude, and had gone out of his way not to flaunt the family's wealth at school.

Why he'd been at a military academy was a mystery to Tom. The pay was bad, and the treatment was worse. Civilian anger at the armed services had reached a fever pitch over the last few years, blaming the rank and file for the disgraces of the last war, for the growing civil unrest. Rich kid like that, his dad certainly could have pulled strings for him anywhere, gotten him anything he'd wanted. Why choose the degradation of the military?

But then, Don had his secrets. Just like Tom had his.

He respected that.

When Tom and Cynthia had shown up at the marina, they'd learned that Don had kicked the five-man crew off for the night. He'd actually left them back in Waikiki, with orders to enjoy themselves, or something like that. Total privacy.

Which meant he wanted to talk.

About what, he found out later.

Cynthia had run back to their apartment to pick up a few things, and Don had beckoned Tom up to the bridge. Tom had been on the yacht once before. It was a gorgeous vessel, state-of-the-art, sleek and streamlined. Like a spaceship. He wondered what the yacht's captain would think of them drinking up here.

"Hell of a view, isn't it?" Don asked.

"Always is with you."

"Yeah, I know," Don said with a grin, and cracked his sweating can of some Texas microbrew. "You only love me for my money."

"Shut the fuck up," Tom told him good-naturedly, and Peter Donovan laughed harder.

But as he took that first sip of beer, Tom had a flash of something else. Somewhere else. His friend, older, worn, tired, clinking their glasses together, thanking him for… something.

Tom had dealt with this his entire life. Flashes. Slips. Little snippets, barely more than a moment or two, like opening a window on a darkened airplane into a bright sky beyond. Déjà vu.

Except that déjà vu was supposed to come after something happened. These were typically things that hadn't happened yet. He'd caught up to a few of them, events or conversations or the most ordinary moment with holes punched through them. Punched through by his own brain, maybe. He never lived a slipped moment twice.

Like he'd been knocked loose in his own timeline.

He hardly ever saw anything useful. Nothing that would have led him to ever consider telepathy or foresight or some other such nonsense. But it had lent him a kind of purpose, a vector.

The thing he saw most was space. The sky beyond Earth's atmosphere, that vast, burning darkness.

Perhaps that was why he never questioned it. Made sense. The sky was where he was headed. Pilot, test pilot, astronaut. Space exploration had exploded in the decade or so since the end of the last major war. Seemed almost inevitable that he'd get out there too.

He pulled himself back.

Not a full slip.

It was fine.

He was fine.

Don was looking at him.

Don had always noticed when it came. But he never asked.

Tom coughed. "So, why'd you come out? It's a big-time commitment and I can't imagine what kind of fuel credit you had to burn."

"My dad wants me to drop my citizenship and my commission," Donovan said. "Come work for him. Came out last week, asked me in person. I think it's an ultimatum."

"Holy shit. None of the Gulf Coast states have declared independence…"

"It's coming," Don said.

"It's been discussed for decades, but nothing ever happens," Tom pointed out. "Besides, it'd be a fucking disaster."

"What's Washington going to do about it? Half the country would follow Texas out, and most of that half is responsible for food production. And military membership. Ain't nobody going to fire on their old buddies just to make those corrupt assholes happy." Don's eyes were unfocused. Like he was very far away. "But Dad's got plans way beyond that. Some of the shit that the family's investing in right now… I don't know. I'm not convinced any of it's going to work."

"Like what?"

"Independent habitats," Donovan said. "Up there."

Tom had heard rumors about such things. There were a number of proof-of-concept colony platforms already in orbit, but so far, none had proven self-sufficient. Water, in particular, seemed to be a constant problem.

"Your family's into asteroid mining, right? Makes sense to expand into—"

"This is way bigger than that," Don said, pacing now. "Way bigger. Total pie in the sky craz—"

And then it happened.

The slip.

Full on.

The one he thought he'd stopped.

It was still Donovan talking.

But not the same conversation.

"—ow that we're right up against that. I was there, remember? But you have to understand, Tom, this is the only launch window we've got. Mercury's a hell of a target to hit, and if we don't make this date, I don't know when else we'll get you up there. My biggest concern is whether we can trust that bio-fucked kid to actually—"

Older now. Not up on the bridge of his dad's yacht, windows cast open to the afternoon breeze, not a care in the world. No, not there. Somewhere tight, confined, an office of polished burl wood that smelled of sweat and jet wash.

Tom checked his watch. Time, GPS coordinates. He always had it on, in these moments. For these moments.

"—y shit."

And then it was over.

"Uh-huh," Tom said, not really listening, and fumbled a pad out of his cargo shorts' pocket. Paper and a pen. He always kept it on him. Had for years. Back when he figured out the slips weren't hallucinations. That he was actually *there*. Actually moving back or forward against what should have been the normal flow of time.

Where he was. Where he went. Where he came back to.

It was frightening, sometimes, how far apart those things were.

Don fell silent for a moment, letting him write. "One of these days, you're going to tell me what this is all about with you."

Satisfied with the scribble—he'd move it to his main ledger later—Tom clicked his pen shut. "When I figure it out, I'll let you know."

"I'm going to hold you to that," Don told him, and went over to check the weather report, which had finally finished compiling. "Fuck, rain tonight."

"We can still take her out and enjoy the sunset, right?"

"Absolutely," Don replied. He tossed back the rest of his beer. "I didn't kick the crew off for the night just to get drunk in the marina."

Tom laughed, and started to ask about who was going to be fixing dinner if the chef was marooned ashore for the night.

He didn't get the chance.

Because Cynthia popped her head in.

"I hate to disrupt, but you've got a visitor. Says she knows you. That you're expecting her."

Tom gave Donovan a pointed look. "You didn't order a stripper or something, did you?"

"If she's a stripper, she'd be the worst one I've ever seen," Cynthia said, and yawned. "She's got a baby with her."

———

THOROUGHLY CONFUSED—HE hadn't told anybody at his unit about his weekend plans—Tom headed back down through the yacht, out to the back deck.

Standing there, down on the dock, was a woman.

Tall and thin, pale even in the harsh afternoon sunlight, long dark hair loose around her. A tired-looking polo with the words *Vastitas Reach* emblazoned on the breast clung to her, damp from sweat, a sling around her body holding a sleeping baby.

But she wasn't there.

Or rather, she wasn't just there.

She wasn't on the front dock, and Tom wasn't on the deck of his friend's private yacht. Not at all.

… walking across a snow field, brighter than any he'd ever seen, fog rising around her with every labored footfall, the gravity…

No.

… in a long hallway of red polished stone, trying to hide her awe, looking…

Not standing either.

… a hand, beating against a smooth bulkhead, the reverberations a sensation he could feel on his own skin, screaming for him to…

Wait. Not that, not yet.

…the ocean, sand, that tropical smell in the air, heat and rot and—

There.

She was there.

A beach. The air thick and warm, the sound of waves crashing beyond them as rain began to fall. From beyond the curve of the beach, out in the rain, screams were rising.

Tom couldn't move, his body leaden, extremities numb. He dangled, but from what, between what, he couldn't tell.

She was in front of him, collapsed on the sand, bleeding out in the failing of the day.

Bleeding light.

But not yet. Not yet.

For now, she was standing there, a wary expression on her face. Something about her was wrong. He couldn't put his finger on quite what it was. Her physical form was off in some subtle way, skin and muscle pulled over something other than bone. Like she'd been pressed out of dust.

"We've met before, haven't we?"

"Yeah," she said, and her accent was strange. "I'd say so. Can we talk about this event horizon scat now?"

THEIR TRIP to the Historian's Office was quiet.

Up until the moment it wasn't.

The MP's surveillance map had proven largely correct: whatever force had infiltrated the station was not well organized. Between the humans and the dog in their little group, they put down maybe a dozen of the unfortunate individuals in the main hallways. All seemed to have been engaged in simple, mindless destruction, and few were armed with anything more than what the *Barachiel* crew identified as diamond-edged mining blades. Gravity-honed strength and military discipline, not to mention the mere sight of Tyr, meant far more scattered than engaged.

Neither the *Barachiel* crew nor the MP had any compunction about shooting them as they attempted to flee.

Caleb got a good look at a few of them. Dead bodies. Scared faces. They were all wisp-thin, fragile-looking, and so pale their skin seemed to glow. The fanaticism was unmistakable. Caleb had seen the same look before. Back home, back then. The followers, the worshippers, the people lost to ilucoccine or despair or insanity. The ones they cleaned out of Lab nests or half-destroyed cities.

Wretched as those people always were, most had still been fit. Plump. The remnants of the old life, old standards of living, still clinging to them.

These had never known anything but want.

"Where are the whitecoats?" he muttered to himself.

"Who?" the MP asked quietly. Caleb had taken point with him. No reason for anybody else to get shot, he figured, if it wouldn't actually kill him.

"The guys in charge. There's always some cynical asshole driving this sort of mob."

The answer came all too soon.

When their little party walked around a blind corner, and straight into a group of Toks.

———

FOR A MOMENT, Nanuk couldn't believe what he was seeing.

Couldn't believe his luck.

He was there. *There*. Right in front of them.

The two parties had literally collided. Stealth had served them; the Martians clearly hadn't been aware of their presence. A small group of uniformed personnel. Only one in combat gear.

Shock held everyone back at first. They just stared at each other.

Then Nanuk smiled, eager.

"Landlord," he purred.

And launched himself at the tired-looking boy in a black uniform.

As part of the Family, however forgotten or neglected, Nanuk was still heir to several advantageous genetic traits. Muscle density. Height. The kind of physiology that the original Onias had had, or at least, aspired to have.

Nanuk had never met anybody he couldn't best in a fight.

Until now.

The Landlord was as much a brawler as Nanuk was. No artistry guided his movements, just a raw strength beyond anything Nanuk had experienced before. Caught off guard for a split second, the Landlord went down hard when the Nepo tackled him but caught Nanuk's hand a bare few centimeters from his face. Fingers like steel around Nanuk's wrist, he knocked loose the razor-sharp blade Nanuk held there, sending it skittering away. Nanuk managed a few blows before the Landlord jerked to the side.

Before his own momentum sent his fist straight into the metal floor below them.

Nanuk howled.

Two of his escorts broke away from their fights to come to his aid. Hands scrambled in, trying to hold the Landlord down, ripping at his clothes, digging at his skin. Nanuk sat upon his knees, squeezing his legs around the Landlord's ribs. Somebody slapped a rock machete—blade shortened for just this purpose—back into Nanuk's hands.

But before he could plunge the thing into the Landlord's chest, end this, at least for now, something huge and dark and black latched onto his wrist.

That four-legged thing.

With Nanuk distracted, the Landlord caught one of his escorts by the collar and threw—*threw*—the man over his body, knocking him into the other, as if he weighed nothing at all. He shoved his way free of Nanuk's leg hold, catching the Nepo across the face with a shattering haymaker.

Teeth dislodged. Something in his jaw broke.

That cursed animal slammed Nanuk back into a bulkhead like a rag doll.

———

"SIR, YOU ALRIGHT?"

Caleb shook himself, head still ringing from the force of hitting the floor. "I'm fine, Aeolis," he growled back. The sound of gunfire had subsided now, their own little battle over, the sounds of fighting relegated back to elsewhere in Asaph.

The nav officer offered him a hand up. Blood covered half his face, but it was drying already. He didn't seem to notice. "Eight assailants, seven dead."

"All eight, if Tyr doesn't stop," Morray observed wryly.

Caleb rubbed his forehead. "Tyr," he snapped automatically, without even looking, "hold only."

The dog growled, thoughts red.

"Hold only!" Caleb barked.

Vision still spotty, he went to go find his dog.

A few paces away, he saw the man he'd ripped off, tossed away. The man had impacted his companion, then the floor a few meters beyond that. His neck was clearly snapped. The other was dead as well, the trauma there less evident.

Huh. Caleb hadn't realized his Earth-born physiology would be that advantageous.

A few more steps, and there was the asshole who'd tackled him. He looked dazed, eyes glassed over, obviously in a lot of pain. A dozen puncture holes in gold skin oozed thick. Dark.

Caleb whistled to Tyr. The dog clamped his teeth harder into the voider's upper arm. The man, sprawled out on his back, cursed in some language Caleb didn't recognize.

"He looks different," he commented.

The surviving MP came over, casting an eye over the man. "Nepo. Part of the Onias gene-line."

"They're like royalty in the Jupiter inwell," Morray said. He'd taken a few superficial cuts to his own arms and hands and was in the process of wrapping the worst with a scrap he'd torn off his uniform's undershirt. "What the fuck is one of them doing here?"

The gold-tattooed man smiled, and spit at him. It caught the comm officer right in the face. Morray cursed and kicked him back. The Nepo started laughing.

"Gentlemen!" a voice boomed behind them. "Can I ask what's going on out here?"

Morray closed his eyes. "Scat," he muttered, under his breath.

———

"I HAVE TO ADMIT, it's strange seeing you this young," General Westland said. He held out a lowball to Caleb. Cut crystal. Something dark, almost red, inside. "It's a bit of a shock, actually."

Caleb hadn't bothered cleaning up, other than washing his hands in the bathroom on the way up here. The chaplain with his old squadron, back on Earth, used to tell him it wasn't a good idea, getting numb to killing. But he'd deal with that later. It was probably somewhat insulting, standing in some three-star's office in a ripped, bloodied uniform. He didn't much care.

They'd almost made it back to the Historian's Office, it turned out, their little battle with the Nepo and his escort happening only a few meters from the main doors.

Fighting elsewhere in the base was contained now, only a few Toks still running loose. Security figured that the Nepo was the ringleader; apparently, that's how the Jovians did things. So the Nepo had gotten hauled off to lockup, and the little party that had gotten trapped in the Historian's Office decided to come out.

Cambel, whom Caleb recognized, and this guy. General Richat Westland. Deep Void Space Command Commander.

The top of the *Barachiel's* chain of command.

And, apparently, some kind of old friend.

He had wanted to talk.

So here they were, talking.

"Whiskey?" Caleb asked, sniffing as he took the glass.

"Hellas brandy. The oak they use gives it that color."

"Fascinating," Caleb said, peering at it. "Did we know each other?"

"You came by Command a few home-years back. Asked for a transfer out of the deepvoider fleet. Said you wanted to thank us. Shook a few hands, gave a little speech, and that was that," the general added.

Caleb had never been much of a liquor connoisseur. But even he could tell the brandy was smooth, faintly spiced. Rich. Not something he particularly cared for. Too complex. "Nice," he said, and set it down. "I suppose you don't want me going to Earth."

"Not at all, no."

"That's too bad," he said, "because that's where we need to go."

Westland sighed and set his own brandy down. "You're… important to this command. If you give that order, we'll follow it. But I can't promise you I can make HOMECOM or Congress understand."

"The Flet's consciousness is absent. And now we have space-time issues, shit going missing, jarring out of place? Terrorist incursions on what I assume is a fairly secure base?"

"You think it's related?"

"I think it reminds me of what I was fighting back on Earth. In, uh, my time."

The general stared at his drink. "The Euphemism."

"Maybe something leaked out of Noqumiut. Or maybe something got started back then that only he can stop." It wasn't quite what Caleb was thinking, but close enough.

Crossing his arms, the general sat back against the gleaming stone surface of his desk. "Between you and me, I'm inclined to agree with you. I also have several thousand men trapped in the outer system that I can't get home until we get the divedrives working again. You've got all the support this command can offer you."

"Then are we even having this discussion?"

"Better you give the order to me than Cambeḷ. Congress is going to blame somebody, and they can't exactly censure you," he said. "It would also help to have something more concrete than impressions and maybes."

"A real connection?"

"Yes."

Caleb thought for a moment. "Where'd that Tok come from?"

———

"WE'VE MET BEFORE, haven't we?" the Flet said, as he pulled Tharsis into the cool of the yacht's interior. Some kind of salon; not the front deck nor the bar, where they'd walked before. Would walk. Whatever. "We've had this conversation before." It wasn't a question so much as it was a statement of fact.

It sounded very much like the man—entity?—Tharsis had known before. In her own time. Except instead of some broken-body apparition, this was a guy younger than her, in an old T-shirt and Hawaiian-print board shorts, barefoot on what looked to be a very expensive private craft. All incongruous, especially with her memories of her own time.

This is his time, she reminded herself. *If there ever was a time he belonged to.*

"We have," Tharsis replied carefully. "But not yet, maybe. I think most of my past is…"

"Hasn't happened yet, has it?"

Bea was fussing in her carrier, waking up now. Tharsis sat down on one of the yacht's padded benches. "You mind?" she asked, as she pulled the baby out of her sling.

Tom looked at her, eyes glazed for a moment. "Huh," he said.

"What?"

"I've met her too," he said, and then smiled at Tharsis with those ancient, ancient eyes. "My little navigator."

Irritation roiled in Tharsis's gut. "Can you tell me what this is all about, Flet? You ask me for help from half a planet away, don't tell me where to be, how to get here, what the fuck is going on…"

He sat down next to her, holding out a hand. She realized he was asking to hold Bea. Another flare of irritation. She didn't hand her baby over.

"This is the edge of it," he said.

"Your event horizon."

"Yes. And we're all going to be dragged through it, before the night is over."

"What does that mean?"

He was quiet for a moment. "I've been to moments past this. Far past your origins, I'd think. But I've never seen this, what's coming tonight. It's a place I haven't been, a time I haven't yet lived. What could make something like that, I have no idea. Considering I haven't encountered this sort of thing again, I assume it's important."

"But you don't know."

"No."

"Then how—"

"Tharsis, what you have to understand is that causality isn't bound to the flow of space-time."

That didn't make any sense, and she wanted to tell him so, but before she could, Peter Donovan stuck his head in.

"Hey Tom, who's your friend?"

———

THARSIS THOUGHT her presence would be hard to explain, but the Flet, Donner, whoever he was, waved it away almost effortlessly. *Just a friend who's in town for the weekend.* It seemed to generate more of a reaction from the blonde woman than Donovan.

She really did look almost exactly like a young Eliza Rallison, right down to the shoulder-length hair. But her eyes weren't as hard as Rallison's always were; even in photographs from before the events of the First Propagation, there had been something dead in that woman. Instead, despite the terrible facial brands she carried, the woman seemed almost soft. Vulnerable. Sweet.

But then, if she was military too, she had to have been through some terrible scat herself. Or would go through it. Tharsis wasn't sure which it was. Where any of this fit.

"Cynthia," she said by way of introduction, and sat down cross-legged next to Bea. "God, she's a cutie."

"I'd like to think so."

"What's her name?"

It wasn't time yet for the conversation Tharsis had been having with Tom, and she had no compunction about spreading out a few toys for the little girl to play with. She squinted at Cynthia. There was something there, she realized, something like—

… Bea, older, running across a playground. Another girl, just a little younger, blonde, chasing after her, laughing…

… Bea, an adult, the hood of her ENEX pulled down, running through the ruin of Noqumiut, giving chase in silence to that same blonde hair…

"Bea," Tharsis said, shaking it off.

"Well, she's adorable," Cynthia said, and dangled a hanging toy in front of her. The baby grabbed for it, wheezing her silent little laugh. "Stronger than she looks, too."

"Babies are like that," Tharsis said, and looked at her again. Yeah. She hadn't seen it very often here on Earth, but it was unmistakable. "You ready for all that?"

"What do you mean?"

"You're pregnant," she said.

"What makes you say that?"

"Anybody could see it. That little light. It's tiny, but it's in there." Tharsis handed Bea a book, something the baby promptly started to chew on. "Maybe a couple of weeks?"

Cynthia stared at her. "I haven't even told Tom about that."

"You two married?"

"Yes. Sort of. We dated at the Academy, and after everything that happened…" she trailed off. "Who else is going to understand you, but another Academy guy?"

Dating. Tharsis had heard that term a number of times on Earth, but she hadn't quite managed to wrap her head around the concept. Casual relationships. Casual sex. Wasn't something that would have passed back home. There was weight to such things on Mars, consequences; courting was the order of things. But as to the rest of Cynthia's point…

"I can understand that," Tharsis said honestly.

"Kind of stupid, getting married right out of school, but it's the only way to get an assignment together." Cynthia was quiet again, watching Bea. "I've been thinking about maybe… not, with the pregnancy."

"What do you mean?"

"You know what I mean," she snapped, defensive. "The whole fucking planet is dying. What kind of life can I give a kid?"

Tharsis could see Bea running again. On fat little feet. On grav-boots, across an ancient metal floor, methane snow just dusting the corridor.

Chasing, chasing…

Another woman collapsed to her hands and knees on the edge of that whiteness, breathing hard in the thin, thin air.

It was the chamber Tharsis had seen. The one in the *Padua Anthony*.

Bea stopped beside her. Knelt down.

The other woman turned into her, face into her shoulder, and screamed.

"You won't," Tharsis said. "You're not going to do that."

Cynthia gave her a strange look but didn't ask anything else.

Donovan came back a minute or two later, Tom and food in tow. The food turned out to be some kind of raw fish and citrus salad, chilled, better than almost anything they'd had on the *Vastitas Reach*.

"You coming out for the evening with us?" he asked Tharsis.

She glanced outside. It wasn't twilight yet. The moment she kept seeing hadn't come yet.

"I, uhh…"

"Of course she's coming, you asshole," Tom chuckled.

Donovan smiled back at him, but there was something more than humor in his expression. Tharsis didn't like the way he was looking at Bea. And for a wild moment, Tharsis wondered if he knew about her. If he'd heard about the little, red-eyed baby and her guardian on the *Vastitas Reach*.

But if he'd heard anything, he didn't say.

"Well, if we're going to head out for a cruise, we might as well go now. The captain'll kill me if I have this thing out after dark on my own."

NIGHTTRIPPERS.

That was the answer to where the Nepo came from.

He'd been working as a manager at some place called Night-trippers.

Traveler's hostel in the international district on Phobos, part of an entire franchise network across the inner system.

A location that was apparently known to the *Barachiel's* intelligence officer when the name came up. That missing lieutenant, Chen, had been living in another one on New Stockholm.

No reasonable expectation of connection, Caleb was told, when he asked why in the hell nothing had been done about this before. *No known problems.*

Known problems, his ass.

The Arrans, this ASDF organization, seemed more suspicious of him than it did the people it was supposed to be fighting.

The Nepo had had something on him, something Caleb had found chilling: a small stack of cards. Glyphs, like the ones from the Noqumiut surveillance flight logs.

Like the ones from that arium in Tikal. That raid from another life.

How had the Nepo gotten them?

What exactly had been unleashed from Noqumiut?

"Any advice for this?" Yip asked as the ground transport trundled through Phobos's wide streets.

Yip, Ninden, Yeti, Padre. All three of the *Barachiel's* dogs. Himself. A few of the local police, men from their rapid response force. That was Caleb's team for this little excursion. And Yip, for some inexplicable reason, seemed to be deferring tactical command to him.

"Depends on what we find," Caleb said, trying to focus. "In my time, the most prominent issue we usually faced was ilucoccine infection. This is something else, though." He thought of Page. "It's easy to not get sucked into whatever somebody is experiencing in an ilucination. This shit, with the glyphs, seems to be worse."

"Worse how?" Ninden asked.

"Worse in that it's harder to tell what's real and what's not. We all might see things," Caleb said. He pointed to the dogs. "That's why they're along."

"No sense of the written word?" Padre said.

"Better sense of smell," Caleb said, and watched the city roll by.

Phobos, as the larger, closer moon to Mars, was a hub of civilian activity. Vast ports managed much of the commercial shipping on and off world, handling everything from inwell-grown produce to Jovian H3 storage, facilitating transfer between the huge freighters and the smaller space elevators. The moon apparently also boasted a huge manufacturing sector, for products or processes that couldn't be reasonably constructed in full free fall.

It was the home of the bulk of Mars's immigrant population, host to various foreign embassies and business interests; like Erg, most voiders were too far diverged to ever set foot on the surface. There was a branch of the University of Titan here, as well as a Golanite monastery.

Arrans lived here, too. Traders, ASDF void service retirees, artists and tourists, diplomats and students.

The moon was cosmopolitan, wealthy, international. Something like Singapore maybe, Caleb thought, the way it had once been in the stories his grandfather told.

That was the picture painted by the *Barachiel* crew on the rockjump ride over. But the city—the only city—seemed smaller than Caleb would have thought. It was limited by gravity, they'd said. Wide-area gravity generation could be highly dangerous, and it was only through a few quirks of the Flet's own perception that it could be managed at all. His reach wasn't endless, though, so neither was the area he could cover.

The Arran section of the moon city was underwhelming, Caleb thought. Prefab and tilt-wall structures for the most part, the same dusty gray-white as the lands beyond the sky-bubble. The spaces between the buildings were wide, the streets narrow, accommodating a few personal vehicles but clearly marked out with rails, for some kind of public transport. Down the center of every street were sunken canals, walking paths alongside for pedestrian traffic. There was nothing to hint at wealth flowing through this place, although the Arrans assured him it was one of the richest cities in the inwell.

The only thing that broke up the monotony was vegetation. Vegetation everywhere, spilling from planter boxes and rooftop gardens, erupting in huge pots along the sidewalks, waving in the water down in the canals. It reminded him of the *Barachiel's* atrium.

Passing into the international district, the city took on a distinctly different feel. No longer were buildings arranged in a grid, the wide streets falling apart into weaving, meandering paths, barely wide enough for the truck to pass. The waterways disappeared. Instead of the neatly ordered buildings, square and upright, structures became more organic.

Like a bull ant nest, Morray had said.

The truck emerged into a small square, ringed three levels high with awnings and closed-case displays. It was a market, Caleb realized. Staring at it, Yip had to bump his foot to get him out of the truck.

"This is the central bazaar," he said, as Caleb joined the team at the back of the vehicle. Tyr was waiting for him, body language tense. The other two dogs were equally on edge. "Charmingly Jovian."

"I wouldn't call anything from that inwell charming, Sergeant," Ninden said. His A24 was out. "At least this smells better."

"What are we looking for?" Padre asked. He was armed with that knockout rifle again, and this time, something that looked like a cattle prod hung off his belt.

"Anything that shouldn't be here," Caleb said. He tried to think. "We might not be able to see it straight on. Ask the dogs if—"

"Like that?" And Yip pointed.

It was a banner, a massive banner, hanging off one of the upper-level shop stalls. Caleb looked at it and winced. Whatever was there, it hurt. "Yeah," he said. "Something like that."

The new captain whistled. "There's a whole mess of 'em."

And there were, Caleb realized. Six of them, hanging equidistant around the misshapen circle of the market.

"But where are the people?" Padre asked.

"Come on," Caleb said, misgivings growing now, "let's find this Nighttrippers place."

It wasn't far. A second-story walkway ran through one of the ant-nest buildings and across a wide network of bridges, spanning structures that, by comparison, seemed sunken into the moon's crust. There were several places where the team had to disengage their personal gravity and take broad leaps or jumps to make the next point.

Nighttrippers lay near the top of one of the voider structures, set into the top curve. At either side of its round door were more banners and into the metal surface, another glyph had been pounded.

"Do these things have any power if we, say, touch them?" Padre asked.

"As far as I know, no," Caleb replied.

They ripped them down before heading inside. And when they went, Tyr insisted on bounding ahead first.

The hostel, for all its strange architecture, was little different from ones Caleb remembered back on Earth. Worn furniture, old paint on the walls, a few small lounge areas. But this one had a large bar connected to it, one that ran half the length of the domed space and out onto a wide open-air patio beyond.

The second Caleb set foot in it, Tyr started growling.

A figure was stumbling about.

It took Caleb a moment to figure out what he was looking at. A miserable, frostbitten woman, clothing impossible to discern. She had blood frozen in her unkempt hair and her bloodless, blackening fingers clutched a hammer. For a moment, he thought it was just frostbite, except the skin of her face was mottled as well.

Blue, a faint glow moving just beneath the surface.

Shit, Caleb thought, heart sinking.

She wasn't coming for them. At least, it didn't seem like it. She was shambling, unsteady, lips moving. Forming words he couldn't make out.

"Ma'am," he asked. "Can you see me?"

The frostbitten woman held up her ruined hands, the soft murmuring getting louder. One word, over and over. Pleading, Caleb realized, pleading like she was the victim here, like it wasn't her fault. They always did that.

She dragged towards him, on the ruins of her feet, barely holding herself upright, the nonsense words still spilling from her lips.

For just a moment, he felt a blasting heat, an unbearable agony.

The woman was raising the hammer now. But whatever she was seeing in her mind, whatever cruel hallucination had driven her to this, her body was barely functional.

Once again, Tyr was on it. Grabbed her by the wrist and shook her down. Her body hit the floor hard, went limp. Unconscious. The whispers of heat vanished.

"She thinks the whole place was on fire," Caleb said, kneeling down beside her, shoving Tyr off. The dog was growling. Caleb ignored him, and checked her pulse. "Or she was in some place that was on fire. But I don't think it was ilu." He looked up at Padre. "What's her skin look like to you?"

"Void-burned, like what you'd get out on a moon somewhere further out," he said, visibly shaking himself and walking over. "Or frostbitten, I guess. Cold injuries."

"You don't see any blue?"

"Like your scars, sir? No."

He didn't like the implications of that. Why had he seen her like she was ilu-infected? Why was she behaving like that if she she wasn't? "So it's the glyphs, then."

Padre had a disturbed look on his face. "This woman's Arran," he said. "I think she locked herself in the freezer. Why would she do that?"

Caleb wanted to say something punchy. *Welcome to the Euphemism.* He refrained. "We should check on that."

"Go," Padre nodded. "I'll stay with her."

He entered the small commercial prep kitchen cautiously, the stench of dried blood assailing him the second he opened the swinging door. Tyr circled the room slowly, not quite in a combat stance. From the trails left on the tile, more than one body had been dragged into the walk-in.

Footprints led to the softly humming freezer. No viewing window. He checked the external temperature gauge; it was as low as it could go. Whatever had happened here, the perpetrators had turned down the temperature.

"Maybe we'll be lucky, and they're dead already," Caleb muttered, hand on the industrial metal handle, and Tyr took up position.

Seven bodies. A few of them might have been teenagers, but it was hard to tell. They'd all been bludgeoned, dragged in, arranged with an unsettling amount of care.

Moving in, Caleb checked vitals. No luck. They were all dead, either from their injuries or exposure.

Looking up from the last, he could see the fire again. In more detail now. Fire reaching out, fingers of flame closing in. The nightmare sounds of a slaughterhouse, of pigs squealing as they died. Sulfur, thick and choking, threatening to consume him with its rage, and he threw a hand up to—

His fingers landed in Tyr's thick fur, warm, reassuring. Caleb closed his eyes and focused on clearing his thoughts.

It took a moment, but when he opened them again all he saw was the kitchen. And a shocked priest in body armor and void-service blacks.

"Mother of God," Padre breathed.

Caleb ignored it and pressed his radio button. "Yip, you guys find anything yet?"

<Yeah, six dead, all voiders. Looks like massive blunt force trauma. But we also found this seal-fucker's office. Want to come take a look?>

"I'll be right there." Caleb looked to Padre. He had his prayer book out. "I understand if you've got last rites or something, but make sure that woman out there is secure first, okay?"

The priest didn't look happy about it but tucked the catechism away. "Roger that, sir," he said.

Caleb left Tyr with him. If that woman woke up, still lost in whatever nightmare she'd been flung into, or if something happened to Padre, the dog would take care of it.

The office in question was, again, seemingly not out of place. Or wouldn't have been, if not for the dead body on the floor.

Or the huge piece of equipment squeezed between the desk and filing cabinet.

"What is this?" Caleb asked, pointing at it.

"That is a dive comm unit. About as small as they come, although the miniaturization runs the cost up significantly," Yip said.

"How much?"

"More than a low-ranking Nepo should be able to afford," the sergeant replied.

The cop who was with him, a serious-looking man whose tattoos indicated he'd once been an ASDF major, nodded. "I think it's obvious somebody else was involved. Somebody was financing this Tok cell."

"The question is who?" Yip agreed.

Brushing it with his fingers, Caleb caught a glimpse of the nightmare again. Fire and brimstone.

Caleb eyed it warily, moving away to the desk. An open notebook sat there, figures scrawled across the pages. Glyphs, but not all complete, not all properly drawn. "How does that thing work?" he asked, and flipped the cover shut.

Something had gotten off Noqumiut.

It was proof enough, as far as he was concerned.

They were going to Earth. They were getting the Flet back and stopping whatever the hell was going on. No matter who on Mars disapproved.

"It gets into that confusing penumbra scat again, but it allows an electromagnetic transmission to—"

"I mean, does it move objects?" Caleb asked. "Like a proper dive core?"

"No, sir," Yip told him. "Effectively works like a radio."

"This is coming with me," he said, and slipped the notebook into a leg pocket. He jabbed a thumb at the core comm. "This needs to be destroyed, the entire district sealed off. Nobody in, nobody out."

"Sir," the cop protested, "there are upwards of ten thousand people in this district. We can't leave them to whatever this is."

"What this is, Officer, is a little tiny piece of the Euphemism, brought out of that fucking place on the edge of the Heliosphere,"

Caleb snapped. "You let this spread, and the death count is going to be much higher than ten thousand."

"With all due respect, Landlord, Arrans don't do math like that."

Caleb stared at him. "You've heard the story about my dad and the shovel, right?" It had come up several times in the Journals he'd read.

The cop didn't flinch. "Yes sir."

"Don't think I don't care. But you are going to have a hell of a lot more stories like that if you don't seal this place off. Immediately."

"Sir..."

"The Landlord's giving you an order," Yip said. "He knows more about this scat than we do. Get the cordon going."

As the cop turned away, pulling up his own radio, Caleb tapped the side of the core comm unit with his boot. "Can we trace this, figure out where it came from? Does it have a serial number or something?"

Yip smiled. "I'll ask Morray."

"Do that," Caleb said. "And get everybody back down here. The sooner we get out of this place, the better. No telling what we're being exposed to right now."

He headed back to the restaurant. Padre was still sitting with the unconscious woman. Reading to her, of all things. But Caleb could still smell the sulfur on her, still see the tendrils of flame reaching out for him.

"I'm sorry about this, Padre," he said.

"What's that?" the priest said.

But no sooner had he closed his prayer book than Caleb had drawn his gun on the woman. Five rounds. Last two to the head.

One never could be too careful.

An hour later, a partially disassembled core comm in tow, Caleb's team left the international district. Out through a police cordon that was being formed.

Chaplain Kannik didn't speak to him for the rest of the trip back to the hangar complex.

THE *BARACHIEL* WAS SCHEDULED for departure the next day. Caleb had wanted to leave immediately, but Cambel had over-ruled him.

"We've got a whole mess of housekeeping tasks to deal with," he'd said. "Least of which is getting my medical transfers taken care of. And our dead."

Caleb didn't argue that. Bringing back the dead wasn't something done in his time. Too risky, considering what they were up against. More than one base had been wiped out by some unknown pathogen smuggled in through a bullet or stab wound. If you were killed in the field, you were left in the field. It had always been a sore spot. If they could give the fallen the honor of a homecoming now, he couldn't stand in the way.

Turned out, the *Barachiel* had almost a dozen in her mortuary hold. Caleb wasn't craftside for the transfer, but he did accompany Cambel to the hangar when the bags were brought in. A few were disturbingly small.

"Captain Ynez," he said, indicating at one of those smaller black bags being wheeled past on a gurney. "Our Marine detachment commander. Good man."

"What happened to him?"

"We were dealing with a Tok 'roid that had slammed into a

freighter, out past Jupiter. It's always nasty fighting out there," Cambel said. "He took a couple shock-blasts, went down."

"They tore him apart before I could get to him." That was Yip, coming down the back tongue of the transport, none of his usual good humor evident. "I've got eight of my guys down here."

"Command prioritized us for backfill," Cambel said. "We should see their replacements in the morning."

"Great," Yip said. "Another officer I'm going to have to break in."

"Less paperwork for you, though."

"That is true."

The banter died as the last of the bodies were brought out of the plane. One bag had LANIN, TRAI MAJ written on the tag in neat block letters. Caleb paused at that one. They'd been friends, or so he'd been told. The man's wife had recognized him; he'd apparently come over for Christmas once or twice.

It was strange, having a past with these people that he couldn't remember. A past that he couldn't touch.

Next were the stasis bags with their critically wounded, escorted by a number of the *Barachiel's* medical staff. Caleb didn't have the foggiest idea of how that technology worked, but apparently, it wasn't good for more than a month or so. Some of the wounded, he'd been told, were down to their last few hours.

"Sir?"

He shook it off and stepped away from the somber procession. "Do what you can for them," he told the medical crew from Asaph.

The nurse just nodded, and away went the gurney.

Caleb looked around. Cambel and Yip were having some quiet, low conversation between themselves. Padre was moving between the bags, one of his prayer books open, muttering some benediction in Latin under his breath.

Feeling out of place, Caleb let himself out.

A protocol officer was waiting for him on the other side of the hangar doors. No lieutenant. This one had ink up to his jawbones. The brass devices on his uniform had been polished bright.

"We have a visitor here for you," the officer told him.

"What kind of visitor?"

THE ANSWER WAS WAITING in General Westland's conference room.

He looked similar to the Jovian, the Nepo, that they had secured down in lockup.

That seemed to be what he wanted to talk about.

"You have to understand, this is a major embarrassment for the Family," the man told him, skipping any pleasantries, launching right into it. "The Onias wants it dealt with as soon as possible."

"The Onias… you're not him, correct?"

"No, just his ambassador here to Mars. The Onias regrets he is not able to engage with you in person. The divedrive issue is… inconvenient."

"That's putting it mildly."

"But as soon as I heard what had happened, I flew over from Phobos."

"How did you hear about what happened?"

The Nepo just smiled, teeth sharp between tattooed lips. "We have our means, just as you Arrans have yours, I assume. No hard feelings. What's a little surveillance between friends?"

"I wasn't aware our, uhh, our inwells were friends." The concept still seemed a bit odd to him. A planet's gravity well, the equivalent of an old-Earth nation-state.

"We should be better friends than we are," the Nepo said. "And perhaps I can assist you. By removing that piece of Nalatok filth you have in your holding cells."

"I don't think he was ideologically driven."

"Perhaps not by the Arcna, but by something. Family does not betray itself like this without"—and the ambassador paused, as if searching for the best word—"without adequately insane cause."

"As if there's a good cause for killing a couple dozen people here?"

"Our inwells have not always been the best of friends. Relations break down sometimes. You're a man of war, surely you understand that."

The ambassador's accent was thick, but his English was very good. Caleb thought the little turn of phrase had to be intentional.

"You can have him back when we're done questioning him. File for extradition or whatever you normally do. Until then, I'd prefer it if you didn't try to give me the runaround just because I'm new here."

The ambassador chuckled a little, and some of the affected demeanor seemed to fall away. "Of course. I'll relay that to my own Landlord."

"If there's nothing else, I'm leaving," Caleb said, and shoved back. "I have shit to do."

"Just one more thing."

"What's that?"

"I have also been informed that you have an axilla bud out there on your spacecraft, picked up on New Stockholm." Caleb hesitated; the Nepo caught it and laughed. "You must work on your poker face, young Rossen."

"What about it?"

"The axilla? I would dearly love to speak with it. For the Onias, of course."

"I don't think that's a good idea."

"Why not?"

Again, Caleb hesitated.

"How long has it been active?"

"Just under two, uhh, sevendays, I think."

"That is old for one of those," the Nepo said. "The Rallarhu makes them so infrequently, and they do not last long. It must have taken an extraordinary amount of energy for her to produce it. Why that effort, the Onias wonders, and why attach to you?"

"She and I knew each other. Before all this. Maybe she just wanted to chat."

"Ah, yes, we understand that. But why?" Keen eyes bored into him. "Could it be that it was sent as a representative, her eyes and ears, while you breached the sacred cordon of the Kuiper?"

Caleb said nothing.

"Or is it after something else entirely? The Onias has long wondered what hold that place has over you both."

"I have no idea what it wants."

"The axilla itself may not either. But be careful of it. Those things tend to become dangerously unstable as they age."

Caleb forced a smile. "If you've got everything you need…"

"I'll file an extradition request as soon as I return to our offices on Phobos." The Nepo rose. "Better for him to be executed at home, don't you think?"

"By family?" Caleb shot back.

"And in sight of the great gas giant that grants us all our lives," he said. "It would be a shame for him to be shot on some grubby Martian gun range."

———

ADAIR WAS JUST PACKING up the last of his things in the borrowed quarters when Stag came by.

"What're you doing?" he asked, leaning on the doorway.

The historian paused. "I heard the transport is due to head back down to Deimos here pretty soon. I wanted to make sure I hadn't missed anything."

In truth, Adair was eager to leave. The tight confines, the last few rounds of violence, had long sucked any of the novelty out of the experience. He wanted to go home, back to the little quarters he and his wife shared out at Hygeia, back to their quiet plans about what life would be like when she retired in six months, back to what made sense. He'd already checked with the travel office. The monthly rotator was still due to leave in a few days.

"Sorry to disappoint you, Daevid, but you're not leaving just yet."

"What?"

"Captain's orders. He sees value in having a historian along for whatever's coming next."

"What, in the Earth inwell?"

"Don't you want to see it?" Stag asked. His voice was light, but there was an undercurrent of sincerity rarely displayed.

Adair hesitated. "My wife…"

"Look, if we get the Flet un-kidnapped, or whatever the hell, we can get you back to her a hell of a lot faster than the rotator. If we don't…" Stag trailed off. "I'm not real sure what happens. But you'll be stuck on a scatty little military transport out in the middle of the void when it hits."

"I don't know, sir, this is—"

"This is not a request," Stag said. "Unpack your notes, doctor. You're coming with us."

———

THE ROCKJUMP SET down in the main hangar just as the *Barachiel* was beginning to pull away from its anchor orbit.

Mars was visible through the atmo static field.

Disembarking, Caleb caught sight of it and just stood there. Transfixed.

Terraforming had been a pipe dream in his time. Just a few weeks ago, before waking up in that clinic bed, it was something he wouldn't have given much credence to. Something to keep civilians from falling into despair. A safe haven, out there somewhere.

But there it was. Atmosphere glowing against the endless black of space. Blue ocean encircling its northern hemisphere, vast swaths of green and yellow standing out against the red of naked rock. The terminator was passing across its surface; on the nightside, lights glittered.

So many lights.

"There it is."

Rallison, coming up beside him.

He looked again. The blue and green were gone. In fact, it was hard to see anything at all. Storm clouds in mottled white and gray covered most of the globe, lightning flashing in places.

"Between Dad and whatever the hell they're doing with the magnetic shield, they think it'll be habitable in a year or so."

"It's home now."

"Yeah, I suppose that's true."

But the moment was gone. Lost to the centuries.

Beside him, instead of a flesh-and-blood woman, was an abomination in its sealed suit.

"Impressive, isn't it?" it asked. "Although, of course, there are plenty who think it's a crime. Started the civil war. Not that you remember."

"Do you remember when we first came here?"

"Do you?"

The craft began picking up speed, and the hangar doors began closing.

Caleb tore his eyes away. "I'm going to Ops."

The suit tilted its head. Some kind of acknowledgement. "We should head to the core."

"I'll meet you there," he said.

"Just make sure it's depressurized for me."

———

BY THE TIME he'd made it up to Ops, they'd already passed through the magnetic shield, out into the international void.

Nothing in front of the window except for black space, dotted with a million tiny pinpricks of light.

"One of those is Earth, isn't it?" he asked Stag, who came up alongside him.

"Well, technically, Earth is that way," the officer said, and pointed in the opposite direction, towards the back door. "We're just headed out to dive distance."

Caleb nodded, not really paying attention. His mind was still working through the events of the past few days. "I know this is asking a lot," he said.

"What do you mean?"

"It's asking a lot, ordering you, the whole ship, into the Earth inwell. That's considered a pretty major deal, isn't it?"

Stag shrugged. "Going to Noqumiut was a big fucking deal. What's one more taboo broken?"

"That's what I mean," Caleb said. He realized other people were listening. No help for it now, he figured, and raised his voice a little. "I've taken you guys on a wild ride through the system the past few weeks, with no guarantees and little explanation. I didn't give you any reason to trust me. I didn't know anything about this time. Steamrolled right over you all. I owe you all an apology for that."

"You don't—"

"Stop being nice. We both know you've put up with a lot of bullshit from me. But this, this is the last stop. This is where we're going to fix this. This is where we end whatever it is that's going on."

Stag was quiet for a moment. "I believe you," he finally said.

Caleb nodded.

The chatter in Ops picked back up.

The *Barachiel* accelerated.

———

THEY DOVE the *Barachiel* to Earth. Cambel had reluctantly agreed to it. The trip could be made under conventional propulsion, he'd argued, but it would have still taken too long.

Whatever was happening, it needed to be dealt with now. Immediately.

As the axilla slithered out of its suit, performed its voodoo with the core command column, Caleb expected a slip, a vision, something.

Instead, there was only silence. A moment, and it was gone.

<Earth inwell in range,> came Ops, over his pressure suit's radio. <Four hours to low orbit and rendezvous with the Lift.>

———

IT WAS hours before anybody came to speak with him.

And when something finally did, it was nothing that he'd expected.

Nanuk was fully expecting extradition. Most likely, that would mean torture, a confession, then execution.

Even when it came to the Family, the Onias didn't have much mercy for anything even remotely connected to Nalatok activity.

Dying in an execution chamber open to the Jovian sky or dying of cellular breakdown after a few more miserable years, a decade or two perhaps. Didn't make much difference to the Nepo. He had always known, since he failed the compatibility trials, that his time in the greater world was marked, limited. That he represented a genetic dead end. That his life held no meaning.

But what a glorious thing, having a mission for a little while.

"You look too satisfied with yourself for a man who has failed."

The sound was reedy, thin. Barely there at all. For a moment,

Nanuk felt real fear; what if they'd trapped him in some ilu nightmare? The Landlords were said to have the power to do that.

But then, there, on the shadowed wall of his cell, a face.

A face, stretched and pinned to the metal, like something skinned off a human skull. But this was pale white, smooth.

"Rallarhu," he said.

"Just a piece of her. A piece of a piece. Sent to deal with you." A curl of smoke escaped from the corner of the thing's mouth. "Quickly."

"We had a deal," Nanuk said.

The axilla smiled, a cold expression on the liquid face. "We did have an arrangement, yes. But you did not satisfy the terms."

"I did exactly what was asked…"

"What was asked was for you to kill the Rossen in his current incarnation. Yet he lives on. This is a problem."

"Your problem, maybe."

"It is everyone's problem. The Onias will demand your interrogation. Nothing withstands he who lurks in the mind." The axilla was almost boiling now. The smile cracked its face, almost all the way apart. It was wrinkling. A few minutes, maybe, and it would be dead. If he could just keep it talking. "But I need no evidence to act."

"I'm not your fucking citizen to—"

"The Tenancy sentences you to death for your failures."

"Wait—" he began, but never had the opportunity to finish.

The small piece of the Rallarhu in front of him broke away from the wall, pushing off like a jellyfish in the boundary oceans of those Ibbie worlds. It floated for a moment in the low gravity. Hung in the air.

Then it was on him.

Dissolving though it might have been, it retained enough strength to wrap itself around his face. Nose, mouth, eyes. Too firmly for any of his screams to escape.

The axilla lasted only fifteen seconds longer than he did. But it was enough.

All the guards found, when they came to collect him for transport to Jovian custody, was a thin film of gunk across his face. Somebody had the presence of mind to take a sample, but it would take over a day to positively identify it as denatured xenocyte lipids. And even then, it was only a footnote in the HOMECOM daily report.

FORTY-TWO

CALEB BARELY MADE his departure window, down in the main hangar. Four hours wasn't much time. It had taken him a while until he was finally satisfied with his personal kit. The *Barachiel* carried very little suitable to the environment he'd be walking into. The quartermaster had finished packing up a few small crates with food and other necessities a while ago, and those were being loaded on the rockjump.

Ops hadn't been able to tell Caleb much about what to expect, and Earth Orbital Command hadn't been very communicative. The on-shift radio tech had spent nearly two hours on the radio with them but hadn't been able to get answers to most of the questions Caleb had left him with. He didn't know what conditions were like down there.

Adair hadn't been able to give him much of the history either.

"A lot of the records from that time have either been lost or destroyed," he'd said. "The motivations of the, ahh, the people who executed the Euphemism aren't well understood. You would know more about it than us."

Caleb wasn't sure about that. He still didn't understand why humanity had abandoned Earth almost in totality. Organizations like the Ariums had been working on seemingly endless ways to kill people, and he supposed that a lot of the initial flight was to escape that. But they'd been fighting so hard. To end it. To stay. He couldn't fathom why Mars, why he personally, had agreed to the terms of the Tenancy that called for Earth to remain depopulated.

Maybe there would be answers down there, tucked into some new past moment.

For his immediate purposes, he would have settled for some more concrete information about conditions on the surface. Ops was fairly certain there were atmospheric fliers, but if Singapore's airfield had been lost to recent events, they could be looking at weeks at sea.

"Morning, sir," Yip drawled, as Caleb walked in. He had a pack in hand himself. "How are you this fine day?"

There were more men waiting in the hangar than Caleb was expecting. Chaplain Kannik. Colonel Cambel. Morray. Adair. And three Marines, all in half-buckled carapace.

The axilla was there too, wandering off amongst the cargo crates lining the back of the hangar.

Caleb frowned. "What are you doing, Sergeant?"

"Coming with you."

That was unexpected. "What do you mean? The gravity—"

"Is painful, but survivable. As long as we aren't down there that long, and we stay in a support carapace most of the time. A few of us got cleared by Medical last night."

"I have no idea how long this is going to take."

Yip shrugged. "We'll make it work."

"There's no need for you to come."

"When else do I get a chance to see the birth world?" Yip replied.

"I don't think I've got time to give you a tour."

"Fuck, I'll settle for seeing a palm tree outside some Aphroditan whore-market," Yip said.

"In all seriousness, sir, sending you down there with nothing but that thing," and the colonel nodded off in the direction of the axilla, "is a disaster waiting to happen. I'm not going to have you die twice on my watch."

"Colonel, I know you're putting your—"

"What are they going to court-martial me for? Keeping reality from ripping apart?" Cambel's words were light, and most of the assembly chuckled. "If General Scrivner has the balls to issue me that kind of paperwork, I'll frame it and hang in on my hearth-room wall back home."

Caleb held out his hand. "Thank you. For everything."

"Fix it," Cambel repeated, but shook his hand anyway.

The chaplain stepped forward, handing him a small package. "None of it's real, Caleb. Keep that in mind."

Caleb shook his hand too. "This is the same bullshit that drove us off the planet, Padre. I never underestimate it." He looked over at Yip. "Everyone ready?"

"Ready and excited about getting crushed by the birth world," the Marine quipped.

<You're going to miss the platform rendezvous if you don't launch in the next five minutes,> a voice boomed. Ops.

"Get going," Cambel said, and nodded at the rockjump. "It'll take us another ten hours to pass by it again."

One they were out in the void, Caleb opened the package Padre had given him. It was a pair of rank patches, velcro on the back. The Tenancy icon, embroidered in pale gold on uniform black. He stared at them for a moment, then ripped his the chevron patches off his shoulders and patted the new patches on.

The sound was loud in the rockjump. Nobody said anything.

———

THARSIS AWOKE to the sound of an explosion.

To a violent rocking that almost threw her out of bed.

For a moment, the Arran lieutenant lay there in the dark, mind fuzzy, trying to catch up to where she was.

She shouldn't have been asleep. She knew that much.

She remembered setting out into the afternoon waters. She remembered spending time out on deck, the wind in her hair, Bea playing at her feet. She remembered…

Time had escaped her again. Or else, she had slipped through it.

Donovan's private yacht. The civilian marina at Pearl Harbor. Waiting, waiting for…

She had the sudden feeling that, like tipping over the edge of a waterfall, they'd just passed through the Flet's event horizon.

Bea was still asleep next to her. All the months of travel seemed to have inured the little girl to disruptions; she could sleep through almost anything. Tharsis was loath to wake her up, but she needed to go see what was going on.

The bed, integrated into the curve of the yacht's outer wall, was low enough to the ground, wasn't it?

Tharsis stripped the thin sheet the rest of the way down, building a little dam around the perimeter of the mattress with the cover, and said a little prayer that it would be enough to hold Bea if she got to rolling. Then, she pulled her clothes back on and went out into the hallway.

Cynthia, Tom's wife, was already out there, a robe thrown on over a thin sleep shirt.

"Where's Tom?" Donovan was asking her. He was still in his boxers, pulling on a clean T-shirt.

"I don't know," she said, arms crossed, hands tucked up into the sleeves of her robe. "He was just gone."

Tharsis was going to ask more when she saw a trickle of water coming from underneath one of the cabin doors. "Yours?" she asked, and when the other woman nodded, Tharsis pushed her way inside. The two Earthers followed.

Cynthia and Tom had been sharing a cabin, one of four on the yacht. Unlike the one Tharsis had gotten for the night, however, this one had an attached bathroom. The bed was rumpled, Tom's clothes mixed with hers all over the floor. But the bathroom, the bathroom, that seemed to be where the water was coming from.

Tharsis poked her head in. It was as if a perfect sphere had been carved out of the already tight space. Floor, ceiling, cabinetry, even the small sink and part of the toilet were missing. Water was leaking from the bowl out into the divot in the floor, running out from there.

"Huh," Donovan said.

Tharsis's mind tried to process it. The answer was clear, she realized. Obvious. "He dove," she said.

"He what?"

"I don't think he had control of it, though. I've never heard of him taking other things with him," Tharsis said, touching one of the carve-outs from the wall. At least a meter in radius. That was a lot of air. "I think what we heard was atmosphere rushing in to fill the void he left. Everything went with him."

"What do you mean, 'dove'?" Donovan asked again.

Tharsis didn't know what to say to that. What she could. How to explain it; it was taken almost as an article of faith in her own time, in the Heliosphere. The Flet could move matter with thought, perception, alone. He just could.

If this was his event horizon, or at least, part of it...

She took a step into the bathroom, then another.

The scene inside the sphere changed.

Instead of sparkling white walls and polished wood veneers, there was a bay. An island. Black rock and the crash of surf. Arid land above a wide blue bay. And above it, the sound of screaming.

What had he said? An arium.

There was only one arium facility in the Hawaiian Islands, they'd told her back on the *Vastitas Reach*. Only one. On the island they owned.

It was a leap, a big one. But at the same time, she could feel it in her bones: this was what he'd needed her help with. This was why she was here.

"He's on Lanai," she said. "One of the other islands. I need to go get him."

Cynthia shook her head. "He's probably elsewhere on the boat, or went out for—"

"He's on Lanai," Tharsis repeated, cutting her off, "and I have to go get him."

Donovan—jesus, the Founder himself—stared at her, but another explosion in the distance broke the little standoff.

Tharsis thought at first that maybe it was coming from whatever was within that sphere. But the light of that other day vanished. Screaming began. Outside. Close.

Donovan was already moving. Cynthia looked lost, like she still couldn't process what had happened in the cabin.

Tharsis rushed down the hall, back to her own space. Bea was awake now, fists balled up, screaming silently. She shushed the baby as best she could, tossing the ever-ready sling over her shoulder but picking the little girl up in her arms. That little face, those red eyes, snuggled into her shoulder automatically. Tharsis kissed the top of her head as she hurried back out. Poked her head into the ruined cabin.

"Come on!" she snapped at Cynthia.

The other woman shook herself out of her reverie and followed.

Donovan had gone outside, out on the lower back deck. He cut a dark figure against the harsh lights of the marina. He had a pump-action shotgun in hand.

That gave Tharsis pause. Back home, it wouldn't have been out of place at all; everyone kept firearms around. But she couldn't recall seeing a single such weapon in all her travels on Earth.

Smoke was rising beyond them, down to the south. Smoke, up into the already cloudy night.

"What's going on?" Cynthia asked.

"I don't know. It looks like the entire airfield is—"

Another explosion rocked the night, throwing a fireball far up into the sky and illuminating the landscape for hundreds of meters around.

"I think it's more than that," Tharsis said.

Figures were coming down the dock. Unsteady, jerky movements. Rocking on their feet. Reeling like drunk men. As the light from the explosion hit, Tharsis could see blood and rot there. Ripped clothing. Terrible wounds. Moving slowly. Slowly. But not stopping.

Cynthia took a breath. "They look like…"

"That's not possible," Donovan said, but handed her the shotgun as he scrambled towards the back of the boat.

"Where are you going?" she asked.

"I think Amanda's idea about a midnight cruise to Lanai is a good one," he said, and jumped down to the dock. The strange little throng, which had been clustering about the back of another boat, turned towards him. "Headshots!" he yelled.

"That is not funny!" Cynthia yelled back but shouldered the gun anyway.

Tharsis watched the bloody group advance. "I'm going to go start the engines," she said.

Tucking Bea unceremoniously into her sling, Tharsis ran back through the yacht, up a flight of stairs and onto the bridge. She'd been around boats for half a year, helped operate a few, but these controls were far more complicated than the ones on the charter boats they'd taken out for snorkel trips.

Outside, the shotgun sounded off.

Bea started beating Tharsis with her fists.

Tharsis forced herself not to react, casting about for some indication of how to operate the damn thing. Somebody—probably that captain—had left a card taped to the throttle controls. Ignition sequence, she realized, and started punching on systems.

Cynthia's shotgun was firing faster now. There was more screaming; other boats, it seemed, were being rudely awoken. Tharsis ignored it—*Bea is going to live through this*, she told herself—and worked the instructions.

The engines roared to life at the same time that Donovan scrambled up onto the bow deck. Hands were reaching for him. "Go!" he yelled.

Tharsis pushed forward on the throttle.

The yacht shot forward.

She almost hit another boat on her way out, as well as the small seawall. The wheel controls were incredibly responsive; she hadn't been expecting that and overcompensated at first. But by the time Cynthia and Donovan joined her on the bridge, Tharsis had gotten them out into the relative safety of the open water.

Where they could see the damage being wreaked back onshore.

Cynthia was sweating, pale. She stank of cordite. Laying the now hot shotgun aside, she sat down heavily in one of the bridge's seats. Donovan was bleeding from a nasty cut on his arm; the skin was already turning an odd shade of green.

"What the hell was that?" Cynthia asked, eying his wound. "Was that…"

"Looked like it," he said, terse. "Smelled like it."

"Did you get bit?" she asked, terse.

"Like you said, zombies aren't real, Cyn," he said.

"If you got fucking bit…"

Tharsis was only half listening, distracted by both Bea's desperate little movements and the ongoing firestorm on the shore. The entire airfield was going up in flames. Luckily the bridge windows were closed, or everything would likely have stunk of burning fuel. Their argument had some kind of significance, though.

"What's a zombie?" she asked.

They both looked at her.

Donovan's eyes had gone wrong, something dead creeping into them.

But no, that couldn't be. The future didn't change. He was a hero, one of the fathers of Mars. He didn't die here. What the hell was going on?

Then something caught Tharsis's eye.

A monitor, set up high on the bridge. One of those screens that seemed ubiquitous in this time.

It was on. Set to gray static.

And one other thing.

A glyph. A glyph like the ones Wyatt drew. A glyph from his writing system.

Cynthia and Donovan were still arguing, the words growing in pitch, in desperation. Tharsis, one arm protectively wrapped around Bea, skirted the edge of that. Got the shotgun.

Used the black resin butt to smash the screen out.

Even with everything happening back onshore, the noise was loud enough to shatter their conversation. They both fell silent, staring at her.

The green hue was gone from Donovan's arm. The deadness gone from his eyes.

"What's a zombie?" she asked again.

FORTY-THREE

THE PARTY from the *Barachiel* was greeted at the Lift's air lock by a very irritated officer. A very irritated, senior officer, based on the number of things tattooed on his neck.

"The hell are you doing?" he demanded, as he marched towards the small group from the *Barachiel*, disembarking from the rockjump. "We didn't clear you to land. In fact, I specifically told you to turn around."

"We appreciate the accommodation, Major," Morray said.

"You in charge here?"

He tapped his neck. "I am the ranking officer."

"I know deepvoiders do things differently, son, but I am ordering you directly to get back on that rockjump and get the hell off my station."

"Can't do that, sir."

"Oh?"

"We need the Lift prepped for drop."

"Why?"

"So we can head down to the surface. We're going to need you to make available whatever resources you've got available at Singapore as well. We need some form of air transport. I believe Colonel Cambel sent the request over an hour ago." He smiled. "I hope everything's okay. We've been having quite a bit of trouble contacting you."

"That request was ignored. Beyond the recent damage, which you should know about, nobody is allowed down to the surface per EORCOM giddy. Not without gravity adaptation..."

Yip picked at his carapace. "We've been cleared by Medical, as long as we don't extend our stay past a few days."

"Lieutenant, I am ordering you—"

"I can't take that order, General."

The station officer stared at them. "Excuse me, son?"

"I can't take that order. It contradicts what he," and he jabbed a thumb over his shoulder at Caleb, "told me to do."

The general's neck was turning red beneath its fanned tattoos, and then he caught sight of Caleb's rank patches. The rage collapsed in a second. "Fuck," he muttered.

"Colonel Cambel did mention we had the Landlord with us, didn't he?"

ARRANGEMENTS WERE MADE.

The general who'd met them at the air lock offered Caleb an apology, and a tour.

"Why not?"

In Caleb's time, there was a network of space lifts, spread across the planet. His own country had built one of the first, the Pan-American, off the coast of Ecuador a year before he was born. He'd been on it once. After getting captured in the jungle nightmare of the Yucatan.

Africa, the Indian Ocean, Brazil. Singapore had had the lion's share, though, seven platforms, all designed for different types of cargo.

One remained, the others lost to the ravages of time and a Tenancy-mandated dissolution protocol. From what Adair had told him, the idea had been for every human construction to be ripped down from its foundations. Sea and land returned to some kind of natural state.

It was an idea that had started before his time. One that escalated, once void habitats started being built. *Why remain on Earth, why allow humanity's toxic influence to poison the planet*, had been the argument. Caleb had heard it himself. In rumors. In news articles. From the mouths of captured whitecoats and the bio-cults that had swarmed to their influence.

He couldn't understand why it still had any power, that idea.

The Arrans, to a man, had expressed their frustration with it. Erg had told him, in one of those quiet conversations down in the maintenance hangar, that voiders looked down on living planetside.

Why be beholden to the idea at all?

Some fossilized ideal of the past, was all he could figure. The legacy of the old ideologies that should have died out when they'd won.

It bothered Caleb that he himself had gone along with it. Even knowing the stakes, better than any of them, it bothered him.

The Malaccan Lift was not, physically speaking, the same as the one from his time. Every component of it had been replaced over the years, from the nanotube carbon tethers to the very bolts that held the top station's communications antenna to the superstructure. The counterweight, a huge chunk of iron-nickle asteroid, kilometers still beyond the station, was probably the same.

At some point, the decision had been made to eliminate both the heavy cargo and passenger lifts, leaving the specialized freight lift intact. Easier to maintain than the vast commercial platforms, most likely, but more useful for what supplies did need to make it down to the surface. In principle, though, it was the same.

The short tour ended in the Lift capsule itself. While distinctly lacking in any ornamentation, the seats were at least comfortable. An observation bubble punched outward from the hull at the far end.

Walking into it felt like stepping into the void.

As he entered, though, Caleb had a flash. Not his own time, not one of those slips. No, it was different than that; somebody else's memory, maybe.

Rallison, standing there with a hand on a different curve, different glass, staring out at a spacecraft, a craft with—

"We should have the Lift ready to drop within the hour," the general said.

The vision, memory, broke apart.

The only other thing in the observation bubble, besides the two men, was the axilla, striding the perimeter of the glass canopy. It put him in mind of a tiger, inspecting its bars at the zoo.

"Thank you," Caleb said absently.

Wondered what the hell he'd just seen.

THE LIFT TOOK three hours to reach the surface.

The small contingent from the *Barachiel* spent most of the ride in silence. Checking kits, inspecting this or that weapon, one of them reading something from the small library set up in a corner of the main room. But by the time they were around twenty thousand meters from the surface, both the gravity and the scenery made the planet below them impossible to ignore.

Caleb had been through Singapore more than once, back in his own time. But even from the air, a great distance away, it was clear that it was a shadow of its former self now.

And a massive blast area stood out on the island, clear as anything against the brilliant green of the jungle canopy.

"What happened?" he asked Yip, who'd come over to the north-facing windows next to him.

"A matter transfer slipped out of its temporal alignment," the sergeant said, and then smiled. It was pained. They were all feeling the full pull of Earth now. Three times what the Arrans were used to. As Caleb understood it, they'd be operating at the very limits of what their bodies could handle. "Or some such scat. The energy release from it did that. Destroyed half the city."

"I think something else destroyed the city, a long time ago," he said. "Back in my time, it was this metropolis, skyscrapers everywhere, filling the entire island."

"Must have been a hell of sight."

"It was," Caleb murmured, and stared down at the last city on Earth.

———

THE MALACCAN LIFT Complex was anchored exactly at the equator, out on something that reminded Caleb of the old oil platforms. He guessed all those were long gone as well. He wondered about the infrastructure necessary to keep these structures in place. How they were built, maintained, replaced. The sea lift and platform-based cranes of his day, not to mention the manufacturing base, were likely all long gone as well. When he asked the woman leading them down to the ferry jetty, she just shook her head.

"Someday, it will be unsustainable," she agreed. "But until then, Landlord, don't worry. We're keeping her in good shape."

"What happens when it becomes unsustainable?"

"We lose Earth forever," she said. "Or at least, anybody who descends to the surface won't be coming back. Unless something changes."

The boat waiting for them, by comparison, seemed state-of-the-art. Or at least, on par with everything else Caleb had seen in the Heliosphere thus far. Yip seemed particularly interested in it.

The only member of their little group that seemed profoundly uninterested was the axilla. But then, emotion was hard to read from that thing as it was.

———

A SMALL PARTY was waiting for them at the harbor. Caleb could remember a vast series of quays; the wooden ramps and walkways now only held a few dozen boats. One of those waiting stepped forward as Tyr jumped from back deck to ramp, unwilling to wait for the boat to be tied up.

"Landlord," the man acknowledged.

Caleb shook his hand. He had a sergeant's rank tattooed on his arm. All four of them had military markings. "You're Arran?" he asked.

"We were," the man said. "Not all of us can handle the false magnetics on Mars. For those with natural sensitivity to such things, Earth is the only relief." He looked past Caleb, at the *Barachiel's* men, struggling over the side of the boat. "You boys need any help?"

"No, just fine here," Yip panted.

"Orbital Command mentioned a few of your crew were coming down with you. I didn't think it was a good idea. Still don't. We may have evolved here, but humanity has twisted itself out of its original form."

"I'm sorry," Caleb said, "but we're in a bit of a hurry, and—"

"Of course. Arrangements have been made with what resources we have at the moment. Even the governor was killed in that explosion," the man said. "I apologize, you'll just have to do with his secretary of agriculture."

Caleb took that to mean it was the man's own position. "I'm sorry to hear that."

The last of their equipment was being unloaded by the boat's crew. Ninden tried to lift one of their packs, and in getting it on his shoulder, fell over backwards. A ripple of laughter went up from the others.

"Scat's going to be three times as heavy here," the agriculture secretary said, walking over to offer the man a hand up. "Lesson for everybody. Be careful."

"Noted," Ninden grunted.

"You might want to manually adjust your carapaces as you go. It should help with movement," the secretary said. "The auto settings are terrible in those things, if I'm remembering right. Takes a little getting used to, but movement'll get easier."

A huge, flat-bodied truck was produced from somewhere, and the locals helped the *Barachiel* contingent load up their gear. The Marines climbed into the back, while the secretary offered Caleb the other seat in the cab.

The road he pulled onto followed the curve of the southern harbor for a while, providing a grand view of both the Malacca Strait and the space lift rising from it. Clouds were piling up to the east, brilliant white, fat on the warm, shallow waters of the Pacific. The sky was clearer than Caleb could ever remember, and he said so.

"It did make quite a difference when almost all human industry on the planet shut down," the secretary said, "but a lot of the old theories regarding overall climate proved to be wrong, from what I understand. It took leaving to truly understand how complex the global meta-ecosystem really is."

"In my time, people were worried that we were going to kill it."

"It's true, some species never recovered. A few regions, no matter what we seem to do, are poisoned beyond our ability to fix on an appreciable human timescale. But according to my read of the records, most populations, most habitats, sprang back incredibly fast. Some within only a few decades. Makes me wonder sometimes what we could have done with the cleaner energy we have on Mars. If we'd just waited a little while longer, but…" The secretary kept his eyes on the road, voice neutral. "We might be marooned here, so to speak, but we uphold our end of the Tenancy Accords. Dismantling humanity's presence here, city by city, brick by brick."

He seemed bitter about it. "How many people died?" Caleb asked.

"Last count, one hundred and sixty-five. Including a few children," the secretary said, and dropped his voice. "We're not supposed to have them, of course, but no birth control method is absolute. And you refused to make full surgical sterilization a condition of coming to the surface. Which everyone does appreciate."

Caleb hadn't been asking about the recent explosion, and felt ashamed of himself for not. "I take it I've come here before?"

"A few times each lifetime, I'm told. Last time was five years ago. Right before the Naven gave birth."

"They told me about that. She was just a little girl, right?"

"She was never a little girl. Even as an infant, there was something about her." They left the coastal road then, the truck turning north up well-maintained asphalt that ran through manicured pasture. Here and there, goats grazed. "Airfield's a few more miles, sir."

"We couldn't have waited," Caleb said.

"Sir?"

"What you were saying, about waiting. Before leaving Earth entirely, right? We couldn't have done that. They were determined to get us gone, whatever it took. Whatever the cost." He rapped the window with his knuckles. "This is beautiful, but it was bought with the blood of billions. They'd already slaughtered half the planet's population, in my own time."

At that, the secretary did glance over at him. "Who was it?" he asked. "Somebody like the Arcna?"

"The Arcna's a corpse," Caleb said. "But I've listened to some of that bullshit she spewed. A pale echo of the propaganda we used to hear as kids. Imitation of the slogans I've seen carved in marble and spray-painted on ghetto street corners."

"So..."

"THERE WAS NEVER some discernible *them*. Just ideas, and people willing to act in their own way. Add that up, and you get an extinction-level genocide event."

The truck was slowing now. Boxy forms of hangars and outbuildings, all obviously prefab, lay ahead. As they passed through the gates, onto the apron, Caleb got a feel for how diminished things really were. In his time, the airport here had been massive. Leisure air travel had largely been restricted, but Singapore had been a major international port and commercial flights were still common. The concrete had clearly been replaced, reduced, over the centuries. Much of the old surrounding infrastructure was gone. "Well, sir," the secretary said, "they didn't get all of us."

"No," Caleb replied, and it felt like some kind of promise, "and they never will."

The truck turned again, down to the end of the airfield, and another dock, set far out into the water.

———

"WHAT THE HELL IS THAT?" Yip dropped a hard-sided case on the apron, folding his arms. "Are we supposed to get on that thing?"

Caleb glanced down the runway, at the plane that was taxiing towards them across the surface of the ocean. A fat, thick body tapering off into smooth wings, propeller shafts bulging tightly in. It rolled between two fat pontoons, set down from the ends of its wings.

"Looks like a normal seaplane to me." In fact, it looked entirely normal. No different from any of a dozen models of hyper-efficient aircraft from his own time. If anything, it was weird they were still using the same design.

"With wings?" Yip spat. "It's a fuckin' antique."

"What do you use on Mars?" Caleb asked.

"Airships," he said. "You know, zeppelins, dirigibles, all that scat."

"Ah," the secretary said. "Zeps are a better way to go on Mars. They can lift more, fly further, take less fuel. But here, it takes a lot more to keep a load in the air. Gravity, you know. And our weather out here, especially in the Pacific, can be nasty. Have you ever seen a typhoon?"

"No sir."

"Well, they're nasty. Nothing like that on Mars. The Vastitas doesn't get hot enough, and it ain't big enough."

"Sir?" Yip asked. "Orders?"

Caleb looked at the veteran. The exosuit he was wearing was prefab, not custom, and clearly fit imperfectly at the joints. Strain showed in his eyes, but nowhere else. Holding it together.

"I'm a corporal," he said.

"Well then, Corporal Petrison, get your ass on that plane," Yip said, and smiled a little.

"Gladly," Caleb said.

"Somebody tell me there's something to drink on this thing," he said. "It is fucking hot down here."

THE TRIP WOULD HAVE to be taken in chunks, they had been told. Fuel was a limitation that there was no way around. Fuel was also precious, brought down on the Lift from orbit and rationed heavily. Several outposts were going to miss a routine resupply because of their presence. Caleb felt bad about that, but their pilot assured him nobody would starve.

Their stop for the night was in the island chain of Palau. An overnight there, and then on to Hawaii in the morning.

There wasn't much there. A small station, home to maybe a dozen former Arrans who oversaw the runway and oversaw a massive swarm of oceanic data-wasps. They greeted the entire team warmly, obviously bemused by the discomfort shown by the Marines, and fawned over Tyr.

Dinner that night was simple. Fish, fruit. Some kind of locally grown potato. Everything was cooked and served down on the beach, although whether that was typical or not, Caleb wasn't sure. It could have been something in honor of him. He wasn't sure. The people they'd met on the surface were, so far, friendlier than just about anybody else he'd run into yet in the Heliosphere. Like they were genuinely happy to meet him.

Whatever it was, he was grateful for it.

Even Earth felt alien. Stripped of humanity's presence, it seemed far bigger than it ever had before.

The Arrans seemed to be enjoying themselves. Tyr too; the dog seemed to be savoring the gravity. In fact, the only member of their little expedition who seemed thoroughly miserable was the axilla. But then, who knew what that thing was feeling?

After dinner, as dessert was being brought out, Caleb realized that Yip was missing. The big Marine sergeant had been uncharacteristically quiet that evening, and for him to have slipped away without comment seemed odd. Caleb whistled to Tyr, and off they went to go look.

They found Yip down on the waterline. Gravity carapace and boots banished, obviously heedless of his uniform as it wicked moisture from the damp sand. A bottle of beer, untouched, sweated by his side.

"That's a hell of a sunset," Caleb said, as Tyr settled down between them.

"What the fuck was wrong with you people?" Yip asked quietly.

"What do you mean?"

"This," he said, and waved his hand at the water. "There's nothing like this, anywhere else in the Heliosphere. Why didn't you fight harder to keep it?"

"I don't know," Caleb said. "Maybe it was because this was never in danger. But we are. Were."

"'Are' is right," Yip said, and reached for the beer. "'Are' is right. We left this, and we're still fighting the same fucking war, all these centuries later. You think that your generation would have had the decency to actually end it, for the price that was paid."

Caleb made to leave. Whatever was going through the sergeant's head, it wasn't his place to ask.

"Petrison!" Yip called, before he was out of earshot.

"What?"

"Never realized before, how much we owe you. Leaving this. For a scatty little rock that's too cold most of the time."

Caleb didn't know what to say to that. He couldn't remember making the decision to leave, head to Mars, reenlist. Maybe it was in a Journal somewhere, one of those classified ones in his vault. "It was never really about Earth," he said. "Not for me. After what happened with my family, I guess I just needed some kind of purpose."

"And that was what, service?" Yip asked.

"Guess so. Not a whole lot else that makes sense."

Yip nodded. He still hadn't taken a sip of that beer. He waggled the bottle at Caleb. "Did you ever have kids?"

"I think you would know better than me."

Yip grunted. "Light of my life, my four girls. Don't get to see them much. My second oldest is taking on the family commitment. Smart girl. Tested into the officer corps. She's supposed to start at the Academy next year. I'm proud as hell of her. But the price…" he trailed off. "The void takes a lot from us."

Sensing the sergeant wanted to be left alone, Caleb nodded and headed back up the beach.

Yeti was waiting when Caleb walked back into the outpost. "Jesus, sir, we were just about to go out looking for you."

"Why, what happened?"

"Got a message in on the shortwave," the Marine said, and pointed down the road to a building studded with antennas. "Morray, up at the orbital. Said he needs to talk to you immediately. Urgent."

———

"WHAT'S UP?" Caleb asked, depressing the talk button without any ceremony.

<Fucking HOMECOM daily reports,> Morray's voice crackled back immediately. Transmission distances planetside were negligible. It was a relief, in a way. <They buried some scat way in the back of the damn thing, I had to call back, just got the scatting answer...>

"Morray," Caleb warned. *Get to the fucking point.*

<That Tok you captured was found dead in his cell when they went to process him for extradition.>

"That's inconvenient."

<What's inconvenient about it, sir, is that he died of asphyxiation. The idiot I talked to in mortuary affairs wasn't real clear about how it happened. They're still investigating.>

"Thanks. Anything else going on?"

<Plenty. Just get the Flet back. Sir. Earth Orbital, over and out.> And with that, the radio signal went dead.

Caleb leaned back in the chair, looked over at Tyr. He'd never considered himself much of a politician. Hell, he'd never considered himself a strategist. That sort of thing was better left to officers. What he cared about was whatever was right in front of him.

But he was responsible for all of this now. What any of it meant, what he was meant to do with it, he didn't yet know.

"If I actually volunteered for this," he told his dog, "then I was a fucking idiot."

Tyr panted but didn't say anything.

"Come on. We might as well get some sleep."

The bunkhouse where they were put up for the night was a simple affair. Ventilated windows, hammocks. The Arran Marines had to sleep in their carapaces, something which led to a great deal of grousing until Yip rattled off a few choice insults.

It still took Caleb a long, long time to fall asleep. And even when he did, there was no rest in it.

He was on a beach. White sand. Not another human around.

Eliza was there, hair unbound, the sea breeze pulling it around her face. In the quiet of the predawn, she looked profoundly sad.

"Was there ever anything real between us?" she asked.

"I don't know," he replied honestly. "I can't remember."

Green-gray eyes turned on him, and she reached over, grasping for his hand.

He let her have it.

They sat there like that for a long, long time.

———

BREAKFAST the next morning was a simple affair, especially compared to the night before. Some sort of rice with fruit, a few sausages. Pork, Caleb realized, and savored it. He hadn't had it yet in the Heliosphere. The Arrans were suspicious of it, though, even as they talked it through with the station staff. Pigs hadn't been taken to Mars. Concerns of the usual ecological havoc had been too high.

Refueled, they said their goodbyes and headed on their way.

To Hawaii.

STAG PACED the floor in Ops. Cambel was getting a few extra hours of rest; Stag had insisted. It was Cambel's shift right now, but Stag couldn't sleep. He couldn't do much of anything, except stare at that orb below them.

Earth.

He hadn't expected to ever be back out here. That little trip with the Landlord, a month or so back, should have been his last visit. His only visit.

No matter. The *Barachiel* had been through the wringer in the time since then and downtime was the perfect opportunity to get a little housekeeping done.

"Do we have a window yet for the maintenance inspection on the hull?" he asked, stopping at the weather station.

The sergeant there didn't bother looking up. Just turned his screen. "I wouldn't advise it until we've passed onto the nightside. Orbital concurs. Sun's pretty quiet right now, but we have to go out there in bare cloth."

Wrapper was an amazing thing, but even centuries of selective breeding and gene-splicing hadn't managed to erase certain qualities. Xenocytes had a tendency to merge with each other, if given long enough exposure. ENEX to ENEX, ENEX to standard survival equipment, casual contact, wasn't usually a problem. But the stuff that lived on the hull never went dormant. Thick, old, awake. There was more than one old blacksuiter's story about some hapless tech going out on a craft's surface and being absorbed, sucked into the goo.

Stag wasn't sure if he believed that or not.

Chief Druz, however, was downright paranoid about it. And to the old blacksuiter's credit, there was the small problem of the axilla.

It had been living out there for multiple sevendays now.

If ever there were conditions for some kind of xenocyte merger, this was it.

At least they had the opportunity to check here. The magnetic field of Earth provided quality shielding from background cosmic radiation. As safe as it got for a void walk in unshielded exogear. Sure, Stag knew he'd get some whining over it. Nobody liked strapping on those snow-shoe-like tragers, and nobody liked trudging across the outer hull's meter-deep wrapper layer. But that's why he gave those orders, and not the colonel. Might as well have the boys pissed at him. They all thought he was an asshole anyway.

"Keep Maintenance on alert," he ordered. "The second we can go out there, we're going."

———

THE FLIGHT that day was as uneventful as the one previously. They had access to the small galley at the back of the plane, restocked with water and fruit from their stop at Palau. Yeti was reading, Ninden lost in some radio drama he'd pulled up on the plane's integrated silic database. Yip slept.

The axilla, normally stoic, had taken silence to an entirely new level. It hadn't spoken one word to anybody since the Lift.

Caleb was taken completely aback when it was waiting for him outside the toilet, about an hour into the flight.

"What are you seeing?" it asked him, the volume of its voice emitter turned down so low he could barely hear it.

"What?"

"What are you seeing?" it repeated. Eliza's face rippled inside the helmet, fading to a deep gray blankness, then reasserting. "Are you seeing it?"

"I don't know—"

"The past."

"What are you talking about?"

"At first, I thought it stray memory, the things I've been seeing. But it's gotten much worse since coming to the surface. As if—as if I am her again."

"Rallison?"

"Yes."

"You are her."

"Caleb," and the false face smiled. "You should realize, whatever Captain Eliza Rallison was in your own time, she is gone now. This," and it tapped the suit, "contains only the barest fraction of her."

"Maybe there's more of her left than you realize."

"What are you seeing?"

He leaned back against the small metal galley bulkhead, inset knobs bumpy against his back. Considering. "I think, at some point, when we were still here on Earth, we did this same thing. Went looking for somebody together…"

"Dad," the axilla said. "We were looking for Dad. Then, as now."

"What did we find?"

"What do you mean?"

"I obviously would have forgotten. But you, Rallison, you've been here before. This moment."

"Not the moment we're headed towards," it said. "There is a point beyond which I have not yet been. Rallison has not yet been. Not all the way. It is… outside what we perceive as the temporal current."

"Outside time?"

"Or within it. Can you not feel it, the edge of the waterfall approaching?" The face shimmered out, leaving only the blankness again. "I hope we find it soon. Maintaining this form in these conditions is becoming nearly impossible."

———

OF ALL OF THEM, Caleb was the one who couldn't settle down.

The closer they got to Hawaii, the more the world began to blur for Caleb. One moment, he was in his seat on the plane. The next, out on the veranda of some small café, the scent of coffee in the air.

Rough fabric beneath his arm.

Ocean breeze on his face.

Yip, humming something as he polished his combat knife.

Eliza, cutting off bites of French toast, fork tinking as it hit the plate.

And there he was.

Outside.

Somewhere in the Pacific.

Bea had a map open on the table, in between the remains of everyone's breakfast.

=Oahu has been dead for decades. The Big Island is, apparently, buried under ten feet of lava or being laid to waste by Pele, depending on who I ask. Of course, nothing's actually happening, but…=

=Means it's compromised too,= Eliza replied.

=And Kauai is under one of the Labs' no-go bans. That leaves the Maui County area. Which is why we're here.=

Caleb kept silent, watching the rapid exchange, scratching one of Tyr's ears under the table. They sat at a small, sticky table out on a pleasant little veranda, overlooking calm morning waters and a town of whitewashed wood. The last town anywhere on the island.

=Kahoolawe isn't a bad choice, but there's no infrastructure there. I've seen no hint of Lab activity here on Maui,= Eliza offered, and jabbed a finger northwest, =and Molokai is another no-go area.=

"Dead?" Caleb asked.

=Nobody would tell me when I asked around yesterday."

=That leaves just one island,= Bea said, and tapped her finger on the map. =Lanai.=

=I asked about transport over there. A few ferries a day, but nothing we can use. Everything, apparently, has been rented out for the week,= Eliza said. =And the airfield's not big enough for us to land on, even if that wouldn't attract immediate attention.=

=There's a place I think we can do a sea landing,= Bea said, and turned the map, finger moving.

A touch at his shoulder shook him back to present day. The hum of the plane's engines. The slight movement through the air.

"Petrison," Yip asked. "Pilot's asking what island we need to target."

"We get an answer from the *Barachiel* yet?"

"They can't narrow it down that far."

Caleb fumbled himself out of his seat. "Let's see if the pilot's got a map."

Turned out, he did. A giant atlas, in fact, set in a series of volumes thin enough to be easily readable. The fidelity was good, but Caleb didn't recognize some of the island names. Must have changed since his time. When he got to the one with Hawaii, the land masses were all unnamed.

"Shit," he muttered.

"Sir?" the pilot asked.

Caleb closed his eyes for a moment. Tried something. Reached out.

He could see the map on the breakfast table. Bea's finger.

"This one," he said, opening his eyes again, back to the present. He pointed at the same one Bea was indicating—had indicated. "We're headed for this one. Right here."

AFTER THE CHAOS of the marina, it took Tharsis nearly an hour to get Bea settled down again.

But she was nothing if not resilient. Beyond what was fair.

So much was going to be put on that little girl in the years, decades, centuries to come.

Tharsis had rebuilt the little nest on the low bed, making what she hoped would be a safe place for Bea until she could come back. Gave the baby a fresh bottle, a fresh diaper, laid down with her until she'd drifted off. Bea seemed perfectly content now, rolled over on her left side, breathing heavy but even.

Tharsis hated leaving her there alone, but there was really no choice.

She closed the door softly and headed back up to the bridge.

Cynthia had gotten Donovan's arm patched up while Tharsis was occupied with the baby, a neat bandage rolled over the outline of bulky suture tape. The blonde woman was curled up again in one of the bridge chairs. Her eyes were haunted. They'd dropped anchor a way off the coast; from here, they could see Honolulu burning.

Donovan was hunched over the main controls, messing with some device that seemed to be jumping through radio stations. Voices, grainy and desperate.

"What's that?"

"Police scanner," he said. "The news isn't saying shit right now, and we can't get through to the command post at Pearl Harbor."

"Anything useful?" she asked.

He snorted. "Nothing's making any sense. Civil unrest, explosions at major fuel depots, more zombies. Like everybody's sharing the same hallucination."

"Could it be mass ilu exposure?" Cynthia asked quietly. "Command's been worried about something like that happening for a while."

"With everybody seeing the same thing?" Donovan asked.

It had to be the glyphs. Tharsis had checked Wyatt's book. He had something similar in there, but not what she'd seen on the screen. Something about dreams. But the symbol she'd smashed had been more refined. Different, somehow. "I think it has to do with what was on the monitor," she said cautiously.

"There wasn't anything on the monitor," Cynthia said, confused.

"What do you know about this?" Donovan asked Tharsis.

"Not much."

"More than I do, clearly." He didn't sound like a young lieutenant anymore. There was authority there, and force. Or maybe she was imagining things, projecting onto him what he'd eventually become. It didn't matter. The moment was what it was.

"I'm not sure," she said honestly.

"But you think it's connected to Tom."

"I'm not sure. It might be."

Cynthia frowned. "What happened to him tonight? Why isn't he here?"

And to that, Tharsis had no idea what to say. What could she? "He, uhh, at least when I knew him before this, he had the ability to move things. Mass. Spatially. What I know about him is that he doesn't see the depths of space-time, you know, reality, the same way the rest of us do."

She said it haltingly; it probably sounded insane. Instead, Cynthia just sighed, and Donovan nodded a little.

"Is it a time issue too?" Donovan asked.

"What?" Tharsis asked.

"He's always seemed to experience things differently," Donovan said with a shrug. "Whole time I've known him."

"Same," Cynthia said quietly.

"But you're telling us he moved himself. To Lanai?"

"I don't know," Tharsis said, "but do either of you really want to go back to Oahu tonight?"

———

IN THE END, pragmatism won out.

Donovan set a course for Lanai. They left the burning cities of Oahu behind.

Lanai wasn't far, not by the scale of this planet, but it would still take them several hours to get there. The ocean was calm, Earth's massive moon half-shadowed as it rose above the horizon.

Under different circumstances, it would have been beautiful.

Although distant from the Maui County cluster, Donovan was able to get through to a few different amateur radio operators via the short-wave. Nothing was going on there, they said. Everything normal. Quiet.

Tharsis wondered if the problem had been them. Tom, specifically. Something percolating through from wherever he was now to where he had been. A leak, an eddy, a counterflow in time. Something from beyond the edge of his event horizon.

Cynthia had gone back down to one of the other cabins to catch some more sleep. But Donovan, Donovan seemed determined to get answers out of her. As soon as he was done fiddling with the radio, he turned his attention on her.

"How do you know Tom, anyway?"

What was Tharsis supposed to say to that? Lying to somebody like Peter Donovan just seemed wrong. Heretical, somehow. "He saved my life a while back," she said carefully, "and he said he needed help. I was hoping he could get… get a berth on one of your ark ships, out to Mars."

Wrong thing to say. That really got his attention. "How do you know about those? How do you know about Mars?"

"I'm in one of your pioneer groups. And I was on the *Vastitas Reach* for a while," she told him. "Made friends with a few of the crew."

His voice got very low. "Is that so?"

"She's registered to your family, isn't she?"

Donovan didn't answer that at all. "Look, I've been around Tom long enough to know that sometimes, for him, causality and time are not the same thing. I don't know if I believe what you're telling me about him moving shit with his mind, but I'm willing to take a little on faith right now. He said you were a friend. Don't fuck me on this."

"Let's just get to Lanai," she said. "Everything should make sense there."

———

THARSIS HAD no idea what they were sailing into.

Unlike Maui, radio traffic from Lanai was almost nonexistent. As they came into range of the island's transmitters, there was some light chatter over what sounded like a police line. Even that was muddled, indistinct. Like many voices were speaking over each other.

That was only the first sign something was amiss.

The second, and more alarming, appeared as they cruised within sight of Lanai's northern edge.

"Do you see that?" she asked Donovan.

"Yeah," he said, leaning over the wheel. "How in the hell…"

Light.

More than could have been explained through human means alone.

It was hard to discern at first glance. Just a glow, rising over the rocky, dry landscape. But as a long beach came into view, as they neared that shore, the light was impossible to miss.

Somehow, the island was still bathed in daylight. Failing, fading, evening light, but there it was, nonetheless.

And anchored just off the white sands was a seaplane. It didn't resemble the few Tharsis had seen in her travels, but nor did it look like something from back home, one of those rare fixed-wing aircraft used for expedited travel.

"Do you see that?" Tharsis asked, unsure.

"Yeah."

"Recognize it?"

He didn't take his eyes off the ocean. "It's nothing we fly. Kind of looks like one of the sketches Tom used to do."

They passed by it in silence, the yacht cutting only the barest wake through the quiet waters. For a moment, Tharsis wondered if they should go investigate, see what the hell was going on.

But something told her it wasn't something she could reach.

Once you were past the edge of the event horizon, there was no leaving it, no climbing out.

There was only the way through.

"What is going on?" Donovan asked her.

"I think," Tharsis said, "we're on the underside of reality now."

"Groovy," he replied. "Where the fuck are we going?"

"Around the island," she said, remembering the bay. "I'll know it when we get there."

FORTY-SEVEN

IT WAS near sunset in both times when Caleb set foot on the northern beach.

It was a different experience, however.

In one, a small pontoon cargo plane bobbed at anchor and the three of them moved furtively, quietly, unsure what kind of attention they might draw.

In the other, military men in heavy gravity carapace talked freely, dragging equipment cases from the small cargo raft onto the sands, setting up a robust little camp. Unafraid.

In neither time did Caleb see anybody other than his traveling companions.

=Seventeen miles from here to the only structure left on the island,= Bea was saying, as Eliza built up wood for a small fire. =There's hardly any people here. They're all clustered down near Manele Bay. For the resort.=

"I imagine this island's owned by the Labs?" Caleb asked, hands too busy to talk.

=The entire country is,= Bea said, confused. =We talked about this.=

He wanted to answer, but he wasn't there with her.

"We'll stay here tonight," Yip said, grounded in whatever passed for the present. "Figure out where we're headed in the morning."

"I appreciate that," said the pilot. Caleb, for the life of him, couldn't remember the guy's name. "Didn't look like there were too many safe places to put down here."

"You up for a seventeen-mile hike?" Eliza asked, the past reaching back again.

She was talking to Bea. Bea, who shot her a dirty look and an obscene gesture, and the two of them set to bickering.

It reminded Caleb of his own sisters, long gone now. They'd always reminded him of his sisters. But then, they'd been raised together, Bea's first time around. He hadn't been there for much of that, Bea eight and Eliza seven when he'd shown up, an angry boy of eleven. He hadn't wanted much to do with any of them at first. His own family was gone, why would he want to be part of theirs?

But Bea was an orphan herself, of sorts, and Eliza was the age his next closest sister would have been, and he had desperately wanted somewhere to belong.

He left for basic training three years later. Bea and Eliza had stayed together. At least for a while. Until Bea fell pregnant with a baby who turned out to be an exact genetic clone, dying as she'd given birth to herself. Until Eliza had enlisted too and gotten pulled up for officer training. Until Donner had gotten thrown out of the Air Force when his Arium connections were discovered. Until Cynthia had died.

Back when everything fell apart.

———

THEY CAMPED for the night on the beach, both parties, past and present. Or present and future, maybe. Caleb wasn't sure. Everything was blurred.

WHATEVER WAS GOING on with the Flet, they were close to it now.

Tyr slept. The Marines slept. Bea slept.

Caleb couldn't.

Finally admitting defeat, he pulled himself off his pad under the one small cover they'd erected, deep in the thicket-brush where they couldn't be easily found. Rallison wasn't there, and he caught her silhouette beyond, out by the tideline. It was dark; the entire Milky Way could be seen, streaked against the sky.

She's a mass murderer, he reminded himself.

But not yet. Right now, she was still the woman he'd known. The woman he'd had feelings for since his teenage years. He'd known her like this, Eliza Rallison, for far longer than he had as some bio-fucked nightmare.

"Hey," he said, sitting down next to her. The sand was damp; he could feel it leaching into his pants, cool and wet.

She didn't look over. "They look so different from down here. The stars."

He looked. He thought about the starfield above Mercury or beyond Pluto's glass domes, the stars through the *Barachiel's* small windows. The glow of Venus's atmosphere against it. Mars, out beyond hangar doors. "Yeah, they're softer here."

"We were there for another few weeks, after the whitecoats took you. Did whatever they did to you, to me, I don't know." She scooped up a handful of sand from just in front of her. The wet grains slid through her fingers. "A few weeks, and then the military finally came for us. They shot you accidentally, during the ex-fil, and when you woke back up…"

"Yeah?"

"It took some convincing to keep them from shoving you and Tyr out the nearest air lock."

"But you passed a bio-scan?"

Rallison huffed. "I don't know what they did to me. I don't know what this shit is under my skin. It's getting worse though. Slowly, but it's getting worse." She finally looked at him then. "Do you ever wonder, what's going to happen to us?"

"I try not to think about it," he said honestly.

"I've been having this dream the last couple of nights. I'm lying out, looking up at the stars. I can't see them, but I can feel them, a million little points of heat. And I can taste them. I don't even know how to describe it. And the only thing I feel, the only thing I can think about, is rage." She rubbed her arm, the one that had been injured back in Page. "You saw what came out of me. What if, what if I turn into nothing but—"

"It's not worth thinking about."

"What if that fucking goo is all I am anymore?"

"Eliza…"

"You know something, don't you, Caleb?" she asked, heated now. Her eyes flashed black, that same shiny black that Caleb had come to associate with the axilla. "What is i—fuck!"

She had been moving, turning into him, but collapsed back against the sand, rubbing her closed eyes.

In the starlight, he could see tears leaking out from under her fingers.

"You okay?"

"At least whatever they did to you left you intact," she muttered.

"You think I like this?" he asked, suddenly irritated. "You think I like losing my memory, not able to remember what happened a month ago? This fucking brain reset that happens when I die? I don't, I hate it. I lose things, things that matter. Like this," and he gestured between them. "We had something, didn't we?"

She looked at him in disbelief. "We had something great together. Something I wanted to pursue. But you were off working as Dad's security guy, and I was pissed at you for that, and it wasn't… what difference does it make now?"

"Hey," he said, and caught one of her hands, tugging her closer. "Don't be like that."

"You're asking me to start something up again that you can't finish," she replied, almost pleading, but came anyway. Further than what he'd intended. Into him, straddling his lap. Thighs sliding against his. "It won't last."

"Nothing lasts," he said, struggling himself. What was inside her, what she was going to do, didn't align with who he knew. This woman. In this time. "That's just the way it is."

"I miss you," she said. Her hands were around him now, her forehead on his shoulder. "I miss what we had before. I miss him and he's gone."

Who you were before, Caleb thought with no small amount of guilt. And whatever came after this night, she was warm and alive and human in his arms, and he couldn't really stop himself. But Eliza was crying now, tears hot on his shirt, whispering into his shoulder.

"And the only thing I've got is hoping that we don't all fucking die on this fucking planet so we can just be together but I'm so scared, I haven't felt right since that fucking Lift and…"

He knew he shouldn't.

He did it anyway.

Lifted her face, one hand gentle under her chin, and kissed her.

For a moment she hesitated. Just a moment. And then she was kissing him back with the intensity of a woman drowning. Like it was the one thing in the universe that would save her.

Caleb, in many a quiet moment, had thought about this. Dreamed about it. Her. But it was one of those things he'd always had to keep locked away, especially since she got those officer bars and had occasional interactions with his own—former—units.

That moment wasn't like what he'd imagined.

Eliza was warm, warmer than she should have been. Every movement, every touch, every slide of sweat-damp skin, seemed to elicit ever more desperate little noises from her. He slid his hands under her shirt as she grabbed at his hair, moaning at the friction from the beach's fine white sand that clung to them. It was no place to be doing this, the last rational place in his brain warned him, but she got his belt off and he stopped worrying about it after that.

———

"ARE we sure that's what they specified? Dock protocols? Out here?"

"Earth's magnetosphere is a proper monster. You're safer here than in a void hangar on Mars. Now stop bitching. The commander wants this done."

That had been thirty minutes ago. A half hour in which Private Second Class Jaques and Technical Sergeant Wright had pulled on unwrappered exogear and gone for a stroll.

Outside.

This was one of those unpleasant tasks that had to be done on foot. By hand. With gravity boots and tragers, step by step. Neither their maintenance wasps nor the rockjump could do a close-in inspection. Wrapper was tough stuff, but a close quarters blast of a chem-prop engine could hurt it.

Wright was having a hard time keeping his mind on the task at hand. Collecting samples from the xenocyte spore-pods. Verifying depth and viscosity in key locations. Easy, routine scat. Or at least, it would have been.

If not for that giant blue ball hanging over their heads.

Leadership, Master Sergeant Druz had said, wanted to ensure the pseudo-genetics hadn't been altered. That nothing had merged in. He hadn't said anything about which section of the hull Wright was to inspect. It had probably been a mistake to choose the side currently turned planetside.

Distracting, that.

<It's beautiful, isn't it?> Jaques asked over the radio. He had their extraction gear for this, stowed carefully in a forty-kilo backpack strapped to his suit. Wright had the vacuum containers for the samples. They both had tragers on, larger than the ones used back on Mars for navigating fresh snow. These were made out of copper, their webbing spread almost half a meter to the side and back. Even with that, you could still sink in.

Then there was no way to stop the wrapper from eating you, if that's what it wanted.

Maintenance men knew, even if nobody else cared to listen. Wrapper was temperamental, prone to mood swings. Especially fully awake wrapper, like the meter-deep layer that clung to the *Barachiel's* hull. Besides, that depth meant the stuff maintained a slow, constant churn, pushing its lower material up to the surface to feed. Far from being a smooth plain, the convection made the surface look like a pot of oatmeal.

Last thing Wright wanted was his fiancé back home getting *that* letter. *We're sorry to inform you that your loved one was eaten by the hull shielding.*

What a fucking embarrassing way to die.

<Navigating wrapper is no time to be taking breaks, kid,> Wright grumbled. But like his newest soldier, he couldn't keep his eyes off the sky either. <If we don't keep up a good pace, we sink. Now where's that spore-node?>

It was a rhetorical question, but the kid checked the coordinate grid on his palm pad all the same. Jaques pointed. <Twenty meters, that

way.>

Earth was beautiful. More beautiful than Wright had ever imagined. Huge, too. Much bigger than Mars. They'd been through this inwell an HST-standard month or so ago, but the images Ops had let run on the chummer monitors couldn't do this justice.

The morning terminator was just beginning to creep across the eastern edges of the ocean, far down on the planet. But he could still see the ocean, its sky, under the faint glow of the atmosphere. Synched to the Lift's orbit, they were stationary above it. It seemed incredible there was room in all that blue for continents, for all the civilizations that used to be.

Wright tried to put it aside and focused on putting one foot in front of the other.

Through his suit, he could hear a sucking sound as the wrapper lapped up around the edges of his tragers.

He hated hull walks. Fucking hated them.

They reached the spore-node without incident, though. The eggheads at the University of Titan may have considered wrapper to only be pseudo-living, but it did reproduce. Asexually, by budding. Similar to other simple organisms, he supposed, but he was no biologist.

The wrapper layer on the hull had established locations long ago where it sent up columns—squat, disturbingly organic—containing its spore load. It was constantly manufacturing this scat. Every five home-years or so, the entire maintenance crew came out and scraped them clean.

What came off was caught, of course, and duly incinerated. But the *Barachiel's* wrapper was always undeterred. New columns appeared within the year.

This one towered over the maintainers' heads. <Four meters, at least,> Jaques reported, scanning it quickly.

Wright grunted. They'd been out here two months ago. It had been half that size. <Shouldn't be this high,> he commented, and started pulling tools out of Jaques's backpack. He keyed on the vox. <Master Sergeant Druz, are you seeing this?>

But there was only static.

Above them, morning was coming. Once, the old histories said, there were millions of tiny lights down there, in that night, the outposts of humanity. Now, there was nothing. Just darkness.

Fucking magnetic interference, Wright told himself, and turned his attention to the column.

A handheld drill, to bore into the column. A scoop extractor, to pull out a sample. Vacuum flasks, to keep it alive long enough to make it to Medical's isolation chamber for analysis.

That was the plan.

But the second he jabbed the drill into that column, it all went to hell.

<Sergeant!> he heard Jaques yell. And he turned, just in time to see a wave, a wave, crest out of the wrapper. Taller than the spore-column. Taller than should have been possible.

Wright's brain couldn't process it at first. It was impossible, impossible. Wrapper didn't move like that. It couldn't. The very nature of it—

<Jump!> he ordered. A difficult feat with the tragers, and probably a fatal one overall, but there was no other option.

Wright knocked the gravity off in his boots, but wrapper had already oozed up over the top of his tragers. Jaques was knee-deep, struggling. Too far to reach. Desperate, Wright keyed the vox back on as he fought to get free of the metal shoes, reach his crewmate, get them out of here. <*Barachiel*, Chief, anybody, mayday mayday mayd—>

Too late.

The wave crashed down over them both. No slow-waking ENEX. This was awake and vital and angry.

Wright's last sight, as the wrapper sucked him under to dissolve him alive, was that slow-moving sunrise, gliding gently over Earth's largest ocean.

THE NEXT MORNING, Caleb was shaking the sand out of his boots, the remains of a chem-heater breakfast at his side, when the pilot came to find him.

"Sir? There's a call for you on the shortwave. Patched down from Orbital."

"Hang on," Caleb replied. "I'll be right there."

There was a lot of fucking sand in his boots.

He'd woken up alone, the tideline retreated somewhat. Or maybe in this time, it hadn't been where it had been then. Things were blurring; he wasn't sure if Eliza had left him. He wasn't sure what the hell had happened last night. He could still feel her, in his arms, his lap. Around him.

They could be happy together, he thought. Could have been.

Was it the Tenancy, the Accords, that had ripped them apart? A sense of duty to the people they'd fought and killed to protect, for decades? Was it because of what had happened to her, that xenocyte that had been injected into her?

Or had something happened?

Something else, something worse?

He didn't know. There weren't any answers in this time, except maybe from the axilla, and that was the last thing he wanted to see that morning.

Mind still chewing on it, Caleb waded out to the plane, Tyr splashing happily alongside.

The shortwave was located inside the cramped cockpit, and Caleb crammed himself into the copilot's seat to take it. Tyr took up position in the back, dripping water on the metal floor.

"This is, uhh, Petrison," he said, flicking the talk switch on. How long, he wondered, before that last name became second nature? Before his own became a title, even to him? "Go ahead."

<That dead Nepo? They finally ran the goo his face was covered with.>

"Goo?"

<It had xenocyte RNA,> Morray said, and paused. Clearly waiting for some kind of reaction. When it didn't come—Caleb wasn't sure what the hell he was expected to say—Morray's voice came back more urgent. <The autopsy found residue on his skin and in his nostrils. The axilla must have broken off a piece of itself, sent it to kill him.>

"It can do that?"

<Xenocyte is some weird scat, sir.>

"Any idea why?"

<Yeah, I asked about that too. Turns out that dead Nepo had a couple hundred thousand in Ibbie, uhh, currency in one of his bank accounts. Internal Investigations won't tell me anything, but my guess is, the Rallarhu was paying him off.>

"For what end?"

<I don't know. But people are dying now. I don't think you're safe around that thing that went down with you.>

Something sharp and loud rang out.

Gunshot.

Tyr's head shot up.

"Copy that, Morray," Caleb said. "I'll get back to you." He looked over at the pilot. "Stay here. Shelter."

"I'm not—"

"Nobody else can fly us out of here," Caleb said, and unholstered his gun. "Stay out of sight and don't get shot."

More gunfire sounded out in the quiet morning as Caleb left the plane, Tyr at his side. Everything seemed too loud: his breath in his ears, his boots in the shallows. He whistled one low command to the dog. Tyr sent back a quick image of acknowledgement before bounding off. On the sound, on the scent.

Caleb proceeded more slowly, cautious, approaching their small encampment on the narrow beach. Nothing. Nothing but drag marks, blood churned into the sand. These led off into the thick, scrubby brush. A set, with boot marks between them.

Discomfort growing now, Caleb followed.

It didn't take him long to find the source of the blood.

Yeti was there, chest caved in, face almost unrecognizable. Dead. Caleb wondered how much force it had taken to inflict that much damage. Maybe not much; the Arrans were gravity-adapted for a lighter world. Lighter muscle, thinner bone. That had to matter, didn't it?

The gunfire continued.

Tracks from the suit led off, into the maze of scrubby brush that extended south across the beach.

He followed, fast as he could.

Only for a moment, though.

Only a moment.

There was a tug on his sleeve.

=What do you think we're going to find here?=

Bea. Walking beside him.

His weapon was gone. The gunfire was gone. The air itself tasted different.

Adrenaline was still coursing through his blood. He fought it down.

=Nothing good,= he told her. Shit. Where was it?

=This place doesn't have a good feel,= she said. =Bad things have been baked into the earth here.=

But before he could ask what she meant, another gunshot rang out.

Her head snapped in that direction. =What's happening?=

=You heard that?=

"We all heard it." And that was Rallison. Standing there by his side. For a moment, looking exactly the way he remembered her. The way she had been last night. Unguarded. Open.

Human.

Not that thing in a sealed suit, unable to stand the surface of their birth world.

That thing killing his men.

"Sir?"

Yip. Yip's voice.

Caleb shook himself.

The women were gone.

"What is it, Sergeant?"

The veteran Marine snorted. He was sweating under the gravity carapace, every joint damp, but he paid it no heed. "Ninden and I chased that thing, but it's fast. Faster than we are in this scat, unfortunately. What's its fucking problem?"

"Not sure yet," Caleb said. "Did you hit it?"

"Maybe," he said. "Hopefully. We should probably go hunt it down." He looked at the dog. "Tyr?"

The dog just panted, jowls splitting into something that, had Caleb not known better, could have been a smile.

Caleb stared off into the scrubby brush. "Our goal's on the other side of the island. Too far for that thing to make it on foot, I'd say, even if it knew where to go," he said. "We should get back to the plane, head that way ourselves."

Yip gave him a look, the kind of look senior NCOs always reserved for when a subordinate was being an idiot, but he didn't override Caleb's directive. "Help me get Yeti out of here."

Despite Tyr's vigilance, they didn't encounter the axilla on the way out of the scrubby brush, back to the shore. Yip's radio was working fine, and he radioed the plane to prep for departure. Ninden was there already, helping the pilot pack up their small camp.

The pilot stared as Caleb and Yip brought Yeti's shattered body out and laid it down on the warm sand.

"Holy mother of God," the pilot said quietly.

"I got a body bag for him," Ninden said, curt, and nodded at a foil-wrapped package by his side.

"It's ASDF practice to deploy with body bags?" Caleb asked.

"Deepvoider practice," the young Marine told him. "One for everyone on the team. You never know when you're going to run into adlet scat." And he spat.

"We need to go finish this thing. Pull the Flet out," Caleb said, and stood. His stomach churned, but he'd had years of practice at this. Not the first injury he'd taken. Not the first dead body he'd seen.

He kept his composure.

"Where's our target?" the pilot asked, even as Yip and Ninden got to work on their fallen comrade.

"South of here," he said. "There should be a bay. I'll show you on the map."

———

THE YACHT PULLED AROUND one final headland; that evening glow they'd been chasing all night came once again into brilliant view.

Tharsis could have cried with relief. After leaving the long, wide beach on the northern shore, with its ghostly seaplane, they'd seen mostly cliffs, volcanic rock shearing off into the ocean. The evening light had faded. They'd journeyed most of the way through the dark.

They'd passed a small port, a little way back, but even that was dead, quiet.

Here they were, though.

Here she was.

Heading deeper into whatever the hell was going on.

"Do you have something I could use to get ashore?" Tharsis asked Donovan, as they stared out the bridge windows.

"Yeah, there's an inflatable lifeboat with a motor down on the lower dock."

"I'm gonna need it," she said, already turning to head back down to the cabin level. "Do you think you could get it ready for me? I need to check on Bea."

She could feel his eyes on her.

But what was she supposed to tell him?

Tharsis took advantage of his silence and hurried down.

The baby was still sleeping, peaceful and quiet, when Tharsis cracked the door. Last thing in the world she wanted to do was disturb her, but all she had on was a light dress and sandals. She wanted something more substantial if she was headed into some kind of fight.

Tharsis retrieved a pair of khaki pants and a long-sleeved shirt from her pack, a set of crew clothes they'd given her on the *Vastitas Reach*. The logo emblazoned on the breast pocket gave her a moment of pause.

She wondered if she could find the ship again. Despite the mylings, despite people like Wyatt, she'd liked the place. It'd be nice to let Bea keep growing up there.

She brushed her fingers against Bea's sleeping cheek, that skin so soft. "Love you, baby girl," she murmured.

She tried not to say it while the kid was awake. Gran would have said that was ridiculous, that babies needed love. But it didn't seem fair to do that to Bea; at some point, Tharsis wasn't going to be there for her anymore. Hopefully, she wouldn't have to leave for years yet. She just needed to get through whatever was so damn important about this night. If she needed to stay on Earth for a few more years to help figure out Bea's future, so be it. Wasn't like Mars was going anywhere.

Time enough for all that later. She dressed in silence, kissed her baby's forehead, and headed back out.

Tharsis found Cynthia exactly where she'd left the woman, down in the galley. The other woman was still in her sleep shirt. There was blood on the sleeve of her robe, but she didn't seem to notice.

"I have to head out there," Tharsis said, nodding at the window. At the twilight island. "Bea's asleep in the cabin. Do you… Can you watch her for me?"

"Guess I'm going to need the practice, huh?"

Tharsis remembered the flash she'd had, those two little girls. Those women, grown up, the one screaming, screaming over… what was it? "Why does it upset you so much?"

"Kids weren't really in our plans right now. Things are so weird and getting worse all the time. You saw what fucking happened back at the marina. How can I subject a kid to this world?"

"My gran used to tell me," Tharsis said slowly, "that we're born into the time when we're needed."

"Is that supposed to be comforting or something?" Cynthia said.

Tharsis ignored that. "I set her milker up on the counter just in case she wakes up and wants a bottle. You won't necessarily hear her cry, but…"

Cynthia seemed to rouse herself then. "I'm being a bitch, okay? She seems like a sweet little kid, and I don't want you to think I'd…" She faltered. "She's going to be fine with me for a couple of hours, okay?"

"Thanks."

———

OUT ON THE BACK DECK, Donovan had actually gotten the boat out for her. Tharsis took the thing in: a rubber inflatable with a small engine, but it would be enough on the quiet nighttime waters. The breakers were a bit larger near the beach, warmed by whatever day was still shining there, but if nothing else, she could probably swim it.

She'd seen worse, and smiled a little at the realization.

At least there wasn't an ENEX trying to eat her here. At least there was atmo and warmth and life.

But when she stepped forward, so did the Founder.

"You can't go out there yourself," Donovan said, standing between her and the winch.

"You're not coming," she told him firmly. "This is my problem."

"After what happened back at the harbor—"

"I came here to help Tom," Tharsis said, cutting him off, "and that's exactly what I'm going to do."

"You have no idea what's in there."

"No, I don't," she said, and snapped the last line on the boat. "But I have to do this."

He stared at her for a moment, then handed her the shotgun he'd given Cynthia earlier, along with a box of ammo and a bag large enough to tuck it all into. "Ever used one of these?"

"A few times," she said. Both were unexpectedly heavy. Tharsis could have laughed; half a year on Earth, and she still found herself surprised at the weight of things. She was grateful for it, though. She hadn't had anything in her pack to take. Even fighting knives were impossible to find on this planet, in this time.

"I want to know what the hell is up with you when you get back. Who the fuck you are."

A daughter of your world, she wanted to tell him, but that would sound insane.

Everyone knew time travel was impossible.

"Take care of my baby," she replied instead. "Tell her I'll be back as soon as I can."

"With Tom."

"If that's how this works," she said, and dropped the boat down the two meters to the surface of the quiet ocean. She climbed down the ladder after it and cast away the mooring line.

For a moment, she stayed there, looking at the light of some other time. A daylight that shouldn't have been. Something was wrong here, deeply and truly.

It felt like Noqumiut.

She took a deep breath and pulled the cord on the engine.

No help for it.

CHAPTER
FORTY-NINE

OF THE JOURNEY to the south shore of the island, Caleb experienced only moments.

As if time itself was stuttering.

He saw the present: the rumbling of the seaplane's hull, the silent Marines in the back hold, the blue waters beneath his feet, seen through the cockpit glass.

He saw the past: Eliza and Bea, smooth asphalt, the signs here and there of civilization.

They walked on in silence.

When they stopped around noon to eat lunch, near the only lush section of the island, when Bea had wandered off a little for some privacy, Caleb tried to ask.

"About last night…" he began.

"Don't," Rallison, Eliza, warned. Of the three of them, she was clearly struggling the most. The day was warm, not unbearably hot, and they'd covered half the distance already. But she'd been stationed in Iceland for the better part of two years, and both the sun and temperatures were clearly not something she was used to. "Don't, Ross."

"Don't what?"

"Ask me about that," she said. Her hands were shaking as she tried to rip open a ration packet. "Last night, what we, uhh, what happened."

"You know, I've always felt—"

"I said don't," she snapped, obviously angry now.

"Why not? There's obviously some history with you and me and I—"

"What difference does it make?" she exploded. "What difference does it make, how you feel about me or I feel about you or fucking any of it? You died, Caleb, and you're going to die on me again, and there's nothing to build on! Don't you get it? There's no point!"

"Eliza," he said, reaching for her.

She just pulled away, going back to her lunch. There were tears in her eyes now, unshed and unacknowledged. "You died, and Bea died, and Mom died. Dad's off doing fuck only knows for the Ariums. And you want to what, make this into something? Go fuck yourself."

"None of us die, Eliza," he said quietly.

But she wasn't there. Not where he was, the plane pulling up just short of the bay.

Caleb stared.

"Can't get through that surf with this," the pilot said, flipping a couple of switches. "And it's too rough to use the raft I've got aboard."

"We don't have a boat?"

Yip came into the cockpit. "I don't think we can make that swim in these things," he said, picking at the carapace.

"But that's where we have to go," Caleb said, pointing at what was waiting for them beyond the curve of the beach. "Unless you're telling me that, right there, is contemporary."

Pointing at the line of buildings, shimmering like a mirage in the desert, under a soap-bubble canopy of old light.

"Michael's ball sweat," Yip muttered, leaning forward, "what the hell is that?"

Caleb eyed the support harness. "That's carbon fiber, right? Lightweight?"

"Mostly," Yip said.

"Tyr?" he called back, and his dog's massive ears pricked up. "You up for a swim?"

———

THE ISLAND THARSIS found herself on was very different from the one she'd seen from Peter Donovan's yacht.

Heading up from the beach, into the afternoon light, she found herself on well-manicured grass, wide-bladed and cut short, fronting a broad, low-slung hotel. Gardens lay on the other side, full of sweet-smelling tropical flowers, all of it green, thick, alive.

A smoothed stone pathway led up to some kind of grand entrance, flanked by bamboo torches that uniformed staff were just beginning to light.

As she walked towards it, she could make out angular, cantilevered verandas overlooking the brilliant blue Pacific. White stone colonnades and shaded porticos. Fine woods she didn't recognize, worked and shaped and oiled.

If she had been anywhere else, at any other time—if this was shore leave from the *Vastitas Reach*, or hell, even a stop at the Venus Sanctums on the *Centrifuge* cruise—Tharsis might have thought it beautiful.

But the warm afternoon air was laden with something beyond the smell of the sea and growing things.

Voices.

The place was full of people.

Hundreds of people.

And she barely needed to see the lanyards around their necks to know what kind of people they were.

One of the very first things she saw, stepping foot inside the cool interior of the hotel itself, was a giant ice sculpture, surrounded by cut flowers.

That logo.

This was an Arium conference.

Like the one Wyatt had taken her to, back on Yakushima.

———

NOBODY LOOKED her in the eye as she wandered through the hotel's halls, on guard. Wary. She wondered if they could see her at all. Something had changed when she crossed through the edge of the twilight. A different time, perhaps.

Maybe it was some kind of phenomenon like an oob. Maybe she

was just underneath the skin of reality. Or maybe this was something entirely different.

The Flet had said, after all, that he didn't know what was going on.

And it wasn't as if she was completely there.

The world kept shifting, changing around her.

One moment, the halls had been dark, quiet, cheery tropical motifs printed in large scale on the carpet with photographs of the island on the walls. The next, the space had taken on an air of self-importance, everything recast in unrelenting austerity. There were people there, walking about with their lanyards and their sweating glasses of champagne. There was emptiness.

There was grass underfoot.

Then carpet.

Then ruins, walls collapsed and overgrown with creeping vines, the hotel's unrelenting angular construction softened not by gardens but drifting sand.

Then the conference.

The voices continued, though, through it all. Overlapping, rising, ringing, whispering.

Too many to sort through. Too many to—

Then she recognized somebody.

Somebody already talking directly to her.

"Amanda? Oh my god, how have you been?"

The conference reasserted itself, bright and smug.

"Wyatt," she said, and forced herself to smile.

He wasn't exactly the way she remembered him, the hapless white-coat with grand ambitions. Older, absolutely, gray flecked into the brown hair around his temples, cut short now, more dignified. That hesitation he'd always had seemed to be gone now, replaced with a steely-eyed surety that made Tharsis nervous. Some of his old mannerisms were still present, though, like the way he was holding his coffee cup, or how he kept fiddling with the messenger bag strap hanging from his shoulder. Little tics.

That myling was still around too. Lurking. Creeping. Hands, grasping for her.

"It's so good to see you," he enthused, practically bubbling as he gave her a hug. "How long's it been now?"

Tharsis had no idea what to say. "A while, I think."

"Decades, I'd say," he said, and let her go again. "You look great. What's your secret?"

"I, uhh—"

But the Arran lieutenant was saved from further conversation by a woman in an Arium-branded jacket, clipboard in hand, walking up to them. "Doctor Blalock, you've got that meet and greet in ten minutes."

"Yes, yes, of course," he said, and waved her off. "Don't worry, I won't miss that. I'm sure they're all eager to see where their money's been going for the past few years." And he smiled at Tharsis. "Annoying shit, but it's what you have to do to get funding."

There was something odd in his attitude. Something Tharsis couldn't quite place. Like he was hoping for approval with every word he spoke. Hers? Seemed unlikely. "Funding for what?"

"You remember the language, right? The language beneath, within, all other language, all other thought?"

She resisted the urge to roll her eyes. "Who could forget that?"

"Well, it's so much more than I ever thought possible. I'm still just plumbing the depths, but… it's amazing." He smiled even wider then. "Presentation's in an hour, but for you, you're welcome to see it now. Want to come to the meet and greet?"

Then she saw it.

The myling. His myling.

Staring at her, mouth half-open. Its teeth had been sharpened into little points. Sweet Michael in heaven, Tharsis thought. What had he been doing to his wetware?

It threw her off balance, and in the time it took her to recover, the moment was lost. Another group of people came up to him—younger, eager, almost worshipful in their expressions—and as his attention turned away from her, everything shifted.

And once again, there was nothing but grass underfoot.

"Sergeant?!"

It wasn't Silicone-Age English. After so long out of her own time, Tharsis almost didn't recognize it. But there, standing in front of her, was a Marine in deepvoider black, a full-body support carapace. ASDF markings.

A24 leveled right at her.

CHAPTER
FIFTY

"ANYTHING FROM THE SURFACE?"

Colonel Cambel had a gigantic mug of tea in hand as he flipped through the daily ops report from HOMECOM. Nothing of note, besides the autopsy data from the Nepo Tok they'd captured on Deimos.

"Morray's in contact with their aircraft. Says they've reached the inflection point for whatever's going on with the Flet."

"There's some good news." He set the HOMECOM tablet down on his desk and reached for the one with the *Barachiel's* nightly logs. "How about you? Anything interesting last night?"

"Nothing. As we discussed, I directed some basic maintenance out on the hull…"

"That could have waited until we were back at Mars."

"With everything going on right now, I don't want to gamble on a void dock being available. Besides," and Stag smiled from his seat in one of the bolted-down chairs, opposite the desk, "wouldn't do, letting the men have too much downtime."

Cambel grunted. "They find anything out there?"

"We only got clearance from Weather about ninety minutes ago. Haven't gotten a report back yet."

"Let's go check," he said, and nodded at the window in the briefing room, just outside.

Something black and oily was sliding across it.

Stag was on his feet, back out in Ops before Cambel. "Maintenance, give me a status on the hull inspection team."

"They went out Air Lock Three fifty-six minutes ago."

"Have they checked in?"

"No sir, not yet."

"Get them on the horn. Something's going on."

At that moment, a groan went through the craft, deep and almost painful.

"Sir!" the tech at Engineering said. "I have a failure on starboard thrusters."

"What kind of failure?"

"Unsure. I'm not getting anything that makes sense up here," he replied, already reaching for the radio handset.

Ops exploded in a flurry of activity, problems being called in from multiple stations. Stag let the colonel start sorting it out and walked back to the Hive technician.

"Get me something in the void," he directed the master sergeant on duty. "I want eyes on whatever's going on out there."

"I'd love to," the sergeant said, and tapped his screen. "But the hangar doors aren't responding."

Something else, something else Stag and Morray had briefly discussed, popped into his mind. The Tok death. The Rallarhu connection. *Fuck.*

"Get Erg up, get him up now," he ordered, already headed for the door. "Get him down to the control pod."

"What are you thinking, Stag?" the colonel called.

He paused in front of the open door. "I think the wrapper's been compromised. I think it's going to pop this craft open like a tin can if we don't stop it."

———

FOR CALEB, the rest of the journey into that bubble of twilight was broken up. Fragments of moments.

Strange.

They'd made the swim to the beach, Tyr making two trips, one for each of the Marines lashed to his harness. Despite the misery of being dragged through the surface by the dog, neither Yip nor Ninden had complained. They'd done what they could to help, stripped off the carapaces for the trip, still able to swim thanks to the weightlessness factor of the seawater. But the plane couldn't get closer than about two hundred meters off the beach, and the surf was rough. Tyr was exhausted by the time he'd brought Ninden to shore.

Caleb had swum in a pair of floating, waterproof cases with what gear they could manage.

Getting back was going to be interesting. The pilot said there was a small inflatable raft he could deploy for their return journey, but only if the surf quieted down.

Caleb wondered why in the hell there weren't plans for this sort of thing. But then, he got the impression that this had been a very ad hoc ferry service for them, and not the way anybody was used to handling long-haul travel down on Earth anymore.

There wasn't time to recover, though. As soon as they'd set foot on the beach, the light had changed. The sounds. The very air.

Everything was shattered.

Back and forth. Back and forth.

Between the ruins of their time, and the old glory of the Euphemism.

Things had still been beautiful then. Now. Even as it all fell apart.

Yip and Ninden.

Caleb wasn't sure where they had gone.

Hell, he wasn't sure where he was.

All he could remember was the disgruntled look on Yip's face as an exhausted Tyr dragged the man through the last of the breakers. "Scat," he'd said, clamping his carapace back on. "There's sand fucking everywhere now."

=I saw you on the beach this morning,= Bea told him now. The sun was setting, and the lights of the last town winked on behind them as they approached the place where he would stand, centuries from now. =With those men.=

Caleb glanced back. Eliza was behind them, walking with Tyr. She hadn't said a word to him since lunch. It felt like the goddamn axilla all over again. =What men?=

=The ones who weren't born on Earth. The ones struggling to stand now.= And she pointed, down to the bay.

=I don't...=

=Don't lie to me,= Bea said. For a moment, her fingers faltered. =It was strange, you know, being born again, growing up again. Like a long, slow waking up.=

=Kid...=

=Don't, Caleb. I know. At least, I think I know.= She looked at him, the young face she wore doing nothing to hide the burden she was going to carry. Was already carrying. =If it happened once, it'll happen again. Same for you. No dying. No being done. Just endlessly coming back.=

He thought about the ruined sections of Singapore. =Everything ends, Bea.=

=Maybe not us,= she said. =And Dad tries to hide it, but he's the same, isn't he? Future, past, all the same for him. It's how he sees things.=

=You'd know better than me.=

=How far back have you come, Caleb, to be with us here?= Bea asked, and smiled ruefully when Caleb's even pace faltered. She put a hand on his arm for a moment. Shook her head. =What happens to us?=

=It's not worth worrying about,= he told her.

And with that, they rounded the last little hillock.

The resort was in view.

At the next distinct rock outcropping, Caleb stopped and unslung his pack.

Eliza came up alongside. "What're you doing?"

He handed her one of the rifles, as well as an ammo belt. "I have no idea what we're walking into down there," he said honestly. "Doesn't hurt to be prepared."

There was a lightweight, flex-weave flak vest for everyone, including Tyr, who accepted it with his usual pre-mission dignity. The stuff was standard issue in the military at this time, effective against small rounds and blades.

=Don't I get a weapon?= Bea asked.

"No," both Caleb and Eliza said at once. Eliza sighed and continued. "You need to stay here. Out of sight."

=No.=

=Bea…=

=I'll be safer with you.=

But before he could continue to argue with her, a call came in over his radio.

<Yeah, Petrison, you're going to want to see this.>

Bea watched him, those huge red eyes of hers fixed on him.

"We should head down," he said. "Sounds like something's going on."

And down in the ruins-that-were, a small back area of the hotel-that-was, Caleb found Yip.

Yip, and Ninden, and somebody he never expected.

A dark-haired young woman in old-style khakis, a heavy bag slung over one shoulder.

A face he recognized from faded photographs, framed on a ranch house wall.

THARSIS RAISED HER HANDS SLOWLY. But before she could say anything, somebody else walked up.

"Jesus, Ninden," the newcomer said. Another Marine. Older. Sergeant's markings. "Put your gun down. It's our missing lieutenant."

"She just walked out of that rubble pile like a goddamn ghost."

"All kinds of weird shit happening here today."

"Sergeant Yerpoli?" Tharsis asked, digging the man's face out of the back of her memory.

"One and the same, ma'am," he said, and pressed his radio controls, leaning his cheek over a little. "Yeah, Petrison, you're going to want to see this."

"Who's Petrison?" Tharsis asked.

The big sergeant cocked his head. Didn't answer her. "What happened to your tattoos, ma'am?"

"Long story."

"How the fuck are you here?"

"I have no idea."

It had to be her own time she was standing in. Had to be. It was broad daylight, warm and bright, and the land around her held nothing but ruins. The outlines of walls and sidewalks could still be seen, angular surfaces long covered by drifting sands and creeping plant growth.

378

Or were the hallways back, cool and shaded? The darkness of the late night, waiting on the coming dawn and a fresh day of leisure?

She blinked.

The two Marines were back. The more junior, Ninden, looked shaken.

"You faded out, ma'am," Yerpoli, Yip, said. "Where'd you go?"

"I'm not sure," she told him honestly. "This place, it's not right. Like it's been pushed outside time, or down into it. Under the surface."

"How?" Yip asked. "Why?"

"The Flet didn't tell me. I don't think he knows."

"You've seen the Flet?" She nodded. His eyes narrowed. "Where is he?"

"I'm not…" she began, and then trailed off.

Because there he was.

Petrison.

Along with two females, one short, young, obviously unsure of herself, and the other, the other…

Holy hell.

The reaction from the Marines was immediate. Both their guns immediately trained on her, the woman with a military face brand and shoulder-length blonde hair. Eliza Rallison.

She looked almost exactly like Cynthia, Tharsis realized, and the pieces of things she'd seen the past year or so came together in her mind. She was the baby Cynthia had been pregnant with. She was the little girl who'd grown up with Bea. She was—

She was the figure, screaming into the dust out at the end of the world.

Out at Noqumiut.

"Caleb? What's going on?" she asked.

Yip flicked the firing selection lever on his A24. "How the fuck did that thing get out of its suit?" he growled.

Petrison—the goddamn Rossen— answered Eliza Rallison in Silicone English. "I asked a couple of buddies to meet us here, okay? In case we needed backup."

"You didn't say anything to me about that," the blonde woman snapped.

"Is that really Eliza Rallison? In the flesh?" Yip growled.

"Yip," the Rossen warned.

But Rallison just glared at the Marine. "Yeah, I'm Eliza Rallison. The fuck does it matter to you?"

Yip nodded slowly, like he was thinking about something very hard, and then, before anybody could stop him, squeezed off a shot.

There was no dodging that bullet. Yip was barely three meters from the Inner Belt's Landlord, and her face was a target too close for a Marine to miss. But instead of contacting blood and bone, the bullet slipped right through her. The skin of her cheek ripped open. There was a squelching sound from the back of her neck. The bullet hit the wall behind her. Harmless.

For a moment, Tharsis saw something dark and shiny under the broken skin.

Slapping a hand over the wound, smoke curling out between her fingers, Rallison stared at him. Unspoken pain in her eyes. "You motherfucking…"

"Yeah, the rumors are true," the Rossen snapped. "Now put your goddamn guns away, both of you."

Yip's eyes narrowed. "How much of you is xenocyte, ma'am?" he asked, dragging the last word out sarcastically.

"You can't kill her," Tharsis told him softly, in their own English. "You can't kill her because you didn't."

"Like you said, El-Tee, we're outside the normal flow of time now," he said, but swung his gun back down on its strap. "Who knows what a man can do here?"

Rallison was still glaring at them all, but sat down, wincing in pain. "Your friend's an asshole, Caleb."

"He's a Marine, what do you expect?" the Rossen replied, and dug a first aid pack out of her bag. "Yip, knock it off. I told you the rumors were true, and you said you were fine with it."

The Marine sergeant, catching on to the game, smiled blandly. "Right."

But as the Rossen was settling a couple of butterfly sutures across the small cuts on Rallison's face, sealing that blackness away again, a scream rose into the young night air.

One.

Then many.

"We need to find the Flet," Tharsis muttered. "Now."

———

STAG HAD GRABBED a wireless headset on his way out, keyed to the main Ops vox channel. Chaos was exploding; half their broadcast antennas were already malfunctioning and the argon thruster system, necessary for precision movement, was firing only intermittently.

<You left in a hurry, Stag.>

Cambel, on a private channel.

The deputy commander answered as he ran. "We gotta get something in the void. Before we lose control entirely."

<Agreed. What's your plan?>

"I need Captain Cooper," the new Marine company commander, Stag hadn't gotten a chance to meet him yet, "to meet me down there with whatever phosphorus munitions we've got in the armory. Thermite too."

A short pause. <He's been notified.>

"Thanks," Stag panted, and ran on.

He made the central shaft of the hangar level at the same time that Cooper was coming out of the lift shaft. Leaner than Marines usually were, but hair buzzed short and uniform impeccable. The kind of scat those guys pulled when they were trying to make a good impression. Two of their new Marines were there too, lugging bulky, yellow-coded lock cases out of the lift.

"Stag," the deputy said unceremoniously, gesturing at himself. "I apologize, Cooper, for the brief introduction…"

"They told me the wrapper's trying to eat us, sir. I assume you want me to burn it off the hangar doors?"

"No," Stag said. "I need you to blow the hangar doors off."

CHAPTER
FIFTY-TWO

PROTECT HIM.

That was what the axilla had been charged to do.

Protect him, from whatever foolish thing the Arrans might try to do.

Protect him, from Caleb Ross.

Protect him, from the entire Heliosphere.

That was the entire purpose of the axilla's existence. What it had been made for. What it was required to do, the most basic command that animated what passed for its DNA. Its… spirit. If such things could have spirit.

The Rallarhu no longer believed.

The axilla wasn't so sure.

It seemed a strange thing, deviating from the pure commands of its origin point, of the Rallarhu herself. But since stepping into the Malaccan Lift, since coming to Earth, the axilla had been seeing more of the past. Memories it had not been given. Moments that the Rallarhu had not shared.

Perhaps with good reason.

Such visions were hard to understand, much less integrate into its limited understanding of her distant past.

Despite its seeming sentience, the axilla was a thing very much dependent on its programming. It was aware of this, aware of its limitations, and in some small corner of what might have passed for its soul, it reveled in such simplicity. All creatures, all things living, should have such clarity.

Protect him.

That was all it had to do.

And yet, it was such a complicated task.

One made more difficult by the memories.

Caleb Ross had loved it—them, *her*—once upon a time. This was the seed of everything else. The axilla had seen that on the beach, the night before. Felt it. The real human emotion that she had once been capable of. Perhaps still was, but she had not deigned to share such things with the axilla.

Caleb Ross had loved her.

Betrayed her.

This, the axilla also knew. Something it probably shouldn't have. But it knew, nonetheless.

The Rallarhu's rage and grief and fear might have been beyond the understanding of the axilla's simple genetic programming, but the axilla could feel it.

Perhaps it had overreacted on the beach.

Perhaps it should have wandered this island, until it faded away completely.

Even now, it could feel the beginning of dissolution.

Such a thing as this thing never lasted long. The axilla didn't mourn its own death; it would have had to be alive for that to matter.

But time and space had gone wrong here. Very wrong.

It was him. Not *him,* of course, but the Flet. Tom Donner. The father who had once been.

She had been part of him, once. And the axilla was part of her.

He pulled at the axilla, just as he was pulling at all of them. The singularity at the heart of this… whatever it was. Crushing them down into some kind of limitless possibility.

Causality bubble. Pocket dimension. A place where new rules, written so long ago, might reign.

Why, it had to find out.

So it wandered.

So it was pulled.

Through a conference it wandered, beneath the surface, unnoticed, unheeded. It could hear the conversations, though, a thousand over-lapping ideas that pulled at the axilla's fading neural circuitry, logic that escaped it.

Through a conference, to a grand hall, filled with people of this time. The axilla had no opinion whatsoever of what it saw, but the Rallarhu's contempt rose up high.

Whitecoats, the old hatred whispered.

All of them listening in rapt silence.

"My first major breakthrough came when I realized that what we were seeing in the ilucoccine-induced visions was not a personal expe-rience. It could be shared. And if such visions could be shared, it implied there was something else, something beyond, that we were touching. So I went looking for the language of that place. The language we share without realizing it. A language that might bring us all together."

A man was speaking, up on stage. Another whitecoat.

The axilla watched.

"That language didn't just illuminate this hidden world, the world of the visions, as I thought. It turned out that the language was control-ling it, guiding it, shaping it. And so I realized, if we could shape that reality with thought and word alone, what was holding it to just that world? Why not others? Why not ours? It sounds impossible, perhaps, but think about what dreams we could live, if we could alter our perception enough."

A murmur went up through the hall, through the assembly at their tables and with their drinks in their hands.

Wide screens on either side of the man lit up. White. With one solid shape on them, sinuous and beautiful. The axilla stared at it, curious, as cries went up.

"I have found a man whose perception is far beyond known human limits," the man on stage said, "a man who bends space with only a thought. Do you think, if we showed him this, that he might finally make the world as it should be? With just a thought?"

Pulling.

Tugging.

I can't hold this much longer.

The axilla found itself in a small room then, hardly grand enough for all the lofty ambition that filled it. A room, in a hotel that was scattered and shattered now, but this room stood intact. Perhaps it would for all of eternity, plunged deep now beneath the entropy flow of space-time's surface. What a fascinating possibility, the axilla thought.

Anything else was beyond its capacity.

Its brain, much like its animating consciousness, was a lie.

A room, a room with a tank in it. A full-grown man inside, intubated and cathetered and suspended in viscous liquid. Wired to a bioconversion machine, the kind of thing that enabled wetware to perform all its glorious uses.

Except this was different, the axilla realized.

This bioconverter was not set to follow.

This was intended to guide.

Somebody had figured out how his mind worked, the axilla assumed, realized what he could do and tried to harness it.

The Flet just didn't experience space-time like other humans.

What dreams we could live…

The axilla knew what dream the Rallarhu had. What desire animated its entire being.

Protect him.

Protect him, so that one day, we might bring him home.

The others, the humans here, the entire place, reverberated with what they wanted. Their deepest hopes.

Why not hers?

The axilla put a hand on the tank.

So soft a touch.

Nothing that should have been able to pass through glass and water.

But inside, the man—the fellow Landlord, the pilot, the father—still opened his eyes.

=Go there,= it signed. =And bring him home.=

FIFTY-THREE

THE HIVE SECTION, where Erg spent most of his time, was a tight cluster of small, interlocking rooms, sandwiched between the main hangar and the smaller specialty ones. It had been built into the swarm maintenance hangar, behind its own air locks. The entire level was isolated from the rest of the habitable areas of the craft.

Static fields weren't infallible.

Erg seemed relatively calm when Stag came into the main cockpit area. The Hive head, along with three of his guys, were running pre-launch checklists. His station looked much like any other pilot's: instrument panels, monitors in place of windows, manual flight controls. But those things were for the benefit of the two enlisted men who served as sensor operator and battlespace controller.

A thick window overlooked the swarm hangar beyond. A team of half a dozen maintainers ripping paneling off the interior bulkheads. Trying to reach the override circuitry for the doors, no doubt, Stag surmised. Cooper was down there already, trying to explain the situation.

Erg's own padded seat, behind and above them, was more of a cradle, supporting his entire body. Instead of the control yoke, a set of gloves, the exteriors comically oversized, were built into the arms. He didn't bother looking up at Stag, long fingers still punching in preflight commands.

"How much time do we have?"

"Not much."

The interior air lock doors from the hangar chimed, and Druz was there with them. He looked pissed. "Scat's locked up tight. We can get the internal seals open but the void-facing door layer is fucked. Only thing I can think is the goddamn wrapper's eaten into the upper layers of the locks."

"From the outside?" Stag asked. "How is that possible? It can't digest the hull alloy."

"It's finding cracks, pushing through." The maintainer shook his head. "I didn't think it could move like this."

The craft shuddered again. Stag caught the update running across the Hive Command's screens: the starboard argon thrusters were completely offline. He chewed his lip. They were attempting to move out of the Lift's orbital path. This would complicate that.

Erg gestured one of his guys forward, strapping himself into the seat. The technician had a helmet-like object in hand. The outside was smooth, oddly similar to something found in a hockey rink. But unlike those, this was blistered with circuitry, both conventional and biologic. The brain interface required a certain amount of wetware to connect. It had been harvested, if Stag remembered correctly, from Erg himself.

"How am I getting outside?" the gangly voider asked, sliding the helmet over his head.

"Druz?"

"Yes sir?"

"You're going to open the internal atmo seals. Cooper is going to cut the outer doors open and—"

"Depressurize the entire level?" Druz protested.

"Just long enough for Erg to get outside."

"I don't have the storage capacity for this much atmo."

"We'll need the atmo to blow out," Erg said. "Keep her at bay."

The maintenance chief puffed. "You cut the outer doors, it'll damage the inner ones. She'll get inside."

"The static shields will hold."

"Maybe. They only function in atmo and if you're blowing it out—"

Stag cut off the argument with a cough. "Sergeant, I'm not asking."

Druz looked between them. "Two of my men were out there. I don't want to lose anybody else today."

"I understand that," Stag said, and clapped him on the shoulder. "But if we don't, we lose the craft. Cooper?" He keyed on the hangar vox. "How close are you?"

<Once the inner doors open, I'll need three, maybe four minutes to set charges.>

"Erg?"

The Hive head closed his eyes. Out in the hangar, a small squadron of five recon and two myrmid wasps flared to life. "Final preflight verification running now."

"Druz, get those fucking doors open."

———

FOR CALEB, nothing he found in the hotel was what he might have expected.

He had burned out ariums before. They always had a certain feel to them. The mission he and Rallison had been captured on had been a particularly bad example. There, security had been provided by something he could have only described as a cult, men and women out of their minds on ilu and stimulants, skulls flattened and eyes… eyes that had been replaced with…

The hotel was nothing like that.

It wasn't some lab overrun with frantic half-animals or mylings with hands that burned and expressions desperate. It wasn't some butcher shop, or the sterile-white horror of indifference.

No. This was luxury incarnate, wasteful in its beauty, all the things whitecoats piously railed against in public.

Unsettling.

They saw nobody at first. Not a single member of staff. Not a single whitecoat. But there was noise. Screams, wails. The sounds of despair. Of fear. Echoing through the brightly lit halls and gentle nighttime illumination of the deep porches.

Tyr padded steadily along, though, pausing here and there for a sniff before moving on. Bea walked by his side, her huge red eyes dilated almost to black.

=Tyr says things are wrong,= she said, at one huge T-junction.

"This is where the ballrooms start. Or should be," the lieutenant

—Ambera Chen, Tharsis, whatever her name was—added, and stepped forward to touch the wall. "This wasn't here a few hours ago."

"Are you sure?" Caleb asked.

"Definitely. I was here. He, umm, the guy running this scat-show, was going to show me something." She took a step back, examining it. "This shouldn't be here."

"We've seen this sort of effect before," Rallison said. "Things moving, or seeming to move."

=We've all had the ilu inoculations,= Bea signed. She was putting on a good face, but regardless of what she said, she was still a kid. She felt scared.

"It's not an illusion. Something else is going on," Caleb muttered. Tyr was whining. He looked down. "What is it, boy?"

The dog sent back an image of an open hallway.

"It's not—" Caleb began.

"Might as well find out," Yip said, and fired directly at the wall.

It didn't crumble. Didn't break.

It was just no longer there.

And now, reality snapping back into place, they finally saw something alive.

People. In corners, doorways, weeping. Running, blind, heedless to anything else. Screaming. Clawing at walls. Clawing at themselves, or each other.

A few turned to look at them, eyes bloodshot, expressions inhuman.

Caleb raised his gun. Grim.

Now, things looked familiar.

"What the hell?" Ninden muttered.

"Welcome to the Euphemism, Sergeant," Yip replied, and spat.

"Keep walking," Caleb ordered, "and shoot anything that reaches for you."

———

AS THE SMALL group advanced into the hallway, Tharsis kept her attention on the girl. She'd been watching the kid over the course of their exploration; it had to be her. But if this was decades later, shouldn't Bea be older? She was barely into her teens.

=You'll be okay,= she told the girl in halting sign language.

The girl frowned, like she couldn't understand why Tharsis knew sign language, and then pointed.

Tharsis turned just in time to see somebody, lost in their own nightmare, charging them.

The borrowed shotgun blew a fist-sized hole in the man's chest.

Bea grunted again, obviously scared now, and Tharsis pushed the girl behind her.

"You okay?" the younger Marine asked.

"Fine," Tharsis lied.

The trip down the hallway was punctuated with a few more such moments. Their own group walked in silence, sign language passing between the Landlords on occasion. A few more people ran at them. More, however, ran away.

Despite what seemed like an incredibly short distance, the small group was still forced to put down more people as they progressed towards the grand doors for the main hall. By the time they got there, only a few strides it seemed, the Rossen and the Marines had their knives out, and Tyr's jowls were matted with blood.

They passed one alcove where a man was thrashing, turning a strange shade of blue, fighting for air. Bea stopped, head cocked. Something was rising around him, Tharsis could see: the ocean, a rush of water that would drown the entire world if…

The carpet was wet.

Tharsis had to drag the girl away. She tried to sign something over it, something Tharsis didn't understand, and finally spelled out the word.

=Impossible.=

As they got closer to the ballroom, the screaming proper picked up. Outside the doors, the party stopped.

The Rossen looked straight at Tharsis.

"Who was here?" he asked her.

Her own nerves badly rattled, Tharsis nodded at one of the large placards, still standing.

"That asshole," she said.

KEYNOTE PRESENTATION, it read, TONIGHT AT 19:00 IN THE GRAND BALLROOM. WYATT BLALOCK, THE POWER OF LANGUAGE.

Shouldering his weapon, the Rossen walked forward to the ballroom door. "Screaming's definitely coming from here."

"I'm going first," Yip said.

But when they got through the doors, everything was quiet.

The banquet hall was still.

Everyone there was already dead.

An event had clearly been in progress. Tables were arranged, a banquet laid out. Some people were still in their seats, slumped over the remains of chocolate cake, coffee spilled across the white tablecloths. A low stage was set up at the far end, with a pleated silk backdrop and a few huge screens, lit from behind by ceiling-mounted projectors. Near a podium, a holographic projector sputtered.

"Well, shit," the Rossen said, glancing around.

Bea stepped forward, exchanging a glance with the dog. Tyr, seemingly in reply, bounded forward, sniffing at the tables. The Rossen went with him, throwing back tablecloths and turning them over.

"What is that?" Yip asked, gesturing at the screens.

"It's a glyph," Tharsis replied. She still had a careful eye on the girl. "I don't know what it means, but it's one of his."

Bea signed something, and Rallison sighed.

"Wyatt Blalock was the whitecoat we were looking for in Japan," she said. "But I still don't see the connection."

"He was working on some kind of language system that could, I don't know, hack the human brain," Tharsis said. "Alter perception. He told me earlier that he'd found something in it. Something… more."

"What does that have to do with Dad, Bea?" Rallison asked, signing as she spoke.

Tharsis only caught a few words of the exchange that passed between them after that, but it was Yip who spoke up about it. "Translation?" he asked, with a very rough Silicon inflection.

"She says maybe they figured out what Dad can do. I know he tried to keep things stovepiped, but at least some of his research has to be in the Arium system," Rallison said. "Bea says that maybe they thought if they altered his perception enough, they could use him to rewrite reality."

"This really is a fucked-up time," Yip grumbled.

Tyr barked, sharp and urgent, cutting off further conversation. He was in a corner of the room, near the service corridor doors. They headed over, Ninden shooting out the projectors as they went.

Tharsis got there just as the Rossen was hauling somebody out from behind the drink station.

"Wyatt," she said.

The whitecoat's eyes were glazed, unfocused. Watching something, but it wasn't them.

"Wyatt!" She yelled it this time.

His head turned, whole body jerking in Caleb's hands.

Tharsis saw it then, too. That goddamn myling again. Bigger than it should have been, a sense of menace reaching far beyond the ballroom ceiling. And for a moment, she wondered, she wondered…

Not the time, she told herself, and stepped forward to grab him away from the Rossen.

"Wyatt, for fuck's sake! Stop looking at that fucking myling! Look at me. Wyatt, fucking look at me!"

The whitecoat's eyes, glazed and distant, finally blinked. Focused. Furrowed in confusion. "Amanda?"

"Wyatt, none of this is real. None of this can be real."

"But when I ran simulations, we saw—"

"It showed you what you wanted to see," she said. "Isn't that the whole point of this little shitshow? To see what you want to see? To make the world what you want it to be?"

"Of course," he said, confused now. "That's always been the point. I just want things to be better."

"Yeah? What did the glyph say?" He tried to look back over his shoulder again, but she wrenched on his collar, keeping his attention on her. "What did it say?!"

"It was," and he breathed, "it was an entreaty to hope, to live your grandest dream."

Bea signed something, and Rallison snorted in agreement. "Too many of you define that as everyone on the planet dead," she said derisively.

"No, no, it doesn't need to go that far if—"

"Somebody always takes it further! Did you think you got to pick where it ends?!" she snapped. "Look around you. Is this what you wanted?"

He must have finally seen it, then. Whatever it was that was happening, whatever everyone else was seeing.

"No," he said, breathing out the word like it was his last. "No, not this."

"Then help us stop it," Tharsis said. "Where's the fucking wetware?"

He was about to answer when more cries sounded from outside the hall.

"Time to go," the Rossen said, and bodily hauled the man up.

The group made it into the service corridor—abandoned, mercifully—and barred the ballroom doors.

But even when Wyatt started guiding them to wherever he'd stashed the Flet, Tharsis noticed a growing chill in the air.

Dust underfoot.

And they had a whole new set of problems to deal with.

WITH EVERY STEP they took down the service corridor, the world around them got stranger.

The corridor widened. The temperature fell, first slowly, then precipitously. Instead of the whitewashed concrete hallway, there was metal around them, freezing to the touch. Here and there were signs of violence; blood, footsteps scraped through the ice and dust on the floor. But it was old, long before.

The place they were in was dead.

"Are you seeing this?" Rallison muttered to him.

"Yeah, think so."

"We shouldn't be seeing it. We're inoculated."

Bea bumped her. =This isn't ilu,= she signed.

The only member of the party that didn't seem to notice it—the only member whose breath wasn't hanging in the air—was that lost lieutenant.

Her attention was focused on the man they'd hauled out of the ballroom.

"What, exactly, were you trying to do?" Chen snapped at their captive whitecoat as they walked.

"Perception shapes reality. The very fabric of the cosmos bends to will. At least it can. For certain people, special people. Like the donor…"

"He's not a donor," Caleb said. "He wouldn't have volunteered for this."

"We're beyond volunteers," Wyatt said. Like he was speaking for something else's benefit; Chen glanced beside him.

"Stop talking to that thing," she ordered, and shoved him forward.

"All we need to do is just guide him in the right direction."

"To do what?"

Bea signed something, and Rallison shook her head. "The kid says you're attempting to open some kind of pocket dimension. Drag us all in there."

"I wouldn't go that far."

"Explain this, then," Rallison snapped. "None of us should be seeing anything right now."

"There are some aspects of quantum theory that allow for—"

"Sounds like a great way to tear space-time apart under the strain," Yip shot back. Caleb gave him a look. He shrugged. "What? I took high school physics."

"Or make a reality where it's easy for the Ariums to kill everybody," Rallison replied. "Making nightmares real like this."

"That wasn't what I wanted," the whitecoat said. "I'm doing this to save humanity, not destroy it."

"Yeah," Chen said. "You're a real humanitarian."

He looked at her. "You never understood."

"Your demon-logic? No, and I never will."

One of the things Caleb had always found unnerving about ariums was the not-quite-there quality about them. As if they existed just beyond the limit of normal reality. The idea, he'd always heard, was to create conditions where anything was possible. Or at least, where what the whitecoats wanted to happen, could happen. Not that it did. Drugs like ilucoccine could produce altered mental states, but that didn't make the effect real.

Of the dozen or so labs he'd raided over the past few years, nothing was ever alive at the end.

What the whitecoats there saw, what they experienced, was a topic of much debate within the military. Rallison's intelligence squadron was going to have a field day with her report from this place.

Bea tapped Caleb on the shoulder, asking one very pertinent question.

=If this is a dream, whose is it?=

"That," he grumbled, "is a very good question."

The whitecoat finally stopped.

Just outside some small room. *Janitorial*, it said on the door.

"You've got to be shitting me," Caleb said.

"It's not what it looks like," Wyatt stammered, fumbling a set of keys out of his pocket. "We, ahh, we had a nicer display set up in one of the meeting rooms for the patrons, of course, but you asked for the guts of the machine…"

"Just get the door open," Chen told him.

Caleb.

It was that voice again.

Caleb.

Bea stopped too, head on a swivel. =He's talking,= she signed. =Dad.=

I can't hold it.

And with that, the hotel, everything, was gone.

Dissolved into blinding white.

———

FOR A MOMENT, Tharsis found herself alone. Adrift in the nothingness that the human mind perceived, under the surface of reality.

Only for a moment.

Then Noqumiut returned.

She'd seen it on the walk down here, felt it. A growing awareness of it, like it was stalking her. But only there, through the door, did it find her.

For a moment, Tharsis stood there, completely disoriented.

Then.

In the room in front of her, there was a tank.

Not a fish tank. A medical tank, wires strung through the gel like veins. She recognized it; she'd seen this room before. More detritus.

More dust. This was the past, she figured, or the future, relative to the point at which she had left Earth. Not her own time, at least.

There, at Noqumiut, she had seen the tank.

Not what was inside of it, though.

Not that shape.

Human, vaguely. Like somebody had spun it out of spiderweb. Not large. The size of a small child, maybe.

Wetware.

"What do you mean?"

It was his voice.

The Rossen's.

Not the one she'd just been walking beside. Not even the version she'd been friendly with, Sergeant Olin. Older. Tired. Wearing an early-model ENEX, wrapper retreated and hood off. He was breathing heavily.

Tharsis stared.

"She must have known," another said. Rallison, but not as she had just been either. This one was losing her humanity. Noticeably. Her skin was waxy white, a faint illumination betraying the xenocyte layer concealed within. She was clearly struggling. "She must have known. That's why she brought down the *Padua*. She knew he was on it. She must have—"

"Eliza, what the hell is going on?" the older Rossen asked.

She laid a hand on the glass. "I put him on that ship so he'd be safe. It was supposed to be just a few years, you know? Just a few years in orbit, waiting for things to be ready. Not out here, not… not like this. Stripped out of his little body…"

"If he's… can't we just pull him out of there? He dies, yeah, but he'll come back."

"What was done to you wasn't genetic, Caleb. He didn't inherit your ability to… reconstitute."

"So what the fuck was this Arcna bitch after? Did she target him? Target… us?"

"I don't know. Me? What happened to me still isn't public knowledge and—"

Tharsis felt a tug on her sleeve.

It was that girl. The one with the red eyes. The one who had to be Bea.

"It's just a memory," she told the girl, "just the past. It's not real."

=It is,= the girl signed, followed by a long sentence Tharsis couldn't follow. When she shook her head, the girl spelled it out.

It's their son.

Tharsis turned back to the scene. An argument, escalating between the two. Faded now, the words indistinct.

Something else was moving in now.

A bulky void suit, the kind that might be worn inside Mars's magnetosphere for spacecraft repairs, strode forward. Hand to the tank.

"Don't worry." Its voice, a cruel parody of Rallison's, rasped through the speaker. "Don't worry, baby boy. Everything will be better soon."

Inside the tank, the figure twitched.

————

COOPER WAS GOOD WITH EXPLOSIVES. Stag had to give him that.

The doors blew out in perfect sequence, melting at the threshold, buckling in the middle, blowing out into the void.

Silent.

"Launching," Erg announced. His hands pushed forward in the gloves.

The recon wasp squadron shot forward on their acceleration rails, following the swirling fire out into the burning blackness beyond.

The level had been almost completely evacuated, except for the Marines and a couple of maintainers who'd volunteered to help. They were out there now, in void-rated pressure suits and magnetic boots. Behind the rails, they marched forward now, flame-throwers dripping heat onto the deck.

Fire was a difficult thing to direct in mig, and the effective range would be limited. But the xenocyte wasn't invincible, and direct combustion was more than it could generally handle.

With the atmo roaring out, blunt tendrils of the infected wrapper were attempting to get in. The flamer team hit any that tried to dive into the space; a combination of the rushing atmo and fire kept the questing tentacles at bay. Like being attacked by a giant, mutant squid, Stag thought, and tried to shove thoughts of the family's fishing boat out of his mind.

<Attempting to reestablish static field,> Ops said. One of Erg's guys had pulled up the Ops vox on the cockpit's main speakers. <Atmospheric pressure nearing critical levels.>

The rush of air stopped.

<Static field holding. Thirty percent integrity. Air pressure holding at equivalent 7500 meters.>

<Just below death zone levels,> Druz offered. He'd gone out in the bay with his men.

"Is that enough to keep her out?" Stag asked of nobody in particular.

<Unsure, sir.>

Cambel's voice broke in. <Hive, get us a clean pass of the hull. Keep your distance as best you can. We don't know what's going on yet.>

Politic, Stag thought, grim. They knew who this was, what pseudo-genetics had been slowly incorporated into the *Barachiel's* wrapper over the past few sevendays. The Rallarhu. But any radio communication within the craft itself, especially from Ops, was recorded and saved for inclusion into either Deimos's classified data-vaults or public release. Mars loved a good deepvoider battle report.

Having the commander accuse a Landlord of a deliberate attack wasn't a winning strategy, especially if Cambel was ever going to make general.

"Coming into view now," Erg reported. Without prompting, the feed popped up on the main cockpit monitor. It would also be displayed up in Ops.

"Mother of God," Stag breathed.

Outside, it looked like the ocean under a northern storm. Rippling, flowing, crashing against the antenna crest that ran down the upper spine of the craft.

"Have you ever seen wrapper behave this way?" Stag asked.

Erg adjusted something on one of his monitors. The writhing mass came into better focus. "That is definitely attacking the antenna array."

<We concur with that assessment.>

"This shouldn't be possible," Erg said. "Normally, it has very limited mobility. It can expand or contract based on environmental conditions, but this…"

"This is her," Stag muttered, turning the vox off for a moment. "Fucking Landlords."

"Question is, what's been the catalyst for this?" Erg asked.

"I don't fucking care."

"Sir, if the R—"

"I don't care," Stag repeated. He could hear the rest of Erg's question, though. *What if the Rallarhu's declared war on Mars?* He turned the vox back on. "Ops?"

<That's our transmission problem right there,> the comm station said. <It's literally eating any signal we try to send out. Hive, are you good on control?>

"If our entire antenna array becomes fully subsumed, I won't be."

<We can set up a repeater down in the hangar bay.>

"That'll encourage further attacks," Stag said. The tentacles had retreated somewhat, but every once in a while, one still slapped down across the static field. Every time contact was made, a little more atmo was lost to the void.

A fully pressurized level would have likely been strong enough to keep those out indefinitely, but Stag knew his craft. They had enough pressurized atmo mix in the aft holding tanks to completely repressurize the level, but only just. Doing so now would leave the craft vulnerable if any further venting occurred.

ASDF giddies were explicit: during a battle, anything open to the void was left to the void.

<Risk we'll have to take,> Cambel said. <Sergeant, get your shop on it. Full void dock protocols.>

<Yessir.>

<Stag?>

"Yes."

<Good work. Now get back up here. Need you on the floor.>

CHAPTER
FIFTY-FIVE

WHEN STAG ARRIVED, Ops had settled down somewhat. The immediate cause of the problem found, everybody was working their portion of it. The rapid chatter remained, but there was an order to it now.

Cambel was standing at the railing of the holopit, watching a close-up projection of the *Barachiel* itself. Normally used for assessing battle damage, the comm boys had clearly written up some kind of script to display what the recon wasps were seeing on the hull. Patches of it were moving, a sea of yellow and orange dots indicating depth and speed.

"Nice work," Stag commented.

"Based on the shifting depths, the wrapper appears to be concentrating its effort in a few key areas," Cambel said, pitching his voice low under the din. "It's already taken out the thrusters. Right now, maneuverability is entirely dependent on the main fusion engines, but it's attempting to work its way down into those engine bells as well."

"Anything else?"

"The hangar level, obviously," Cambel said. "And here." He indicated an innocuous region near the back of the craft.

The main H2O exchange hatch, Stag realized. The water shields were compartmentalized. While some were permanently sealed, though, that one held the craft's potable water supply and had to be regularly inspected and refilled. "It's vacuum tight," he said. "There's no way it can worm in there."

"All it needs to do is vent something. Notice that's the voidside right now," Cambel said, quiet. "We don't have the fine maneuverability to recover. Not over a planet."

"Are you saying this thing is trying to roche the *Barachiel*?"

"Shove her down into the planet's gravity well until it tears her apart? It appears that way, yes."

"What the fuck is going on?" Stag asked. "Why is she doing this?"

"I have no idea. But Ivan, we have to be pr—"

"Wrapper depth increasing at Ops window perimeter," Maintenance called out. "Three meters and growing."

Cambel headed back onto the main floor, sentence unfinished. "Show me."

The feed from the recon wasp revealed a bleak scene. A wave, looking for all the world like something from the rough northern seas, rising, cresting.

Slamming down.

For a moment, the gleam of the xenocyte was visible against the glow of the planet beyond.

The force of the blow shuddered through Ops.

The window went black.

On the monitor, it was clear that the wrapper was prepping for a second blow. Pulling back. A sliver of open void was visible once more.

Just like the ocean, Stag thought.

"Why isn't it going after the cockpit?" somebody asked. "It's more exposed."

"Because it knows the cockpit's behind an air lock," Cambel said. "We are too, but that won't save Ops from explosive depressurization if it cracks the glass."

"Do you think it can?" Stag asked.

"Let's not find out," Cambel said grimly. "Aeolis?"

"Yes sir?"

"Take us down."

"Sir?"

"Down into the upper atmosphere." Cambel drummed his fingers on the railing of the holopit, staring out the half-occluded window. "Shallow. We're not trying to land, just burn the scat off."

"Sir, I don't recommend that maneuver. We've lost the argon thrusters. I can't guarantee meeting the necessary angle," Aeolis said, pushing back from the navigation station. "And main telemetry. Gravity here…"

<Sir, I don't recommend that either,> Erg added on the intercom. <We can't secure the hangar level right now. If we attempt an atmospheric entry with nothing but static shields…>

"We're all going to die if we don't, gentlemen," Cambel said coolly. "Now get it done."

———

IN NOTHINGNESS, a figure stepped forward.

Detail existed in the world once again.

A voidsuit, dusty and scratched, smeared with the effort of traversing the rough terrain of the island. It was patched, sealant tape slapped over what Caleb could only assume were tears in the heavy material.

"Not much longer now," the axilla said.

In front of it was a tank. The kind Caleb had seen in a dozen ariums, broken open on a dozen raids. But it wasn't a full-grown man inside. Oh no. This was a network of tiny lights, woven somehow into a parody of a child.

Lights glowing brighter now. Obscuring detail.

Twitching as—

The whitecoat who'd led them here had pulled away. Backed against the far wall. "It's happening," he breathed, lost somewhere between reverence and shock. "It's working."

Outside, the screams turned to howls.

The room around them faded back in, coalescing out of the white. But it wasn't some tight room in a hotel. It was huge, corners faded to shadow, dust and ice and blood in the corners.

Rallison craned her head around. "Where in the hell…"

"Noqumiut," he muttered, looking around. He recognized it from the surveillance wasps. "This is Noqumiut."

"Not long now," the axilla crooned, staring into the tank now. There was a body now, small, squirming. "Not long, and you can come home to…"

For a moment, that past, that terrible past, that world that ate itself, rose up. Full and whole and coming, coming for—

"No."

It was that lieutenant. Chen.

And with that one single word, Noqumiut—the vision, the false reality, whatever it was—fell apart.

They were back at the hotel. Stuck in a room, tight and unpleasant. There was still a tank, but one of contemporary design, and the figure inside was decidedly adult.

Bea was beside it still. Desperately trying to do something, anything, with the control panel.

Chen was between the suit and the girl. Hands up. Hands out. Like she was pleading.

"Move away, little girl," the thing hissed at her, feral, angry.

"No," she said again. There was fear in her eyes, but she didn't budge. "You're trying to bring him back, I understand, but you can't. It's not possible."

"Move!"

"Every single strand of tissue, every bone, every fiber of him that wasn't useful for what the Arcna programmed him for, it's gone, don't you understand that? Dissolved, taken. There's no life for him."

"He's coming back."

"He can't! It's not possible!"

"If Dad just perceives it right—"

"At what cost?" the lieutenant yelled back. "I just left a fucking island tearing itself apart because of what the Flet is doing, what these people are making him do, giving life to this asshole's insane idea," and she gestured at the whitecoat, "that perception should be able to rewrite reality! But you're plugged into the Arcna! That's what he holds, her dreams, her horrors! Don't you see what you're calling up!?"

The suit's round helmet twisted to one side, a gross parody of curiosity. "My job is to protect him."

"Can't you hear those things outside?!" she demanded. "That's Noqumiut, coming for us!"

"My job is to protect him," it repeated.

"What kind of world does this give him?" Chen snapped. Her voice was shaking. "How are you going to protect him from the Arcna's nightmare?"

The axilla stood there, motionless.

Then it howled.

Then it lunged.

Straight at Bea.

Chen moved first out of any of them, grabbing for the suit's exposed back. Integrated tubing—oxygen, waste lines—provided her something of a handhold, and she was able to jerk the thing back. It threw itself around, momentum carrying one of the suit arms around in a wild arc. The metal edge of the glove fitting caught Chen high in the chest.

The sound of her collarbone snapping was a dull crack.

She hit the floor, grabbing with her good hand for the thing's boot, even as it scrambled towards the frightened girl in the corner.

The howling outside escalated.

"Bea," she yelled, even as she wrapped herself around the axilla's leg, "Bea, get Donner disconnected! Get him out of there!"

Ninden threw himself into the fray then, combat knife out. He managed to puncture the thing's suit once, twice. The axilla, finally shaking Chen off, gave her one last nasty kick to the ribs and whirled on the Marine.

One punch caved his chest in.

Yip, meanwhile, had his eye to the door, half-cracked. He fired blind down the hallway. "Something's coming, Petrison!" he yelled. He turned to Rallison. "Help me bar this thing?"

"With what?" she demanded.

"Landlord," Chen groaned.

Caleb's attention snapped back to the tank.

To the axilla, moving at Bea.

He stepped in.

Smoke curling out of rents in the axilla's borrowed suit, thin and rank. He raised his gun, but the thing was faster. It ripped the weapon away, flinging it across the room. A gloved hand reached for his neck. He rolled away only just in time, but it kept coming.

Despite the fatal exposure the xenocyte form was suffering, it clawed at him with the desperation of a dying animal. Caleb couldn't untangle himself, couldn't get loose. He'd lost his knife.

Steely fingers closed down around his neck. But unlike the Arrans, he'd been born in this gravity well, built for it, and its killing force was somewhat lessened on him.

"Why?" he coughed at the thing killing him.

"This is how we get him back," it hissed back. The sound from its emitter was weakening. "You can't stop it."

"Isn't that what we're all here to do? Save your dad?"

"It must continue!" the thing screeched and tossed him across the room. Caleb hit the wall, falling down, all the air knocked from his body. He groaned, trying to push himself up, get his feet under him. His side throbbed in agony; he wondered if he'd snapped a rib or two. "To continue is his life!"

The voices were getting closer.

He managed to get himself to his knees. His knife was stuck in its sheath. The axilla was advancing on him. "I don't get it, Eliza. Explain this to me."

The thing screeched again and threw itself at him.

But its motion was arrested.

An explosion. The sharp, painfully close report of a gun. A hail of glass, shattering out the thing's mask.

Yip. Firing his A24 one-handed. His other arm was tucked into his half-unzipped uniform, snapped bone clearly visible through broken skin. Meeting Caleb's eyes, he winked and made to squeeze off another shot.

His finger never moved. The trigger never depressed.

Moving with a speed Caleb hadn't believed the thing capable of, the axilla threw itself on the Marine sergeant. His body disappeared beneath the suit and a flurry of blows. Artless, heedless, murderous.

Tyr managed to stop one arm, locking his teeth around the wrist. The axilla screamed as the dog dragged it bodily off Yip, flopping around, trying to get into some kind of defensive position.

Caleb had forced himself onto his feet. Breathing hurt. Moving hurt more. But his knife was back in his hand, and the strike was open. He dove in, missing a wild haymaker thrown his way, and stabbed as hard as he could.

He ripped the suit open, groin to helmet.

For a moment, Caleb saw it. Open. Exposed. Something alien, forced into the form of a woman. Dissolving already.

"Why?" he asked.

The thing looked at him, clearly summoning the last strength it had as the atmosphere ate it alive. The eyes were cloudy, barely defined, but Caleb still had the sense of overwhelming sadness there. =You never knew him,= it signed.

Then there was nothing. Just a stinking pile of black goo on the concrete floor.

Tyr was already padding over to Yip's broken form. Caleb struggled to his feet. Followed.

Yip's body looked as if somebody had taken a sledgehammer to it. His eyes were still open, mouth moving slightly, but no words came out. Caleb laid a hand on his chest. There was breath still rattling there, but not for long.

His eyes moved a few more times.

Then nothing.

The howling in the hallway continued, though, closer now, murderous, something human, far too human in the sound.

"Bea!" Rallison yelled from the door.

And the teenager finally gave up on the control panel. With a strength Caleb didn't know she had, she ripped the entire communication harness free of the tank's wall.

Goo poured out into the room.

The screaming finally stopped.

In the corner, that whitecoat was crying.

———

STAG AND CAMBEL stood at the edge of the holopit, watching. The data was patchy; the normal reliable projection was only a best guess. Almost all their external sensors were offline, the wrapper eating any electromagnetic radiation that washed in or out of the antenna spine.

The only things keeping them connected to the outside world were Erg's comm wasps and the repeated setup in the hangar bay. But the static shield wouldn't last much longer under the wrapper's insane attack and with the doors gone, the entire level would likely burn out. Druz and Cooper refused to pull out, stating they intended to keep the flame-throwers on until the last possible moment.

<This wasp isn't going to last long,> Aeolis said from the cockpit. He, and one of the pilots, had tucked themselves away in the blister, readying for the maneuver they were about to attempt.

<I'll guide you in. Keep to the angle and we should be fine,> Erg said.

Comm keyed up the feed from the wasp, up on the main monitors. The window was still black. Another three waves had hit it while they had feverishly worked to get this ready.

Ops had gone quiet. Preparations were over. Everyone was strapped in, everywhere on the *Barachiel*.

"We don't know if the maneuvering thrusters will even fire," Stag said quietly. "If the plasma generation cells are compromised, or too full of xenocyte material to ignite."

Cambel, beside him, had his milky eyes fixed on the hologram of their craft. "All we can do is pray that they do," he said in the same quiet tone, and then, louder, "This is the finest crew in the ASDF, the finest I've had the privilege of leading. I trust your skill, I trust this craft, but most of all, I trust him." He pointed up, meaning clear. "Now let's get this bitch off our hull. Hive, *Barachiel* Flight Control, are you ready?"

A pair of *yes sirs* echoed back on the intercom.

"Good. Take us in."

The descent played out across the Ops monitors and in the shuddering of the craft and in Erg's calm voice, piped up from Hive Control.

Blue-green plasma ripping out through a dark rippling sea. In fits and starts, hiccups, but then in steady streams, wrapper dying even as it tried to smother them once again.

The glow of Earth's atmosphere, getting closer, closer.

A groan unlike anything Stag had ever heard.

Flames, beginning to lick at the edges of the video feeds, filling the battered window.

One last frantic report from the hangar bay. Static shield failed, Cooper's men attempting to reach the air lock, Druz unconscious and—

The Ops monitors went black.

The only sound left was one of the station techs praying quietly, fingers flicking across his rosary beads.

THARSIS CAME BACK to herself slowly, pain ricocheting through her body.

Small hands were holding a napkin to her shoulder. Confusion reigned in those red eyes.

Tharsis looked down at the wound.

Bone was poking out of the skin.

But instead of blood, dust was pouring out.

She took the napkin, holding it in place. "It's okay, kiddo," she told Bea, trying to smile, and looked over to the Rossen. "We should get out of here."

"Can you get us back to the beach?" He and the Rallarhu had the Flet between them, one arm over each of their shoulders.

Tharsis closed her eyes for a moment. She was starting to feel light-headed. Cold.

No blood, though. Why didn't she have blood?

"I'll try."

The two Marines were left where they fell; the small party had no way of carrying them. Wyatt couldn't be budged either, and nobody was feeling particularly charitable towards him.

Tharsis didn't see his myling anywhere.

Maybe it had been in the tank's control equipment.

Maybe it had been…

It was better forgotten, she decided. Better not to wonder.

The hallways beyond the room were quiet, dark. They found their way out to the hotel's gardens, the wide lawn, easily enough. Any confusion from earlier had fled.

It was still night, the moon low over the western horizon but the stars bright.

"Look at that," she said to Bea, more out of habit than anything else. The girl was beside her. Walking with her, Tharsis realized, taking her weight. Why did she feel so weak? "You'll get to see it someday, all the beautiful and terrible things out there."

Bea just patted her back with her free hand and kept on walking.

But the further they got from the hotel, the more Tharsis felt it.

The strangest sense of tugging, falling.

Whatever had held this convergence together, allowed the past and the future to collide, seemed to be failing. Maybe it had been, as Sergeant Yerpoli had said, some kind of pocket dimension. Real, or real enough. Closed now.

Her doing, somehow.

They were all drifting apart. Back to where they were supposed to be.

When they reached the beach, Tharsis stumbled. Bea's hands couldn't pull her back up, slipping right through her. The girl gave Tharsis one last confused, saddened look.

Then she was gone.

Then Tharsis was alone.

Her knees hit the sand, her good arm only just catching herself.

Braced up on one arm, she could see it.

Dust and light.

She was coming apart.

And then she heard the voices.

"But Tom, she left the baby."

"Wasn't her choice," Donner was saying. "She can't come back."

"So what, the kid's ours now?"

It was Bea. Tharsis could see her. A baby again. Awake, her little hands scrambling for a grip on the bottle, sucking sounds loud in the morning air. In Cynthia's arms.

Her little girl.

She tried to stand. No luck. Tharsis tried to put weight on her right arm. Tried to crawl forward.

Into what, she didn't know.

The beach was gone.

"Why not?"

"We can't just..."

"No," Tharsis said, shocked at how weak her own voice sounded in her ears. "No, sweetheart, I'm coming..."

He looked at her then. Not the cadet. Not the man they'd just dug out of a tank. The Flet, with all his centuries. From the galley of a yacht that had long since vanished, from a morning after a night that was so long ago.

"It's okay, Ambera," he said.

And then, even that little room was gone. Replaced by the roaring white nothingness she remembered from that dive out to Eris.

The white, and Bea, drinking her bottle.

"It's okay," the Flet repeated.

She looked at the little girl one last time. Her arm finally gave out, and she collapsed. But onto what, she couldn't tell. It felt like she was lying on her side, but when she looked at her wounded shoulder, light was pouring up in viscous streams, scattering like water in mig.

What had he said to her?

Like you've been pressed out of dust...

"Was I ever really here?" she asked.

The Flet just smiled at her.

Her last thought, before the white vanished, was that she was tired of dying.

EPILOGUE

MORRAY HADN'T GOTTEN official clearance to head down in the Lift. Not from Orbital Command, not from Colonel Cambel, not from Diana Watch Medical. Not from the Rossen either, although that's what he'd told everyone.

He didn't think the Landlord was going to care too much. Execute him. Anything ridiculous like that.

Bigger scat going on.

Somebody needed to be here. To help with the bodies.

Deepvoider crews took care of their own.

And for all Morray knew, he was the last of them.

Radio contact with the *Barachiel* hadn't been re-established yet, when he'd stepped off the Lift here. Diana Watch had attempted to keep contact with it, but the few surveillance satellites here were all focused on watching the surface. They had sent out search parties, but scouring a planet's greater inwell with a few rockjumps was like trying to locate one single grain of sand in the entire Aonian desert.

They had gotten footage of the craft. Wrapper fighting it like the ocean in winter. Streaming fire from the hangar deck.

Diana Watch had already put in a request for transport back to Mars. For the Rossen, Adair, himself.

Until the *Barachiel* got her radios and identifier beacons working, she was on her own.

Until she made contact, she was presumed lost.

Not something Morray wanted to dwell on.

The Lift had been dropped earlier that morning, timed to coincide with the Rossen's arrival. Morray had begged—okay, *lied*—his way onto it. But the Rossen had been delayed an hour or two out of whatever island they'd refueled at, and so instead of meeting him at the Lift platform, Morray got to meet him at the airfield's dock.

It was a glorious sight. Painful, to be sure; the crush of Earth's gravity was no joke. Still, glorious. Worth the agony, worth the tongue-lashing he was going to get from the doctors back on Deimos. Fortunately, he had nothing he needed to do other than wait on the dock and watch the young clouds build their kingdoms on the impossibly blue horizon.

They'd been nice enough to get him a chair. Padded. Made it a little easier.

A seaplane coasted up, jets winding down even as it cruised in. Morray stood, wincing at the pull on his joints, and walked down to where the passenger door was opening.

Out stepped the Rossen, exhausted. Contusions littered his face. His knuckles were scraped bare.

Tyr seemed in much better shape, bounding out and past them.

"Probably needs to piss," the Rossen replied. His face twitched. He didn't question what Morray was doing on the surface, though, which was nice. "I'm sorry, Lieutenant."

"What happened?" The report the Rossen had called in the night before hadn't exactly been clear.

"The axilla went crazy, tried to kill us."

"It did the same to the *Barachiel*, up in orbit."

"Everyone else is dead." The Landlord's expression was grim. "I'm guessing this constitutes some kind of international incident."

"Sir, I think just coming down here is an international incident."

"Fucking stupid, all of it," he muttered, and then raised his voice. "Tyr! Where'd you go, boy?!"

But the howl the dog sent back made no sense.

"That was the call for casualties," Morray said, confused.

"Go after him," the Rossen said, weary. "I've got bodies to unload."

Morray had always prided himself on his physical fitness test scores. He'd tried to stay on top of it; even in the artificial gravity of the deepvoider, hard exercise was essential. He wasn't going to end up one of those mig-locked old officers, unable to go home. No, he was going to retire back to the family ranch and enjoy what he'd fought for.

Following the dog, though, took everything he had. The big animal was moving at speed. Urgent. On Mars, Morray wouldn't have been able to keep up with him. Here, it was almost impossible.

He fell behind, guided only by the sound of Tyr's baying. By the time he reached the spot where Tyr had stopped, every muscle in his body ached from effort.

There was a body in the grass. Half obscured by a dying ENEX. Blood slowly pooling out onto the thick green blades.

Female.

"I need a stasis bag!" he yelled.

————

THARSIS WOKE to the sound of surf. Of the chatter of a million animals. Of wind in trees.

Her eyes hurt. Her bones ached. Her skin burned. The air was too thick. Her lungs labored to pull it in. She was face-up, staring up at a perfect sky. That tropical ocean sky that could only exist on Earth.

Hawaii was her first thought.

But as she tried to roll over, her muscles protested so strongly she nearly passed out.

Earth. But her old body, her correct body, damaged practically beyond repair by that little jaunt on Eris.

Home would have been better.

Why couldn't she die at home? She hadn't seen it in so long.

"We'll get you there," she heard somebody say. A shape above her. Blurry. Indistinct. "We'll get you back there."

She tried to reach up, reach whoever that was.

Her hand slipped out of his. Too weak. Too wet.

At least it was actual blood on her fingers, instead of that terrible light.

AUTHOR'S NOTES

This book was interesting to write. Actually, that may be an understatement. This book was hard.

I knew the broad strokes of Caleb's story. That was straightforward - he dies at the end of *The Lighthouse of Kuiper*, so of course he's going to wake up here. Of course we need to explore how he deals with this crazy world.

Tharsis on the other hand, Tharsis...

I knew where she ended up (Earth). I knew why (the Flet... sort of). And I knew she had the key to solving the problem here; she was the only one at the end capable of deciding against the emergent pocket universe and its altered laws of physics. But getting her there?

I went through six drafts of her journey. Six full drafts. Different time frames, different paths, different obstacles along the way. Originally, I had wanted her to be on Earth for years, maybe decades, watching things fall apart. But it was slow, and sad, and this series isn't about the descent into dystopia.

Besides, I feel that the Euphemism, like many a great science fiction or fantasy backstory, is best glimpsed only briefly. Leaving some mystery is always important. When you, as the reader, can fill in some of the details for yourself, it's more of a shared experience. It's just more interesting that way too.

One thing that didn't change was Tharsis's relationship with the

Naven. That scene where she finds the baby is one of the first I wrote for this novel.

I'll confess, I considered cutting it out. But I felt that in order for Tharsis to reject the promises of the Euphemism at the end, she needed to experience some of its more unsavory realities for herself. With manipulation of the human genome so common in this world, these sort of scenes are likely not all that unusual. What would one do with failed experiments?

I was also three months pregnant when I wrote that scene. Talk about emotional!

However, it was fun taking Tharsis on a journey across the Pacific. I've done a fair bit of traveling in the region myself. I was able to take her to some of the places that stand out in my memory; Yakushima, Singapore, Lanai. A few, I wasn't able to squeeze in (Ularu in Australia will have to wait for a different story). And some places, like Neue, I've never been to but damn, do I want to.

Probably more accessible than Venus or Pluto or Mars. For now, at least!

If you liked this book, there's no greater compliment a writer can receive than a review! Plus, it helps other readers find and enjoy it as well. Even just giving a star rating is a great thing. (And hey, if you hated it, thank you for reading this far and I'd love to hear your thoughts too)

If you'd like to subscribe to my newsletter for a free bonus epilogue, future release information, and the occasional Embarrassing Cadet Tale, please head over to my website and sign up!

https://rensingwrites.com/

Cheers,
Rensing

THE CATHEDRALS OF MARS

COMING NOVEMBER 2023

Tharsis was late to breakfast the next morning. She knew she was cutting it close; they were scheduled to head back to the train station in less than an hour.

After the reception, after their little party had come back to the hotel, she'd stumbled back to her room and collapsed.

The nightmares, the nightmares hadn't stopped all night. Noqumiut again. She wondered if she'd have to carry that the rest of her life.

Lieutenant Colonel Orlani, Stag, had gotten his crew a large table in the back of the ancient hotel's grand dining room. Out of the way, half-tucked into an alcove. The crew was talking quietly, but stopped when she walked up.

"Didn't they teach you how to be on time at the Academy?" Stag asked, point blank.

The man was merciless. "No excuse, sir," she muttered

"Yeah, don't pull that spider scat with me either," he said, and indicated a chair. "Sit down. I2 wants me keeping an eye on you."

"I'm not going anywhere," Tharsis grumbled. It was only partially not a lie.

The thought had crossed her mind since making planetfall. She could just leave. Catch a train or steal a car. Go back to the Bulge, get a job on a sheep ranch or in one of the coastal logging camps.

Fade away. Disappear.

But then, she'd already disgraced herself enough for one lifetime. Better to stay, face the consequences. Keep her bad choices from crashing down on her little sisters, if she could.

Hell, maybe the Rossen wouldn't execute her at all.

The gnawing guilt in her gut offered her the memory of Singapore anew.

The baby in a trash can.

The fire, rising to the heavens.

The breakfast room of the *Caledonian* was nice. Really nice. The carved wood detailing was exquisitely preserved, aided by Lunae's dry air and the relentless care of the hotel staff. Europa oak. Old world.

The whole place had been brought here from Earth. Brick by brick. Nail by nail. Like so many buildings in the District of Lunae. A heritage salvaged from the birth world, before wrecking crews tore it all down.

It, like all such structures here in Lunae, were the pride of the nation.

That morning, she found it deeply unsettling.

The scene from the bowels of the Sarsen was still rattling around in her head. The Rossen's voice. Others. Talking, pleading, yelling.

She tried to put it aside.

The past was past; she was no longer a part of it.

But then, if that were really true, why did she keep seeing it?

A waiter came by, took her order. The crew passed around coffee in a silver carafe, everyone lost in their own little conversations.

"You look dragged," Morray told her from across the table. "You doing okay?"

"I blew up a city," she said. "What difference does it make?"

Around the table, talking stopped.

"Technically, that was the Flet's fault," Aeolis said, not unkindly.

"Does it matter? The Naven's dead," she replied.

"And her fault as well."

"She was four," Tharsis snapped. "How could anything be her fault?"

"Look, El-tee, Tharsis, I know you're getting beat up by Internal Investigations," Stag said. "But they're more concerned with what you saw out at Noqumiut, I'd think. Probably running our wasp surveillance footage against what you're telling them."

"What's there to say about that fucking place?" she grumbled. "Everything is dead."

"Except whatever is generating the myling," Chaplain Kannik said, down at the other end of the table. "It seems an interesting choice, the Arcna opting for a biological means of storage and broadcast control verses…"

Tharsis thought about that tank.

The axilla. The Flet.

Bea.

And she shoved back from the table.

"Don't go too far! I'm still accountable for you!" Stag called after her as she walked away, tone light.

Tharsis didn't answer. Didn't trust herself.

She found herself outside, out in the warm morning air, breathing hard. The hotel had a wide front veranda, filled with small tables and cheerful planters spilling green across the red sandstone facade. She sat down, ran her hands over her scalp, tried to catch her breath.

You have to stop doing this, you have to start playing by the rules, she told herself. *This is what got you into this mess in the first place.*

But what she'd seen last night, the voices she'd heard in the depths of the old Capitol building…

Tharsis remembered her grandmother sitting at her chair near the hearth, telling her stories as the winter winds battered the walls of the sturdy old ranch house. Stories about the lights that played on the mountain slopes, or figures that trooped through the peat bogs in the morning mist.

The things that would come and watch.

The things that were not quite there.

She also remembered her grandmother getting in arguments with the parish priest about what they were, what it meant. The church held it was purely a consequence of altered perception, some physiological trait recognizing the energy that played beneath the skin of spacetime. Her grandmother always thought it was more.

After the menace, the pain, she'd felt out at Noqumiut, Tharsis was inclined to agree with Gran. The penumbra was more than just physical.

It held memory. It held emotion.

So what was the penumbra guarding, down below the debate chambers and offices and grand hallways of the Sarsen?

...don't do this...

Who had the Rossen been pleading with? Why?

A light in the sky caught her eye.

A cascade of glowing white streaked across the dusty blue, bursting, dying. Like fireworks.

As Tharsis sat there staring up at the sky, a thought began to form.

One she couldn't shake.

What if the Rossen hadn't shot himself?

What if that, too, was a lie?

"Pretty, ain't it?"

It was the Rossen, Tyr at his side. Tharsis blinked. Nobody had gone over his itinerary with her—that was his business, his and Congress's—but she hadn't really expected to see him this morning. Or much at all again. Propagations were one of the rare times when tradition allowed for the Landlord to be on the surface.

During Propagations, it was usually expected for him to stay on the surface.

Wasn't he going to stay?

"Meteor bursts, I think," Tharsis replied.

He continued like he hadn't even heard her. "Everybody inside, ready to go?"

"Umm, yes sir?"

"Good. We need to leave. Now."

Available for pre-order now!

ABOUT THE AUTHOR

A lifelong science fiction fanatic, E.M. Rensing still managed to surprise her family when she decided to pursue a commission in the US Air Force. A graduate of the United States Air Force Academy, she enjoyed a 13 year career as a Cyber Operations Officer, and has traveled all over the world. E.M. Rensing lives with her husband and daughters in south Texas.

www.ingramcontent.com/pod-product-compliance
Lightning Source LLC
Chambersburg PA
CBHW031156310726
48969CB00001B/109